UNDER THE MOUND

For my parents.

✠ ✠ ✠ ✠ ✠

Published in 2011 by Be Read
an imprint of Simply Read Books
www.simplyreadbooks.com

Text & maps © 2011 Cynthia Heinrichs
Cover illustration © 2011 Atanas Matsoureff

Library and Archives Canada Cataloguing in Publication

Heinrichs, Cynthia
Under the mound / written by Cynthia Heinrichs.
ISBN 978-1-897476-62-8
I. Title.
PS8615.E365U54 2011   jC813'.6   C2011-903026-8

We gratefully acknowledge for their financial support of our publishing program
the Canada Council for the Arts, the BC Arts Council, and the Government of Canada
through the Canada Book Fund (CBF).

Manufactured in Canada
This product conforms to CPSIA 2008

Book design by Elisa Gutièrrez
Typesetting by Natasha Kanji

10 9 8 7 6 5 4 3 2 1

UNDER THE MOUND

By Cynthia Heinrichs

BE READ

foreword

I was first drawn to Orkney in 1998 by the five thousand-year-old megalithic monuments for which it is famous. Great solitary standing stones and stone circles, ancient houses, vaulted tombs hidden under hills—these were the mysteries I sought.

But as I waited for a tour of the chambered tomb Maeshowe (also known as Orkahaugr) another mystery was lurking. On an information panel I read:

In 1153 Earl Harald and his men took shelter in Maeshowe during a snow storm and two of them went insane.

And then what? Not a hint was offered. Not the whisper of a clue.

Inside the mound the guide described its structure and history and offered theories about the purpose of its builders, but it soon became apparent that for all the available theories, there could be few proofs. It is difficult to know what people intended fifty years ago, much less five thousand. I was glad. I liked the idea that there would always be an abundance of wonderfully wide gaps in my knowledge of Maeshowe and its builders. I was glad of the mysteries that refused to be solved.

But for every mystery that won't be solved another demands it. I had to know what had happened to the earl and his men. The guide informed me that the earl had ruled Orkney for fifty years after the incident in question, but as to the mad men she could offer no answers. Perhaps superstition had gotten the better of them, she suggested, or perhaps they had been mad all along.

Gaps can be so annoying.

But gaps are also where dust settles, and then soil, and then, if the wind blows just right and happens to be carrying a seed, and if that seed finds purchase and is blessed with enough sun and just the right amount of rain, and if you are very, very lucky … something grows.

This is what grew out of that day under the mound.

ON THE TENTH DAY OF CHRISTMAS,

svein asleifarson was on gairsay drinking with his men, when he started to rub his nose.

"i've got a feeling," he said, "that earl harald is on his way here to the islands."

his men said that was hardly likely with such a gale blowing, and harald being such a land-lubber.

svein said to his men, "i knew that was the way you would think. so i'm not going to give earl erlend a warning based purely on intuition," he said, "though i doubt if i'm being very wise."

that was the end of the conversation and they got on with their feasting, just as before.

earl harald set out for orkney at christmas with four ships and a hundred men. he lay for two days off graemsay, then put in at hamna voe on hrossey, and on the thirteenth day of christmas they travelled on foot over to firth. during a snowstorm they took shelter in orkahaugr and there two of them went insane.

year 1153

ORKNEYINGA SAGA

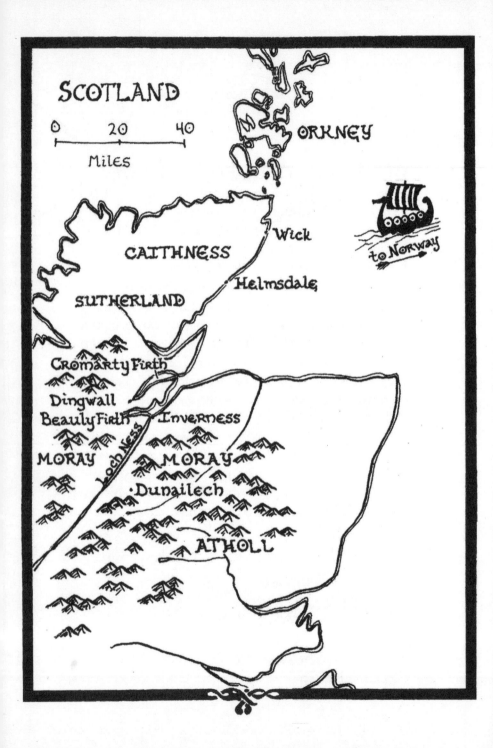

SCOTLAND

0   20   40
Miles

ORKNEY

to Norway

Wick

CAITHNESS

Helmsdale

SUTHERLAND

Cromarty Firth

Dingwall

Beauly Firth

Inverness

MORAY

Loch Ness

MORAY

Dunailech

ATHOLL

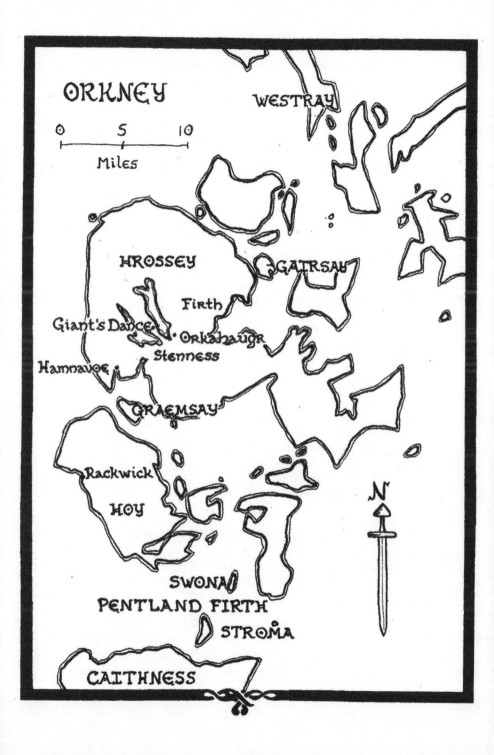

CHARACTERS *(in order of appearance)*

✢ *people recorded in history*

MALCOLM MAC ALASDAIR
a young man of Moray

ALASDAIR ROY
his father

MAIRE
his mother

MARJORY · SEONA · EITHNE
his sisters

THORIR HONEY-TONGUE [thor EER]
Earl Harald's skald

✢ **EIRIK**
Earl Harald's cousin and lieutenant

✢ **BENEDIKT**
Earl Harald's cousin and lieutenant

✢ **SIMON**
Earl Harald's nephew and heir of Atholl

ANGUS · FERGUS
men of Atholl

✢ **HARALD**
Earl of Orkney, Shetland, Caithness and Sutherland

✢ **THORBJORN KLERK** [thor BEE'YORN]
Earl Harald's foster-father and chief advisor

✢ **MARGARET**
Earl Harald's mother, widow of Maddad (Earl of Atholl)

✠PAUL
former Earl of Orkney, brother of Margaret

HAERMUND HARDAXE · OFRAM · EYOLF ARNFITH · VERMUND · OGMUND
some of Harald's men

SIGRITH
a young woman of Orkney

MENTIONED:

✠MADDAD
former Earl of Atholl, and father of Earl Harald (d. 1152)

✠KING DAVID
the late King of Scots (d. 1153)

✠KING MALCOLM
the new King of Scots

✠KING EYSTEIN
King of Norway

✠EARL ROGNVALD
Earl Harald's cousin

✠EARL ERLEND
Earl Harald's cousin

✠SVEIN ASLEIFARSON
chief advisor to Earl Erlend

✠GUNNI ASLEIFARSON
Svein's brother and Margaret's former lover

OUR LIVES ARE A SERIES OF DAYS *that usually run smoothly together, blurring one into the other, so that it is almost impossible to point to the particular moment when the change occurred, to say* this is where my life took a turn. *But in truth nothing begins on a single day. Our fates are woven, complete, at the moment we enter the world.*

Yet the strands of that weaving are taken from the days that came before. A man inherits much of his fate from his father, and he from his father before him. All a man can choose is how he spends it.

In 1130, eight years before I was born, my father joined with the men of Moray and the chiefs of the Highlands in rebellion against David, the King of Scots. They were a proud and powerful lot, those rebels, and did not like that he would have them bend a knee to him, southern king that he was. But pride is not a sword, nor power a shield against a greater force, and they were defeated, utterly. On that day the lifeblood of Moray was drained into the soil and those who survived were banished to poorer lands, far from the ancient kingdom that had given rise to their disastrous pride.

My father escaped the battle with his life and, in those days when Moray was filled up with men loyal to the king, he somehow managed to retain his ancestral home and a small portion of his lands. There was the air of a miracle about it, but if he ever spoke of it, it was only to say we owed much to Earl Maddad of Atholl, cousin to the king, his chief advisor and intimate friend.

Why would such a man choose to intervene to help my father, a rebel against the crown which he upheld? There was never a hint of an answer, just the evidence of a long and constant relationship, the letters that came and went with regularity and my father's frequent visits to Atholl. I recall a large, dark man who seemed to stand twice as tall as other men, who swung me high to the rafters once and made me cry before he made me laugh. My father might have been in service to that powerful earl, and yet I sensed friendship too.

But friendship requires the exchange of gifts. No man is a friend who only receives.

When Earl Maddad died in my fifteenth year, I found myself attached to his son, Harald Maddadson who was the Earl of Orkney. Or he had been, until his cousin, Erlend, stole his lands from him, with the blessings of both the Norse and Scottish kings.

Some men might have accepted it as fate. Earl Harald Maddadson did not and so I was drawn into a world beyond my imaginings.

Into that world I took my own inheritance: the crumbling fortunes of my family and the burden of redeeming them. And a bond and a debt, and a gift as well. ⏣

PART 1

1

*let the man who is wise, and would wise be thought,
both ask and answer with care.
tell one thy secret, but never another,
if three know, a thousand will.*

~WISDOM OF ODIN~

The fire crackled loudly on the hearth, lighting my father from behind and making it appear that his red mane of hair was ablaze. It was not, but it might well have been. He was in a temper and I had put him there.

"You will go to Orkney and you will make yourself useful! That's the last word on it!"

"But, Father," I cried, "it's still Christmas, and the celebrations … and for pity's sake, they're Vikings!" It was that last part which bothered me most, but I mentioned the holy celebrations in hopes he might change his mind for their sake. I was, as usual, wrong.

"The last word, boy, and if you don't believe me, keep talking and you'll go with stripes on your backside." He looked angrier than he actually was, but that could quickly change. "A party from Earl Harald's brother in Atholl will arrive in the next few days. Before the end of the season is what I've been told. They go north to support him, and you will go with them." His tone did not brook argument.

Now I knew why he'd told my sisters to leave the room where we'd been sharing the fire that afternoon. Seona and Eithne had picked up their sewing and gone quickly enough, whispering about venturing out on the new-fallen snow, but Marjory had stopped to grin at me from the door to say *what trouble you're in!* I had ignored her, of course, looking pointedly down at the tiny oak deer I had carved for my mother and was now oiling. I had carefully hollowed out a hole in its back where she could store her sewing needles, for she was always losing them and sending me to find them.

When I looked up again Marjory was gone, but she was, as usual, right.

"And as to their being Vikings," my father was saying, "you're always one to judge before you've learnt about a thing. They're as Christian as we are, for the most part, and Earl Harald is more Scottish than anything, and with royal blood in his veins at that. He's a good man. It's his mother who's the Viking!" He laughed without mirth at his joke.

I did not laugh at all.

"Margaret's the one to watch out for," he said, "but *she* won't be going with you!" His voice struck those last words emphatically. "As for the others, if they still go viking, it's no business of yours. On this venture they'll serve the Earl Harald, as will you."

I looked desperately to my mother, who sat by the window. The last rays of faint winter light fell on the embroidery in her lap. With a quick shake of her dark head to quiet me, she turned to my glowering father with a smile.

"Husband, Malcolm is barely fifteen years old. There is some time yet to make him a man, is there not?"

My father shook his head with exasperation. "Not you too, woman. You know that I would lay the world at your feet for a glimpse of that smile, Maire, but not in this. I was not much older when I went to war! If I had a more likely lad to send, by God, I would. But I don't, and so he must go! I have let him be long enough. He will go."

A more likely lad … you mean you, yourself, I thought as I stole a glance at my father's left foot. Alasdair Roy—Roy for his red hair—was tall and muscular, a warrior Celt in every way but one. His left foot could hardly be called a foot at all, with so much of it shorn away by a sword twenty-some years before. It held him upright and he could ride a horse, but he would never go to battle again. And I would never be the warrior my father had been …

"Father—"

"Enough!" he exploded. "Are you a fool? Do you not see what goes on about you? The world is changing! King David showed us some mercy, but he's gone and this boy king, this King Malcolm, he has no love for me, not with my enemies whispering venom into his little ears. We will not fare well under his reign. Word is spreading. He will have all former rebels gone from Moray, though we have not been such for twenty years! His grandfather could forgive, but this one, who was not even born when it happened, he will use our past deeds against us to steal our lands. If he does it, Malcolm, we will have nothing. Nothing! No dowries to get good husbands for your sisters, nothing for you to inherit to pass on to *your* sons.

"If we still had money we could persuade him to leave us be, but it was spent long ago keeping King David's wolves from our door. We have nothing. This is our chance," he said with a shake of his head. "*Your* chance. We need the good favour of powerful men. This Earl Harald will be a great man and this is the time of his making. Those who aid him in recovering his earldom will be rewarded and you will be among them!"

I knew he had been more troubled than usual since the spring when King David had died, but I had given it little thought. The convoluted topic of Scots politics was not one I enjoyed. I preferred the honesty of my tools and a sure piece of wood in my hands. But it had been a winter of many visitors, I suddenly realized. Lone men, and sometimes a few together, who had come to our hall to sup, but shared the news with my father behind closed doors rather than before the fire with the family as most guests were wont to do. I had hardly noticed. Now I wondered.

He was glaring at me, knowing I had wandered in my thoughts. His look sparked a kindred flare of temper in me, but I reined it in. I was no match for him when he was in full boil.

"Father," I said, carefully, "may I speak?"

"If you must."

"Father, I do not doubt your wisdom," I began, treading softly, "but did this earl not lose the earldom he was given? Why do you think he can take it back now?"

"You do not doubt my wisdom, you say, yet you come very close to a whipping, boy!" He scowled down upon me as if he were weighing what to do with me, then sat suddenly on his low stool. I saw then how tired he looked. My father seldom looked tired.

"But to answer your question, there will be fire and blood in Orkney if Harald is not at the helm. And fire in Orkney spreads, like all fire does."

"To us?"

He shrugged. That was more of an answer than words. He ran a hand through his hair. "Why must you try me so, Malcolm? Why can you not just do as I command?" What I saw in my father's eyes, heard it in his tone, was not simple anger or weariness. It was fear.

I had never known him to be anything but fierce, brave, strong. I looked at him now, sitting on his stool. *We will have nothing*, he had said. *Nothing*. The fullness of it all came down on me then and that fear found its way into me. My father, without his land, would die.

"I'm sorry, Father," I said quietly. "I will obey you. I just want to understand and I do not. The earl is not much older than I. He was tossed out of Orkney on his ear, yet you believe he will regain his lands. Why?"

He gazed out the window over my mother's head. "You say you will obey me, so why should I give you my proofs?" he said to the slit of darkening blue that showed in the falling dusk.

"So I can grow to be as wise as you, Father. How else will I learn?"

That snapped him out of his gloom. He glared at my mother, who was trying to hide her smile. "You have too much of your mother in you, boy. But I'll tell you why I believe it." He sighed, then seemed about to change his mind. They exchanged a look. She inclined her head slightly, a gentle encouragement. He sighed again, then he caught my eyes with his and said, "I believe it because I have seen it."

"Seen it?" I burst out with a laugh. "What do you mean?

You have seen the future?"

Too late I saw my mother's eyes widen in warning. My father sat as still as stone. I looked down at the object I held in my hands. I had been rubbing it rhythmically, automatically, throughout our exchange, but now my hands froze on it. A deer does not move when the arrow is aimed at its heart. I wished myself anywhere but there.

When my father finally spoke his voice was soft. "Yes, my son. I have seen the future. And you in it, though at this moment I begin to doubt the truth of that small part. You'll have to learn when to keep your tongue still if you're to live as long as I have, seeing the future or not!"

I suddenly felt ill. Was he truly claiming to have second-sight? Second-sight was a thing for old maids and madmen, not warriors, not men who lived in the world of flesh and politics. Ishbel, the old kitchen biddie, claimed to have it, with her predictions of death and the doom of the world coming every other day, but none of it ever fell out as she said. No one died, at least not when she said they would, and the world went on its way.

Still, everyone knows there are those with the ability to see the future, to see more than most men do. They are seldom left in peace, those ones. Everyone wants them for their gift, and to blame them when it does not provide for them to their liking.

"Father," I said, hardly believing I was even asking it, "Are you telling me that you have second-sight?"

"Call it what you will. This is what I know: I have seen Harald Maddadson dying in his bed, in Orkney, an old man." He started to say something and then changed his mind. "Harald would never be allowed to live in Orkney unless he were lord of it. No, he will be earl there again and a man of means. And you will share in it, if I have my way. Which I will!"

My head spun with it all. Enough that I was to leave Dunailech to go to the ends of the earth with a band of wild Vikings—whatever my father chose to call them—and in the dead of winter, at that, but now my father had second-sight? I felt then the way I did when I awoke from a nightmare and could not tell if I still slept or not.

He was watching me. "This is much to take in, I know. But you will get used to it. When you are a man you must learn to take things as they come and find the grace to deal with them. That is something I have learned only late in life," he said, smiling at me in that way he did when he was treating me like a child. "Fate comes as it will. Accept it."

He sat back, crossing his legs so that his maimed foot rested on the whole one. "My gift came upon me when I was not much younger than you. It has not always served me well, in part because I have struggled with it, tried to deny it. Feared it even. Perhaps it is a blessing that you've shown no signs." He smiled wryly. "Few know of it, Malcolm, and I think you know what would happen if they did. At the very least I would be a subject of the satirists, but even that would likely mean our downfall. You must not speak of this to any. Do you understand?"

"I do, Father, and I will obey you in this and in the matter of Earl Harald." My words were as wooden as the deer sitting in my palm.

He sprang up and clapped me on the back so hard he

almost knocked me over. "I never doubted you would my boy. I told you, I saw it." Alasdair Roy of Moray laughed aloud. I tried to smile. My father had second-sight and I was going to Orkney. My happy life was ending.

"Be ready when they come for you," he said. "And don't forget, this venture with Earl Harald is a secret. It will fail if the wrong parties learn of it. If any here at Dunailech ask, you are going north to Earl Harald's lands in Caithness. You are going to … to repay the debt I owe his father. Now, go pack your things. Wet and cold, it'll be, with wind unlike anything you've ever known, I can promise you that. They don't call Orkney the Islands of the Boar for nothing, my son. You must be strong as a boar to survive it. If Orkney does not break you, it will make you a man."

• • •

I sat on my bed among the linens and furs I had slept in since leaving the nursery. The chest at the end of the bed had belonged to my mother's father. It held a Bible and a few books of tales, along with his journals. He had been a bookish man. I seldom took the books out of the chest—they were too precious to be handled often—but I had read them all.

On a small table by the slit of a window lay lumps of wood that were slowly becoming birds and fish and all manner of animals. In the long winter months, when my mother and sisters worked with their needles, I worked with wood. Even when the winter light was too dim for the womenfolk to do their fine stitching, I could work by touch. I loved nothing more.

When will I have time to carve again? I wondered. Soon I would be on the sea, and then in Orkney, perhaps even helping to kill other men. I had never seen a man die. The thought made me shudder. I shook it off and reached for my best whittling knife. *For carving wood, not men*, I thought, as I put it in the leather bag that would carry my few possessions.

I wondered how many more nights I would sleep in my own room. If fate did not favour me, I might never sleep there again. Fear welled up in me, fear of the days ahead and what they might bring, fear of travelling friendless among men known for their savagery. I murmured a prayer of protection, but it did nothing to clear the tempest that swirled in my head.

How can he send me off like this? I thought furiously, then stopped myself. I was my family's only hope. That was what he had been telling me and I knew it was no lie. They needed me to go out into the world and find a way to save our lands, our very lives. The thought was no comfort. *What could I possibly have to offer an earl?* I felt the edge of my anger again. *Might I make him a comb for his hair? Perhaps I could entertain him by whittling kindling into pleasing shapes?*

And then there was the matter of how long this plan had been in the making. Why was I only learning of it now? And second-sight? I could not decide if I was more angry that he had never told me or that he had told me now.

A sound at the door roused me from my thoughts.

"I hear you are finally going to be out of our hair," said a voice, light and sweet.

"All those tangles have had me trapped almost beyond bearing," I growled.

Marjory, my younger sister by a year and my dearest friend in the world, though I would never have said as much to her, grinned back. She was used to comments about her unmanageable mass of hair. In truth, it was a thing of beauty, an auburn tumble of curls that shone in sun and firelight. It would bring men knocking at our father's door in a few short years.

"Father says you are leaving us to serve the Earl Harald Maddadson and to find good, rich husbands for your ugly sisters."

I laughed. My sisters were anything but ugly, but her words took me back to what my father had said. Even Marjory with all her grace and wit and her lovely face could not hope to find a good match if she had no tangible wealth to bring to it. With two older sisters to be married first would there be money for a dowry for the youngest? Was there even enough for the eldest? What would happen to them if I failed at what I was meant to achieve in Orkney, whatever that was?

"You will, I suppose, have to come back some day," said Marjory. She had strolled to my worktable and was fingering a coiled figure that was becoming a dragon.

"Someday," I replied, as I assessed the state of an old tunic, old because my mother had cut down one of my father's. I ran my fingers along the frayed edge of one dark green sleeve and took a deep breath. Marjory had broken the spell of my anger, but it would not do to reveal too much to her. She was as quick of eye and mind as she was soft of foot. "But who knows," I said. "Perhaps I will like it in … in Caithness."

"Yes, Caithness. That's where Father tells us you are going," she said as she gently took the tunic from me, glanced at the tattered edge and tucked it under her arm. She could work magic with a needle; my tunic would be looking respectable in no time. "They call it Headland of the Cats, don't they? I should like to see it someday, to know why," she mused, chewing on her lip. "I would go there now," she added softly, "if I weren't a girl."

"You would probably like it better than I will," I replied.

"It will be a wonderful adventure!" she scolded. "And since I cannot go, you must like it for both of us!"

She sincerely wanted to go. I was amazed by her, as always. "It might just be a long nightmare of bad food and weather and even worse men."

"It won't. I know it. It will be brilliant. You will see."

"I should take you along," I retorted, feigning surliness. "You can tell me what a wonderful time I am having, no matter how miserable I am." But her excitement was like the heat from a new-made fire radiating into the room. I felt the first stirrings of it in me and was grateful to her. And at the same time I realized how much I would miss her. I covered this quickly, though I knew she would be aware of it.

"I could," she shot back, "but I would not waste my time. When do you listen to me?"

"Always," I said, and that was not in jest. I might not like what Marjory said to me, but I knew it was usually both wise and true.

"Well, just think of what I would tell you to do and do the opposite, as usual." Then, in a different tone entirely, she added, "But do trust Father, Mal. He has been out in the world. He has seen things you have not."

Now I was annoyed. "If he could see me coming home in one piece, I'd be happy to trust that."

"If he could tell you how it all falls out, what would be the fun of it?"

What did she know? To her I said, carefully, "Well, he can't see what will fall out, can he?" I watched her closely to see if she gave anything away.

"Don't be silly!" she snorted. "And even if he could, how could he know *all* of it?"

I was quite sure she was not lying and I was relieved. The thought that she might know about our father's supposed gift, when I had just learned of it, angered me more than I was willing to admit. I had never had secrets from Marjory. With our worlds parting, at least for a time, I supposed it was inevitable.

"You are right."

"Of course I am." Her eyes sparkled. "I envy you, Malcolm. I must sit here and wonder about you the whole while you are gone, with nothing but sewing and the end of the holy days to entertain me. It will not be easy. Nor will your part be. But you will be *doing*. You men, you are so fortunate. You will come home and tell me *everything*."

"I will," I said. We stood, face to face, regarding each other. There was no more need for words. I knew all that she was saying to me. As did she.

"Well," said Marjory. "I do not want to take you from

your packing. I came with a small gift, to keep home in your heart and strength in your soul."

I reached out to take the small figure from her hand. It was one I had carved, part of the menagerie of wooden creatures inspired by nature and, the more fantastical ones, by stories and my imagination. This particular figure was of a small boar with very sharp tusks. It sat in my hand, tiny and harmless, and yet the very sight of it made me shiver. The boar is the most dangerous of creatures, lurking undetectable, hiding its great bulk as if by magic, until the moment it bursts out to run down the unwary comer. Marjory had been gored by such a beast while picking blackberries beside the stream on the very day I'd given the figure to her.

"I had forgotten all about this," I said as the memory came ringing back to me in all its cold horror. "It could have killed you."

"But it didn't."

"Still, is this your idea of luck? I gave it to you in the morning and by noon your leg was a bloody mess. It seems to me it bears a curse, not luck."

"On the contrary, dear brother, I believe it saved me. A boar to protect me from a boar. Does it not make sense?"

I rolled my eyes. "In some strange female way, I suppose it does. But it does not explain why you are giving it to me. And you can't give it to me anyway. It was a gift."

"Then I'll ask you to hold it for me till you return," she said and before I could stop her she had snatched my dirk from its sheath. Ignoring my protestations she cut a lock of her hair which she deftly braided and then wound around the belly and through the legs of the boar. I watched her wonderingly as she tied the ends in a loop, pulled a thong from a pocket in her gown and knotted the amulet she had made to it.

She put up her hand to silence me when I started to speak, gesturing to me to lower my head. I did so, knowing very well that there was no point in arguing with her. I watched her face, calm but serious, as she pulled my tunic away from my chest so that the small boar dropped against my skin, still warm from her hands.

"Wear it next to your heart and do not take it off," said Marjory. "I pray it will protect you where you are going."

My head snapped up. "But this is a boar, Marjory. Should you not give me a cat?" I dissembled, trying to turn it to a joke. "For I am going to Caithness, sister."

Marjory reached the door and turned to wink at me. "Of course you are, brother. Godspeed to you, and sleep well." ☙

2

let a man never stir from his road a step
without his weapons of war,
for he never can know when the need will arise,
of a sudden, for his sword.

~WISDOM OF ODIN~

he sound came from the other end of the room.
Far off the wind moaned and howled, but inside
the footsteps came, lightly tripping across the
floor, coming closer, then closer still. I opened my eyes,
searching the blackness. There was no one there. My heavy
lids fell closed again. Then, the drop of a foot, and another,
soft and quick and close, running … someone was coming!
Shadows loomed above me … I sat up and stared into the
dark but I could not see anything, anyone. I was alone.

And so cold! I couldn't bear for my own frigid fingers to
touch my skin. I moved closer to the wall and felt blocks
of stone like ice against my back. The fur I pulled up to
my ears was not a fur, but a woollen cloak and my bed had
become a stone floor without rushes to soften it. The footsteps began again. Hooves, not feet, clattering on stone,
rushing at me, a stampede of horses bearing down, hounds
howling and voices moaning on the wind, and I lay in their
path, paralyzed. The pounding hooves drove at my mind,
tearing at it, while I lay, frozen, unable to escape. *No, no,* I
moaned. *It's not time. It's not time.*

A sharp pain bit into my arm. In one motion I leapt up
and swung at my attacker, only to be knocked back just as

suddenly onto my bed.

Marjory scowled down at me, rubbing her arm where I had evidently hit her. "It's time to get up, you bloody brute."

"What happened?" I gasped.

"You were taking too long to wake up so I gave you a good pinch. And then you flew at me like I was murdering you! You get a mite carried away with your dreaming, brother," she said. "You'll want to watch that. I'm sure your new friends will teach you your manners if you behave this way with them. They're very interesting, by the way."

"Was there a storm last night?" I muttered, staring around at the grey stone walls, thinking there was something familiar about them. *Of course they're familiar, half-wit. It's your chamber!*

"There's not a cloud in the sky," she said, tossing my mended tunic at my head. "You'll start your journey off dry, anyway. Now get yourself up and dressed. They're waiting!"

"They? What are you talking about?"

"Harald Maddadson's men. A small gaggle of them came in the night. They've eaten. They'll be ready to go soon, or so they said to tell you. And I doubt they're as patient as I!" she said as she tore the bearskin off me and dashed from the room.

I swung my feet to the floor. So soon! A suspicion crept up in me. *Why did Father only tell me last night? Did he think I would run away?* The thought made a sour taste in my mouth. I could not deny that I would have been glad to find a reason not to go, but did he imagine me such a coward, so lacking in love for my family that I would abandon them?

And where would I ever run, alone, that would be less dangerous than going north on this mad venture? A Highlander without kin is nothing, no one. He might as well be dead. No, it made no sense, either that I would do it or that he would think it. Perhaps he had not known they were coming so soon. I hoped that was the truth as I began to dress.

My practice sword lay on the table where I had placed it the night before. I made to reach for it, and stopped. I stared at it a long moment, then slung my satchel over my shoulder and went out the door. I had my knife. It was enough.

The hall was empty. Only the remnants of a quick meal remained. I followed the sound of voices out to the courtyard.

I heard them before I saw them. Marjory's gaggle consisted of at least a dozen men, judging from the voices. Deep voices, some of them speaking accented Gaelic, the rest clearly my own countrymen. *Thank God,* I thought with relief. *I'm not being sent alone with a horde of Vikings!*

"Who are we here for?" one of them asked.

They hadn't seen me yet.

"Alasdair's whelp. A boy along for the ride," said another.

I felt my face grow hot.

"Well, if he's anything like his sire, he'll do."

I stepped out from the arched doorway before they could say more. They all turned to look at me.

Every man in the group had that air of confidence that

comes of training in arms from childhood. Even the youngest, a youth of maybe seventeen, looked like he would feel very much at home swinging a heavy sword. These were men of my father's breed.

One of them approached me with a friendly look and the open palm of greeting. "You must be Malcolm," he said. "I'm Thorir. I welcome you into our company." I gripped his hand firmly with both of my own as I had seen my father do, hoping that I would give a first impression of a character I knew I did not possess. I searched my mind for something to say but all I could think was that I felt like a sapling in a circle of broad oaks.

Thorir was tall, but of middle height compared to the others. His hair was unruly and darkly blond, his face shaven but for the beard on his chin, which ended in a short braid. His eyes were wide and blue, childlike, his dimpled cheeks and disarming smile adding to the effect.

Another man—this one looked more like a Viking—stepped forward next. "I'm Eirik Stagbreiller, Earl Harald's lieutenant and cousin. I am in charge of this sorry band, though I hardly get to show it with this upstart taking over from me all the time." He grinned as he slammed Thorir on the back. Thorir grinned back.

Friends. I had never thought of Vikings as having friends. I had never thought of Vikings as being anything but pirates and murderers.

"Thorir," Eirik continued, "is the earl's *skald* and fancies himself something special. A sort of Odin among men."

"Don't blaspheme, Eirik," said Thorir. "Odin does not like for men to raise themselves above their station. My poems are but a poor shadow of the god's thoughts."

Pagans? I was shocked. I had never met a man or woman who did not believe in the one true God. Surely, the Scots had their old beliefs sprinkled in with their faith in God and the Church, but none that included other gods! Did my father know that he was sending his only son off with a band of pagan cutthroats instead of Christian ones?

"Note, a shadow of Odin's *thoughts*, not his mere words. Still a high mark, is it not, Thorir Honey-Tongue?" The speaker was another tall man, much like Eirik in his face, but darker, with a leaner, more serious countenance.

"My brother, Benedikt the Priest," said Eirik, gesturing at the large cross that hung from his neck, heavy, ornate and costly.

"Hardly," snorted Benedikt, "but I am a God-fearing Christian. One god, mind you," he said, winking at Thorir.

So, I thought, *pagans and Christians together, and all friends. Marjory was right. They are interesting. Troubling, but interesting.*

The youth I had noticed earlier stepped up to me and gave a shallow nod. "And I am Simon," he said, his eyes running up and down me once before he smiled in a way that made me feel even smaller than I had before. "I am son and heir of Earl Malcolm of Atholl and nephew of Earl Harald."

I took in his rich clothes, the fine embroidery of pale flowers decorating cuff and collar. My own tunic was trimmed with my mother's perfectly regular knotwork. Simple, but Scots. I wondered just how Scottish young

Atholl was, he who lived in such close proximity to such a Norman court.

"I'm glad to meet you," he said. "Don't look so surprised. Your father has been to Atholl many times and has spoken of you often. It is good to finally have the opportunity to know you for myself."

I nodded in agreement, but could not rid myself of the sense that he'd said more than one thing with only one set of words. Still, his look was friendly and we were of an age, and, judging from the fine silver cross he wore, he was a Christian.

As I moved among them, losing their names as quickly as I learned them, I realized that a few of their faces were familiar to me. Angus, a long-limbed man with copper hair, had been to Dunailech before. He acknowledged my flash of recognition with a slight smile. Fergus, a small and grizzled man who reminded me of a badger, had been in our hall not long ago.

All greeted me civilly enough, though I could not quite forget who the Vikings were, with their ice-blue eyes and high cheekbones and yellow hair. They looked and smelled cleaner than I'd expected.

"I see you have met my son," came my father's voice from the doorway. The men crowded forward to greet my father with much laughter and comradery and I drifted back.

"It's a shame you won't be joining us," one man said.

"It is," said my father. "I'd give my other foot to go."

His words jarred me. I'd never heard him refer so lightly to his injury, indeed he rarely spoke of it at all, except sometimes in winter when he murmured something to my mother and she rubbed oils into it. I had always imagined it must ache more when he thought of it and so I avoided mentioning it. As had he. But now he joked with strangers about a subject that had always seemed barred to me.

Strangers to me, not to him.

"Your father is a good man," said Thorir, who had come to stand beside me.

"Yes," I said, watching as my father made a joke that had them all howling.

"You are much like him."

"What?" I said, scowling up at his friendly face. Did he think that was what I wanted to hear? My father and I couldn't have been more different. While I showed little promise of swelling to grander proportions, Alasdair Roy was a bull of a man, built to wield his will with his body. He was entirely capable and passionate in all his actions, from eating to singing to fighting and though he had a keen intelligence, his real strength was his determination, his faith in his ability. And I? If my father was a blustering storm, I was a mild spring breeze. We were nothing alike.

"Not in form, of course, but in the eyes. That is where the soul lies, you know."

Why that angered me so much, I do not know. "It may be where your soul lies," I snapped, "but mine is in the hands of God. My God, not yours. And I am nothing like my father!"

I was surprised at the force of my words. And appalled at their volume, for all eyes were now on me. There was silence in the courtyard.

"And I was little like mine," said my father. "But life has

still been good enough to me for all that I lack of his character." The smile he cast my way made me glad, for the first time, that I would be away from Dunailech for at least a few weeks. He turned to Eirik. "My son is a good lad and quick in the mind. He will be obedient and will do his best. He always does."

I flushed at his praise, spoken as it was on the heels of the insult I had just paid him. But I burned too at the unspoken message in his words: He is a good boy, his words said, but he is no warrior, no fighter, no man to have at your back in a fight. He is but a boy. ⚭

3

most blessed is he who lives free and bold,
and nurses never a grief.
but the fearful man is dismayed by all,
and begrudges every gift.

~WISDOM OF ODIN~

*T*he women appeared magically just then. *Or perhaps not so magically,* I thought, catching Marjory's eye. She was giving me the look she reserved for me when she thought me stupid due to petulance. Well, she wouldn't be saving me from myself much longer.

My mother touched my cheek briefly. "Take good care," she said in her low, quiet voice. My sisters were providing an unwitting distraction for the men from Atholl, who had attempted to extract kisses of parting and were being spiritedly rebuffed.

"I say that with a mother's love and not because I fear for you. Not really," she added, looking me in the eye so that I would see she spoke the truth. "I know your pure heart will guide you," she said, "and that you will be back here with us again." When my eyes went wide, my eyes that were a reflection of her own, she laughed lightly. "A mother has no need of second-sight, my son. She has her own ways of knowing. You will fare well. Very well."

I did not know if my mother spoke to keep my heart high, or if she truly saw anything of the future, but her words went some way to dispelling the storm clouds that had hovered at the edge of my thoughts since I'd learned of my impending voyage. She kissed me then, but did not cling, for which I was grateful. It would not do to be unmanned in front of my new companions.

My elder sisters were less considerate, each taking turns to embrace me heartily, amid mock and a few real tears. Marjory, when her turn came to wish me a safe journey, simply tapped my chest where the amulet rested and brushed my cheek with hers.

Then came my father. "A minute more," he called to Eirik, who nodded as he mounted his horse.

"We have little time, son," he said as he drew me away from the others, his hand pressing on my shoulder for balance as he limped beside me. "Listen carefully. I did not wish to say these things with other ears to hear them. I do not know who is a friend and who is not."

Alarm sang in my ears. "You said that Earl Harald was a good man," I said. "Are these men not all his?"

"Do not be naïve, son. Good, bad, no one is all one. But some are more of one than the other. And a friend to Harald may not be a friend to you! Mark it!" He wagged a finger in my face. "And yes, Harald is more good than not, by my eyes, but he is young and he is still overly reliant on certain others. That could be a danger to you, for he has strong-willed people about him who influence him much. I believe he is a good leader, or at least he will be, but he has not learned yet who should have *his* ear. Do you understand me now? Be wary with Thorbjorn, Harald's kinsman and foster-father. He does not like any to get between him and his earl, and of Harald's mother, Margaret. Her beauty belies her danger, and the two are equally great!"

"But you said she would not be with us," I interrupted.

"Let me finish. Eirik has informed me that your party will stop at Wick and that Margaret is likely to be there, now that Harald has separated her from her lover. She has been … stretching her wings since Maddad died. She will not like being fettered again." A look I could not decipher passed over his face, then was gone. "It is unlikely you'll even see her, which would be for the best, but if you do, keep your wits about you."

"Is that all?" I asked. I could not imagine why, of all the possible dangers I might face on the coming journey, he chose to warn me against a woman.

"It is not all," he said. "I cannot be as specific with the rest of it. Just be wary of those who love power overmuch. Few of these men are Vikings anymore, but the man who is Viking at heart serves no one but himself and his own desires. He will despise any who get in his way. You must beware of him."

"Who is it? How will I know him?"

My father shook his head. "That's not the way of it. I don't command my gift, but a man like that will make himself plain to you soon enough, if you keep your mind open. Now go."

It was good then that he'd taken me so far from the others, for all the anger I'd stored up in the past day overflowed. "And that is how you send me off into the world, with dreamy warnings against evil men?" I cried. And then, because I had no desire to discuss the subject of my father's newly revealed gift, I attacked from another angle. "And how long have you known of this plan? Why did you not tell me sooner? I had a right to know!"

Everyone was looking at us by then. I fully expected to feel the back of my father's hand. But his voice was surprisingly calm when he spoke. "You are right," he said.

That nearly shocked me out of my fury. "Then why—"

"Because I was not sure."

"Of me."

"What?" He looked at me with confusion, then with comprehension. "Ah! My foolish son! I have never understood how you see things in such a different light from the way I do. You are ever quick to think the worst. No, I do not doubt you, whatever I might say when I get to talking. I was not sure what folly might be planned. *That* was my concern. Surely, Harald has the makings of a solid leader, but I will not ally myself to my detriment again. We have suffered enough for that in the past. I was waiting until I knew more. Until I could be sure of this path."

When I did not respond he growled in frustration. "Do you hear me? You are not my concern. Ach, that's not my meaning! You are *all* my concern! I will not send you off to the wolves if they are but throwing themselves into the fire. I send you off with every hope that you will return to me!"

"How can you say that?" I cried, knowing the answer even as I asked the question. *Oh, God above, don't let him start about second-sight again.*

But God has His own will.

He searched my face, as if he were memorizing me. "I wish I could tell you that I had seen you returning, but I cannot. You call them dreamy warnings, and that is just what they are. Some are easy to understand, others less so. All I can do is decipher them the best I am able and trust that fate will be kind."

Hard as I found it to accept his claim of second-sight, the thought that he had not seen me returned safely home disturbed me more than I cared to admit. "This is madness, Father!" I cried. "I don't even know what you expect me to do. How am I supposed to restore our fortunes? What do you want of me?"

"You are a faithless wretch, Malcolm. To start, you will lead these men to the cove on Loch Ness where we usually fish. I have left boats there for you to cross in. As for the rest of it, do your duty. Serve Earl Harald and do it *well*. It will be enough. You shall see. Now, it is time."

His arm, falling about my shoulders, cut off any protestations or questions. He walked me to my garron, one of our nimble mountain ponies. As I swung myself up onto her round back he said, quietly, "Malcolm, you must accept the path fate has laid out for you, but how you walk it, the choice is all yours."

I did not see a wealth of choices open to me just then, but I nodded respectfully.

"And Malcolm," he added, so low that I hardly heard him. "You may deny my gift all you like, but when your own comes upon you, no matter what it might be, do not shun it. If you do, it will be to your shame. And futility! You cannot dismiss what is within you, what is given by God. At least not for long."

His words followed me as I rode away from him and my home.

• • •

My new companions rode along, talking and laughing together, in a mood very different from mine. Even the grooms who would retrieve the horses we rode fell in with the others, clearly enjoying the excitement of men embarking on an adventure. I would not need to guide them until we reached the end of the valley so I kept a rein on my garron and dropped to the rear.

I did not turn to look at Dunailech as we rode away, though for a time I thought I could feel Marjory willing me to. I would not have any of the men think I was already homesick so I kept my eyes ahead, but in my mind's eye I was memorizing the place as I left it. Now it was blanketed in a new fall of snow. Perhaps when I saw it again it would be its usual green. I might even be home soon enough to see it white with the snowdrops that would signal the coming of spring. It was Marjory's favourite time.

The men had spread out where the valley floor widened, their voices echoing across the flat, white stretch. One rider lagged behind the main body of the group. *Or not a rider*, I smiled to myself. The man seemed to be having some difficulty with his mount. It was Thorir, the poet. The skald. His horse, a beautiful specimen from Atholl, stood with legs stubbornly splayed while he kicked its sides, to no effect. His curses, colourful as they were, had no impact either.

"Is there trouble with the beast?" I asked as I rode up beside him.

"It won't go," said Thorir, in irritation, but when he looked at me he was grinning. "I think it knows that I would rather be on a ship. This is not a comfortable way to travel!" he grimaced.

"The ride will not be long," I said.

"So they tell me," said Thorir, squirming, "but I'd still rather be riding a sea horse of ancient oak than this fleshly one. Pretty she might be, but her gait leaves something to be desired and I am beginning to know how the wishbone feels when it is being split!"

I grinned. I had been riding since I could remember, for my father had always insisted we have horses. Costly as they were, they protected us from the appearance of poverty, and my father insisted that appearance could be as important as reality. Whatever his reasons, I had benefitted, for I was an excellent horseman and could sit all day in the saddle. Still, I could sympathize with Thorir. "You will be sore tomorrow," I said.

"I am sore today! We rode from Atholl on these blasted beasts and I don't know if I'll sit down for a week after this. Can you believe that I thought it would be fun to go so far south? I was going to scour the heart of Scotland for a tale worthy of growing into a full saga, but all I've gotten for it is a flaming red rear end."

Again I laughed. Then I helped him adjust his position and gave him some advice on how to better encourage the horse to obey his commands. Something about how well he took my lesson led me to suspect he was not really so inexperienced a rider. We set off again together, spurring our beasts to close the distance between us and the others.

Thorir gestured back in the direction of Dunailech. "The hill your family home is built atop—is your ancestor buried under it?"

"What?" I exclaimed, taken aback at the question.

"Well, it's quite a good-sized mound. Where I come from the founder of a farm, when he dies, is placed in such a mound, to be a guardian of the land and those who come after him."

Dunailech did sit atop a hill. I turned to look back at it. We were far enough now that I could not see if Marjory watched.

"We bury our people in the churchyard, not in the mounds. Those are for the Good People, the fairies. No Scot in his right mind would want to live on one. Men have been known to enter them and return a year, a hundred years later. Sometimes not at all."

"So they are not really good then, these Good People?"

"Well, they are good enough if you don't displease them."

"Then they sound much like our mound dwellers," he said. "There is one in Orkney I have heard tell of. He was a great dragon-slayer in his day. They say he still watches over his descendants, that he still speaks for the land. There could be the makings of a saga in his tale."

"The dead man speaks for the land?" I asked.

"Yes. The land registers all sins, you know. Crimes against the soil, against the blood. And the mound dwellers, they remind the people when they go astray."

I gave him an incredulous look.

He held my gaze, then winked. "I shall enjoy getting to know you better as well, I think. Now, tell me, how did your father injure that foot of his? There must be a story there also."

My father's foot had been cut away in battle during the rebellion. From what I had heard of that brutal day, most men worked hard to forget it, which would explain why my father never spoke of it.

I told him as much.

"I know little of this Moray rebellion," he said. "I was a boy when it happened, living in Dingwall, mind you, but it might as well have been a world away for all I cared."

I looked ahead. We were climbing now, but the path was still wide and did not diverge. My services as guide were not needed as yet. I had no cause to deny him the story.

"It was twenty years ago when the Mormaers of the Highlands, our *Ri*, decided that King David, who was of the Roman faith and not of our Columban church, should not have dominion over them. He was the *Ard Ri*, the high king, but they are kings in their own right. David's ways smelled dangerously English to them, for he had spent much of his youth in that land. These Highlands belong to the Picts and the Dalriada, who come from Ireland, and both are Celtic peoples. We will not have others rule us with their foreign ways."

Including the Northmen, I thought, but did not say.

I went on to describe the valiant battle and utter defeat of Moray and then how King David had scattered the survivors, sending them to the barren reaches of Sutherland and other places where they would be forced to expend all their energies on survival, leaving no time for rebellion. Thorir listened in silence.

"My father was maimed in the battle. He was one of the lucky ones, I suppose."

"He truly was," said Thorir, "though I'm sure he would have been welcomed to Valhalla with great anticipation had he fallen."

"My father is a good Christian," I snapped. "He will be in Heaven, not your pagan hell."

"It is no hell, my friend, but I understand your misgivings. Go on."

I had lost the thread of my story.

"It was on this battlefield that your father met Earl Maddad?" he prompted.

"All I know is that my grandfather died in the field and my father inherited and then lost most of his lands all at once. He managed to keep some of them with the help of Maddad of Atholl, or so he has always said."

"And his wound. How did he receive that?"

I bit the inside of my cheek. "He never told me. All he ever said was that it was worth the cost." My telling had holes of which I was becoming acutely aware.

Thorir nodded. "An interesting story there, I am sure."

"Father said we survived because of Maddad. That is all I know."

"It is good, I think, this connection between your families. Some serve others for the coin they earn, others for love, but perhaps indebtedness is not such a bad form of loyalty, and it is more likely to lead to love than will a bag of gold!"

I shrugged. Loyalty was not an issue. I knew my place.

The ridge where we rode had begun to stretch itself thin around the mountain's side, forcing the riders into a narrow file. From here the trail would not only be less clear, but it would diverge in a number of places. The riders had come to a halt.

"Malcolm, I believe it is time for you to show us the way," called Simon. I rode up past the other riders to the fore. Thorir followed.

"It is a good thing we have a guide, isn't it?" said Simon to no one in particular, as I went past him. "Always good to have a man who knows what is coming."

I was inclined to tell him that it was not so difficult to find one's way to the edge of the loch, but decided against it. What little value I had I would keep. "I seldom know what is coming," I said as I passed him, "though I do know where I am meant to go, at least for now."

"Ah, well, that's better than most," said Simon. Again I was quite sure I did not know what he meant. He did not add anything as Thorir and I rode on ahead.

"You have told me of your past," said Thorir. "Shall I tell you of your future?"

I swung around in my saddle.

He met my look with those wide eyes. "A man should know as much about his path as he can, shouldn't he? Do you know what has been happening in Orkney, about why we are going there with Harald?"

There was no guile in him. I relaxed and made room for him to ride by me.

Scots politics are complicated even for those who enjoy the convolutions of power struggles and broken alliances and the weighing of possible outcomes. Orkney politics were dizzying. But Thorir was a good teller of tales, and from him I developed a basic understanding.

In short, it seemed that Earl Harald's cousin, Erlend, had managed to steal his lands with the support of the kings of both Norway and Scotland. Those two kings liked to keep the powerful earldom of Orkney off-kilter, for it was a viable threat to them both. But there was a third earl in the picture, one Earl Rognvald, who was the senior of the three, and he was away in the Holy Land. None knew when he would return, but when he did, if he came home to find Harald no longer in possession of Orkney, he was within his rights to dispossess Harald of his position entirely for failing in his stewardship.

And so we were going, in secret, to find this Erlend and take back Orkney from him. The problem was he was no easy man to find.

"Then how do we know Erlend will be in Orkney when we get there?" I asked, hoping I did not sound foolish.

Apparently I did not, for he answered me straight. "The good Earl Harald has his ways of learning such things. Or shall I say his foster-father does. Thorbjorn is certain of his spies. We will go north as quickly and quietly as possible and take Erlend wherever he happens to be drinking Yule. The man likes his feasting. He won't give it up, no matter what Svein advises."

"Svein?" I asked.

"Erlend's chief advisor, a most brilliant man. Svein Asleifarson was once in Harald's camp, but there was a falling out. More than one, really. It is a long story. Be advised not to mention Svein's name in front of Thorbjorn when you meet him, for he hates the man as much as he once loved him. They were brothers-in-law and good friends, but since

Harald was expelled from Orkney, Thorbjorn's hatred has reached new heights."

I was looking at Thorir with some consternation. "So, Svein is the enemy?"

"For now," he answered, with a grin that I would come to know well.

"You mean that one day he may not be?"

"Fate will tell, but I hope so."

"Would he become Earl Harald's advisor, then?"

"He could be mine," said Simon, from just behind Thorir. "Who wouldn't want to use a man like that? It is unfortunate that by the time I am earl of Atholl he will likely be dead, for my father is a young man."

I looked around in surprise at his bluntness but there were smiles on a few faces. Was this usual talk for nobility? It was rather cold for my liking.

Thorir seemed to have followed my line of thought. He smiled. "It would always be good to know what that man has puzzled out, but Svein's sense of honour is somewhat skewed. He can keep an eye on the truth even while he skirts the edge of it. I believe Harald needs someone a touch more to the sharp point of it."

I was about to ask him what he meant by that when Eirik spoke from close behind. "Svein's sense of honour may be his own, but he is a man of his word. He has no qualms about killing a man who deserves it, but he does it outright, not piecemeal or for pleasure! Unlike Margaret. What she did to her own brother ..." He cleared his throat. "You would think that Svein would have known what was coming there, would you not? I mean, they say he has the witchery in him, that he can see what will arise from men's actions."

The path widened and everyone clustered to look out at the view. The Monadhliath Mountains rose up around us in rounded humps like waves on a great ocean. The sky was a sheet of pale blue, unmarred by a single cloud, and the sun on the white-capped mountains dazzled my eyes so that they ached.

"They say he has that power," said Benedikt. "But how far do you expect a man can see? And besides, how often is such a gift used for good, coming from where it does?"

"And where is that?" asked Thorir.

"From outside the realm of men," answered Benedikt.

"But from above or below?" Thorir pressed. "And can you see far enough to tell?"

"Ah ha!" cried Benedikt. "I like that, though I cannot say I am at ease with men's claims to see through time. I say leave it to the women, who are already strange creatures to us."

"I think the stone falls where it does. There is little a man can do once it is in the air."

"Except to deflect it onto some other man's head!" laughed Eirik. Others joined him in laughter.

As I rode I fingered the boar under my tunic. Why had Marjory given it to me? And why all this talk, suddenly, of second-sight? And what had this Margaret done to her brother to make a man like Eirik uncomfortable? These questions were in my mind as we rode in file along the gently curving slope for a time.

It was near midday when we rounded the western side of

the mountain. Fading from sight in the distance was Glen Mhor, the great, long gash of lake-filled valley that cuts Scotland in two. Directly below was Loch Ness, the largest of all our lakes and a mysterious place, even in the bright light of day. Its waters are said to be deeper than the ocean, its source a magical spring.

I found the head of the trail. It led down between two sloping hills whose feet were shrouded by a fog that clung to the valley floor. An eerie silence crept over each man as he descended into the low cloud. The sun had risen to its highest position, but inside the mist, it was as if it had never risen at all. At times my horse's delicate brown ears disappeared as I wound my way down the steep, narrow track. Sounds were muffled and distorted but they were all that confirmed I was not alone. A muttered curse from Thorir, just behind, sounded from out where the water should be. The slip of a hoof on a frosty rock seemed to echo from before me, though I knew it was only a trick of the mist, for I was the first rider in the party.

And then, as if by magic, the air cleared and Loch Ness appeared, long and slender, its waters cradled by the surrounding hills, bright as a metal mirror. A final white wisp lingered briefly in the middle of the lake, and then it, too, vanished. Almost immediately the placid water began to ruffle into a light chop that sparkled with diamonds. We had reached the cove where my father's boats waited for us.

I stood on the narrow strip of beach, feeling, for the first time, the hard truth of where my path was leading me. Once I stepped from the shore of the loch into one of those boats, I was leaving Moray, perhaps for good. ⊕

4

*he hath need of his wits who wanders wide,
aught simple will serve at home,
but a gaping fool is the one who sits
with the wise and nothing knows.*

~WISDOM OF ODIN~

I sat in the prow of the small boat with the wind in my face. The others talked quietly about sundry matters while I tried to calculate when my father might have secreted the boats in the cove. He might have apologized for keeping this venture a secret from me, but that did not mean I was quite ready to forgive him. I was also hoping to distract myself from the fact that I was on the water. I liked water well enough, but not being upon it. In the middle of the lake the waves had grown into whitecaps, tossing our boats about less than gently.

No matter, I told myself, *I will be on land soon enough. With such expert oarsmen as Vikings must be, Lochend could only be an hour or so away.* From there we would travel on foot to Beauly Firth. On land I was as agile as a goat, bred for the hills as God bred the goats for the same. I could tramp overland like any fit man of the Highlands, running for half a day without stopping. Moving over water was another matter. My belly would not feel settled until I was on solid earth again.

"I have heard there is a demon in the depths," said Benedikt, fingering his cross in an absent-minded gesture.

"A demon?" said Angus, dragging back on his oar. "Perhaps you mean the water horse."

"What sort of beast is that?" asked Thorir.

"I've never seen it myself," Angus replied, "but some of the fisherfolk say it comes often, stealing their sheep if they let them stray too close to the shore. Girls have vanished, too. Once I heard a child tell how a serpent-like creature lured his sister away into the water as she bathed. Others say there never was a thing in here but fish. What do you say there, Malcolm?"

"I have heard all those tales," I said, reluctantly, "but there is only one I believe for certain. St. Adamnan wrote that St. Columba, he who brought the one true God to our people, subdued the monster with his word, in God's name." The Life of St. Columba was one of my grandfather's books and among my favourites.

"It seems all the stories agree that there is such a creature in these waters," said Thorir, "so perhaps we should not speak of it. Better not to summon it with our talk, no?"

It took me a moment to realize his words were not in jest. "You do not believe you can draw this creature here with words, do you?" I scoffed.

"You say it was turned away with words, so why do you doubt that it could be drawn here that way as well? Words are more powerful than any sword, my friend," said Thorir.

"Aye," I said, more irritated than I should have been. "Those spoken in God's name are."

Thorir's response was calm and certain. "Those, I'm sure, good Christian, but not only those. Words are the greatest gift of our lord Odin. They give us much power over our world, over other men. We can call others to us with them, men, as well as the spirits and the creatures of the other worlds. We can fill another with courage or drain it from him, all with words. Do not mock the power of a word."

"Those who practice the old ways would say the same, but God resides now in Scotland," I replied tersely. "And it is just a story."

Thorir gazed out at the water with a distant eye. "My people tell a story too, of a great serpent that will destroy the world. Not even the gods can defeat it; indeed, it will destroy the mightiest of them. When that serpent is summoned, with a word, the end is near."

"Pagan nonsense," I said and turned away to cross myself.

"There are things beyond your knowledge, my friend, and beyond your power," he said.

"I know it," I answered bitterly. Just one day earlier, I had been happily going about my life in the home I loved, never dreaming I would do else. "What you speak of is superstition and blasphemy." I spat the words over my shoulder.

"You must bear with Thorir," interjected Benedikt. "He believes in the old ways, the ancient creatures and the spirits. I do not know that he is wrong about their existence, but, Thorir, young Malcolm is right, too. The saint turned the creature away with his command and in the name of God. All you must do is accept Christ and you have his protection."

"Thank you, my friend, but I do not think that the creature that lives in this lake knows who your Christ is. It is much older than he is and subject to other powers. And it would not do for me to forsake Odin now, would it? He would not look on it kindly with so many turning their backs on him these days."

"In time, friend, in time. At least you are ever loyal," said Benedikt. There was no condemnation in his voice. I was dumbstruck. I knew of witches and the spirits of stone and water, and of the Good People, of course, but a Christian man had nothing to fear from any of them if he knew how to call upon the power of the Church. No man with an education, with any sense in his head, showed any true fear of such things. Yet Thorir was a poet, like our wandering bards, and as such was among the best educated of men. And Benedikt, whose cross said he was a Christian, was either humouring him or gave his fears stock. It disturbed me greatly, I who had been raised to believe in God and that all who did not were doomed. I was beginning to wish the water horse would rise just to command us to leave it in peace.

"Whatever it is that lives in the water," said Angus, "it is unlikely to show itself to a score of men, words or no." He nudged Thorir, who shrugged in response.

But I could not let it go. His mind was not changed. If he insisted on having his gods and serpents I'd give him one of our good Scots demons to play with. "It is unlikely, yes," I agreed, "but if you see a dark head coming out of the water, tell me and I will help you row faster."

I was rewarded with volley of laughter. I grinned, feeling happy for a moment.

"So, do they all have dark hair then, these water-folk?" said Thorir, softly.

"Aye," said Fergus. "Fair heads are thought to bring ill luck. A water horse wishing to lure some innocent would disguise itself more wisely." His own grizzled hair was a colour that defied definition.

"But they can appear in any shape as well," I said. "A handsome man or woman, a horse or a wolf, a serpent as long as the loch is wide." Thorir was silent behind me.

"So, would these fisherfolk welcome you coming out of the mist then?" Eirik asked, waving a hand at my dark curls.

"More likely they'd flee at the sight of your brand of gold," I retorted bravely. "Men hereabouts welcome few things coming out of the mist. Longships have been up the rivers and through this loch."

Thorir spoke. "I think the people of the lake have less to fear from us today than from your water horse."

I did not answer him. It vexed me that he took the story of the water horse so seriously, or perhaps it the way he held so devoutly to his foreign beliefs that made me afraid, and therefore angry. And then it may have been that he awakened a kindred fear in me, one that I had learned to deny, for the stories of the nursery and the hearth driven home in children's hearts are never totally wrested from their place there.

There was silence again. The shores sped by as the oarsmen hauled us north with practiced strokes. The choppy waters set up their own rhythm on the hull of the boat. I would be glad when the only motion I must countenance was my own. I breathed deeply of the fresh air to soothe my complaining belly and watched as passing clouds dimmed the sunlight and cast shadows on the dark water.

Of the dancing shadows on the water, one caught my eye. It moved strangely, differently from the others. It was darker and grew larger as I watched, a shadow hidden within the lake running alongside our boat as if racing with us. I glanced back and saw Thorir's eyes widening in surprise. The hair on the back of my neck rose up. Had we indeed summoned the beast simply by speaking of it?

A touch on my shoulder made me start. Benedikt pointed to the sky with a grin. I looked up to see a raven there, flying in tandem with our boat, just out of reach. Not far behind was a second one, flying above the first and behind. Then, as if they knew we had seen them, they swept up high in the air, catching the currents above and sailing away till they were dark specks against the sky. Then they were gone.

I smiled at Benedikt and the others who were all enjoying the joke. The teasing went on a while, but it was light-hearted and I took it as such. My thoughts were on the words I imagined I had heard whispered from behind me. A quick glance showed me Thorir rowing steadily, his eyes on the water, and far away.

The wind plays tricks with my ears, I thought.

But they were strange words for my mind to conjure on its own. I knew I had not misheard.

The whispered words had been distinct: *He sees all, he knows all.*

• • •

The sun sets early in midwinter giving only six, perhaps seven hours to the day. It was nearing dusk when we set off on foot from Lochend along the river Ness and then across the low hills to the northwest, easily covering the half dozen miles to Beauly Firth.

The moon was new, so only starlight, cold and distant, shimmered on the waters of Beauly when we arrived on its southern shore. But the warmer light of supper fires flickered within the scattering of fishermen's huts, and the gnarled men of the sea loch welcomed their guests with proper hospitality and shared their meager stew. Then we all curled up in our woollen cloaks to sleep and to prepare our bodies and souls for the next leg of our journey. ⚜

5

brand kindles brand till all be burned,
spark is kindled from spark.
by the words of his mouth a man is known,
and the speechless by his silence.

~WISDOM OF ODIN~

I bolted up out of my sleep, my heart pounding in my ears. *Where am I?* I lay on a dirt floor, shivering. *Not at home.* The air was heavy with the stink of grease and smoke and the unwashed bodies of men. Those same bodies and the close confines made the room surprisingly warm, yet my bones ached with cold. Wind whistled through the many chinks in the walls of … *Beauly Firth,* I remembered with relief. I was in a fisherman's hut on the shores of Beauly.

I turned onto my back and pressed my fingers into my throbbing temples.

The driftwood fire had burnt down to glowing coals. In the faint light I could see the humped forms of some of my companions and a few fishermen sprawled in sleep around me. Except one. The glow of the embers glittered in the open eye of the wizened fisherman who sat hunched near the fire. The rest of him was only a shadow.

"Had a dream, you did," he grunted.

Had I? If so, it was gone now.

"You were speakin', speakin' to one in your dream."

"It was just a dream," I muttered, but a strange apprehension was stirring in me. I wrapped myself in my cloak and rested my head again on my satchel.

The old man's gaze pressed like fingers into my back.

"What is it?" I muttered as I propped myself up on my elbow. The drumming in my head increased.

"You must strive to waken within your dream. Wake in the dream, not in the world."

Wake in the dream? What nonsense is that? The old man has lived too long in his hut in the wind, I thought, but even as I flopped back down and closed my eyes, I felt as if I were being pressed towards the edge of sleep by his words, by his eyes.

"Dream," said the man.

I did not answer. I slowed my breathing to feign sleep, even while I fought the waves of drowsiness that washed over me. I would not sleep. I would not dream.

The fisherman's words had awakened a memory in me that hovered just out of reach: a sensation of hoofbeats, of footsteps, of a bitter cold that crept inside me like an icy finger reaching for my heart.

• • •

I did sleep, but if there were dreams they were quickly lost. I lay awake for a time, trying to recall them, before the others stirred. Then Thorir was leaning over me with a hunk of stale bread soaked in fish oil. Unappetizing as it smelled, I gratefully made quick work of it, sweetening my mouth with the shriveled apple Benedikt tossed me. I was eager to leave the shore of Beauly and especially to leave the little hut.

The sharp air outside stung my nostrils with salt spray.

It cleared some of the ache from my head. In the predawn light I could see the rest of our party leaving the ragged line of wretched hovels, making their way across the sand to the fishermen's curraghs.

We would cross the Beauly water in the fishing boats and then hike over the narrow arm of the Black Isle to meet Earl Harald in Dingwall. The fishermen moved purposefully to get their passengers under way, hoping, no doubt, to have a full day of fishing on the return part of their voyage, turning the payment Eirik doled out to them into a true boon.

The curraghs, wicker-framed boats covered in skins, were strung out along the shore like beads on a string. I drifted towards the nearest one and helped to push it into the water as I clambered in. Too late I saw that I had chosen the boat of the fisherman who had spoken to me in the night. But though the man had me move twice as he made his preparations, he gave no sign he recognized me. It was as if our conversation had never taken place.

Perhaps I dreamed it, I thought as I watched him expertly playing the wind in the small boat's sail and we began to move steadily across the water. Once I thought I felt his eyes on me, and I waited a time before I stole a glance his way but he was looking at the horizon. In the dim light he was like a knotted branch, his skin darkened and etched by the elements, ageless and ancient all at once. He worked the sail with a grace that seemed at odds with his looks.

We scudded northwest on the choppy water, my head and belly rocking with the boat. Though the wind made my eyes stream, and sent tears whipping off my cheeks to fly behind me, I closed my eyes and gave myself up to that lashing, for it kept the nausea at bay.

I breathed deeply of the salt air. The only sounds were the waves slapping the sides of the skin boat and the constant exhalation of the wind. My mind drifted back, again and again, to the image of the fisherman by the fire and of the uncanny sense I'd had that he had been able to see me perfectly in the darkness, that he had seen *into* me. *Maybe that was a dream too*, I thought, annoyed that it should have followed me into the day. All men have dreams. It was foolishness to give them any power.

The sun had just begun to hover low over the sea, burnishing the waves with gold, when I felt the sudden grinding of the boat on rock and sand. We had reached the northern shore. The others were already leaping onto the shingle and I quickly moved to join them, impatient to feel the steadiness of earth beneath my feet.

I was throwing one leg over the side when the old man gripped my arm, knocking me off balance, almost pitching me into the water. I jerked my arm from his grasp.

"What do you want?" I demanded. My voice sounded ugly to my own ears.

"I have naught to say but that I wish ye well," he said, unaffected by my tone. Only then did I see that one of his eyes was milky blue and sightless. The other one made up for the lack, examining me thoroughly enough that I squirmed. He did not smile, yet I thought I detected an amused note in his voice. "Aye, lad, fare thee well."

He leapt lightly into his curragh and maneuvered it back onto the water where it was joined by its sisters who, having released their catch of men on shore, set off eagerly to their true work. Nets flew overboard, splaying open on the surface before vanishing into the black depths. The small boats scattered like dancing leaves on the waves as a watery sun rose up over us.

And I stood on the shore wondering at the chill that had crept into my flesh at the touch of the man's hand and at the hairs on my neck standing up like hackles on a dog.

• • •

It was good to run, to warm my blood and stretch my limbs. When Thorir edged his way towards me and fell into step at my side I wondered at it, considering how I had spoken to him on the loch, but I did not protest.

He grinned in greeting. At first I hoped he would drift away and not irritate me with any of his outlandish notions, but he kept apace with me and remained silent. Now and then I glanced over at the large pagan loping at my side and after a time I found myself relaxing and even feeling oddly comfortable with him there. We ran easily in step, despite the difference in size, our breath puffing out in parallel clouds of vapour. We ran that way all the seven or eight miles across the Black Isle, until Thorir called out suddenly as the main tower of the castle of Dingwall appeared in the distance.

My nerves tingled with excitement and a twinge of apprehension as we neared the fortress. It was built solely of stone on a scale that spoke of enormous wealth and power. The town was the birthplace of the great MacBeth, Mormaer of Moray and later, King of Scots, more than a hundred years earlier. It had also become the seat of his cousin, Thorfinn the Mighty, a fearsome earl of Orkney with the unlikely reputation of being at once a terrible Viking and an ally to MacBeth. Now it was a kinsman of Earl Harald who ruled there.

Entering Dingwall felt like venturing into the wolves' lair. I had grown up on stories of Viking marauders sweeping down on Moray from this stronghold. The threat of the yellow-haired barbarians in their dragonships, with their keen thirst for the blood of Scots boys and girls, and for burning houses down around the ears of innocent families, was one frequently wielded by many a frustrated mother and nurse. And I could see why my people both feared and envied the place. My father had included military strategy in my education so I knew enough to appreciate Dingwall's excellent situation. The harbour, shaped as if God Himself had carefully sculpted it to be a safe haven, was filled with a multitude of upthrust mast and prow, signifying great sea power; the fortress, towering above the south end of the town perfected the natural defenses. Dingwall was inviolable, at least to my admittedly inexpert eye.

Hurrying to keep up with Thorir, I entered the stream of people moving in and out of the enormous fortress gates and a moment later I was swallowed by them.

The courtyard of the castle lived up to the promise of its exterior. It was open and spacious, yet still managed to seem filled with a wide assortment of men and women and children. Here were men practicing with swords and spears and axes while others wrestled. All seemed healthy specimens, many going shirtless despite the cold.

The women were tall and fair, with high cheekbones and light eyes. The younger ones wore their hair long and loose or in braids, while those I took to be married had theirs bound up in knots that sat on their necks, some simple and others in a complex weaving of braids and twists. Their long apron-like garments, dyed in a wide variety of bright shades, were strange to me, but it was not their dress or their beauty that drew my eye. It was their jewelry that told me, beyond a doubt, that I had entered an alien place.

Scots brooches, for both men and women, are of much the same design, a circle or half-moon with a long pin, which holds a cloak or shawl at one shoulder. These women wore two large oval brooches, one below each shoulder to hold together the straps of their dresses. Between most of them were suspended chains, from which hung an assortment of objects, so that each woman wore upon her breast the tools she required to fulfill her household duties.

I cannot say why it struck me so at the time, but this was the thing that fired home the truth of my situation. King Malcolm might rule in name, and there were Scots men and women in Dingwall, but this was no land of the Scots. I had entered the land of the stranger.

As we marched in a pack towards the main building, my eyes were constantly drawn back to the ornate jewelry on display all around. It was not greed or envy, but a deep appreciation for the excellent craftsmanship evident everywhere that awed me. Animals were not all I carved. I was glad when a man approached and Eirik and Benedikt stopped to exchange greetings. Standing only feet away was a woman whose silver brooches made me wish I could have created something so lovely.

She stood with a few others, wealthy couples dressed in their finest, probably on their way to festivities. She waved her white hands as she talked. I could not understand her words. When I edged closer I knew it was because she spoke a foreign tongue, but I had not moved to hear what she said. I wanted a better look at the patterns that swirled on the surface of one of her brooches. I squinted to see the animals etched there, fantastic, serpent-like creatures that gave birth to others from their mouths, and held yet others fast with their sharp teeth. I sought to memorize the design, that I might use it later. I was so engrossed in my study that I did not notice that the brooch's wearer had noticed me as well.

She shouted something at me I did not understand, but the curl of her lip gave me the nub of it. I felt my face turning red.

"No," I spluttered. "I was only looking … your brooch …" I protested, but she waved me away with a flick of her hand. Everyone around me was laughing. Explaining would only invite more of the same.

The shout that rang out a moment later was like an answer to prayer as all eyes turned away from me.

"What have we here?" came a deep voice. "Terrorizing the womenfolk already?"

"You would think the boy had never seen a real woman before, what with his eyes falling half out of his face," laughed Eirik as he slapped my back. "How goes it with you, my lord?"

"All goes well, and now that you are here it promises even

to improve! Introduce me to these men, and this one who has such a way with the ladies first of all."

I turned to meet the man who was to be my lord and master.

I had to look up, for Harald Maddadson was half a head taller even than my father. He was broad-shouldered but not thickset, and when I took the hand he offered I found its grip strong, the long fingers calloused. It was a hand that would be equally at home holding a silver goblet or a thick oar. *He is no pampered young lord*, I thought.

He was dressed like the others, his garments simple and unadorned, but well made. Gold flashed on breast and from under sleeve, but there was nothing ostentatious about him.

The thick, dark hair that hung to his shoulders was normal enough, but his deep-set eyes had the look of a predatory bird. Those eyes took careful stock of me, even while a smile danced in them. As I met that gaze I tried not to stare at his most striking feature, for the earl's face was dominated by a nose like an axe blade and it drew my eye the way only the loveliest and ugliest of things can. There was something noble in the harsh angle it cut in his profile but it was a nose I imagined a child would have to get the better of, to learn to defend. *Or maybe earls don't have to worry about teasing*, I thought. This one didn't have sisters. My own had helpfully catalogued all my imperfections for me long ago.

His wide slash of mouth grinned down at me. "I see you are making yourself at home here already." He nodded at the woman whose angry scowl had become a coy smile.

The large blond man beside him gave a great laugh and the earl grinned at him fondly. He looked younger when he smiled. I recalled that he was only five years my senior. After Simon and myself, he was the youngest man there.

"I didn't mean to offend anyone, sir, I was just looking at …"

"We know what you were looking at, boy," boomed the blond man at Earl Harald's side. "And well worth looking at, it is," he added with a lewd wink. The object of his regard smiled back with a raised brow, took the arm of one of the men and drifted away.

"No, I, that's not what I was …" Now frustration rather than shame was blazing hot under my skin. *This must not be the earl's first impression of me*, I thought, but any excuses I made would only make me look more foolish. I didn't know which was worse, to be thought lecherous, or to tell him I'd been so intent on a brooch.

"Look at the blush on that rose!" cried the blond man, and I felt a new rush of blood darken my face as the earl and the others laughed again.

The earl's laughter abated. "Leave him be, Thorbjorn," he said, but his grin had not faded.

Thorbjorn, I thought. This is the man my father warned me not to get in the way of.

"The girl who warmed my bed last night didn't blush so prettily," he said with a broad wink, "nor had she for many a year, I'm sure!" He guffawed. The others joined in. I trembled with the effort to restrain myself.

"Shall I ask the lady if she has plans for this night?" asked Thorbjorn, playfully clapping a hand on my shoulder.

His touch was like a spark in tinder. "Ask her for yourself if you want," I cried, "but don't make *me* out to be a pig!"

His smile fringed in yellow beard and mustaches remained in place, but as I looked into the ice-blue eyes, they grew impossibly colder. Thorbjorn looked down his long, handsome nose at me. "So, you do not desire ladies, then," he said mildly. "It was all you needed to say. I'm sure we can find someone more … to your taste."

Shame and rage made a great rushing sound in my ears. I fought to contain the flood of words that threatened to pour from my mouth, for a part of me knew I was on the verge of an irretrievable error.

It was Thorbjorn watching me, a sly smile playing on his face, that cooled my ire. *He is baiting me*, I thought. *This is not a man I want as my enemy! I must stop this!*

I drew a calming breath. "I agree the lady is attractive," I began, but just then Thorir roughly threw his arm around my shoulders, cutting off my next words.

"And what red-blooded male wouldn't?" he grinned wolfishly, his eyes locked with mine. "But there is no need to explain. An experienced woman is a good thing, to be sure, but she's no match for your girl at home!"

What is he doing? I was about to speak when his grip on my shoulder tightened. He was warning me. *I was only going to tell the oaf that my people have a higher regard for their womenfolk,* I grumbled inwardly, but I kept silent.

"My foster-father is just making sport, Malcolm," said Earl Harald. "It is Malcolm, is it not? Alasdair's son?"

"Yes, my lord," I said, bowing stiffly, wondering how he had guessed.

"Another Malcolm," said Thorbjorn, the jest gone from his voice. "Will we ever see the end of creatures called Malcolm? And Alasdair's son, to boot. We are deeply honoured."

His sarcasm took me aback. My father had warned me about this man, but had not said he knew him. I watched his face as he looked me over; there was curiosity there, and something else I could not define.

The earl darted a glance at his foster-father before turning back to me. His expression had changed as well, from teasing to thoughtful. "Yes," he said. "Alasdair's son indeed! None could be more welcome. Our fathers were excellent friends," he said, "and so shall we be."

I returned his smile and if mine was forced, it was not wholly a lie. The genuine friendliness on his unattractive face right then was like cold water on my heated temper. First impressions are one thing, but instinct, that is another. It might be early days for promising friendship, but I felt a surprising pleasure that the earl had voiced such a thought.

I took his hand and knelt, for the first and the last time in his presence, though I did not know it then. I pledged obedience and loyalty to my new lord, and then he drew me to my feet again, his keen eyes searching mine, again.

I do not know what he saw in me that day, but for my part, I felt a glimmering of hope.

That hope was tempered, though, by another sight. As I rose from my humble position I glimpsed the look that flashed across Thorbjorn's face and I wondered what sort of friend I would need to protect me from my new enemy. ❦

6

*friendship is made when a man can utter,
to another, his true mind.
there is nothing so vile as a fickle tongue,
that only speaks thee fair.*

~WISDOM OF ODIN~

he hall of Dingwall was large enough to house all of Dunailech, at least so it seemed at first glance. The smoke-blackened beams of the ceiling were vaulted far above our heads and hung with long banners that decorated the dull room in vivid red, green and blue. *Not banners*, I realized. *Sails.* The sails that would, in spring, clothe the masts of the ships in the harbour.

At the far end of the hall the enormous Yule log smouldered dully red on the stone slab that served as hearth. It would be kept alive throughout Yule and the last of it saved to light the next year's log. The flint never touched such a log. Indeed, flint was not to be used at all in the season. If it were, it was because the Yule fire had died, not a good omen for either my people or these.

Enough benches to seat more than a hundred men lined the stone-flagged floor, all aimed at that hearth and the head table that sat before it, the seat of power.

Eirik, Benedikt and Thorbjorn were absorbed in a heated discussion. I could not hear what they said, but their displeasure was unmistakable. The earl glanced frequently in their direction as he spoke to us.

"My kinsman is in Norway and has graciously opened

the doors of his castle to me for this gathering of men," he said. "Tonight we will all celebrate Yule together. I know that many of you have left warmer fires to lend me your aid and I would show my appreciation for your sacrifice."

A voice rose up from the little knot of the earl's lieutenants and he turned towards them. "Is all well, my friends?"

"I was asking these two where the rest of the men are," said his foster-father.

"And I have told him," interrupted Eirik, "these are the men your brother sent. He said that there were troubles starting, with Atholl still struggling after the loss of your father. He could send no more."

"He could. He *would* not," growled Thorbjorn with disdain.

"He has his own trials these days," said Earl Harald. "But it matters not. We have what we have and they are all clearly worth two men each."

Flattery. My fellow Scots would see through it, but would enjoy it.

"And if each of them could hold two swords and two shields I'd be satisfied, but this is not the support we expected from him," answered Thorbjorn. "You're too easily satisfied. Perhaps your brother is not as loyal as you think."

The earl raised a brow but did not comment. He turned to his nephew. "What word from your father, Simon?"

Simon shrugged. "He sends his love, uncle, and as many prayers as he wishes he could have sent men, but as you say, he has need of them himself these days. Scotland is a whole new world with Grandfather and King David dead and we must find our feet in it."

"Prayers instead of men. Excellent. And was that last part your own or wisdom from your generous father?" said Thorbjorn.

"My own," replied Simon haughtily. "My father's business is *his* own, but if you want to know my position, I will tell you: I will rule Atholl one day and I would have it intact when I get it. He has done what is right for his line. And I have come to offer what support I can, including my fighting arm. Perhaps if my uncle is successful he will return the favour one day."

A part of me admired how effectively Simon defended himself, though another part wished he could have defended his father's name as well.

Thorbjorn's approval was more complete. He looked Simon over a moment and nodded. "Willing to fight, are you?"

"At any given moment."

Thorbjorn snorted. "And can you fight?"

"Better than you can imagine."

The earl's foster-father snorted once more, but he seemed pleased with Simon's boast. "I still say Atholl could have sent more, but it is done. With these, we have fifty to add to the ones at Wick—it's half what I'd hoped, but it will have to do."

"They'll more than do," said the earl.

"Not if it's an army we're needing," said Thorbjorn.

"Then let's not need an army," answered Earl Harald. The look that passed between them said they were continuing an old conversation. To us he said, "We depart early tomorrow for Wick, but until then your time is your own. Leave your gear with the chamberlain and return at nightfall for the feast."

With a nod he went to Thorbjorn and they moved off, talking together, Eirik and Benedikt trailing behind. I watched as my companions dispersed, wondering what on God's earth I was meant to do between noon and nightfall. Just then the earl called over his shoulder, "Thorir, choose your own companions and take your old chamber. And I expect you to earn your keep now, instead of traipsing around the countryside collecting tales and entertaining yourself."

"But that is my work, sire," said Thorir cheerfully.

"Only if you share your treasures, and well," said Earl Harald with a laugh, as he led his lieutenants through the door at the far end of the hall, and was gone.

Thorir chuckled to himself as he slung his satchel over his shoulder and made his way past the benches towards the far wall. *His usual chamber*, I thought. The others were all disappearing out the main door. Only Simon remained.

"Come on, then," he said. "Let's see what this place is all about."

I hitched my satchel up on my shoulder, prepared to follow him.

"Malcolm?" Thorir stood in front of an enormous tapestry, tipping his head to one side in a gesture of invitation.

"It's up to you," Simon laughed, "though why you'd want to spend your day with that pagan I cannot imagine."

I could hardly imagine it myself. Perhaps it was the sense I had that Simon felt he was doing me a great favour by taking me under his wing, but the thought of spending the afternoon with him did not appeal to me. I thanked him and mumbled something about having already been invited by Thorir. It was untrue, but I could live with a small lie.

Simon shrugged, wished us a good day and was gone. I grabbed up my things and followed Thorir as he disappeared behind the enormous tapestry. As I lifted a corner of it I glanced a moment at the image stitched there in colourful thread. A man rode an eight-legged horse into what appeared to be the gaping jaws of a wolf. A serpent encircled the outer edge of the tapestry, biting its own tail. *Pagan indeed*, I thought, and wondered if I might not be better off with my fellow Scot, but it was too late now.

The flicker of oil lamps showed Thorir vanishing around a corner. I followed him up the steep, narrow turn of stairs. He whistled a thin tune as he led me down a dark passageway and into a small chamber where he marched straight to the slit of a window.

I dropped my gear and sat down on one of the sleeping benches. It was a simple room, no larger than mine at home. The ashes in the grate were cold, but it was bright enough, for the sun was on a level with the window. The slanted beams shone in like pale fingers, illuminating a multitude of dust motes.

I joined Thorir at the window. Below, I could see people bustling about in the courtyard and in the streets that twisted down to the harbour. The long arm of water that linked Dingwall to the North Sea curved eastwards, freckled with small craft. To the north rolled the mountains of Easter

Ross, dazzling white against the blue sky. The horizon was smudged with grey clouds, too distant for concern.

"Do you know the place well?" I asked.

"I've called it home much of my life. But I was not born in Dingwall. The sea brought me here, if you will."

The words dangled between us, awaiting my invitation to continue. I gave it with a look.

"I was only a small boy when my family left Norway. We were caught in a terrible storm and our ship was wrecked. I was the only survivor. My uncles' ship landed safely and they found me on the shore, but they were off to … trade, and could not be burdened with a child."

I knew he meant raid, rather than trade, but I did not interrupt.

"They found a woman to keep me and said they would collect me at summer's end. They did not. I heard later that they died raiding an Irish monastery.

"But the god was watching for me. Hrafn's father ruled here then, and he took pity on me. When my talent began to show he had his own skald foster me and when I was old enough he paid my passage to Iceland, where I trained with masters. Wise Odin planned well for me, placing me in the path of a man who could sense and then draw out my gifts. When I think that I might have been raised by a tanner or an uncultured farmer …"

But at that moment I did not care who had raised him. "What is all this talk of pagan gods?" I exclaimed. "All your fellows are Christian and yet you give thanks to this, this …" I stopped, for I did not want to utter the name.

"Odin. His name is Odin."

"It is a sin to worship false gods."

"And yet you call them gods nonetheless." Thorir smiled as he gazed out the window at the town and mountains and sea. "It is only a sin for you. For me it is truth."

"There is only one truth."

"Is there?"

"Then why have almost all your people taken up the Christian faith?"

"Because as one world dies another must take its place." When I did not respond, having no idea what he was saying and not wanting to know, he went on. "I was a Christian before the wreck."

"You must not …" I began, but he waved me off.

"Let me finish," he said. "I was a Christian, or at least my parents were. And then we crossed the sea and the storm came up from a windless day and it struck us like an axe blow. I remember it so clearly, though I was very small." His voice became softer. "My father prayed that we would be spared. Fervently he beseeched his god. Your god. The next wave that fell from the heavens carried away all our goods and most of the crew. But he was a man of faith and he got down on his knees and prayed harder while the storm lashed down on us. And as he prayed that his family would live to walk on the land again my mother was swept into the sea. Then it was only my father and I, and he looking already like a dead man. His eyes bore into me and I saw the change in his heart as it transpired.

"He leapt up and held his arms to the sky and cried out to Odin to save his only son, to give him life, to make him his own. I remember him standing there, pelted with rain, begging for my life. And the god answered. Lightning struck the mast and the ship slew about. The last I saw of my father was him standing, arms raised with the mast sheering off above him as the ship broke and fell under the waves.

"All I knew when I awoke was who had saved me. Believe me, Malcolm, they fought me on my faith. They nearly whipped it out of me, those first ones. Later my guardians were more open of mind. I know that you cannot see it, that it reeks of sacrilege for you, but I know who saved me. Your god took all I had, except my life and my gift. Those *my* god gave to me. I belong to him. So we differ." He winked suddenly. "And yet we can laugh together. Let us agree that if I allow you your faith, you will allow me mine."

All my experience said that his words were evil, but I could not summon up my own words to argue against him.

"Is it so hard to let someone believe in a thing you do not?" he asked when I was silent.

"It is," I answered, "when the belief goes against all I hold to be true."

"Then perhaps you should change what you believe!" Thorir said, merrily.

"And perhaps you should do the same," I retorted, but I was grinning, despite myself.

"We shall see," he said. "But in the meantime you should not let such things torment you. All is well and all will be well."

"Now you know God's will?"

"I know it is beyond my power to control it and so I give myself up to it. To fate."

I rolled my eyes.

He laughed but then he grew sober. "You mock fate, too. Ah, Malcolm, you have seen so much of the world that you mock all that is new to you? I do not think you are so arrogant. No, I suspect you know just enough of fate to fear it and not enough to have faith in it. I remember feeling that way. So far you have had little choice in your life, but you will. Follow the path laid out for you. The time for certainty will come, when the paths diverge and you must choose. And when you choose, that decision will define all that comes. But until then, you should be kind to yourself." He turned back to the view. "And that includes not making dangerous enemies, at least not until you are strong enough to overcome them!"

"What was I supposed to do?" I cried. My earlier anger flooded back. "And why did you stop me? I was only trying to explain."

"Any explanation would have been fuel to that man's fire. He was only teasing until you insulted him, though I do believe he disliked you at first sight."

"Then we share something."

"That doesn't mean you should make an enemy of him."

"What can I do if he hates me right off? I don't even know why he would. I've never met him before. He has no reason."

"He does have a reason. You just don't know it."

A thought came to me. "I think he knows my father, but

I don't know why Thorbjorn would dislike him. All the others seem to like him quite a lot."

"So they do. He has a good reputation, your father. But he is also well-liked by certain very powerful men, and there must be a reason for that. So maybe that's it?"

When I didn't reply he said, "Well, you'll have to ask your father when you return home. And who knows, it may simply be that you are oil and water. Sometimes it is just like that. But don't provoke him, unless you want to make real trouble for yourself."

"So I should just be silent when he shames me …"

"No one can shame you but yourself, Malcolm. Each man's actions testify for him."

I wondered if he knew how much he sounded like my father. I was glad when the talk turned to other things as we ventured out to explore the town.

• • •

The sky grew more overcast by the hour, but that did not discourage Thorir from proudly revealing every fine point, and some not so fine, of his precious Dingwall.

Around mid-afternoon, bellies rumbling, we caught the scent of roasting meat and tracked it like hounds to the stall of a rotund vendor with beady eyes and a large, upturned nose. When we whispered too loudly that he looked much like the tender boar he turned on his spit, Thorir played peacemaker and paid the man more than he was due. It was Yule, Thorir explained, and Yule meant goodwill and generosity … and boar!

Of course, that led him to tell me about the boar the

warriors of Valhalla feast on daily, which is restored each night for the next feast. And then about a holy golden boar that flies across the sky in winter, restoring light to the world. He very much enjoyed tormenting me with such pagan talk. For my part, I tried to pretend it did not bother me. This did not rob him of any pleasure. We spent much of the afternoon with him teaching me about his Odin and me trying to change the subject.

I did not admit to him that his stories fascinated me as much as they troubled me.

He led me to the outskirts of town. Now we stood in a large field covered in short grass, flanked with trees that were turning black in the failing light. It was not plough land, that I could see, yet its purpose was not evident. The sun was nestling down between two hills to the west and far off smoke rose from the chimney of a farmhouse. A flock of birds flew black against the sky, then disappeared again in the trees. It was a dark place. *The perfect site for some pagan sacrifice*, I thought with a shiver.

"This is where we hold the *Thing*, our parliament," he said. "Where all men gather and are heard. Where men may even decide the fate of their lord."

The idea was almost as strange to me as Thorir's god was. "How can it be that a man should decide the fate of his lord? It is not natural."

"Is it not? Are you sure? At the Thing no one man decides anything. Each may speak, and none may silence another. Together they decide what the course will be. That is what happened to our Earl Harald in Orkney, you know. True, there was trickery and when the men of Orkney voted they thought they were buying the best peace, but they were swayed by lies. That is how Erlend was allowed to rule in place of Harald."

"But I thought that King David and the Norse king both supported Erlend's claim."

"Certainly, but in Orkney, as in other lands of the Northmen, if the people do not accept a man, he cannot rule them, at least not for long. It is not just the people who serve their leader. A leader has responsibilities that he may only shirk to his detriment. A true leader earns his place and, in turn, the love of his people. "

"The ways of your people are strange," I said, but something in his words excited me. What a wonder it must be to have a say in your own fate. To choose your own master! And how frightening, also. What would happen to the kings of the earth if all peoples allowed such a strange practice?

I took a last look around before following him. The shadows of the trees mingled on the black field as the sun sank behind the horizon. The wind made them waver, so that they looked like men moving quietly in the darkness, men tending the land, men gathering to fight. Fields were for such things. That they should also be for making peace, and for such a warrior people, was a peculiar thought indeed.

As if he read my thoughts Thorir spoke over his shoulder, "And then we are alike again, for all men want peace and yet we are caught in a round of strife, often despite our best efforts. I will tell a tale this night that will make it clearer. Harald's story is not just his own. It is old, Malcolm, very old. And as with all things it will end and then it will begin again. All that was done before will be done again. It is the way."

"What do you mean?" I asked.

"All stories are repeated. Each time they are changed, yet in essence they remain the same. All things end and are reborn. The story begins anew. And not only for men. One day even Odin the One-Eyed will die, as will all the gods and men and the dark creatures. It is what the warriors of Valhalla wait for, what they are chosen for. To fight on the final day, when even the World Serpent, Jormungard, will die. And after the world has grown silent there will arise life again. New men, new gods."

"How can a god be doomed?" I demanded. It made no sense.

Thorir was laughing. "He is a god, is he?" he teased. "My, how easily you are taught to deny your religion." At my cry of protest, Thorir closed his mouth with a pleased look and refused to speak. A short time later we had entered the castle, where torches were lit and servants rushed about preparing for the feast.

"How can a god be doomed?" I asked again.

We had reached the hidden doorway. Thorir pointed at the image on the tapestry. "That is how he is made. It is Odin's fate to be devoured by the Fenris wolf on the last day. He goes to battle knowing how he will die, as do all the gods."

"Why does he fight if he is doomed?"

"Because, to do less, would be to *be* less."

Thorir's words stilled my tongue and rang within me like

the final note of the lute wavers in the air of the hall. His words came from a source forbidden to me, yet I found I could not deny them. This did not stop me from trying.

"What hope is there, if not even your gods are immortal?" I asked, looking up at him. "If there is no promise of Heaven, of eternal life? How can there just be *nothing* afterwards."

"Who said there was nothing? There are the other worlds Odin will go to, the worlds I hope to see when I die, and there is the world that will be born from the ashes of the old one. And as for hope, mine is that Odin, who has gifted me with much, will not remove my gifts without replacing them with others. I pray I will always have an honourable lord to serve and words to make music of, and friends, friends who would sacrifice their all for me, as I would for them. But most of all, my heart's desire is that I should become a wiser man, that I should grow closer to the god and to know him better, and that I should acquit myself honourably always, and be afforded the grace to accept my fate as it comes. The god is just.

"And now, my friend," he said with a smile for my own bemused expression, "I go to make myself irresistible to the women and I promise you there will be no justice there." With that he ducked under the tapestry and climbed up the stair, singing a rowdy song. His words still played in my mind but I knew I would receive no more answers that night.

In our chamber a fire was lit and there was water to wash with. We applied ourselves well to our ablutions, Christian and pagan both, and, as day turned to night, we went down to our mutual feast. ❧

7

good is not, though good be thought,
mead for the sons of men,
for the more they drink, the less can they think,
and a watch keep over their wits.

~WISDOM OF ODIN~

horir was right. Yule in Dingwall was not so different from our celebrations, pagan in origin
though it was. Both Scot and Northman shared
a wild exuberance, a flaunting of their vitality in the face
of a dark, cruel winter. Where we differed was in degree. In
Dingwall that night the men danced on the edge of abandon and still danced madly on, almost out of control but
never quite, as if their life's training had been in maintain-
ing that balance. The strange flavour of it alarmed and fascinated me by turns. Dunailech had never seen the like.

We were seated, to my honour and some discomfort, at
the head table. I knew I was only there because Thorir had
pretended to misunderstand the earl's gesture to be seated amongst his highest-ranking advisors. He had boldly
gripped me by the sleeve and half-carried me along, me
fearing greatly that I might be sent away in shame in front
of all of Dingwall.

But Earl Harald was little concerned about who sat at
his table. He laughed when Thorir squeezed me in on
the bench near the earl's large, ornately carved chair. His
cousin's chair, but his for the night as the man of highest
rank. *Cousin of kings*, I thought, watching him. The others

who shifted down on the bench did so readily enough, for which I was glad.

The hall was bursting with men. There were Hrafn's men, those who had not gone home to their farms for Yule, and the others who had gathered—for the party from Atholl was not the only one—to join the earl in his venture north. Men lined the benches and crowded up before the head table where they waited to offer their support and loyalty to the earl.

Four servants entered the hall with an enormous platter. They were greeted with a resounding cheer that only thundered the louder when they lowered their burden of a great roast boar onto the heavy oak planks before the head table. The Yule log burned high now, spitting sparks to the blackened ceiling. The benches echoed with shouts of laughter and bursts of song. Platters of roast meat and fish, cheese and fruit, baskets of bread and amazing quantities of wine and winter ale and mead were constantly replenished so that the flow was not halted for many hours.

I ate and drank my fill a few times over that night and decided that a Yule feast was a splendid thing, even better than the Scots variety, telling that to Thorir more than once. He laughed at me, and I joined him in his laughter.

Half the night had passed when the earl turned to me and held out his horn. "Malcolm," he said, "I would toast our fathers and friendship. Will you drink with me?"

I nodded, puffing up a little with the honour of it. Of all the men there, he wished to drink a toast with me. I watched as the pale gold liquid flowed into his exquisite drinking horn, intricately carved and leafed in precious metal. *Gold within, gold without.*

The earl drank and then handed me the horn. It was heavy in my hand. I tipped it back.

I had been expecting ale, but the sweet, spicy drink that hit my throat was mead. Rich, potent and heavenly. I knew that it would not take much to make me wish I had kept to the ale. I turned to the earl with his horn.

But Earl Harald shook his head with a grin and leaned over the table to speak to someone. A drinking horn cannot, I discovered to my dismay, be put down while it still holds liquid.

"Why don't you pass that here, boy," laughed Thorbjorn from Earl Harald's side. "It's a man's drink. I'll show you how to do it justice."

"Actually, it's a god's drink," Thorir murmured softly beside me.

"Here, let me show you," urged Thorbjorn. "And perhaps one day we'll teach you to wench as well. Oh, what a man you'll make!"

Grins flared. The mockery in Thorbjorn's voice burned in my heart.

I downed the lot. Simon, who sat beyond Thorbjorn, cheered me on, as did the men clustered before the head table. At first I feared I might well drown in the stream that flowed without cease down my throat, but finally the last of it was gone. Quite satisfied with myself, I returned Earl Harald's horn to him, my victory somewhat dampened by having to decline a second draught.

The earl laughed, not unkindly, and put the horn in Thorbjorn's waiting hand. Then he leaned back to give instructions to the chamberlain who hovered at his shoulder. Thorbjorn, his eye on me as a servant refilled the horn, gripped it expertly and called out, loud enough for all to hear, "*This* is the way a man drinks." He quaffed the contents of the horn in one smooth motion and then held it out to be refilled, his yellow beard glistening with drops of mead. But when the horn was full again he did not drink. Instead he held it out to me.

Had I been wiser I would have accepted the ridicule in his eyes instead of the challenge, but drink makes men fools and I was none so wise even when sober.

The earl was still busy with the chamberlain or he might have passed the horn. As it was, Thorbjorn held it out just far enough to be offering it to me, but too far for me to reach without leaning across the earl, an act which I was quite sure would be considered ill-mannered and disrespectful. Thorbjorn watched my face with growing delight. Other eyes were on me. I knew that if I did not take the proffered horn soon I would be humiliated in front of the entire hall.

If I do it quickly, I reasoned, *Earl Harald might not even notice.* He was leaning back far enough in his seat. *Surely he will not care and I will have the horn and win this petty battle.* I drew myself up awkwardly and stretched as far over the table as possible, hoping the earl would not suddenly lean forward and find me there.

Standing made me realize the potency of what I'd already consumed. I'd been drinking throughout the feast, reassuring myself that I drank far less than any man there. I should have made other comparisons. I swayed on ground that felt more like water than stone.

The horn hovered just beyond my reach. Thorbjorn's expression was all patience, but even drunk I could detect a smirk hidden there. *Well,* I thought, *if I take the horn I will have won. What can he do? I will have won.* That decided it. I lunged.

But even as I wrapped my fingers around the horn and began to pull back, I knew I had miscalculated again. Thorbjorn, instead of releasing it to me, was gripping it all the more tightly.

Perhaps it appeared to onlookers that we made a toast, or that we held the horn together in a gesture of hospitality. But he and I both knew the truth. He was pulling back on it with a strength far greater than mine. I would have to either release it or attempt to wrest it from his much stronger hand.

That he was punishing me for my words earlier that day I had no doubts. His eyes taunted me and my pride leapt up in reply. *He will not beat me!* I thought furiously. I pulled hard at the very same moment that Thorbjorn let go.

I fell back, the horn flew up and golden mead rained down on the head table.

The earl looked down at his fine, drenched tunic, then from Thorbjorn to me and shook his head ruefully as he beckoned a servant. "It is a wise man who knows when to stop with the drink," he said to me as the servant mopped up what wetness he could. "Thorbjorn, the boy is drunk. Leave him alone, will you?"

"Just when he is proving himself to have some mettle?" answered Thorbjorn. "Well, I suppose you are right. Let him nap now."

All those near enough to hear burst into laughter. Even Thorir was grinning. I desired greatly just then to slip down to the flagstones, to find my bed and bury myself in it.

Thorbjorn fired one last barb. "Bring some warm milk for the young pup and save the good drink for the men." I bit my tongue. I could not beat him at this game. When he saw that I had given up, he snorted, picked up a haunch of venison and began eating. Simon leaned past him to grimace sympathetically at me. The men in the hall had already turned to other things, but I was sure I had lost a battle in their eyes. A battle for what I was not sure and I was too tired to sort it out. My only wish was for the night to end.

But it did not. It wore on and on.

I drifted into a reverie, indulging myself in a dream of lying in a warm bed and sleeping for days and days, being left behind in Dingwall while the others sailed to Orkney. I would find my own way home. My fantasy was a pleasant alternative to the scene in the hall. The voices had turned raucous and the figures who danced to the fiddles and the drumbeats seemed to roil and contort, like beings of smoke, like beasts even, rather than men of flesh. I could not look at them without thoughts of hell swirling in my mind. I kept my head on the table, which, though it was sticky with spilled liquor, was at least solid and steady. With my eyes closed the noise receded from my ears until I could almost imagine myself far away.

I do not know how much time passed that way, with me secretly absenting myself from the celebrations, but at some point a conversation that had been going on for a while intruded on my wandering mind enough that I had to open my eyes to see who was speaking. When I looked around me I knew that I was not alone in my inebriation. Minor contests of wit and boasting erupted into short-lived bouts around the hall. There was singing and dancing, games of dice and knucklebones and some sport involving women that had me averting my eyes.

The revelries in the hall had not subsided but spirits at the head table were more restrained. It was the Earl Harald and his foster-father who spoke, quietly enough for their conversation to be considered private, but close enough that it was not private from me. I turned my head so that I faced in their direction.

"You must agree that more would make it easier." That was Thorbjorn.

"Must we debate while we're in our cups?" sighed the earl.

"The sooner the plan is laid …"

"Can we not celebrate one night?"

Thorbjorn shook his head. "There are times when I think you are soft, Harald."

"Soft? You think so? With you raising me, I doubt it is a possibility." They both chuckled. "Here is my softness," he went on, his voice so low I strained to hear his words. "I feel a thrill like lust at the thought of my cousin's blood on my sword. If he—"

"Then what stops you?" Thorbjorn interrupted. "The people want rid of him. They'll welcome you now with open arms."

"Then why kill him?"

"Because he'll never give up his claim."

There was a pause. "True. He won't. You are probably right."

"He usually is," came a new voice, one low and blurred by drink.

"Arnfith has the right of it," said Thorbjorn, though I detected a trace of disdain for the speaker, who was clearly having difficulty focusing on what was before him. "Even when he's the worse for wear, he knows what must be done."

"That I do," slurred Arnfith, "and I say burn the man's house down over his head. Crops are bad, weather's worse. He deserves to die."

"You blame Erlend for the weather?" asked Earl Harald, with a look of curiosity.

"Ah, blame him for everything. I don't care." The man took another swig of drink. "All I know is the people will be blaming him, and that's for your good, isn't it?"

"I suppose it is," answered the earl, "as long as I don't invite the same sort of blame!"

"Don't talk that sort of nonsense," growled Thorbjorn.

"The people believe it. Poor overlords make for poor crops."

"The people are cattle. They believe what they are told. You're a Christian and a noble, Harald. You're educated. You can't believe that what you do has any effect on the land."

The earl did not answer but I watched his face as he nursed a thought and then put it aside. "I will take Orkney whatever way I must. That is what I care about. And the truth is, kin or not, if Erlend entered the hall now, with weapon drawn, I could not be more pleased."

I suppressed a shudder.

"It is good to know you have the heart of a man, Harald."

Earl Harald gave him a wry half-smile. "Ever my tutor, aren't you."

Thorbjorn shrugged, "I serve my lord." He extended his hand and the younger man took it, holding it for a long moment. It was a pact they made and not a new one. These two had been united in their cause for a very long time already. If I had not known better I would have thought them father and son in blood, not just in fosterage.

"And I would serve my lord as well," came another voice.

I turned to see Thorir standing beside me, hands clasped, quietly regarding the hall. It was only moments before a hush fell upon all there, as if by magic. Among both our peoples a poet is esteemed as highly as a warrior. I wondered if a warrior could command such silence.

Thorir's voice was only as loud as it had to be to carry to the dark corners of the hall. "It is fitting that we gather here with our lord under the roof of his ancestor. From Dingwall Earl Harald will strike out to regain his lands. He will bring peace and prosperity not seen since the time of the magnificent prince, Thorfinn the Mighty, Earl of Orkney, Shetland and the Hebrides, Caithness and Sutherland. It was that noble man who built these strong walls, more than a century ago, for war, but also as a place of meeting. He formed the bridge between two peoples, two peoples who join here today in common cause as they did once before. Now it is time to relate the history of that great man, that we might honour him and the son of his line."

Thus Thorir began the story of Thorfinn the Mighty.

He told of how the Scots king had no male heir, so he married his three daughters to powerful men, and in time they produced three grandsons: Duncan, MacBeth and Thorfinn.

"People said the young Thorfinn was fierce and hard, strong and intelligent. He had a nose like an eagle and eyes as shadowed and sharp. That was no timid boy who ruled Caithness and Sutherland, and his ambition grew as quickly as he did. He set his sights on his father's lands of Orkney and Shetland, lands ruled by his half-brothers."

A nose like an eagle, I thought, stealing a glance at Earl Harald.

The story went on to tell how Thorfinn's half-brothers did not want to share their inheritance but the people of Orkney saw his great spirit and many of them flocked to him. One man of good reputation became Thorfinn's foster-father and greatest supporter. They called him Thorkel Fosterer.

"Thorkel went to make peace between Thorfinn and his eldest brother, Einar. He feasted Einar to make him his friend, but when it came time to go to Einar's hall, a voice in Thorkel's heart warned him of danger. His instinct was true. When he sent men to spy the road, they found Einar's men waiting in ambush in three places. Thorkel delayed, still hoping for peace, but fate beckoned. Einar grew impatient, insisting that they must leave. Thorkel knew his choice and struck Einar so that he fell into the hearth, dead.

"It is a mark of a man how others speak of him when he is gone. None cried foul at the death of Einar. He had murder in his heart, murder of his guest. Thorkel had killed in defense. The matter was done.

"Soon Thorfinn was lord over all lands north of Moray. Then the king died."

Thorir related how Duncan was given the throne, but his cousins did not let him sit easily there. This I knew from my own history, for my father had told this story to me many times, though from a different perspective: MacBeth of Moray was always the hero in his version.

Thorir's tale wove itself into a complex web of the three cousins, Thorfinn, MacBeth and Duncan, detailing the battles they fought against each other and against other comers who hoped to fight their own way to the throne of Scotland. Thorfinn reached southwards from his perch in Orkney, ravaging the lands of Ross and Sutherland and Moray in his quest for power, breathing fire across the land. The people cried out in grief at the sound of his name and he left in their hearts an undying hatred.

Thorfinn hardly sounded heroic to me, but the Northmen in the hall hung on every word spoken of him. The Scots kept their allegiance to themselves, which was probably wise, considering the current state of their company. The story went on to tell how Thorkel killed again to remove a distant cousin of Thorfinn's who vied for some of his territory.

My eyes drifted to the tapestry. What had Thorir said about Harald's story? *All that was done before ...*

"Finally Thorfinn and MacBeth united against Duncan and pursued him deep into the heart of Scotland and they killed him. And though it was MacBeth's sword that struck the blow, he was made king. Kin-slaying it was, but in arms, in battle, and to supplant a weak king with a strong one. The people would never take Thorfinn, not with all the kinsman's blood that was on his hands, with all the cruelty he had shown the people and the land.

"And so, MacBeth ruled as king and Thorfinn returned to his lands in the north where he must face yet another rival. Thorkel slew this one too, making Thorfinn the sole ruler of Orkney and keeping his hands clean, yet again, of kinsman's blood, and in the holy Yule, thereby assuring he would not bring a curse down on his head and lose all he had fought for."

I stole a look at Thorbjorn. His expression was a mixture of satisfaction and reflection, as if what he heard was being filtered into a pot he quietly brewed, just out of sight.

"From then on Earl Thorfinn was settled in his titles and he visited the kings of Europe. When he grew old he went with MacBeth to the Pope in Rome and both men received absolution for their sins. Once he was home he sat down quietly and lived out his days in peace, an earl almost seventy years, and he died in his bed an old man.

"Such is the story of Thorfinn the Mighty, forefather of Earl Harald Maddadson, ruler of nine earldoms, a man of such strength that none could stand against him, none but the people who refused him."

Thorir raised his drinking horn. "My prayer this night is that the heir of Thorfinn the Mighty will know such peace as his ancestor found, but that he might come by it sooner and hold it even longer."

Thorir was about to sit when Thorbjorn stood, horn raised. "A good telling, Thorir Honey-Tongue!" he said. "High praise for foster-fathers who are seldom praised. And fitting, I say, for on this journey we face enemies the likes of Thorfinn's in his day." He looked around the hall. "Remember it, all of you. There are battles in store for us. This will be no easy venture, but victory does lie at the end of it." He turned to Thorir. "I would reward you for your story." He passed the horn to Simon. From the scrip at his waist he drew a half dozen silver coins, a small fortune, at least in my eyes.

I had been watching Thorir's expression throughout Thorbjorn's speech but it told me nothing. He hesitated only a moment before graciously accepting the gift from Thorbjorn's hand. "I thank you Thorbjorn Klerk for the honour of your gift. I hope my story will bear good fruit."

"It will," said Earl Harald. "Men have said I am much like my ancestor. It is good to be reminded of his success. It is a sort of blessing, I think."

A blessing? I had never heard a story in which more men were slain by their own kin.

"I, too, would reward you, Thorir Honey-Tongue," said the earl as he reached for his own scrip. Then he stopped and smiled. "The way my ancestor would have. I would be as great as he was so I will follow his example." Instead of coins he reached beneath his sleeve and drew out a thick gold ring from his wrist.

"Ring-giver," said Thorir with a twinkle in his eye as he accepted the bracelet, a heavy twist of gold. Even in the days when a skald was paid with ring-money he would only have earned a portion of such a ring. It was a great honour. "I am well pleased that you find my telling so beneficial, to both inspire and to warn."

"To warn?" Thorbjorn interjected. "Thorfinn was the most powerful man in the North and the longest-lived earl Orkney ever had. Following his example can only lead to great heights!"

"No man lives a perfect life," said Thorir pleasantly. "Our lord can surely learn from Thorfinn in many ways, from his victories, and from his mistakes as well, even if that only means to not raid the lands he passes through in coming days!" He said it as if it were a joke, but I knew him well enough already to know there was more meaning to his words than a light jest. I nodded my head in agreement. While the story of Thorfinn seemed to have inspired the men in the hall, it had left my own heart a little cold. *Thank God it was MacBeth who was made king and not that bloody-minded Viking!*

"Did you have something to add?"

Silence. I looked about and discovered many eyes on me.

"I didn't say anything," I said, quite sure it was true.

"You were nodding rather vehemently," said Earl Harald. "With what were you agreeing so … strongly?"

I looked from him to Thorbjorn to Thorir, regarding their expectant faces with consternation. It was a simple enough thing, what I had been thinking, but I was quite sure it would be unwise to speak my mind just then, especially considering the fact that I was having some trouble keeping it focused on any particular thought for long. And I knew Thorbjorn would not like it. I did not much care what he liked after the way he'd treated me, but I was in no condition for any more of his punishments, so I tried to think of a small lie to put in place of the truth, even while I fought down the desire to simply spit out what I'd been thinking. After all, it was the truth, was it not, that this Thorfinn had been brutal and bloody and cost himself a kingship? And if it was truth, should it not be told?

It was Thorbjorn who helped me make my choice. "He looks a bit like an addled cow when he's mulling something over, doesn't he? Speechless, mindless."

All hesitation left me. "I was thinking," I said, "that the Earl Thorfinn might have been king of all Scots had he only the good sense to restrain his foster-father."

No one made a sound. There were no grins, no cheers, only a few raised brows, the verdict of which I was unable to ascertain. The silence threatened to swallow me whole.

How many times had my father told me my tongue moved quicker than my mind?

"Well, you have proven you can both think and speak," Earl Harald said, finally, "and your opinion is certainly an interesting one."

My eyes slid to Thorir. His look was blank. He had warned me against making an enemy of Thorbjorn. If only he had told me how to accomplish that feat.

But Thorbjorn's face bore a broad smile and his tone was

humourous when he spoke. "He has a temper like his father's. I like that. Perhaps he will share more of his views in the daylight hours, and when he is able to hold his head upright." I was being dismissed, along with my opinion. He smiled at me, looking much like a dog does when it bares its teeth. He had not liked me before. He would like me even less now.

I asked leave of the earl, to find my bed for the night.

"Your wisest choice of the night," he said, without emotion. "And Malcolm," he added, as I rose to leave, "I appreciate a man who will speak his mind. Men of truth are invaluable. But so are men of good judgement." And with that he turned his attention to his foster-father and I made my way from the hall. ❦

8

from the lips of some thou needn't look
for reward or good will;
but a righteous man by praise will render thee
firm in favour and love.

~WISDOM OF ODIN~

I had hardly put my head down before I was getting up again and wishing very much that I had never tasted mead. While the others broke their fast in the hall I made my way down to the harbour. I would satisfy myself with lungfuls of fresh air and leave the food and ale to them.

I waited on the dock as men loaded the earl's ship. My hands were kept busy with a small piece of wood I was carving into what was likely to become a bird. It was not uncommon for me to carve blindly for some while before I knew what would come out of the wood. My hands carved, but my eyes were on the ship that sat long and low in the water before me, her curves broad and full, sweeping upwards at each end. She was wide enough for four large men to sit side-by-side in her, two to an oar, with room to spare between them for gear and passengers. With a dozen or more oars on each side, the ship could be propelled by fifty men and whatever aid the wind provided.

But what shot me through with awe was the prow of the ship, for while the stern jutted up to the sky, the prow curved forward and over into the fierce head of a dragon.

I had never doubted the instinct to flee a Viking attack,

but now I understood the sheer terror that would inevitably course through the veins of any man, no matter how brave, at the sight of such a fierce, golden beast driving out of the mist carrying death in its belly. And yet it was so beautiful! I could hardly draw my eyes from the intricate carvings of cavorting beasts and precise knotwork, adorned with red and blue paint and fine gold leaf, all expertly wrought.

I looked up to see Earl Harald standing beside me. "What have you got here?" he asked. As I handed the figure to him I realized what it was. An eagle breaking free of the wood, head thrust forward as one wing fought to catch the air. He turned it about in his hand, examining it carefully. "You carved this?" he asked.

I nodded.

"It is very good." He gestured towards the ship. "Inspired by her, were you?" When I shook my head, not understanding him, he said, "She is called Sea Eagle."

Had I known that?

"There are few like her left. Thorbjorn insists on using her, as a mark of my station, you know, and I confess, I do not mind. She is beautiful, isn't she?"

"Very," I agreed.

"She is a fearful-looking creature, but for me, well, she seems a protection."

I could see how that might be, as long as you were on the right side of the dragon.

"I was not told you were an artisan."

I chuckled. "I am hardly an artisan, my lord. It's just something I like to do."

"You do it well." He thought for a moment. "I will commission something from you."

"Commission? You mean for pay?"

"Of course, for pay. You are not a slave, are you? And it will keep Thorbjorn from complaining about you."

"Yes, Thorbjorn—" I began, intending to apologize for the trouble I'd caused.

"He thinks that I am doing your father a favour and that this is not the time."

I bit my cheek.

"He doesn't like your father much, for various reasons. That's why he's behaved as he has towards you." Before I could ask what reason Thorbjorn Klerk could have for disliking my father, the earl said, "It has something to do with my father and their friendship."

I had not expected that.

"So he is right, I am doing your father a favour, but it is only a favour to repay the many your father did mine. After all, I would not be here now if not for Alasdair Roy."

Now I was staring at him. What on earth was he talking about?

He laughed at my expression. "You know the story. How your father saved mine in the battle during the rebellion? I was born in the year after it, you know. If your father had not defended mine I would not be here now." He looked at me thoughtfully. "And I suppose you would not, either, since it was your father who collected the ransom that allowed him to save your home. Dunailech, isn't it?"

My head was spinning. My father had saved the great Earl Maddad? How was it I did not know this? It stung that I should hear these deeds of my father from another man.

It seemed I did not know my father at all.

"Are you sure of all this?" I asked.

"Sure of it? It is one of the few things my father took the time to secure in my memory. I hardly knew him, you know. I grew up in Orkney. But this story he insisted I know. He always said that I should remember if I ever needed a friend who would tell me true, I should look to Alasdair Roy." The piercing look he gave me passed in an instant. "You didn't know."

"I knew they met during the rebellion and that Earl Maddad saved my father."

"Saved him from the wrath of the king, yes, but it was Alasdair who did the saving first."

I shook my head. It would take some time for this newly written history to sink in.

He was perceptive enough not to dwell on my ignorance and the possible reasons for it. "The rebels were defeated and knew it. My father was caught up in their retreat and cut off from his own men when the rebels discovered him. They wanted revenge. No ransom for this man, the king's right arm, they said. He fought hard, but he was alone. It was only a matter of time. He was weakening. And then Alasdair leapt up and stood between the rebels and my father. All he said to my father was 'if your life ends here, then so does mine' and proceeded to defend my father's life against his own men. I believe that was the day he was maimed."

I was speechless.

"So, Thorbjorn is a hard man, I know, but now perhaps you see where his dislike comes from." I shook my head in confusion at his swift turn. He expanded. "He does not like that you have a claim on me, and I on you. There is a bond between us, forged by our fathers. He resents it. And he will punish you for it, I'm afraid. You must understand, Thorbjorn has been very good to me. He has been my teacher. He has been my father. I was only five the first time I went to Orkney. Did you know that? Thorbjorn went with me. I could not do any of this without him. It is best that you stay out of his way. I'm sure that his temper will soon cool."

He was telling me that he would not stop his foster-father from bullying me but that he was sorry for it. It was something. "And as for your words last night, you should know that I do appreciate honesty in a man. You made me think. But perhaps you will be more cautious in the future?"

"I will do my best," I said with sincerity.

"That is what I have heard of you," he said, grinning. So, there were no secrets from him. Somehow, coming from him the words did not shame me. At that moment I knew what my father had meant about Harald Maddadson's qualities, his ability to lead men.

The loading of the ship was done. The earl turned to me, "May I keep this?" he asked, holding up the eagle.

"It is unfinished."

"I like it this way."

I agreed, feeling more pleased than I wanted to let on.

He put the eagle into the scrip at his waist. "So, when asked, you are my carver, at least until we find out your other talents." He left me just as Thorir came striding down the wet planking of the docks looking as fresh as if he'd slept a full night and only drunk a single cup.

"There you are," he said. "I thought you might have wandered off to drown yourself to avoid the hangover you are sure to have."

I growled at him. As if inspired by his words, my head began to thunder again. The longship writhed with all the men who were now clambering about in her, adjusting her various ropes and sails. My stomach began complaining. It was just coming to me that I would be on that ship soon, and with the head and stomach I had given myself the previous night.

"I do not think that I will enjoy this journey very much," I said.

"The sea air will do you good."

"The sea air might, but the sea itself is likely to kill me."

He grinned. "Ah, you do not have sea legs yet. Well, if the motion of the waves sickens you then you will surely be sick this day. But we should arrive at Wick before morning."

"Of *tomorrow?*" I gasped in horror.

"We must go the whole way as quickly as possible or risk Svein's spies getting wind of our coming. We would have stopped at Helmsdale, but Harald is worried. There's a man meeting us at Wick who will tell us where Erlend is now, but Erlend will not stay put forever. And if Svein hears us coming he'll have Erlend aboard ship and hidden away in some secret cove, leaving Harald to scour all those scattered isles for him. It was difficult enough for him to drum up this support. No, Erlend—and more importantly Svein—must not catch a whiff of Harald's coming until he is upon them. Besides, there is some brilliance to this plan. Orkneymen," he added in a quieter tone, "call our earl a Scot when they speak of his reputation for avoiding the sea. No one would expect him to cross the Pentland Firth at this time of year."

I was already queasy with the thought of being sea-borne for a whole day. "The Pentland Firth?" All I knew was that it was very far north.

"It is only the most treacherous body of water in the world," Thorir said lightly. "But these Orkneymen cross it as if it were a little pond. Thorbjorn captains our ship and is an expert seaman. He will bring us across safely. Besides, you shouldn't worry about that quite yet. First you must survive the North Sea!"

Thorir's confidence in Thorbjorn's ability to captain a ship only provided moderate relief. The possibility of drowning was not one I had entertained, but it did put the impending bout of seasickness into perspective.

"Odin will protect," said Thorir.

"Odin the One-Eyed?" I asked, sardonically.

He winked. "Indeed."

For some reason I thought of the fisherman at Beauly, of his words to me, his blessing, and then I forgot him as the men began taking up positions at the long oars that fanned out like flaring wings on a giant wooden bird. The chests I had seen the men load earlier were now being used as benches. Shields formed a regular border of decorated circles along the side of the ship. Thorbjorn walked down the aisle between the chests, barking orders at the men. As I scrambled onto the ship I prayed for a swift, smooth journey.

The first stage was east up the long arm of water that connects Dingwall to the sea. The oarsmen struck a quick pace to the rhythm of Thorir's drum and his chant, pulling in unison, their muscled bodies working together in an impressive show of strength. Dingwall faded behind us until it was a speck on the western horizon.

From my place on the foredeck, out of the way of the crew, I watched as the shores slid by with increasing speed. Smudges of blue smoke against the sky spoke of crofts in the low hills where men could raise their cattle on the land and still be close enough to the sea to reap its harvest. Ahead, the water corridor narrowed; the sea lay beyond it. A small child ran along the south shore, waving madly. I waved back but he did not see me. He kept running and waving until we left him far behind.

I immediately felt the difference as the sea caught us up. Among the crew there was a moment of adjustment as the waves dragging at the ship so that the oars on one side did not meet water when they pulled, briefly ruining their balanced striding. As the helmsman strained to angle the ship to the north, Thorir adjusted his chant and the men fell, with practiced skill, into a new and even march.

Earl Harald paced the deck, calling to me as he passed. "Your shade of green blends in with the fields." He didn't look well either. We exchanged grimaces. "Well, they say I have a talent for turning the shade of the water I'm sailing on," he added. "So we are alike." I had gone beyond the point of laughing, no matter how kindly the jest. I fought back a wave of nausea and then lunged for the side and was sick.

"He looks about to die," quipped Thorbjorn. "You

should let him. Coddling does him no good, nor does it serve you."

"I'm not coddling anyone," said the earl, "only sympathizing."

"There should be no sympathy between one such as you and one such as him."

"Ah, Thorbjorn! Can I be a man as well as an earl?"

"As long as you are more earl than man, and do not weigh yourself down with weaklings."

"Malcolm is strong in his own way," said Thorir.

"You see something that is not there," said Thorbjorn with disgust as I hung my head over the side again.

Thorir's knuckles rapped the solid timber of the dragonship by my head. "The use of the oak cannot be spied in the acorn. But its uses are many and great."

• • •

I do not remember much after that. In the times that I was awake an image of my father came to me, over and over again. I could see him, barrel chest and red mane, but not his face. The more I tried to see him, the more his face evaded me. It added to my nightmare. Trying not to think of him only made it worse.

Once, late in the day, I lay on my back watching the low sky as the sun that had not shown its face all day painted it violet. The clouds shifted rapidly and from their shadows two dark forms burst free, flying above the flapping sail. I watched them through half-open eyes. I saw Thorir catch sight of them, too, and our eyes met for a moment.

Then I slept. ☉

9

be wary, the stranger who comes to a door,
keep silent that he may hear.
with his ears let him listen, with his eyes let him look,
only thus will he keep away harm.

~WISDOM OF ODIN~

A light stood out from the blackness. It danced, disappeared and shone out brightly. It could have been a star but for the degree to which it waxed and waned. A voice barked an order. I felt the ship heel about sharply as the helmsman aimed it at the faint spark glinting on the horizon.

Wick. It didn't matter. I just wanted to die, and quickly. I would never rid my mouth of the taste of vomit, or my ribs of the ache of a day and half a night of violently heaving up my insides.

A shout from the ship brought an answering cry from what must have been land. I still could not tell where water ended and land began. A torch flared, close, then another, and voices sparked with them and men were greeting each other from ship and shore. *Definitely Wick*, I thought, and was surprised to feel hope. I had forgotten hope since losing all desire for life somewhere in the North Sea. But at Wick I could sleep on solid land and eat and—the thought of food had me retching again.

"We've arrived, land-lubber," said Thorir, laying a hand on my arm. "You'll have just enough time to get your guts back in shape before we set out again." He was laughing, but he hauled me up and passed me a wet cloth. "Wash your face," he said, "and rinse your mouth, too. You'll feel and smell better. Whew!"

I felt like an old man, taking the cloth in feeble fingers and passing it over my face. I was glad of the dark, that none could see how my hands shook. But Thorir was right. It helped.

The rowers suddenly hauled in their oars and the ship was carried by its own momentum and by slapping waves towards a loose line of torches that burned high above us. It shuddered a moment later as it scraped against rock and then was caught and held fast. Torchlight illuminated the men who reached out strong arms to steady the vessel. As my eyes adjusted to the faint light I saw that they stood on a stone shelf that stretched out very low into the water. Another taller spur extended towards the sea behind them.

"We'll settle her in for you, my lord," said a voice, and then Thorir was shoving me up and over the side where I was all but trampled as everyone eagerly piled out of the ship. My whole body swayed with the remembered motion of the sea. Thorir caught my arm and propelled me along in the wake of the others towards the black face of a cliff. Where a wall of rock appeared suddenly before us, we turned sharply and I saw rough-hewn stairs lit by torches set into rough stone brackets. The stairs were narrow and high and exposed to the sea on one side. I took care with the placing of my feet, for I had no desire to slip and fall. I had not survived the trip over the waves to die under them.

As I stumbled up the last steps I saw a sprawl of small

wooden houses with firelight glowing from ill-fitting doors. We passed them and then I felt wood beneath my feet. A drawbridge spanned a wide ditch and led into an open area where there was a stone gatehouse and a few more wooden shacks. Another drawbridge led across a shallow ditch to the inner yard.

Earl Harald's keep at Wick was a simple blockhouse, square and solid. Men disappeared through the seaward-facing door into the warmth and the light of the hall and I followed, but as the smells of cooking wafted into my face, I whirled back outside again as if struck. I fell to my knees, gagging, and leaned my face on the wet stone. There is nothing as wonderful as the scent of food when one is hungry and healthy, but when one is sick from the sea, it is as welcome as poison.

"Not feasting tonight?" asked Earl Harald as he came up the stairs. He patted my shoulder sympathetically. "No water either, if you want my advice. You'll only throw it up. Best wait until morning."

I nodded, unwilling to risk speaking.

"Believe it or not, a night's sleep will make all the difference. Find a warm corner before they're all taken," he advised, then turned to the servant who had appeared in the doorway and stood waiting, rather nervously, at his side.

The earl listened to the man, his eyes on the ground, and then jerked his head up to look him in the face. The man nodded unhappily. Earl Harald's jaw locked hard on the news he had just received. He spun on his heel and strode into the keep.

Thorir looked thoughtful. I sat with my back against the

wall staring out into the night. The wind rushed past me, graciously taking all smells away on it. I shuddered with cold but nothing could induce me to return to the hall again.

"Go in, Thorir," I said. "There is no need for you to freeze."

Thorir crouched down beside me. "You'll not last a night out here, fool. Just come inside the doorway. The air is fresh enough there."

I shook my head.

"Then we'll find a nook for you, somewhere you won't be tempted to spew on anyone," he chuckled. He was enjoying himself too much for my liking. He laughed even harder at the name I called him. "Perhaps upstairs. Harald's quarters are on the top floor, I recall, but there should be room on the second. I expect Eirik and Benedikt will sleep there. If they find you asleep they won't bother to send you away. Get up before you shiver yourself to death."

I acquiesced, grumbling as I followed him inside. There we were immediately shuffled to our left and pressed against the wall. The hall was smaller even than ours at Dunailech, perhaps the length of four men lying end to end, and the width of three. I held my breath against the stench, a part of me hating the men a little for enjoying the food so heartily. I heard my name shouted and a burst of laughter, but I did not look to see who called.

The wall of the keep was thicker than I was tall. The stairwell was built inside it, curling upward in a spiral, like the pink-hearted seashell a wandering priest had once given my father as a hospitality gift. Torches set in sconces lighted our path. One turn of the stair left the world of the hall behind, the next turn and we entered another.

I heard something. At first I thought it was a trick of the walls playing with the sounds of the sea, but then I knew it to be a woman's laugh, then a man's voice, murmuring. Thorir rounded the column of stone ahead of me and stopped, blocking my view. I peered around him to see Earl Harald standing in the pool of soft light that spilled out of a doorway.

He did not turn, but put up a hand to warn against speaking. A moment later he looked to Thorir, and a message passed between them. Thorir nodded and the earl moved aside so that we could both see into the chamber.

We were to be witnesses. I moved to get a better view.

A roaring fire crackled and threw sparks from the hearth near the far wall. The room was partitioned on two sides by heavy curtains. A heady scent tingled in my nostrils. Perfume. The floors were strewn with bear and deerskins instead of the usual straw, and on the walls hung colourful tapestries of figures enacting strange scenes, glittering with gold thread. The wooden chests that lined the walls were elaborately carved, as were the other furnishings. Whoever lived in this room was a lover of beautiful things.

A man lounged with one leg thrown over the arm of a high-backed chair, his blue-black hair falling back like a raven's wing to reveal hooded eyes, eyes that rested on the woman before him. One corner of his handsome mouth was turned up in a slight smile as he sipped wine from a beautiful goblet.

The woman's hands gripped the arms of the chair as she

leaned towards him, her low-cut gown hanging open, a long strand of jet beads dangling down between them. She returned his look with one equally suggestive.

Her thick hair was the colour of wheat. It hung like a shawl over her shoulders and down her back, unbound, like a maiden's, though I did not believe for a moment that she was one. She was tall but not slender, a study in curves, her narrow waist accentuating hip and breast, her bare arms softly rounded, glowing golden like her hair in the firelight. She looked like a cat, a lioness, sleek and powerful.

It was not just the warmth of the fire on the hearth that crept into my veins and flooded my skin with colour. The woman radiated an energy that made my heart pound. I could not take my eyes from her. She leaned forward to kiss the man on the mouth and I hoped very much that the earl would not look at me just then.

He did not. Instead he stepped forward abruptly. "Greetings, Mother."

She only hesitated a moment before straightening.

"If it isn't my dear son," said Margaret Hakonsdottir. "I thought you'd deserted me."

This was the earl's mother?

"You know where I was, Mother. Let us not play games."

"What else is a poor woman to do when she is left all alone for weeks on end?"

"Alone? Leave us," he said curtly to the man in the chair, who had been sitting motionless since the earl had announced his presence. Now that I could see him better I realized with a start that Margaret's companion was very young, little older than Harald. He sat on the edge of the chair, watching Margaret, waiting for her command, I realized, not the earl's.

He reveals whom he respects more, I thought, *or perhaps whom he fears?*

"Don't go." Margaret dismissed her son's order with a wave of her hand. The man slid back into the chair, his expression hidden by its carved wings.

"Darling boy," said Margaret as she crossed the room, "this is my guest. It is not for you to ask him to leave."

"Get out," Harald said, ignoring her. There was iron in his voice.

The man did not move. *Is he an imbecile,* I wondered, *or does he have such faith in his ... lover?*

Harald's hand clenched and unclenched on the pommel of his sword. As he took a step into the room I saw Margaret judge her son's face in the firelight and make a quick decision.

"Leave us, darling," she said. "I will call for you later."

The young man got up with obvious reluctance and made for the door. I half expected Harald to strike him as he approached, but if the man feared the same he did not show it. He stopped before Harald and bowed slightly. Harald nodded stiffly and then the man was pushing past Thorir and myself and was gone.

Margaret stood before the fire, perfectly composed. *Her beauty belies her danger* my father had said. But how could anyone so exquisite be as treacherous as he had suggested? I wanted to believe, as I gazed on her, that she was as lovely in spirit as she was in form.

"Let me pour you wine and have food brought up. Then we will talk of our plans," she said. For the first time she turned her attention to Thorir and myself in the shadowed doorway. "Go down to the kitchens and be quick about it."

My nausea had miraculously left me and been replaced by a strong desire to escape the tension that ran between the earl and his mother like a bowstring. That same tension had also kindled my curiosity, to be sure, but I knew my place. I turned to go.

"They stay," said Harald. His fingers toyed with the hilt of his sword.

"If you insist," said Margaret, a slight smile played on her full lips as she turned to pour wine into the goblet her lover had used.

Harald crossed the room with long strides and sat down. "You are not in the quarters I assigned."

"I cannot imagine you intended me to stay in that shack," she replied.

"I chose it myself. It was the best of the lot and larger than this room, which I need."

"You must have had many things on your mind that day," she said, handing him the wine, "for you forget what I am used to. I am of noble blood. I do not live in thatched huts."

He swallowed a deep draught of the wine. His eyes rested on the cup in his hand, where the flames of the fire danced along its surface. "You are not here at my request, Mother. This is an inconvenience for me, having to deal with your antics."

"At your request? No. But you have never known what was best for you, as I have. I am here to help my son, as a mother should." She ignored his other remark.

"I have help."

"Thorbjorn is a good man, yes, but he is rather … unrefined. And Eirik and Benedikt will do what you tell them to. I ruled Atholl with your father for as long as you've lived. You need me."

The earl was about to respond when she stopped him. "I know you are upset by the trouble with Gunni and Svein, though it was partly your fault, you must admit. If you'd only let Gunni be—"

"If *you* had let Gunni be, I would not have had to banish him."

She exhaled sharply. The smile had not left her face, but anger was in her eyes. "Harald, these things are done with. It is foolish to revisit them. Let us deal with the present and with the future. I have good news. Your man was here. He told me where Erlend is expected to spend the rest of Yule and, even better, that Svein is not with him. It is perfect. You can slip across, kill Erlend, and it will all be done. Then we can begin again, in Orkney. I have many plans, all of which will both strengthen you and your rule. Harald, I am so pleased to finally—"

"It was not for you to question my informant."

Now she was angry. "Stop being difficult and let us get on with our plans."

"Our plans?" His voice was cold.

She heard it too. I could see in her eyes that she was feeling for the ground, the way a cat does it when it unexpectedly drops from a height.

"What are *our* plans?" he asked again.

"You will go to Orkney and dispose of Erlend. I will follow with the child, and together we will make of Orkney what it should be, a kingdom in its own right. No more being subject to Norway and Scotland. You don't need to be a mere earl, Harald. With the right advisors at your side you could be a king."

Harald let her finish. Then he said, quietly. "Where is the child?"

Did Harald have a son?

"Fraternal love. I am so pleased." She refilled his cup of wine.

Not a son. A brother.

"The child, Mother."

"Your brother has a name."

"Your bastard is only my half brother."

"You should not say such things. I have told you—"

"I am losing patience, mother. We both know he is Gunni's, not my father's."

She shifted course, watching her son's stony face carefully. "Why would you see him?"

"To assure myself."

"Of what? His existence?" She gave a small laugh.

"Of his well-being. I am not you, Mother. *My* half brother has nothing to fear from me," he said with a wave behind him. Only then did I see the man who sat in the corner opposite the makeshift bedchamber, behind the half-parted curtain. My skin crept. I suddenly felt he had been watching me all along, though his features were too shadowed for me to see his face.

An angry snarl transformed Margaret's lovely mouth for a brief instant but when she spoke her voice was level. "It is good to know you have your brother's interests at heart. I am eager to discuss his future. I have sent him for fostering as is natural for noble children."

Harald exploded. "Not before they are weaned, it is not. Or before they can walk, talk, know their own name!" He caught himself, took a deep breath, then said, "It may well be for the best. Perhaps *he* will escape his inheritance."

"Escape it? Did you not hear me? It will be the three of us in Orkney, a family."

Harald stood up. "Will it? Mother, once again you have made your plans and neglected to ask me mine. I will go to Orkney, I will deal with Erlend as I choose to, and I will rule there, alone, until Rognvald returns from the Holy Land.

"As for you, it is bad enough that your belly is hardly emptied of one bastard and you have another oaf in your bed. You will not meddle in my affairs anymore. This plaything of yours will go and you will stay away from my men. *All* of them. The next man I find in your bed will not leave it a man. One way or another you will stop whoring your way through my lands!"

I gasped at his words and the rage in them. Harald didn't move, but Margaret's eyes swung to find me in the shadows of the landing, fixing on mine. "You should be careful what you see and hear," she hissed, before disposing of me with a scornful look.

He spoke through clenched teeth. "You have been in

control long enough, Mother."

That was when the rage Margaret kept so carefully contained almost leapt its boundaries. For a moment I thought she would fly at her son and claw at his eyes. He saw it too. He smiled as he watched her fight to regain her composure.

The two stared at each other in a silent duel. In profile they couldn't have been more different. One curved and golden and lovely, the other angular and dark. Only in the set of jaw and unflinching gaze was there indisputable evidence that these two were mother and son.

"Harald, be clear about what you are saying."

"I will go to Orkney without you and without my brother."

"You will sleep and see how wrong you are in the morning. You will change your mind." Her words were calm, reasonable, and yet I sensed that something had shifted in her, like water turned in an instant to ice. I felt it as surely as if it had occurred inside of me.

"Nothing will change. Good night, Mother," said Harald as he rose and moved towards the door. "And good night to you, Uncle," he said over his shoulder. "We will speak soon."

"Yes, nephew," rasped a voice from the shadows. "Soon."

I followed Thorir away from the keep, wishing I had indeed been more careful about what I'd seen and heard. ⊕

10

the end of a man is easily made,
by the words of a wicked woman.
her baleful tongue will work his bane;
his goodness matters not.

~WISDOM OF ODIN~

I awoke the next morning under a thatched roof hung with clusters of dried herbs, onions and garlic, meat and fish. Sunlight peeked through the gaps between the wooden planks of the walls, letting in the voices of men calling to each other over the cries of wind and wave.

Thorir's things lay in a pile in one corner, but he was not to be seen. I suspected he had gone to eat. I wondered what the kitchens of Wick might be serving up and was quite pleased to hear my stomach growling in protest at its empty state. I felt remarkably well. I lingered a while longer, stretching like a contented cat, not yet ready to leave the warmth of my makeshift bed.

I had not even dreamed, so deeply had I slept.

• • •

Wick sat on a narrow finger of rock as high up from the sea as it was long, dropping down in sheer cliffs. From the door of the keep I could look down the alley between the buildings that lined the edges of the promontory, all the way to the tip where men were finishing the wall that would enclose the outer courtyard and garden. Beyond that was the sea and then the land of the Northmen.

A few men lingered in the hall. Even empty, it did not seem much larger than it had when full of men. Clearly, Wick was not meant for comfort, whatever efforts the earl's mother had made in her chamber. But it was a solid fortress against enemies. Earl Harald would at least have Wick to fall back to if he failed in Orkney. What would happen to my family and I if that happened was not a thought I wished to entertain.

I settled in to a meal of dark bread and cheese and copious amounts of the wonderful buttermilk a servant offered me. She nodded with approval at my untiring appetite. Hunger and thirst restored my faith in my own mettle as much as the food and drink did.

"I see you have survived the night." Thorir dropped to the bench across from me, a grin on his open face, his skin red and glowing from the sting of the wind. I waved a hunk of bread at him as I downed more buttermilk.

"Slow down, fool," he exclaimed. "You must be more moderate. Your belly has too recently been in the business of sending its contents the other way." He took the pitcher away with a laugh but watched like a proud mother as I put away the last of the bread and cheese.

"Our lord informs me we will rest here at least a day, maybe more, though we must be ready to leave at any time. In the meantime we are all to be put to use. I am helping the smith with some repairs. It seems his horse didn't like being sparked in the rear quite so hotly and ran amuck. The roof almost came down on the poor man. An earl can do without a poet, you know, but he must have his smith and the smith's handiwork!"

"As long as he always speaks such truths, the poet is as valuable to me as the smith," said Earl Harald, as he drew near. He looked tired and preoccupied. "I can hardly believe my eyes," he said to me. "You must be a warrior of Valhalla, rising from the field of battle to be reborn. I assumed you would be recovering for days, but here you are. So will you be out hauling stone with the men or shall we find you some more moderate employment?"

Before I could answer that I was well and fit to haul stone, a thing that was not likely true when I was in the best of health, he said, "Right, so you'll run errands for me."

"And later he can help me move some boulders. If he's as strong as he smells, we'd all do well to watch ourselves!" laughed a man from the next table.

They were right. I reeked. I was properly embarrassed.

"At least water can wash this away," said the earl. "But what will we do about you, Vermund? We'll have to keep you in the rear so Erlend doesn't get a whiff of you and run off." The man laughed and raised his cup in reply.

"Consider it your first errand to get yourself to the kitchens," said Harald. "The girls will provide you with water for bathing. And send your clothes to the washerwoman, though I doubt if she'll accept the job."

I left the hall to the sound of their amusement, eager to wash the last of the ocean voyage off me. The servants had their fun with me, but they were kind enough. Once I was clean and in my spare clothes, my other set carried away at arm's length by a scowling washerwoman, I felt much restored.

But if the earl intended my morning's work not to tax

me overly, he miscalculated. I did not rest that morning for more time than it took him to articulate a message, or for the recipient to formulate a reply. By midday I knew the grounds of Wick as if I'd always lived there. I scurried like an ant on its foraging, darting back and forth from the keep to the bake house, to the smithy, to the storehouses, and back again. I searched out merchants in the tiny village that had sprung up outside the gates. Wick was looking to buy meat from the surrounding farms; boys were sent out to the countryside to learn what livestock might be had, as well as oats and all manner of food needed to sustain a hundred fighting men and those who served them. Hosting such large numbers in the dead of winter was no easy task, nor a cheap one.

The grounds were a hive of activity. Servants fluttered about like mad butterflies while warriors-cum-workmen constructed the outer walls and dug the second ditch, the one that pressed at the back of the keep itself. The way they delved into the earth with such vigor, I could only imagine how they would go to battle. Nothing was done by halves. Now and then a light rain fell, blown at a slant by the north wind, but no one paid it much heed.

Thorir was enjoying his efforts at the smithy. The ill-tempered grey which had caused the trouble stood munching his oats in the stables next door while the men sweated to point the central roof post back at the sky. I waved to Thorir as I walked by. He rolled his eyes in reply.

The earl's quarters were on the top floor of the keep so every message I carried that day took me past Margaret's closed door. Each time I hurried past, I wished I had not witnessed the previous night's ugly scene, even while I wondered about it. Earl Harald had shown a side I did not much like. His mother had disturbed me as well.

But if Earl Harald had been harsh the previous night, he was not that day. It was nearing midday when I arrived in his quarters and, instead of sending me out on yet another errand, he told me to rest myself. I took off my cloak and sat.

He finished what he was doing, then said, "You have done well, Malcolm, but I have other work here for you. The boy has a talent," he said to the others as he placed a wrapped object in my hands.

I opened it to find an axe head.

"This is a weapon I had forged on Orkney, by a master craftsman, but there was not time for it to be finished." I knew that he referred obliquely to his being forced out of Orkney. "I wish for a handle that fits it, both in function and form."

My hope that I might prove useful to the earl as a craftsman suddenly shrank. What did I know of weapon making? I made toys for children, combs for women's hair. I felt foolish, as if I had arranged my own shaming. I examined the axe head as I searched for something to say.

It was a delicate thing in design, its curved blade arching back to a narrow span where the handle would fit. It wasn't much larger than my hand, but it was heavy. The well-forged metal was almost black, the surface decorated in hammered silver, a complex pattern of the wildly contorted beasts the Northmen loved to display on any ready surface. It was a pagan design, ungodly for certain, and so beautiful it brought a catch to my throat. Already it had stirred my imagination so that I could see what should be on the handle that had this as its head.

Benedikt came to admire it and nodded approvingly. Meanwhile the earl had taken out the eagle I'd carved and, to my embarrassment, was showing it to the others. My discomfiture was quickly mixed with pleasure. They thought it was wonderful and were disappointed when I admitted I had no more of my work to show them. The boar stayed, small and solid, under my tunic. I would carve something for the earl that would make them all gasp with admiration. I could feel my station rising as I thought it.

"Find Hrothgar," said Earl Harald. "He will provide you with wood. Oak, tell him. And Malcolm, I would have liked it for this venture, but I know there is not enough time. I prefer the work to be done well. If hurrying it will lower the quality then do not rush."

I nodded, already immersed in designs that writhed on the handle in my mind. All that was needed was the wood. The longer I looked the more my fears were edged out by a familiar excitement. I could see how it should be, as if it already were.

As I reached the door the earl called, "There is one more thing, if you will."

His words were cold water on my sparking imagination, but I did not let that show when I turned to receive his order.

"Please wait on my uncle. Ask him if there is anything he needs, anything that I may attend to on his behalf."

"Your uncle, my lord?" The whole morning I had willingly run every errand he had asked of me, but at this one I balked. The man in the shadows was not one I wished to visit.

"He is in my mother's chambers, Malcolm. You saw him last night, did you not?" He sounded irritated.

"Yes, of course," I answered, wondering if I might still find a way out of it. Bad enough that the man had seemed to look right through me, but if Margaret was there ... And why could the earl not visit his own uncle? He had said he would, so why did he send me?

"Ask if he needs anything. And if you see anything of concern, anything that is not as it should be, come to me." The way he looked at me as he said it, I knew he was referring to his mother, perhaps to her lover being there. I did not think I wanted to report if that man had returned. I had not forgotten Harald's threat.

Eirik and Benedikt both looked intrigued. They did not know what had transpired in Margaret's chamber. It seemed Harald did not share everything with his lieutenants.

"Now go. And when you are done there, tell Thorbjorn I wish to see him. We have matters to discuss."

I wondered what I had done to be punished twice over, but I hurried away before he could round it out with a third trial.

It took longer to walk down that one flight of stairs than it had to walk up the whole height of the keep at any time that day. I paused on the landing before shifting the axe head and lightly rapping on the heavy door.

There was no sound. After a brief interval of silence I reasoned that if none answered my knock I was free to leave.

I was on the third step down when I heard a voice, dry as autumn leaves underfoot. I was about to hurry away and pretend I hadn't heard, but some need of mine, whether it was to be obedient or to keep my word, or perhaps, more likely, to know what was hidden from view, forced me to turn back. I hesitated with my hand on the latch, then pushed the door open.

A quick glance around the room assured me that Margaret was absent. The curtain that had hidden her bedchamber the previous night was drawn back, revealing a tousled, but empty, bed. I looked away. The man I had been sent to wait on sat in the high-backed chair in front of the roaring fire instead of in the dark corner where he had been the night before.

There was only one narrow slit of a window in the room and no lamps burned, but the fire was high enough to cast a flickering light on Harald's uncle.

He wore a simple garment, a full and heavy cloak with a hood draped over his head, like a friar or a monk might wear. I was surprised, both because it was terribly hot in that room for a cloth of such weight, but also because it was dyed the deepest black, not one of the usual earthen shades of the godly men of my experience. Black dyes, I knew, were among the most expensive; the cloak was a costly one.

"Well? Do you speak or only stare?" His laugh was like a knife being whetted on stone.

"My lord," I said awkwardly, "the Earl Harald, has sent me to ask if there is anything you need, anything that can be done for you."

"Done for me?" Another laugh. "We are beyond that,

my young Scot. Far beyond that."

I had edged towards the door while he spoke.

"I shall tell him as much. A good day to you, my lord."

"Aren't you in a hurry, then." It was not a question. "Is it my sister you fear? She is off punishing the washerwoman. The poor creature knows nothing of silk, though she'll be an expert soon, I'll warrant. So you need not run off just yet. Unless you are under strict orders to be elsewhere at this very moment?"

"No, my lord, I just thought you did not need anything of me, so I …"

"I said nothing could be done for me by my nephew, but you may be able to offer me something. You serve my nephew, do you not?"

I nodded reluctantly.

"You'll have to speak when you answer, boy. Dumb nodding is for the sheep of the field, whereas you are born of a higher realm. And besides, I'm afraid my eyes aren't what they used to be." This time his laughter caused a flurry of rattling sounds in his lungs. When his coughs had subsided he whispered, "Come closer."

I obeyed. Thus far I had seen nothing of him but one bone-white hand clutching the arm of the chair, not so much old as frail. The hood still hid his face when I stood directly before him. Even when he tilted his chin up at my approach, the light from the fire only outlined a prominent brow and chin, an angular nose. His other features were shadows in the valleys between them.

"You are from Moray," he said.

"I am. How do you—"

"I have an ear for accents. Good ears, I have." He chuckled unpleasantly. "Sharp as the knife that gave them to me."

A sick realization came over me. Someone had spoken of Margaret's brother and what she had done to him. I thought now I knew what it was. I wanted very much to leave just then, for there was also something horrible *about* him, something almost dead, as if he but lingered on the doorstep and a breath of wind would put him through it and away. No wonder Harald wished to avoid him.

"You are going north with Harald then?" he asked. "To Orkney?"

I was not sure how much I should say to this man. My father's warnings played in my head, to be wary, to keep my secrets. I chose my words carefully. "I am here to serve Earl Harald as he sees fit."

I thought that would choke him, his laughing and coughing were so merciless. The sound made my own lungs ache.

"My lord," I said with alarm, "you are ill! I will tell the earl you need to see a physician, or perhaps there is a healer in the vicinity."

"You will not! And you will stop calling me your lord. I ceased to be anyone's lord long ago. My name is Paul. You will run down to the kitchens and fetch me some mulled wine. Put a large dollop of honey in it and get it back here still hot."

I did as he commanded, wishing as I waited in the kitchens that I could ask one of the servants to run up with the drink. But I did not. Though my revulsion for him was undiminished, a queer sort of pity had come over me.

Whatever he had done, he hardly deserved to be treated as badly as he obviously had been, and by his own kin. I carried the steaming cup back up to him and watched while he drank it.

His face never showed the whole time. His hands were steady but with a heaviness in them, as if the simple movements necessary to life were a burden.

"A piece of advice … what is your name?"

"Malcolm mac Alasdair, sir."

"Mac Alasdair." He grunted. "My advice, Malcolm, is that staring is rude in the least and deadly at its worst. For my part I don't mind your scrutiny, but others might take offense. Might think it a challenge." With that he pulled the hood back from his face.

It was much the same as the firelight had shown it to be: sharp planes and deep hollows with the same heavy brow that overhung Harald's features. But under that brow the shadows were darker than they should have been. The eye sockets were two empty pits of blackness where eyes should have been. I gasped in horror.

"Do not grieve yourself, young Malcolm," he said softly. "It was done long ago. Before you were among us, I'm sure. This was not even the worst of it," he whispered, and his voice trailed away. He cleared his throat, "If you wish to help me you will return later to bring me news of the world. That is something I do miss. Perhaps that is what I miss most from my old life. Choosing my own company. Now, off with you. Margaret was not pleased that you saw her last night. She will not like finding you here."

I gaped at him.

"Close your mouth, boy. I may not have eyes, but the knife affords a man a wide view of the world. A dark view, but a wide one. Now go, and return before the day ends."

I rushed down the flight of steps to the hall, stumbling down the outer wooden staircase. My shock at Paul's revelation was retreating in the light of another thought. *How did he know I was there last night?* He had not seen me and no one had said my name. The thought lingered like a bad smell, following me into the yard as I went to fulfill my other unpleasant task.

But Thorbjorn was not so easily found. I went first down the narrow alleyway that ran out toward the sea, looking in each doorway, but I reached the garden enclosure without finding him. It was bitterly cold. I had forgotten my cloak in Harald's chambers.

When I finally found Thorbjorn he was berating a bear of a man who looked as cowed as a small child anticipating a whipping. I decided to retrieve my cloak first and then pass on the earl's message when there might be a chance Thorbjorn's temper had cooled.

The hall of the keep was empty but for a few servants. I dashed up the first flight of stairs. Voices reached me before I arrived at the landing.

"Give him part of Caithness, then. When you kill Erlend you will take back the portion he stole." Margaret's voice was cool, businesslike.

"Caithness comes to me from my father. I will not share it. Do not press me further, Mother. The boy will be provided for. Now, where is the man who came with word of Erlend? I have not been able to find him."

I was edging back down the stairs when I heard Thorbjorn bellowing like a bull in full fury from somewhere near
the keep door. I decided to stay where I was.

"I let him go."

"You let him go? Mother, I warn you now. If you try to
undermine me I will banish you to some convent where
you will have only a covey of whey-faced nuns to command
and control. And do not mistake me. I will do it!"

"I gathered the information he brought and sent him off
to his family. It is Yule, after all. Now, let us continue our
discussion of last night. I want to know your plan."

I noticed that this time she said *your* plan. The thread of
tension I'd sensed the night before was near to snapping,
though mother and son both spoke in perfectly controlled
tones.

"Nothing has changed from last night," said Harald. "I
do not need you. You will have no part in my future, nor
the future of Orkney."

Thorbjorn was entering the hall. At any moment he
would come up the stairs. I cursed my luck. My father
would have called it fate and said not to bother cursing it.
But my father was unlikely to be throttled by Thorbjorn,
however Thorbjorn might feel about him. I moved as quietly as I could past Margaret's door.

Not quietly enough for sharp eyes. "What is he doing
here again?" Margaret asked.

Harald looked at me. "Malcolm, I am busy. Go."

I was happy to obey.

"Malcolm? Alasdair's boy?" The curiosity in Margaret's
voice took me by surprise. She knew my father, of course,

but how did she know my name? She was regarding me now with new eyes which made no sense to me at all.

"Yes, he's Alasdair's."

"You have brought him here. How interesting. Does he show promise?"

My face was burning red at this point. *Promise at what?*

"He belongs to me, Mother. Malcolm, go."

I obeyed gladly, dashing up to the earl's chamber to retrieve my cloak. I was on my way back down when I realized I was about to find myself in much the same position I had been in before. All I needed to make matters worse was for Thorbjorn to come thundering up the stairs. I sat down on the stairs, out of sight of the door, and ran my hands through my hair, thinking of what to do.

Harald's voice carried to me. "Mother, we are done here. My plans are my own."

"Are you certain?"

"Very. Now, tell me where Erlend is."

Margaret's voice had a smile in it. "Erlend is in Orkney, drinking, without Svein, waiting for you to run him through with your sword or burn down the thatch over his head. That is, if you can find him."

I could not help myself. I stole forward in time to see him grab her arm roughly. "Where is he, Mother? I am getting tired of you hiding things from me!"

"You said you do not need me, my son. As you wish. You will learn nothing more from me."

"What do you want?" he shouted.

"Now? Not a thing. You have made up your mind. You will cut me from your life. So will I cut you from mine."

Harald shook her furiously. "What do you *want?*" he bellowed.

Triumph was in Margaret's face. "What do I want? I told you last night. To be in my rightful place, steering the ship of Orkney with a son on either side of me. And," she eyed Harald, weighing her position, "I want Erlend dead. I want you to prove yourself to me, prove that you deserve to be the Earl of Orkney, that you are the man your father and I produced. If you do not, I will not show you favour again, ever."

Harald had stood unmoving throughout her speech. Now he gave a small laugh, more of an exhalation of breath than anything. He nodded his head and took a few steps towards the fire, where he turned to face his mother.

"I am glad I asked you that question. If I was unsure before of who and what you are, I cannot be now. I know exactly where you stand, and where I stand with you." He nodded again. "But you see, I only asked so I would know these things. I have no intention of changing my mind. Moreover, though I had few qualms about it before, I have decided that I will do my utmost to avoid killing Erlend. Yes, I think that I will try to sue for a peaceful resolution to this matter. That would bother you greatly, would it not? Then I will be well-satisfied. You have tried to make me less than a man, as you are so wont to do with the men about you, Mother, and I will have none of it. You have given me enough. I will find Erlend myself and I will deal with him as I see fit."

Without another word, he stalked out of the room and out of the keep. ☙

each man should be watchful and wary in speech,
and use his might in measure,
lest when he come fierce foes among,
he find others fiercer than he.

~WISDOM OF ODIN~

harald had disappeared by the time I got out of the keep. I made my way to the smithy, hoping to find Thorir. He, too, was gone. Just as well. I needed time to think.

The smith's hammer rang in steady rhythm, his fire roaring like it must in hell and nearly as hot. The hut was set aright again, though I noted the smith's horse had found new lodgings: its rear stuck out from the stable next door, the long tail flicking back and forth contentedly.

How did Margaret know I was Alasdair's son? A small part of me was pleased, even while the rest of me knew it was folly. *And what was between the earl and his mother?* The way they spoke to each other curdled in my stomach. I wished I had not witnessed it.

I watched the birds that floated on the gusting wind above the keep. They hung there effortlessly. I felt a pang of envy at their simple, stupid existence. Wind, food, flight. Not for me. I was a fish with an attraction for nets.

In the practice yard two men were circling each other with fighting axes much like the earl's, small but lethal, with long handles and finely-honed cutting edges, only these were simpler and plainer.

One of the men was squat and bulging with muscle, his hair sandy and frizzled, his face as ugly as a toad's. He carried a second axe on his belt. His opponent was Angus.

"You think you can best an Orkneyman with the axe, Scot? You should stick to your pikes and your dirks."

Thorir dropped down on the bench beside me and leaned forward expectantly.

"We were using axes when you were still in your rightful place, north of the sea," Angus replied softly, the hint of a smile in the corner of his mouth.

"And you still don't know how to use one!" grunted the frog man as he lunged at Angus and then feinted and put his shoulder into the taller man's groin. Angus lost his balance and staggered back. He was up again in an instant, his axe at the ready, eyes glittering. His opponent barked a laugh, not of ridicule, but of pleasure.

Angus took that moment to drive forward, spinning to his right as he caught his axe in his left hand and aimed a blow at the other man's shoulder. But the Orkneyman had seen his intent and had already swung out of harm's way; as he did he hooked Angus' heel with his axe, in the space between the shaft and the blade, and threw him to the ground. Angus lay on his back with the second axe poised above his head, ready to cleave his skull in two. Victor and vanquished regarded each other silently.

"Then perhaps you will teach me, Master Haermund," said Angus.

"It will be my pleasure to teach a Scot a lesson," grinned Haermund as he lowered the axe and extended a hand to help Angus to his feet.

"Ah, Haermund, I see you are showing hospitality to our guests," said Thorbjorn as he strode into the courtyard. "Just don't maim any of them. We will need all able hands in Orkney."

I had forgotten about Thorbjorn.

Angus gave Thorbjorn and Haermund each a nod which only Haermund returned.

"I see the pup is still breathing," said Thorbjorn, eyeing me. I watched Angus drift away, wishing I could go with him.

"And eating," said Thorir with a wink to me. "He mends quickly and well."

"Good. Then he can spend some time on the practice field today. We will see what he is made of." Thorbjorn drew his sword. "Have you been trained, boy? Do you know how to use a man's weapon?"

"I do," I said, gritting my teeth. "But not so well," I added honestly.

"Then you are fortunate you heal well," laughed Thorbjorn.

"He is," interrupted Haermund, "because the boy was waiting for a lesson from me. Earl Harald would have him learn to use the axe and I'm the man to teach him."

It was a lie, of course, but Haermund proved a good liar when the cause was worthy. Clearly he thought mine was. If Thorbjorn had his doubts about Haermund's story he didn't say. He shrugged and walked away.

He was half way to the keep when I remembered Earl Harald's message. *Perhaps he knows already*, I told myself hopefully. *Well, he will know soon enough, and sooner than*

I can tell him now even if I run, I added, rounding out my excuse. With luck neither would learn of my omission.

I slumped back down on the bench. I was suddenly very tired.

Haermund stood before me, his thick fists on his hips. "I see Thorbjorn has set his sights on you. Avoid him if you can, at least until you are fit to meet him fairly. If he wants a contest I am here to test him," he added with a grim look. "Until then, it will do you no harm to train in the axe. It seems fate must love you very much, for here I am, a master of the weapon, at your disposal. They call me Haermund Hard-Axe for good reason! Now, I think that you and I had better start our lesson, for your friend is looking on."

He was right. Thorbjorn had stopped and was talking to Simon, but he was watching me. Reluctantly I handed the axe head to Thorir and followed Haermund to a pile of weapons where he selected an old, worn-looking axe for me. When I looked up again both Thorbjorn and Simon were gone, but I did not have the nerve to beg off from my lesson.

I ran my finger over the dull edge of the blade and looked questioningly at Haermund. "I don't want you to cut my arm off or open a vein if you actually hit me," he said. I raised my brows at his own weapon, which was deadly sharp. "Don't worry, boy, I won't hit you. I'm too good to hit you unless I want to." He said it without arrogance. "Now, give me your name. I like to know the men I fight."

I told him.

"Malcolm mac Alasdair," he said, as if he were tasting it. "A good name. Now, hold that thing properly, like this."

He demonstrated how to grip the handle. I was following his example when he swung at me so swiftly I heard, rather than saw, his weapon fly by my ear. It stopped just in time but I had dropped to the ground nonetheless, my axe skidding along in the dirt.

"I told you I will only kill you if I want to. I do not make mistakes with this charming creature." He caressed the axe lovingly and raised it for my next lesson.

• • •

When Haermund was satisfied with my efforts he let me go. Thorir, who had been cheering me on, returned the earl's axe head to me, clapped me on my bruised back, and announced that he had work to do. He loped away in the direction of the courtyard garden at the end of the promontory. Well enough, I had work of my own.

Hrothgar had already prepared a slender shaft of oak, almost the length of my thigh, for the handle. It curved slightly along the lower middle and widened almost imperceptibly at the ends. He also gave me some pumice and a wonderful piece of sharkskin for smoothing the rough edges later. I took a few lumps of wood that he said he had no use for, and returned to my warm place by the smithy. The wind had come up again. I wrapped myself in my cloak and prepared to begin.

I rested my eyes on the wood, waiting for the designs that had swirled so readily in my mind to reappear, that I might capture them with my knife. I could see much of it: knotwork would cover the majority of the wood, all enclosing a form on the middle part of the shaft where the earl's hand would grip it. The trouble was that that central form eluded me and the harder I sought it, the more stubbornly it hid. I took a deep breath to settle my impatience. Forcing it would do no good. I laid wood and metal on the bench beside me and edged closer to the fire, hoping that if I relaxed, my inspiration might be fooled into returning.

Maids scuttled across the yard to the laundries, their chattering carrying to me in snatches. There was a farmer in the yard, bargaining with a servant about some pigs. Now and then a light rain fell, a scattering of drops from the winter sky.

"Does my son encourage such lounging?"

I jumped, startled to see Margaret standing over me, her hair bound close to her head. She was dressed in trews like a man, though there was nothing masculine about her appearance. I wondered that I had not been warned of her presence by the musky, rich scent of resins and flowers that she exuded. I remained awkwardly mute. Her smile did little to put me at ease.

"Well get up then and saddle my horse. I am going riding."

She followed me into the small stable and indicated a giant roan tethered in the warmest corner, closest to the smithy. Her nearness disturbed me so that I fumbled with the leather straps. She did not speak. Her silence only made it worse. I hid my face in the horse's smooth flank as I busied my hands with adjusting saddle and blanket.

As I led the mare out of the stable I stole a look at her face and found she was regarding me with quiet amusement. "You are a curious creature," was all she said. Then she was swinging her long leg expertly over the back of the horse. She immediately kicked it into a canter and was gone, without another glance in my direction.

When she got to the gates she drew the large beast to an abrupt stop. Someone approached. Simon. *Of course*, I thought, *he is Maddad's grandson, Margaret's by marriage.*

Margaret laughed at something he said. There was none of the tension I'd sensed between her and Harald. Of course, Simon had grown up in Margaret's household. I wondered how Harald would feel, seeing another so clearly in possession of his mother's love.

A minute later Margaret rode out of the gates at a gallop and I sat down again, determined to begin work on the earl's handle. But nothing came to me. Frustrated, I picked up one of the small pieces of wood and began, absently, to pick away at it.

I had been working for a while when I heard my name and realized that it was not the first time, that someone had been hissing warnings at me which I'd been too preoccupied to hear. By the time I saw Thorbjorn bearing down on me, his look black with fury, it was too late.

"Did you forget something?" he growled.

I groaned. Harald's message. I began to explain.

"Don't waste my time. You cannot even follow a simple order. Or was it intentional! You think to worm your way in with him, do you? Well, your father was one thing, but I'll not have Harald saddle himself with weaklings."

I was angry now, but I did my best to keep my own tone even. "The earl does not think I am useless. I am doing the work he gave me to do," I said, holding up the naked piece of oak.

"Work?" he said, scathingly. He did not give me time to respond. "Get up! You can do your *decorating* by the fire in the evening like the other women. In the day you won't get off so easily. I won't take mewling puppies with us to hold us back when we're in the thick of it."

Even in practice he could hurt me, perhaps badly, but there was no avoiding him now. I took a deep breath and stood up. "I do not know why you hate me," I said, "but I will fight you if I must."

"Hate you?" he snorted. "You are beneath my hatred. I despise your weakness and the way it spreads about you like disease. Harald is talking of making peace with Erlend now! Was that your doing?"

So that was the source of his anger. "How could that be my doing?" I cried.

"How indeed. I know why you are here," he hissed in my face. "I know you think to make a place for yourself. Well, you had better prove yourself then, hadn't you? Are you your father's son, or are you not?"

"I am here because—"

"Do not take me for a fool."

"I never would," I said, and meant it. Thorbjorn Klerk was many things, but he knew his business. I could protest my ignorance all I liked; he clearly believed I was up to something.

"Where is your sword?"

"I have none."

"Are you going to fight me with your little knife?"

"I will."

A small crowd had gathered. The presence of witnesses would not save me from what I knew would be a sound beating.

Simon, leaning against the smithy wall, yawned. "It hardly seems worth the effort though, does it, Thorbjorn? I mean, he is clearly no fighter. When you are done with him I would like very much to test my arm against yours. I promise to be more of a challenge and more of an entertainment too." He sounded as if he were making an invitation to supper, all courtly and pleasant.

The veins in Thorbjorn's face bulged frighteningly as he glared from Simon to me and back again. But the fire had gone out of him, just like that. "We'll fight later," he said to Simon. "I have more important work to do." And off he went without a word or look back.

It was my turn to stare at Simon. "How did you do that?" I asked, wonderingly.

"I only turned the bull," he said, with a conspiratorial wink. The others were dispersing, the promise of entertainment gone. "His pride overcame his wrath. I like to keep the peace where I can. Now, shall we?" He tapped the pommel of his sword.

It was a friendly enough gesture and after what he'd done for me I should have accepted but found I could not. I did not want a fight just then, even in sport. "Perhaps another time," I said. "I was not looking to fight. He was."

"Certainly," he replied with a polite nod.

"I'll fight you," said one of the men who had been exercising nearby. The man was enormous, like an old bear just come out of his winter sleep, large but lean enough to move well. "The name's Ofram. You can move fast, I assume?"

"I can," answered Simon.

"You'll need to."

The match began immediately. I sat next to Thorir to watch.

"So, Harald is talking of peace with Erlend?" asked Thorir.

"What? Yes, he said something like that to his mother."

"Hmmm. That's interesting. Thorbjorn can't like it much."

"Clearly. And somehow I'm to blame," I said wryly.

"Do you like the idea of Harald killing Erlend?"

"Of course not! But I have no say in the matter. It's his business what he does."

"I suppose it is. Why did Thorbjorn blame you then?"

"What are you getting at?"

"Nothing. I just thought it curious."

Simon and Ofram were dancing around each other, swords raised. Every time Ofram swung I winced. A blow from that arm could knock any man's lungs clean. But Simon was quick, his instincts sharp. Ofram's weapon never met its mark.

"I think Harald was just saying it to upset his mother."

"It worked, I'm sure. She is one to clear the field of competitors. For her, keeping Erlend around only begs future trouble."

"My sense of it was that she wanted Harald to kill him just to prove he would do her bidding."

"And that is likely as well. So, you have met her. And what do you think?"

"I think I am like a bird trying to fly through water," I remarked. "I do not understand these people. I do not belong here."

Thorir thought about that. "You feel out of place," he said, "but you are not. I am sure of it. You belong here more than you know. Look up there," he said, pointing to the birds that still hung in the air above the keep.

A great shiver passed through me for no reason I could determine. One enormous bird dropped down from the sky and landed on the wall a few paces away from us. It was settling itself when another came, as large and blue-black as the first, to sit beside his brother. I saw the shadows sweeping across the waters of Loch Ness and up the coast to Wick.

"Odin's eyes," murmured Thorir, breaking the silence.

"What was that?" I asked. I could not take my eyes from the birds. I felt cold all over. They were *watching* me with those eyes like jet beads.

"The ravens. The two ravens of Odin, Huginn and Muninn. They report to the Allfather on the news of the world. What news do you think they are gathering here?"

I stared up at him, my hard-won calm broken. "You are mad," I said, exasperated, and I marched away from him, through the compound of Wick and out the gates.

• • •

I headed westwards, straight for the sun that hovered low. I had an hour or so before dark. The weather was mild for early January, but the day ends in the mid-afternoon at that time of year and I did not wish to be caught in the wilds of Caithness alone at night.

Thorir's words ran through my head, as did Margaret's. And what of Thorbjorn's puzzling accusation? Why did people keep mentioning my father? I had a very strong suspicion that his great secret had only been secret from me. So what did that mean? What did they know of him and what did they *think* they knew of me?

I stretched my legs with ever-lengthening strides until something inside me broke free and I was flying across the land, leaping the rocks where they burst from their carpet of green, flecked with frost where the sun had not reached for weeks and months. In the distance I spied a grove of trees. I ran in among them, darting between the tall trunks, dancing over the undergrowth. The harder I ran the lighter I felt, until I was gasping for breath, my throat raw with the cold air. But my heart was finally right again. I slowed to catch my breath.

A movement between the trees caught my eye. It did not belong to the wind, nor did that particular shade of colour belong to a winter day. Gold. Gold hair upon a russet cloak. I knew whose it was. Margaret was unmistakable with her long hair unbound, falling in swirling coils around her shoulders. She was a golden flame in the forest.

And the man before her was her black-haired lover. She put her hand on his chest. They kissed and then began to speak again. *If you see anything of concern, anything that is not as it should be*, Harald had said. They were too far away for me to hear their words but I was certain they were saying goodbye. Whatever Margaret was, whoever the man was, they deserved their words of parting. And no man deserved what Harald had threatened.

I moved away as quietly as I could. Once out of the grove I fell into a trot towards Wick. I need not hurry too much. They had not seen me, and they would undoubtedly take what time they could together.

I could see Wick clearly and was able to make out the tiny figures of the men and women going about their business, when I felt the beat of hooves drumming the earth behind me. Suddenly I was running, like a deer leaping over the heath, not even knowing why, except that I knew I must run, that I must be seen by those people in the distance. The feeling came upon me as suddenly as she did.

The distant figures were growing larger. They saw me. They had to see me.

Thunder descended, shaking the ground. *She will run me down*, I suddenly thought, and then I felt the heat of the roan as it thundered by and Margaret's cloak whipped out at me. Throwing my arm up to protect my face, I staggered, then slowed to a stop, chest heaving. When I looked again horse and rider were entering the gates of Wick. ◈

12

*the unwise man lies awake all night,
thinking of this and that.
when morning comes he is weary and worn
and no lighter of his load.*

~wisdom of odin~

T hat night I avoided Thorir long enough to be sure I would not be dragged up to the earl's table. I joined my fellow Scots and a few of the Orkney-men at a table at the other end of the hall. It was pleasant to be among my own kind, even though they were almost strangers. There was something of home in their speech and manners, a sensibility that set us apart from the others in the hall.

And while I kept watch on the entrance to the stair for fear Margaret might appear, they talked of nothing else. They gossiped like women at their spinning, only quieting themselves when the earl, moving about the hall to address various individuals, came near. I understood better now why he had been so concerned about his mother's effect on his men.

"I hear she'll bed any who come to her," said Fergus with a lascivious grin.

"But not you," said Ofram, the man who had fought Simon in the courtyard that day. "She told me so last night, she did."

"She will not bed just anyone," said Angus, quietly. "She is a woman who will take her pleasure, but do not make the mistake of thinking that she is a wanton, a kitchen maid who'll do your bidding for a quartered coin. The earl's mother is like a man. She does as she pleases. If she were a man, you would think nothing of it."

"But she is not a man. Her behavior is not proper for a woman," said Ofram.

"Proper? Who are the men to bed if women are not willing to join them?" said Angus with a smile. "But you are right to a point. The matter of her lover has caused much trouble."

"Margaret's affair with Gunni has cost our lord dearly," said Ofram.

"It was not the affair that cost him. It was the earl's ending of it," replied Angus.

Was Angus defending Margaret?

"Sure enough," said Fergus. "If Harald drove my brother off like a criminal I'd be outraged too. Svein may be a devil, but he has his duty to kin aright, if you ask me. Harald should have swallowed his temper."

"You're right there, but if he had we wouldn't have this chance at some sport! Speaking for myself, a little warring in winter helps pass the time," said Vermund.

"You'll take warring any time you can," grunted another man, Eyolf. "You're just hoping to fill your purse, perhaps to ransom someone? Well, you'll not get that this time around, for I hear there will be no fighting, if Harald has his way."

"Is that what you heard?" said Vermund. "Well, I say he has the blood of his family in him and so the odds of a fight are better than good. Remember when Paul was earl? His own aunts tried to kill him with a poisoned shirt. It was his Yule gift! These nobles, they think the rules of kinslaying don't apply to them. They kill for convenience, and if it conveniences me, how am I to blame?"

"There is killing and there is murder," said Angus.

"And the difference?" retorted Vermund.

"Intent," answered Angus. "Even an accidental killing of a kinsman requires a blood price be paid, unless a man is slain in battle. It is forbidden for your people and mine and for good reason. How can family ties be maintained if we kill the very brother we are required, by law, to avenge? It is not possible. It has been the greatest of sins since Cain slew Abel."

"Bah," snorted Vermund. "Laws or no laws, a man must serve his needs. Mine are a full purse. Harald's are Orkney without Erlend. Simple. I like it simple."

"Even Margaret avoided killing her brother," pressed Angus.

"Did she avoiding killing him or did she avoid letting him die with dignity?" Vermund was getting irritated now.

"Whatever she did, I'd still like to try for the prize myself," said Fergus.

It was highly unlikely that Fergus, who was far from young or handsome, would ever have a chance at that prize, but I felt a duty to warn him nonetheless.

"The cost," I said, "might be higher than you are willing to pay." And so I told my companions how our lord intended to deal with any of his mother's future companions. The rest of what I had heard outside Margaret's chamber I kept to myself.

There was much cringing at my news.

"And how did you hear all this?" asked Ofram.

"I happened to be there and the earl did not care that I heard."

"You might take more care with what you hear," said Vermund with a raised brow. That was the second time I'd heard those words since arriving at Wick.

"It seems the son takes after the mother then," said Og-mund. I gave him a puzzled look. "You know how Harald became earl, don't you?" he asked. "And of his uncle, the Earl Paul, who ruled before him?"

I know he sits in a room above us and that he has no eyes, I thought.

"It's not a happy tale. Earl Paul held all of Orkney at one time. The people liked him a great deal. There was some trouble with Erlend's father, but he died and it looked like Orkney would have some good peace out of Paul."

"There might have been a lengthy peace under him, if it weren't for Margaret," said Angus. *So, he was not defending her.* "She had Svein kidnap him. He took Paul to Margaret and Maddad in Atholl, where they called him guest. I was about your age then. I remember how he sat at the banquets those first days with a patient smile on his face and was civil to all. Then one day he disappeared, though no one had seen him leave. When Svein heard he was terribly angry for he had not sought to harm Paul, though what he thought was to happen to the man, I don't know. It was not long before we heard Paul had abdicated, sent word that he would never return to Orkney, and that none should come to bring him back, for he was maimed and not fit to rule.

They should accept his nephew, the child Harald, as their earl, along with their cousin, Rognvald, who would rule for him."

My mouth grew dry. I had seen the empty sockets that proved part of the tale. Blinding was not an uncommon way of disposing of competition among the nobility, but that was not all. *The son takes after the mother, Angus had said.* I was afraid I knew what he meant.

Angus sighed, "Some say Margaret did it herself, others that she only watched. They say he was unmanned first, and then blinded, in that order, so that he might bear witness to the proceedings and see himself no longer whole. To that I cannot testify, but I do know he was blinded, for I saw him when he left Atholl at last."

"But why?" I demanded.

"Who knows. The only reason I can think, beyond hate and cruelty, was to be sure he never made any sons to vie with her own later on."

"They say he's here," said Fergus.

"No one's seen him, but if he survived the voyage, he's here," said Angus. "As soon as Maddad died, Margaret flew north like a bird into the arms of Gunni and left orders that her brother was to be brought here. He was frail, though. It is a long way from Atholl to Wick, especially for a man who has been imprisoned for more than fifteen years."

From there the talk moved on to other subjects. It was an old tale for everyone but me, and concerns of Erlend and Svein and what was to be done in Orkney were more immediate. In time the discussion turned, as it usually did, to embrace the women who served our meal and who among them might serve later as well. Margaret's name was not spoken again.

But I still had to wait on Paul and risk meeting Margaret when I did.

I was given a reprieve when Thorir stood to indicate the entertainment was beginning. It would be impossible to slip away without being seen until he was done.

That night Thorir told the story of how Odin received wisdom from his mother's brother, the giant Mimir, from the spring at the roots of Yggdrassil, and how he had willingly paid for that boon with an eye. I wondered if he had ever begrudged the loss.

He told how Thor, Odin's son, fished for the World Serpent to destroy it and save the world from its destiny of destruction, but the giant who went with him in the boat was afraid and cut the god's line and doomed the whole world with his act.

He told one tale after another, enthralling his hearers, binding them to him like lovers. My friend—for that is what he had become, a friend—was a true master at his trade.

Finally he rested for a time, one foot up on the bench, his back against the wall behind the head table. Musicians played while he eased his throat with a cup of mead. He caught my eye, gave me his customary wink, and began:

"Now is the story of Sigurd, son of Sigmund, told.

"Sigurd became the step-son of King Alf after his own father was slain in battle by Odin. He grew to be the best-loved of King Alf's sons. The king would have made him his heir, for Sigurd had the makings of a true king, but

Sigurd had no claim to the throne.

"So King Alf sent Sigurd to the dwarf Regin for foster-age, and Regin asked Sigurd why he accepted a low place at court. Sigurd answered that he sat among kings and was treated as their equal. But the dwarf kept on at him, telling him what a shame it was that he would not rise as high as he was made to because he was not of the king's blood. It was not hard for Regin to persuade Sigurd to seek adventure. He asked his foster-father where he should go to find the greatest danger and the highest reward.

"Regin answered, 'My brave and glorious Sigurd, I know just the place and a task only you can fulfill. There is a dragon named Fafnir who sits on a hoard of gold in a cave. He is so evil and strong that none can best him. I know, for Fafnir is my brother. He became a dragon after he slew our father for his gold. Now he robs me by keeping it all for himself. But there has been none like you in the world before now, Sigurd. Perhaps you have the strength to defeat him and take the gold.'

"Fafnir was away when they reached the mountain. Regin advised Sigurd to dig a pit and to hide in it, and when the dragon walked over the pit, to pierce his soft belly with his sword. Then Regin ran away to hide, for he was a great coward.

"While Sigurd dug the pit Odin came to him in the guise of an old man and told him to dig a deep ditch to catch the blood of Fafnir and to bathe in it. Wherever the blood of the dragon touched him, he would be invulnerable.

"So Sigurd did as the old man advised and then he hid himself in the pit and when Fafnir returned, Sigurd thrust his sword into the serpent's belly and slew him. But as the dragon lay dying, he told the hero that the gold was cursed, and that any who laid claim to it would bear that curse and be destroyed by it, as he had been.

"'I will accept my fate as it comes to me,' said Sigurd. Then Fafnir died and Sigurd bathed in his blood so it covered all of him, but for one place on his shoulder where a leaf had become stuck.

"Then Regin bade Sigurd cut out the heart of the dragon and build a fire and roast the heart, that Regin might eat it. And Sigurd did as he was asked, but when he took the heart from the spit he burnt his finger. He thrust it into his mouth. Suddenly he heard the voices of the birds and he understood their words. They said Regin had murder in his heart, and that he meant to slay Sigurd and take all the gold for himself. Such was the power of the heart of the dragon.

"So Sigurd slew Regin, his foster-father, and he ate the heart of Fafnir and was imbued with great wisdom. And when Sigurd entered the cave to claim the gold he claimed the curse of kinsman's blood with it, with full knowledge and acceptance."

The men were still drinking to Thorir and applauding his tale when I slipped out of the hall and up the cold spiral stair. I wondered briefly, as I stepped onto the landing, for whom his story had been intended.

I knocked at the door. A voice spoke, so faint that it could have been the wind. For a panicked moment I thought it might be Margaret expecting someone else.

The voice came louder. "Come in, Malcolm. And hurry.

She will return soon enough." Dry coughs followed. It was Paul.

I went in.

"She saw you."

I knew that, yet the way he said it filled me with dread.

His hood was pulled up again and I was glad. I had not been able to erase the image of his ravaged face, of those empty black pits. Still, standing before him I had the sensation again that he was examining me. I knew it was not possible but the feeling persisted.

"My sister will call you to her chamber, tonight, tomorrow."

"What does she want?" I asked.

"She wanted to kill you, but I told her that I would not allow it, that I would tell my nephew of her meeting myself. I surprised her there. She is always taken aback by a man who denies her what she wants." His laughter was painful, bitter.

Kill me? My knees felt weak and my head whirled. *Over seeing her with her lover?*

"Why would she want to kill me?" I cried. "She met her lover on the moor. I don't care. I won't be responsible for any man being ..." I could not finish that thought, not to this particular man. "Tell her I won't say anything."

"She thinks you were spying on her."

"I wasn't. Tell her, please."

"I'm afraid it is not so simple," said the former earl. "Go now. She will return soon. Only meet with her here, in my presence. I will protect you as I am able. But come alone. The simpler this is, the better."

I tripped down the stairs as quickly as my feet would take me. In the hall the fire still blazed. Men were stretching out on benches and bedrolls or talking quietly over their ale. There was no sign of Margaret. Thorir sat with Angus and the others at our table. I went to join them.

Margaret entered the hall a moment later. I knew because everyone around me stopped talking to look her way. She, in turn, exchanged a look with her son and then swept her eyes around the room, settling them on me a moment before she turned and disappeared up the stairs.

Thorir offered me his cup. "Are you well, my friend?"

"I took a short voyage on open water," I retorted, gulping down a large draught.

The others burst into laughter and someone poured me more ale. I sounded cocky enough, but my mind was on the moor and in the room above. What mess had I stumbled into? Dread filled me even while I forced my face to show contentment. Margaret wanted to kill me. Why? Perhaps it was true that these people of noble blood cared so little for the lives of others that they would dispense of them for their own convenience.

That night Thorir and I elected to sleep in the hall. Cramped as it was, the temperature outside had dropped and the storehouse was a drafty alternative. I lay on my back, staring up into the shadows cast by the smoldering Yule fire, wondering what the coming day might bring.

• • •

A sound of scratching woke me. A woman stood in the shadows with a broom, sweeping, her head bowed. I thought it strange that she should be working while we all slept. Then I noticed something familiar about the shape of her shoulders, her stance. Suddenly I knew her. Marjory.

Her face was hidden in a cowl. I went nearer and touched her shoulder, but she did not look up. Her broom brushed at my foot in its unending rhythm across the patch of floor before her. Back and forth it swept, yet the dirt remained unstirred.

Dread dropped into my heart like a stone in water. Something was wrong. My hand reached hesitantly to pull back the tattered hood.

I jerked back in horror from the crone I had unveiled. Her face was wrinkled and rough as an oak bough, her hair a mat of rusty grey. She gaped up at me, eyes wide with surprise, lips flapping around a toothless mouth, speaking words with no sounds.

A bony finger darted out to scratch the skin over my heart with a twisted yellow nail. My hand flew to where the blood welled up in a beaded line. My amulet was gone. The empty mouth grinned at me as the crone stepped back. I lunged forward desperately but my hand passed through her, as if through water. She faded until I could see the stones of the wall behind her. She was as insubstantial as mist, retreating to a place where I could not follow, like dust, blown away on the wind, grey and then gone.

But not her eyes. The eyes that were locked on mine were blue and clear as a summer sky, and they beseeched me. After a long moment, recognition flared in me. I laughed aloud as those blue eyes flashed with the triumph that I knew so well. She knew I had seen her. This was Marjory before me, distorted, disguised, but there was no doubt. She was my sister and no crone.

But she was almost gone. And what could have happened to her? She was old and worn … suddenly I knew. I had failed in my mission and this was her fate. I bowed my head in grief.

I felt a touch like wind on my hands. I looked down to see the ancient fingers on mine and then their rough calluses and ridged scars were melting away and the sagging skin grew white and soft. I raised my eyes with joy but it was not my sister's face that rose up above me. I was holding the hands of a woman whose head nearly reached the stone roof.

Her eyes were blue too, but blue like a winter sea. I had lost something in that sea but I had forgotten the name of it. The woman was very beautiful, with the face of a lion and a mane of gold that cascaded down in shimmering waves to clothe her naked form and carpet the floor. It swirled in a pool around my feet. I reached to touch it and then drew back in pain but she caught my hand in hers and kissed my fingers and they were healed. She smiled at me with her large, sharp teeth and pulled my dirk from my belt. She cut a lock of her hair, throwing it up in the air to let it fall in a shower of glittering gold that landed with the tinkle of little bells.

"Take what you need," she purred. Her half-lidded eyes were gentle.

If I took the gold Marjory would not grow old and die. If I took the gold I could go home and all would be well. I had no choice. I must have it. With it, all would be well.

Without it …

I filled my hands with gold but it kept spilling back onto the ground. I had no sack to put the pieces in, not even a pocket or a scrip. There was gold everywhere, and I could not carry any. I almost wept with despair.

Then, as if she read my thoughts, she said, "How may I serve you, Malcolm?" and before I could answer, she said, "Shall I take you home?" and I did not need to answer, for she knew my heart. She threw her head back and laughed with a roar like summer thunder. I ached with the sound.

"Your journey is ended," said the lion-woman. I saw then that she had powerful wings on her back and sacks of gold hung there. She stretched herself out and I climbed on her back. She launched forth into a starry sky.

"South," I said, and we flew.

We flew over the raging sea and the speck that was Dingwall and the dazzling waters of Beauly. Finally we reached Loch Ness. I was almost home. The lion dove from the heavens to skim the surface of the water. Another creature rose up from the depths to meet her, a dragon with golden scales on its breast, and it kissed her enormous mouth.

Then, Dunailech was before us, perched on its hill. My heart shouted with joy as we descended. There was a shimmer of dark red-gold in a window and then familiar blue eyes. But there was no joy in those eyes. We drew closer and they widened in fear and horror and I suddenly knew what Marjory had been saying with her old crone mouth. "No, Malcolm, no!" she had said, and I had not heard. And it was too late. The lion that was a dragon was laughing with a deep rumble that shuddered along her entire length. She opened her mouth and spat flame at the stone keep on the hill. I cried out and fell into the cold air.

A hand pushed me down, gently, onto the solid ground.

"What is it?" whispered Thorir, his hand still on my chest.

I could hardly hear him for the sound of my heart. "Only a dream."

"Tomorrow you will tell me about it."

"It is already gone," I lied.

Thorir's face flickered in the firelight. "Tomorrow," he said with finality.

I would tell him. It could not hurt. It was only a dream. I grunted my assent and he rolled over and was snoring in moments.

My hand went to the amulet. I clutched it fiercely, as if it were an anchor. *It* was real. The dream was not. That is what I told myself over and over again until I finally drifted into sleep. By morning the dream would be gone and so would the scratches etched into my chest. &

13

*if haply a fool should find for himself
wealth or the love of a woman,
his pride will grow, but his wisdom never,
and onward he fares in his folly.*

~WISDOM OF ODIN~

One winter a cat at Dunailech took up the habit of coming into my chamber and curling into a purring ball on my chest while I slept. At first, in my dream or my half-slumber, that warmth was comforting, but as I lay there it would change, growing heavier and heavier, as if the cat were growing as it sat on my chest, and I would suddenly wake in a flailing panic, desperate to relieve myself of its smothering weight.

That is how I felt that day. The world was sitting on my chest and I could not thrust it off. I waited until Thorir and I were alone at the table and then I began to talk.

I told him about my dream of the previous night, of Marjory and the woman who was a lion, then a dragon. And once I'd told him about that, the rest rushed out like birds freed of their cage. I told him of the cold stone chamber where I'd woken, more than once, and of the sounds I'd heard there. I told him about the fisherman and his strange words and that I was afraid to sleep, lest I dreamed.

"Well, there is no use in that," said Thorir. "The one thing no one can avoid is fate. Your dreams are only a reflection of it. What is happening in your dreams echoes, or perhaps presages, what happens in your waking life. Frightening as it may be, you must dream and then learn what the dreams can teach you. They may well prove to be the most precious gift you have."

I saw my father sitting on his stool shaking his head wearily as he confessed his gift.

"When did the dreams begin?" he asked.

"The night I learned I was to go to Orkney."

"And before that, did you ever have strange dreams, dreams of the quality you describe?"

Had I? How did I know what was strange, what was normal?

"Most dreams," he prompted, "they fade in the first moments of waking. But these are different. They stay with you, as if they were real."

I thought of the Marjory in my dream and of the strange golden woman. They had been so real. Suddenly my hand flew to the amulet. It was as if a taper had been lit in my mind.

I pulled out the tiny boar and told Thorir how I had given it to Marjory the morning she had been gored picking berries. I had never thought of it before, what had inspired me to give her the carving that morning, or at all; it was not a very typical gift for a girl. But if I had dreamt it …

It still did not explain why I had given her the boar, nor why she had given it back to me.

I shook my head in frustration. "My father called Orkney the Islands of the Boar. Maybe Marjory somehow knew where I was going."

"You two are very close," Thorir said with a smile. He leaned forward to look into my eyes. "Malcolm, do you recall yesterday, when the ravens appeared in the yard, that I called them Odin's eyes?"

I began to apologize for my outburst but he waved me off.

"New ideas stir the emotions," he said. "I know you are a Christian and I swear to you I have no desire to tamper with your faith. But I think I may have some answers for you, or, if not answers, then a window into this mystery of yours, one that may show you a clearer view than you had. You must promise to curb your temper and your tongue and hear me out," he said with a knowing look.

I had a good idea that I would not like what he had to say, but I assented.

"Every morning Odin sends out his ravens, Huginn and Muninn, Thought and Memory, and they fly the world over gathering knowledge for their master. When they return to him, they tell him all. Even the Christians among my people know that a raven in the sky means they have been seen. Some beliefs linger." He smiled. "Ravens are also birds of the battlefield and can mean death is coming to a man, but when there are two, and always only two, well, I do not believe that is an omen of death. There is something otherwise at work."

He sat back a moment and regarded me. Then he leaned forward, his eyes alight with excitement. "Malcolm, since you joined us on this voyage, I have seen two enormous ravens, together, every day. I have only seen the like once before. The day my parents were taken from me. I did not tell this before, but the morning we left Norway two ravens lit on the mast and flew away when we lost sight of land.

You know the rest of it."

A chill had crept up through my limbs as he spoke. "I do not believe in such things." *I cannot believe such things,* I told myself, *or I must deny all I have ever believed!*

"You do not, but I do, and I believe that the ravens follow us for a reason. I believe that events are unfolding around us that Odin has an interest in. They may be very dark events, for he is the god of death, but he is also the god of wisdom and of poetry. That will mean little to you, of course. I only wish for you to understand what I am about to tell you. Malcolm, when you left, when you went out on the moor, the ravens followed you and did not return."

His words hit me like a wave. *Pagan nonsense,* I told myself stubbornly, but in the back of my mind another voice whispered.

I drew a deep breath to regain my footing. "What has all this to do with my dreams, Thorir? I have not dreamt of ravens."

"No, but I believe you may have dreamt of the spirits of others, and perhaps this is why the ravens have such an interest in you."

I did not want to hear such things. Angry words rose to my lips and I was about to voice them when I saw Thorir's face, his guileless expression, so kind and earnest, and I swallowed them. I knew I would not have done so with my father.

He waited until I was ready for more, then asked, "Do you know what a varden is?"

I groaned aloud.

"Every man has a varden," he explained, enjoying himself, despite the fact that he was being serious. "It is a part of his spirit, his soul. He cannot live without it, nor does it live when his body dies. And those with the gift and the skill can use it as they do their body of flesh.

"North of my homeland live a people called the Lapplanders. Among them are people who can travel in the spirit, while their bodies lie in sleep. We have such people too, usually women, but sometimes men as well."

Was this what my father had meant when he said he had dreamed of Harald an old man in Orkney? And the fisherman, he had told me to wake within the dream. The weight on my chest pressed harder.

"It was only a dream," I protested. "And besides, I did not go anywhere. I flew on the back of a dragon, Thorir! There was nothing of the real world in that."

"You are ever the impatient one, Malcolm," he scolded. "When the spirit leaves the body and voyages, it sees with the spirit's eyes. The spirit has a form too, a form that can only be seen by another spirit and by animals. You have seen a dog bark angrily at one stranger and lick the hand of another? It sees what we do not." He looked at me expectantly.

"So," I laughed, "am I now a dog?"

"You may well be," he answered with a grin. "Do not laugh! The dog, the wolf, they are creatures known for their devotion, their fierce loyalty to kin, to those they love. The varden of a man, or a woman, bears the form of an animal that represents the true heart of that person. A clever woman may be a fox, a mild one a deer, an angry man a bear or, dear Malcolm, a dragon!"

I gaped at him. "A dragon? You think I am a *dragon*?" This was too much.

"I don't know what you are. You cannot see your own varden, of course, not unless you are dying. I only tell you about dragons because you have dreamed of one. Fafnir could not overcome the darkness of his spirit so he committed his great sin—killing his father—and was transformed in body. He was not unusual in succumbing to the dragon within him. It is the most challenging of spirits to battle. It usually takes a lifetime to be defeated completely. But as far down as a man can fall, so high can he also fly. Had Fafnir wrestled with his spirit and won, he might have been a truly glorious man."

"Glorious? Why are you telling me this? Men who are dragons? Dragons are fell creatures—"

"Was it not your god's most beautiful angel who became the cruelest devil? Dragons are fell creatures, yes, but they are also the purest of creatures. They are brave, strong, passionate, they love single-mindedly and they love truth above all. When a dragon chooses wrongly his purity is tainted in a way that it is not with others."

"Are you sure you are describing a dragon, Thorir?"

He ignored my interruption. "Most of them stand apart and can be very secretive, private. Have you ever heard tell of two dragons together in a place? That seldom falls out well! They are often leaders, though with such power most are unable to control their nature and become harsh and cruel. I suspect Thorfinn was one."

I had just been thinking the same thing.

"We are affected as much by the traits of our varden as

we are by those we derive from our parents."

"Are you saying Harald has a dragon varden?" I asked.

"I do not think he does."

I was surprised by his certainty. "Why do you say that?"

"His troubles would be different. That is all. He could have. I don't know."

I could see that he was finished. He was waiting for my response.

I sighed, making light. "You have actually gotten me to discuss dragon spirits with you. What a true master of your craft you are, Thorir."

He nodded in happy acknowledgment, then was serious again. "Malcolm, whatever form your spirit may have, your dreams seem to be a warning. A man who is warned is wise to take heed."

For a time I said nothing. He pushed himself up from the bench. "I know," he said. "You do not want to hear these things. But I am your friend. It is my duty to tell you that which you do not want to hear."

He was halfway out the door when he called back. "I almost forgot. Harald wanted to see you in his chamber." Then he was gone.

• • •

I sat alone at the table, the clatter from the kitchens below comforting me with its ordinariness. My mind raced with Thorir's words. I'd been furious with my father for setting far less bizarre ideas in my mind, but fantastical as this talk of ravens and vardens was, even knowing none of it could be true, I was intrigued. With thoughts of spirits travelling the night and dragons in men's bodies, I mounted the stairs to the earl's chambers.

As I rounded the first part of the spiral I saw with relief that the door to Paul and Margaret's chamber was closed. Voices came from the earl's apartment above. Each step brought them closer and clearer. By the time I reached the landing I knew a debate was waging. Thorbjorn's voice was all edges and anger and I flinched at the thought of what would happen if I vexed him with an interruption, but he would like it even less if I lingered outside the door. I stepped into the doorway and waited until I was seen.

Harald sat at a table by the one window. He nodded to me. There was much crosstalk so I could not tell what the dispute was about, only that all had opinions and all were speaking them.

"Cousins, let us discuss this matter calmly," said Benedikt. "It does not benefit anyone to debate in anger. Thorbjorn, do you not care that this is a holy time?"

"That is religion, this is war. There should be no debate at all," snapped Thorbjorn.

"Yet you insist on pressing the matter," said the earl in a tired voice. "I am the earl here, am I not? It seems that certain people forget that quite regularly. Perhaps because I am at present the earl of nothing?"

"You are still earl of half of Caithness," said Thorbjorn, "and you'll have all of it and Orkney soon enough. But you cannot do this thing in halves! A man must be decisive and his acts must cut as cleanly as his blade, in one fine and final stroke. And then it is done!"

"I will think more on it," said Harald. He gave a brief smile when Thorbjorn shook his head with frustration.

"Now, Malcolm, what do you need?"

"I was told you asked me to come," I said, wondering suddenly if Thorir had played some sort of trick on me.

"Of course. I had forgotten. You waited on my uncle?"

"I did."

"And what does he want of me?"

"He wants nothing." I did not add that he wanted my company and perhaps my soul.

But Harald was not pleased. His face went dark. "Well then," he said angrily, "ask again on your way out and then find yourself something to do for the day. Have you made way on the carving?"

"Not yet, my lord. But I will today. I promise."

"Fine then. And if my uncle needs anything, tell me and I will see to it."

The door closed behind me as I made my way down the twisted stair. What was wrong with him? If Earl Harald was so concerned about his uncle why did he not visit him himself? He had all but ignored the man that first night and then he used me as an intermediary. *That is the way of power,* I thought. *He does as he pleases and I go where I am bidden.* And why did it bother him that Paul did not want anything of him? I would never understand these people.

Suddenly it came to me that Harald's order to visit his uncle just then might not be a bad thing. Was it not better to surprise Margaret than to come when she called? I sat down on a stair to think. Yes, it would suit me fine to go now. And I would hold my tongue and weigh my position carefully, taking time to think. I would listen well and be silent and find my way out of whatever trouble I had stumbled into.

When I arrived on the landing I found the door open.

"I have been waiting for you," said Margaret. She was standing before the fire. Paul sat in his chair to one side. "Come in and close the door. It seems that our paths are destined to cross, over and over. Why do you think that is?"

"Wick is not a large place, my lady. Perhaps it is simply coincidence."

Paul snorted. Margaret smiled at him, her eyes narrowing briefly. Then she swung her gaze to me. As she stepped closer the light of the fire cast a rosy halo about her, illuminating the silhouette of her body within her silk gown. Amber, like the heavy strand of beads around her white throat. The room was very warm. I fumbled with the folds of my cloak.

"Coincidence is what fools see when they close their minds to the threads that bind all events together. So they think the spider can fly and catches her prey by magic. Only when the sun illuminates the web do they see it is another sort of magic altogether. But you are a bright boy. You will learn to see, I'm sure."

I knew she was not a good person but I still could not believe she wanted to kill me.

"I am curious as to why you are here. You are much … younger than the other men."

She meant to humiliate me. I gritted my teeth. She saw it.

"I apologize, my dear. I did not mean to make you feel ill at ease. I do not question your worth to my son, only the reason that your father sent you. I know your father, you know. A handsome man. You have a more refined look to you." Her eyes never left mine. "I recall your father to be quite charming, intelligent. And stubborn, with a temper. All the best qualities of a Scot, no? Are you like him?" She smiled into my eyes.

I have heard of snakes in the barbarian lands that cast a spell over a man with their eyes so that he falls into their power, standing immobile while they strike with their deadly poison. If I held my tongue just then it was only because I could not speak.

"What I cannot understand," she went on, "is what Alasdair hopes to gain. Can your family really be in such dire straits that he was forced to send you away on this desperate venture? I mean, Harald's coffers are not exactly full. What can he possibly give *you*?"

She was right. What *did* my father hope to gain? It had never made any sense to me. Now it seemed the height of madness, worse than ridiculous.

Still, I felt the need to defend both my father and Harald. "I do not think my family or this venture are so desperate, my lady. Your son is an able leader from all I am told."

"I know exactly how desperate your family's situation is. And as for Harald, yes, he is able enough, but every man finds defeat when fate decrees it, and Harald is hasty and young. My instincts are excellent, Malcolm, and they tell me that Harald's plans will not fall out as he desires, that peril lies at the end of this escapade. If Harald fails where will you be? And that's not all! If, God forbid, you should not return for some unforeseen reason, what will befall the family of Malcolm mac Alasdair?"

She spoke all my fears aloud. I saw the dragon soaring down on Dunailech, Marjory's eyes widening in terror.

Margaret's expression was compassionate. "Sit, here, my dear boy," she said. She took my hand as she drew me down beside her. Her arm against mine was warm. I breathed in her honey-rich scent. "Do not be dismayed," she said soothingly. "As I have said, your father was a favourite of ours. There is a small favour I would ask of you, and in return I will speak on your behalf to the king. I have known him since infancy. Did you know that? I have sat in the queen's chambers with him on my knee when he was very small. He will heed me if I ask him to pardon an old friend his very old treasons."

I already knew what she wanted. I thought I was wise to offer before being asked. "I never intended to tell Earl Harald about seeing you," I said. She had almost ridden down upon me but now I understood. She had been afraid, afraid of what I would do and what Harald would in turn do to her young man. I knew she was dangerous, yet I could hardly blame her for wanting to protect the man! "He is my lord," I said, "but I will not be party to a man's maiming—" I could feel Paul sitting in the shadows. Neither of them gave any indication my words were amiss.

"I am so very pleased," Margaret said, squeezing my hand. "Harald is angry but he will regret many of his actions later. Your wise choice will save him from his own rashness. And now, I feel that you have done me a very good turn and I should do you one as well."

"You have offered to help my family keep our land. What more is there?"

"There is much we could do for each other. For instance, you should have a few coins to make a jingle in your purse. And I, well, I would hope that you could offer some of what your father used to."

"And what was that?" I asked, puzzled.

The web sparkled in the firelight. I did not see it until much later.

"You know that he worked for us for many years."

"I know he was a friend to your husband."

"And to me. He was very valuable to both of us."

A wave of nausea passed over me. "How so?" I asked.

She watched my face closely. "I can understand why he did not tell you about it. Such things are best kept quiet, but he was with us, nonetheless."

"He was friends with the earl," I repeated.

"And with me," she added softly. "You seem upset. Did he say differently?"

I shook my head. Something here was wrong.

She smiled. "I said it before. You are much like your father. And I hope you will be in this also. I require help for certain matters that I cannot address myself, you know, being a woman." She got up from the bench and went to the hearth, prodding the logs there into a shower of sparks. There was a lie there, but also a truth.

"I can do nothing for you," I said.

"You can help me," she said. "You can help me with my son. I expect him to see that he has been very wrong in doubting me, in turning against me—"

"What does that have to do with me?"

"What it has to do with you is that you can be there,

perhaps to persuade him that he would do better with me at his side—"

"Why would you think he would listen to me?" I interrupted, fear creeping up in me.

She turned to look me directly in the eye. "You ask why I think it? Perhaps for the same reason my husband—and I—listened to Alasdair."

That old question had returned. Why *were* my father and Earl Maddad friends? My father, a maimed, defeated rebel with no power. But the true mystery was why anyone, Margaret, *Thorbjorn*, would think Earl Harald would listen to me. I was afraid I knew the answer.

Margaret was asking me a question. She repeated it. "Do we have a bargain?" she asked.

"A bargain?"

"You will, when the time comes, help Harald to see the error of his ways, that he needs me as much as ever and that my way, my plans, are the best path for him to find himself Earl of Orkney again."

I stared at her, trying to think but the thoughts in my head were twisted, unclear.

"Your way? What do you want him to do?" I asked.

"I want Erlend dead. That's all."

"But why?"

"Do you care?" she snapped.

"No," I lied.

"Then you will do it?"

"I do not think he will listen to me," I said, trying to think of how I might free myself from this part of the bargain without losing her help with the king.

She ignored my protest. I could feel impatience in her, though her face showed only that she waited for my reply.

In that moment it seemed a small matter to agree to do a thing that I could never imagine achieving anyway. My father had advised Harald's. That did not mean I would advise Harald! And what would she know of it, what I said and did once I left Wick? I could keep silent and she would never know. It was not honest, but this was a matter of saving my father's very life. He would die without the small patch of land that was Dunailech. It was his heart, that land. I did not like what I was agreeing to—the sick feeling in my belly told me that it was not right—but I saw little other choice.

The life of my father, of my family, was worth the sacrifice.

"I will do what I can to encourage him to follow your plan," I said, suddenly feeling empty, hollow.

She smiled, satisfied. "And perhaps when you return we can talk more. I think we could give much aid to each other. But you have given me two things now. I should give you one more."

I had gone against Harald in the matter of the lover and thought nothing of it. And this other matter had seemed small as well, but now that they were compounded I was feeling less easy about the whole thing by the minute. I must ask a favour that would benefit him. But what? What was there that Harald wanted that she could give?

The whereabouts of Erlend. I had seen Margaret's reaction when she withheld that information. It had been to spite him. Surely she could give that small thing, and start the bridge being mended?

"I have one request," I said.

"Ask," she smiled.

"I would like to know where Erlend is."

She flew at me, grabbing the front of my tunic. "What did you hear?" she cried, enraged. "You little sneak! You have been toying with me? I *should* have killed you!"

If she'd had a knife in her hand right then she would have.

Paul spoke. "Margaret, your head is too hot. The boy simply thought he'd help Harald. He is an ignorant wretch. He has no idea of how things work in this world. Malcolm, my sister has no intention of giving your lord anything that will help him. Not now. If she could withhold wind from his sails, she would, just to spite him. Is this not so, sister?"

She did not take her eyes off me. "Yes, brother," she said. She did not let go. She was thinking, scouring my face for information. I could only stare back at her, blank with shock.

"You are impudent, Malcolm mac Alasdair. I thought you had courage, perhaps some talent, but now I see that your father's blood has been wasted in you. Yes, you are simply impudent. A boy. I have no use for boys.

"It would suit me well to discover what you really do know, but I lack the time and the ... circumstance, so I will deal with you thus: what has happened here today, what you saw yesterday—all of it—will stay between us. You will not speak of it to my son, not in any way. If you do, not only will I not intervene with the king for you, but I will do quite the opposite. I will see that your family loses all, land and lives. I will tell the king that they are all plotting against him, that they work towards a new rebellion, and he will have them cut down, all of them."

"If I say nothing—"

"I will still speak to the king on behalf of your family."

All I could do was nod.

"Now get out," she commanded, and I gladly obeyed. ☙

14

the pine tree wastes which is perched on the hill,
no bark or needles to shelter it;
such is the man whom none doth love;
for what should he longer live?

~WISDOM OF ODIN~

I spent the next few hours carving by the blacksmith's fire in an effort to sort myself out. At first I tried to work on the handle for the earl, but I only got as far as marking out the pattern of knotwork I had envisioned for it, and even that was a struggle. My conversation with Margaret played itself out in my head, over and over again, confusing me as much as it had when it had taken place. Whether Earl Harald won Orkney back or not my family stood a chance of being saved. I should have felt some relief. And yet I did not.

The fire heated my face until it hurt, but I sat staring into the high flames, determined to understand the implications of what I had done, and, if God still loved me, the solution to it.

After a time I picked up the other piece I'd begun the day before. A cat. The eyes in its head had become too large to be lifelike, but I liked the way its sinuous tail curled up and across one hip. I fell into this work with ease. Thoughts of Margaret still plagued me, but the more I carved, the clearer it became to me that I just needed to determine exactly what it was that I had misunderstood and I would find my way out of the trouble that I could feel pressing down on me.

But whatever that was continued to evade me.

Margaret appeared in the yard near midday. I watched with interest as Angus approached her. I could not tell what passed between them, but it was clear that they knew each other. And why not? He had been Maddad's man.

Angus gave an elegant bow and Margaret walked straight to me.

"It is good to know that you are so predictable," she said. "I realized after you ran off that I had forgotten to tell you something very important." She smiled, and for one foolish moment I hoped she might say she was sorry for her outburst, for her threat.

She sat down beside me. Only the blacksmith was near and he was deafened by the pounding of his hammer. "It came to me after you left that you might not be as dim-witted as I thought. That you might entertain the idea of confessing all your little sins to my son once you are out of Wick. I thought it was only fair to warn you of what will happen if you do so. You should know that I have more eyes and ears than the usual woman. If you speak of this to anyone, I will know it." She leaned closer to whisper in my ear. "Speak of this to anyone and I will destroy your family, as promised, but you will never know of it, for my eyes and ears will use their hands to take your life as well. I will end you all."

Any confusion I had ever felt in her presence was wiped clean.

She smiled, seeing realization take hold. "It's done then. Fare well, young sweetling. Perhaps we will meet again. Perhaps not. Fate will tell, no?" She got up and went into the stable. A few minutes later she came out, leading her mare. She did not even look at me. I watched as she walked to the gates. She stopped to talk to Arnfith and Vermund who behaved with much more respect now than they had the previous night. Vermund cupped his hands to lift her onto the horse's back. She kicked the beast hard and was off.

A raven perched above me on the blacksmith's roof. I glared at it. In turn it regarded me quite calmly before flying off in the direction Margaret had gone.

Margaret had become a splash of red and gold on the bleak Caithness moor when I went to find the only person who could help me.

"Why did you let me make that bargain?" I cried out, when I burst into the chamber that had become all too familiar to me.

Paul slowly turned his head, as if to look at me.

"Sit, Malcolm. And do not fret."

"Do not fret? This could mean the end of me! Of more than me! She was not meeting her lover, was she?"

"Malcolm, if you insist on behaving like a fool, at least close the door so none can hear."

I ran out to the landing and listened hard, but the only sounds I heard were the muted voices from behind Harald's closed door. They did not seem to have been disrupted.

"Come back in, boy. None heard you. Still, it would do you well to learn some discretion. It may keep you alive longer, assuming you also acquire a sum of patience."

I closed the door, chastened, and sat down.

"It was her lover she met. As for your bargain, you must believe me when I say that I wish you no ill, but it was a grave error to ask her for that particular boon. Why did you ask about Erlend?"

When I told him he sat for a long moment with an odd smile on his face. "Of course. I had forgotten what innocence was like. How sweet these little twists of fate can be." His smile was far off. He was not speaking to me.

"If you don't wish me ill then you will help me. I can't do what she wants. I am betraying Earl Harald."

"You should have thought of that before." His tone was harsh. "But I did promise that I would not sacrifice you on the altar of my revenge and I am a man who must keep my word. I am not long for this life and cannot heap myself up now with sins. At least not against innocents. Now, how to help you. You have betrayed your sworn lord and you cannot tell him a thing. What a conundrum. My sister has done well."

I recoiled at the admiration in his voice. "You said—"

"Patience," he interrupted. "My sister has come, over the years, to think of me as less than a man, in more ways than one." I could see the corner of his mouth lift in the shadows of his hood, the way Margaret's had so recently. He talked in a meandering way, as if telling himself a story. "There is a benefit to any circumstance, if you are willing to seek it out. Some people find solace in solitude. Margaret finds it in my ever-presence. We have become brother and sister in the end." He smiled that crooked smile. "I do believe she will miss me when I am gone." He coughed again, a dry rattling from deep inside. I thought I heard his death in it, not far off.

"But she forgets that she has wronged me, that I have

my honour to think of, that I might yearn to restore it. She forgets that I still have ears and a tongue. She has under-estimated me. She defeated me by knowing my weakness, but now I have done the same. I know what she will do and it will be her downfall." His voice trembled as it rose. "Margaret has made a pact with her old friend, Svein Aslei-farson."

I had gotten up to pace the room while he spoke. Now I stopped. "How do you know?"

"I was here when she made it. I heard it all. But she did not hear all. I told you, she underestimated me. She left us alone together."

I began to tremble. I had truly sold my soul to the Devil.

"Breathe, boy. Svein agreed to leave Erlend alone through the Yule season so he might be vulnerable. He is tired of the man ignoring his advice; he also likes a good leader to serve. And he knew, of course, that her talk of making parlay with Erlend was a farce, that she would want to kill Erlend and put herself in power through Harald. But, as you know, Harald would have none of it. A surprising turn."

"So what does she plan now?"

"You have heard Harald and Margaret argue about her bairn. That child is safe and well and *waiting*. Waiting for Harald to be out of the way." He laughed. "Not that the child knows any more than Harald did when he was made earl, but he waits there nonetheless. The irony is delicious, if you think on it. She sacrificed me for Harald all those years ago. Now she will sacrifice one son for this bastard of Gunni's. And for both she uses Svein. Is it not poetic?"

"It is vile," I answered.

"Your purity is enviable," he said sardonically, "but you are less innocent than you were a day ago and your field of battle is near at hand. Now let me finish. It would not do for Margaret to return before I have it out.

"Margaret is not the only one with more than one plan. Svein did not like the part he played in what was done to me. He has added some of his own flavour to the stew."

My mind was racing. "You must tell Harald about all this."

"Did he come to see me?" he snapped. "He feels guilty. I cannot blame him. But I do not blame him for what she did. I am even glad he defied her. He may become the sort of leader I failed to be. Peace-loving *and* strong. He has farther to go, but he may do it. But some things must be left to fate. And to what is in the hearts of those playing in it. Now, do you want to know what you can do to save your lord?"

I sat down again.

"Stop him from killing his cousin Erlend, at least until the end of Yule, until after the twelfth day of Christmas."

"How do I do that?" I cried. "Margaret will have me and my family killed!"

"Yes, well, that is an added obstacle. All I can tell you is that the people will not support Harald if he takes that route. Svein has sown the seeds. If blood is shed during holy Yule, and kinsman's blood at that, they will never forgive it. He might have a chance, if they are allowed to forget again, but not now."

That was too much for me. "I do not understand what this is of Yule, that it is so much more abhorrent to kill now than at any other time," I exclaimed.

He shook his head disdainfully. "You think you know so much, you who have lived among your sheltering mountains, with your sheltering family. Orkney is not Moray, boy, and the people of Orkney are not Scots. They may be Christians now, most of them, but they have the old gods and the old ways in their blood. They have turned a blind eye to the ways of their rulers, but that is changing. Svein has stirred up their dissatisfaction. The people suffer when the land is defiled. They will know where to point the finger of blame when hardship falls on them. They will not abide more murder."

"What are you talking about?" I spluttered. "Your people have been raiding mine for generations! Murder is in their blood. You say they are Christian. If that is true then this pagan nonsense is just that, nonsense! You have been too long locked away from the world."

He lunged to grip my wrists in his bony hands, cutting off my words. His voice, formerly so brittle and weak, suddenly deepened and was infused with a new strength.

"Those pagan ways you speak of are alive and the ancient powers do not stand aside because you deny them. In Orkney the old powers work and men bow before them or they pay the price. It is imprudent to go there thinking otherwise. Harald goes to *take* Orkney, but he will only ever have a part of it under his control. The land is weary of this line. Orkney's earls have killed, time and again, to get power. We are tainted with our greed, with the spilling of our own blood. No, the land will choose this time. And may it not choose blood. May it not choose fire."

Blood and fire. War.

He leaned toward me, his face a leering mask, ugly and unearthly. "Beware of the stones," he hissed. "Heed the people. Follow the old laws. Listen to what lurks in the silence. You will be very surprised at what you hear. But not for long. Soon you will know the path you have always trod, though you have been blind to it all your days. I know," he whispered. "I know." The last words were almost inaudible.

I wrenched my wrists free. He slowly leaned back into his chair. When he spoke his voice had returned to normal.

"It is not just the sway Svein has over the people. The land is rising up too. Men of power draw away from the land and from the other worlds, but the people do not. Their lives are always intertwined with the truth. They are the land! Land, people, spirits, they are the body, the mind, the soul ..." His voice drifted.

"Earl Harald will not kill his cousin," I said. "He even argued with Thorbjorn on it."

"You are both foolish and very wrong, Malcolm, my naïve boy. Trust me. When Margaret hunts she empties the forest. Are you not pledged to convince him yourself? My sister has baited that trap and she will feast from it. If Thorbjorn lost this battle with my nephew, rest assured, there will be another."

Did he mean that Thorbjorn was involved too? If he was, Harald was surely doomed.

I felt as if all my strength had been drained from me like blood from a mortal wound. If he spoke the truth, if Harald could not vie with those who plotted against him, what could I possibly do?

"One more question. What was your weakness?"

"Ah, you pay close attention after all. That is good. My weakness. I did not believe that anyone could be more cruel than I was, than I could imagine."

"And Margaret's?"

"She cannot imagine that anyone would do a thing that did not serve them."

We were both silent.

"Now, I do have a small gift for you. I shall tell you where Margaret hides her little bairn and I shall not tell her you know."

When he told me I cried, "But how does this help me? How do I stop all this? Who has Margaret got in among Earl Harald's men?"

"Besides you?"

I was suddenly furious. "She called him her eyes. Who is it?"

He smiled. "Her eyes. I like it. Well, if you cannot find him yourself there is no hope for you. You have a man's task before you. It will not serve if I treat you as a boy. Now, it is time for you to go, though I have enjoyed your company. In all these years my only visitors have been you and Svein Asleifarson. How fitting that the two of you who can see so much better than other men should visit me in my darkness."

I froze. Of all the shocks of that day, that may have been the greatest. "I do not know what you mean."

"You do."

"Do you have second-sight?" I whispered.

"I do not. I have the sight a blind man acquires when he

is shut up in his mind. Do you?"

Before I could muster any words a soft chuckle came from behind me. "That is a very interesting question."

I whirled to see Margaret standing in the doorway. How long had she been there and what had she heard? And would she let me out of the room? The way her body filled the frame of the door I had a sudden fear that she would not, that she might truly have decided that I should not leave Wick alive.

She walked towards me and I detected an eagerness in her, a curiosity. I could have answered her, but I did not think my answer would serve me. She wanted to hear that I had second-sight. I knew it in my bones.

"Well?" she asked.

I stepped past her and she let me. I went to take her place in the doorway. *Let her curiosity serve me,* I thought.

"There are many good questions in my mind, too," I said quietly, and I went away.

The sound of coughing followed me down the stair. It lingered in my ears as I stepped into the hall where the evening meal had begun. I found a bench and sat quietly while the hall filled with raucous laughter and ribald jokes, and the smells of food from the kitchens below, all mingled with smoke and the sweat of men. I sat in that crowded hall and I had never been so alone.

• • •

There was no great feast that night. Rumours swirled that we sailed at dawn. I could not wait. A sea voyage, even one across deadly waters, was welcome to me.

After a time Earl Harald stood. The hall grew quiet.

"My good men, I am glad to tell you that all plans are now in order. On the morrow we sail for Orkney to settle matters, finally and justly. We will keep our meal brief tonight, that we might ready ourselves to leave before dawn tomorrow. But I promise you a victory feast, on Orkney, when our work there is done."

That produced a resounding cheer and Harald smiled as he sat.

I was confused. "So, does he know where Erlend is?"

He shrugged. "I don't know. I suppose we'll find out soon enough. Harald has more than one spy in Orkney, you know. I see you are still eating. Are you sure that is wise?"

"Even a man who is to die is allowed a last meal, is he not?" I retorted. "Word came too late to stop me from filling my belly, but I am keeping away from the drink."

"He only made his plans just now," said Thorir, quietly. "We'll go tomorrow, but we'll lay off Graemsay for a few days. Why, I do not know."

But I did not care why. Paul had said to stop Harald from killing his cousin Erlend before the end of Yule. Two days on Graemsay would take us to the end of the holy season. The news was an answer to prayer. Two days might even give me time to figure out how to save Harald without destroying myself.

It was not long before the hall was filled with men lying prone on the floor and on benches, and if any worried about leaving the security of Wick, there was no sign of it in the soft snoring that soon filled the room.

• • •

"Thorir," I whispered, sometime later.

"What?"

"What happened to Sigurd after he slew the dragon?"

A pause. "He had many great adventures. And then he was murdered in his bed, as he knew he would be."

"What do you mean?"

He rolled over to face me. "Sigurd knew when he went with Regin to find the dragon that he would seal his doom by his actions, by taking the gold that was not his. And later when he met the woman whom he would love and then the one he would marry, he knew what would come of it, just as he knew when he swore an oath of brotherhood that the man with whom he swore it would bring about his death, that he would find the weak place in his shoulder where the dragon's blood had not touched and cut him there."

"Why did he not go away, avoid them all?"

"Whatever his errors, Sigurd embraced his end with his honour intact. There is nothing else."

I wanted to ask if it was not more honourable to try to struggle against one's fate, to defy it, but I knew I would not get the answer I wanted.

I did not ask my other question for the same reason. *How does a man regain his honour once he's lost it?*

That night I dreamt many things, all dark and fearful. Once I dreamt a figure slipped through the hall with a lit taper and for a moment I thought it might be Marjory again, but it was not. I slept fitfully. Once I woke from a dream that I was buried alive under the cold earth. This time I did not cry out. ⚭

15

The sun had not yet risen, but a thin veil of snow glowed pale on the black rock of Wick as we sat waiting for Earl Harald to appear.

All four ships were loaded with gear and men. Thorbjorn had been stalking the deck of the Sea Eagle impatiently for some time. Thorir was whispering something to me about the need to catch a particular tide later that day when the earl and Eirik finally came down the cliff stair. The earl's expression was black. He climbed onboard, spoke a few words to Thorbjorn and then stood aside as his foster-father gave the orders to set out.

The crew of the Sea Eagle fought a minor battle to bring us out of the rough harbour of Wick; the sea convulsed violently in the close space between the fingers of rock, penning the ships in like sheep until it finally spat them out, one by one, into the sea. With a sudden rough jostling we were underway.

I looked up at Wick Keep as we drew away from it and wondered if Margaret watched.

The first blast of wind made me clutch at my cloak. The cliffs had been a danger, but they had also been a shelter. The deck grew unsteady and my legs with it. It was not long before I lunged for the rail.

When I had completed my business there I lifted my head to find the earl beside me, looking grim.

He went straight to the matter. "Malcolm, how was my uncle when you saw him last? And when was that?"

"I saw him yesterday, shortly before the evening meal. He was well enough."

Harald nodded.

"Is something wrong?" I asked, suddenly afraid. Had Harald finally visited Paul? What might Paul have said to him?

"He is dead."

"What?" I was aghast.

"I went to speak with him this morning and he was dead."

No wonder he looked so grim. I stared stupidly at him. "How?"

"You said he was ill."

I heard what he was asking. *If my uncle was so ill, why did you not say?* My mind was racing. Paul had been ill, not far from death, surely, but not so close …

"What else could it be?" I asked.

"Or who else?"

"She would not …" I said, shocked, even though my own thoughts had already gone there.

"No? You don't know what she is capable of."

I knew more than he imagined, but I couldn't correct him for fear of unravelling the whole story.

Suddenly I wanted to do just that. I opened my mouth to tell him everything, to free myself of the lies I had trapped myself with. Whatever Margaret wanted kept secret, it was not good. Harald might be flawed but he was not evil. I must do what was right and trust that he would as well.

But what if doing what is right is not enough? Who do I trust more, Harald to protect me and mine or Margaret to destroy them?

I thought, for only an instant, of what would happen if Margaret learned I'd confessed to Harald. Only for an instant, because I could not entertain the thought longer, it pained me so deeply. I could not risk it. I would find another way. I spoke carefully. "He was very ill, my lord. If your mother harmed him I cannot say. Nor can I say why she would have."

"I should have done more for him."

He felt guilty. It was a sign in his favour.

"She might have done this, or she might not. I cannot say. But at least you know that you could not. You had concern for his well-being. You are not like her."

His laugh was abrupt and harsh. "Am I not?"

I was startled. "No. Even with what Erlend has done to you, you choose not to kill him."

The look he gave me was incredulous. "Ah, Malcolm, you are so young. I said that, yes. I needed to break free of her, to show her that I was not under her thumb. And I thought about it for a time as well, but the truth is that if I must kill Erlend to regain Orkney, I will, so I suppose we are more alike than you think." He turned on his heel and stalked away.

I was numb. I could see from the looks on the faces around me that word had spread. Thorir, on the foredeck, was watching me. I could not tell what he thought.

"Are you all right?" asked Simon, who had come to stand by me.

"I'm fine. Why do you ask?"

"For one you look more than seasick. For another, you spoke to Paul, did you not? Did you know he was so ill? What did you talk about with him?"

So many questions. I looked at his small, unreadable eyes. He was Margaret's grandson. If she *had* done this ... "He was a lonely man. He wanted company."

He squinted at me, then nodded deeply. "Yes, I can see it. Poor man. I did feel sorry for him, you know. All those years at Atholl. He would have been better off dead, I suppose. Well, he is at peace now. I will say a prayer for him. He deserves a prayer or two, don't you think?"

I did. I turned to face the sea and put my hands together to say a quick word for the dead man's soul, though I doubted my prayers could aid him at that hour. Those of us still living and under Margaret's influence were the ones in need of help, and so I prayed that what Paul had told me would save both me and Harald, as it had not saved him. I prayed for a safe voyage and for God to be with us all and that Harald had not meant what he had said about killing Erlend, that the two days on Graemsay would cool his ire.

When I looked up Simon was gone, which was wise of him, for I was sick again for some time. But it was nothing to the sickness of heart I felt. I could not know if Paul had died of poor health, but I could not take the chance that he had not. If Margaret had killed him she could have me killed. She could kill my family. Paul's death sealed my mouth as surely as it did his.

I was not as ill that day as I had been coming from Dingwall. I was able to watch the black cliffs of Caithness as they sailed by, and to see the flocks of birds as they reeled like clouds over the sea. A part of me even felt a thrill of excitement at the sight of four ships coursing the waves.

I was watching the oarsmen pulling when Thorir came to sit by me. That they could row, for hours on end without pause, always awed me. He watched with me for a few minutes, then said, "We're not far from the Pentland Firth now. We must enter the stream as it goes to the west. We started late, which is why Thorbjorn is pushing so hard just now. If we miss the tide we must wait for the next one. That would mean sitting out here until after nightfall or putting in to land."

The thought of being onboard for the better part of another day made my stomach quiver.

"Once we're on the … stream, then all is well?"

"Well?" grinned Thorir. "Of course. Barring any trouble with the riptides, any overly large waves, a sudden storm and of course there's the Swilkie."

I glared at him, refusing to ask what the Swilkie was.

"The Swallower, they call her. She lives at the bottom of a giant whirlpool that can suck the greatest longship to the bottom and grind it up to salt the sea." When I rolled my eyes in reply he threw back his head with a merry laugh.

Thorir took up the drum and I took a turn at bailing but it was not long before my fingers were useless with cold and I gladly passed the pail to another man. The sail snapped sharply in the wind that gusted from the southwest. The water seemed to be growing rougher. I spent some more time at the rail.

Suddenly Thorbjorn shouted a command and all the oars swung up towards the sky at once. Thorbjorn scrutinized the sea ahead with narrowed eyes, the sea, which, I suddenly realized, looked like a pot on full boil, a great churning wall that rolled towards us like rapids on a flooding river, like an army on the attack.

Thorbjorn shouted again. The oars went down and we plunged straight into the contorting waves. The great ocean stream swept us up in its might and sent us winging westwards.

"It is a great storm!" I shouted to Thorir as he came to crouch by me. "Should we not turn back, wait it out?" That devastating turmoil looked as if it might take us in any direction, including under.

"Wait it out?" Thorir shouted back, eyes streaming. "This is no storm! This is the firth and as good a winter crossing as we could pray for! Besides these men have seawater in their veins. To turn back, for them, would be cowardice! Do not fret, Malcolm. You are in the hands of a good crew and of your god, or mine, as the case may be. And if we die, we'll know which one all the sooner!" He laughed joyously and clapped me so hard on the shoulder I knocked my chin on my knees.

"This is life, Malcolm! This is poetry, love, friendship, adventure! All the best the gods can give! Let it lift you up from the earth that binds you!"

He is mad, I thought, but I loved him in his madness.

I gave him a look of defiant nonchalance and he laughed

as he turned to make his way through the obstacle course of crew and gear and ropes, as graceful as if he were on land.

But there was truth in his words. Truth like magic, for as he had spoken I had felt my fear turning to something more akin to anticipation, even exhilaration. The power that roiled beneath the flexible planks of the Sea Eagle could swallow me in an instant and there was nothing I could do to stop it. I could pray all I liked, but if God wanted me to die there, I would. It was as simple as that. I was puny and powerless and suddenly free. As I gave myself up to the wind and the raging tide I had the oddest sensation of being carried to a place, of being drawn towards something, rather than being pushed along as I had felt since my father had informed me that he was casting me forth into the world. I rode the waves more lightly on that new feeling.

At one point we veered north and I looked to see where Thorir pointed. Off the tip of an island ahead of us the water seemed to curl inwards on itself. The Swilkie. I thought I saw a long, thin arm of water reach for us as we passed. If we were in danger I did not know. We went on, veering ever more to the north, until land rose up from the water.

The rain that had been falling ever more steadily as the day progressed turned to snow and the ever-present wind intensified, as if to say: *This is the land of Orkney. It is a different land. Remember it.* And indeed it was a different land, a land more of sea than of earth, with the hump-shaped islands only barely distinguishable from the low swells of waves.

We angled north again, though I cannot say how anyone

could tell direction at that point, for the sky was low and white by then, and the snow obliterated all but the nearest sights. Islands rose up and disappeared again like whales breaching and diving. Orkney was no Moray, but it had a beauty unique and compelling.

The island of Hoy rose up in the west to shelter us from the main force of the wind. The snow still fell. The sea was calmer and did not send such gusts of spray up to douse us from below, but it was terribly cold. Even the sun was cold, sitting low on the horizon behind a blanketed sky. The wool of my cloak was heavy with water. I wiped at my face with the cuff of my linen tunic, which did me no good at all. I wondered if I might never be warm or dry again.

Only a few short days ago I'd been at home, safe with my family and ignorant of the earl and his venture. My first fears upon learning I was to be sent away now seemed childish. Few of my companions were as vile as I'd expected them to be.

What had happened at Wick was another matter. The earl planned to kill his cousin, his mother hoped he would, and his uncle warned me he must not. Now Paul was dead and Margaret might have had a hand in it. It was a mess! But what could I do? One of my companions was Margaret's spy. If I told Harald what I knew my family would die. But if Paul was right and I did not, we might all be doomed.

To the north I caught glimpses of a broad, low hill rising up from the sea. Hrossey, I was told, the main island of Orkney, where Erlend sat in some farmhouse drinking Yule. I squinted to see it better but it lay well hidden by the lowering sky and the rain and it was not long before another island blocked my view. We were nearing Graemsay.

And then we were moving past it. "I thought we were stopping here," I said to Eirik, who stood nearby.

"There has been a change of plans," snapped Harald from directly behind me.

I had not known he was there.

"But why?" I asked, feeling my two days grace slipping away.

"Why?" he demanded. "How is it that you think you should be privy to my plans?"

I was shocked at the harshness of his words. Why was he so angry with me? Did he suspect that I knew more about Paul's death than I had told him? Or more about Margaret?

Of course he did. And could I blame him? He was right not to trust me. I kept secrets from him. I told lies. How could he trust anyone, I wondered. How could I?

He didn't wait for an answer, stalking down the length of the ship, his thoughts already elsewhere.

As were mine. I had thought there were two days in which Harald might be convinced, by me or some other, to choose another way to deal with Erlend. Now there were none. ☙

PART 2

16

he hath need of fire, who now is come,
numbed with cold to the knee;
food and clothing the wanderer craves
who has fared o'er the rimy fell.

~WISDOM OF ODIN~

by the time we navigated around the low-lying bulk
of Graemsay the world around us had disappeared.
The heavens descended, snow falling so thickly it
filled the sky and covered the land. Even the water paled to
a pearly grey. Earth, water, sky—all were one.

There was no chanting or drum-beating now. There
might be those on shore who would warn Erlend of our
coming, and that we could ill afford.

It was not long before a shape reared up on our starboard
side. We edged carefully alongside it, keeping out of the
pull of the waves, until it dropped away and Thorbjorn
called out softly. The helmsman angled to starboard, hug-
ging the coast. Shadows rose up on our port side and then
directly ahead. We had found our way to Hamna Voe.

When we gathered on shore we appeared as an army
of ghosts, white and hoary, otherworldly. The earl had
to shout to be heard. Even then the wind carried half his
words away. I moved closer to hear. "It is midday. We leave
now … arrive … Firth … nightfall."

Enough men to crew two vessels would remain at Hamna Voe. They would guard the ships and, if needed, they
could round the island to Firth to meet us.

Ofram pushed forward. "My lord," he cried. "Are you sure we can arrive in Firth by nightfall? Would it not be better to camp here, perhaps? Go in the morning?"

"We are finally here," said Earl Harald. "We go now."

His orders were passed through the ranks. We should take provisions for a day. God willing, we would feast at Erlend's expense by sundown.

As the men began to equip themselves Thorir drew back. His usual smile was gone.

"What is it?" I asked.

"Nothing," he said.

"If I must answer your every question," I retorted, "so must you answer mine."

He smiled slightly, then leaned to speak into my ear. "To reach Firth from here we must pass through Stenness and that troubles me, especially with this," he said, waving a hand at the sky. "Weather is in the hands of the spirits during Yule."

I gave him a quizzical look.

"Stenness is a place of the ancient peoples and their spirits, their stone dances and their tombs. It is a haunted place in the full light of a summer day. But during Yule … the spirits wander at will now and some are brazen. It is their time, and they have great power. Wise men stay by the fire at Yule."

I could see he was greatly disturbed. "Why didn't we go by sea to Firth?" I asked.

"That is the way they will look for us."

"You could stay here," I suggested.

"I cannot very well compose a poem to commemorate the event from a guard posting. Besides, it is not just for myself that I fear," he said with a strange look. Then he raised one hand in a gesture that said to leave the matter be. I could get no more out of him.

My toes had grown numb and I was stomping my feet and walking in little circles to keep myself warm when the order came to depart.

And so we began our trek across Orkney.

At first the wind was a help. It travelled northeast with us, so that it pushed us along like ships navigating the sloping hills of the island, each one in its own world of snow and wind. I inhaled a flake of snow that tickled my nose and made me sneeze. No one heard me. The only sound was the howling wind, a constant low moan that sometimes rose up in piercing screams. Any lull proved brief, just the storm catching its breath in order to prepare for another chorus of wailing.

It was not long before the sound began to conjure up images, visions of tortured souls crying out for release, crying in agony. *Hell must sound like this,* I thought. I told myself it was just Thorir's talk of haunted places, but I began to wish fervently for even the briefest respite.

We trudged along in snow that quickly piled halfway up to my knee. My feet were soon wet, even though my footgear had been well oiled and I wore the wool stockings my mother had knitted tight to keep out the cold.

Just ahead of me Thorir's form was ethereal, appearing and then hidden again by a veil of snow. A glance behind me showed only the ghostly hint of Haermund as the wind eddied and swept the snow away long enough for me to see him plodding determinedly in my fading tracks. I hurried to catch up to Thorir.

I must have tripped on a rock hidden under the snow, or it may have been that I turned too quickly, but in an instant I was on the ground and sliding, grasping for purchase, to no avail. When I finally stopped I could not get up; the breath had been knocked clean from my lungs.

I lay there, my chest heaving with rough gasps. I tried to call out but no sound came. Even if it had, none could have heard it.

For the first time that day I felt real fear. I sat up, my eyes strained for any suggestion of a shadow moving nearby. Snow blew into my mouth when I called out, and blanketed my shoulders and my legs where I sat. I got to my feet, shouting with all my strength, knowing the effort was in vain. I slogged a few more paces and then stopped.

I had rolled, that I knew, but from where? To my horror, I realized that I was in a shallow depression, and that the ground rose up on two sides, not one. In my rolling I had gotten turned around. Somewhere, likely very close, my companions marched by in file towards Firth, but they might as well have been across the sea for all the good they did me. I thrust down the urge to run and breathed deeply, willing myself to be calm.

Once, when I was small, I had ventured out alone in the woods after a fresh snowfall. I had been told to stay by the fire with my mother but the purity of snow and sky had beckoned. The world had become a pure, crystalline fortress of snow-laden evergreens, roofed above in dazzling cerulean blue, the ground carpeted in shimmering white. It was irresistible. I ventured ever farther from home, reveling in my adventure.

But the currents of the sky often hide their intentions behind mountain faces. One moment I was tracking the soft prints of a rabbit and the next I was caught in a blizzard.

I tried to run home but unwittingly worked my way deeper into the woods, farther and farther from any human abode. Finally, terrified and exhausted, I crouched under the sheltering boughs of a giant fir with my eyes shut tight to pray for my father to come for me, willing him there.

And when I opened my eyes I saw frost-rimed faces peering through the heavy branches, familiar eyes creased with worry and then brightening with relief. I remember vividly how my father gripped me so hard the air was forced from my small body as he berated me with a ferocity that made me sob. And then he carried me home, warm and safe against his chest, each step taken with his maimed foot an awkward lurch, an agony.

I had no father now to rescue me, but I remembered the lesson. Someone would notice I was missing and search for me. *Like a child,* I thought, but there was nothing for it. I did not give ear to the voice that said, *How will they find me?* Nor to the one that caused panic to flutter in my belly, *Will they give me up for lost?* If none came before full dark I would find a farmhouse where I could take shelter and find the others the next day. I told myself that unlikely story and others like it as I waited for what stretched into an endless length of time. I could no longer feel my toes. Darkness was falling and the wind blew more savagely. I began to stamp my feet again.

At first I just pounded the ground, hoping to knock some

feeling back into my lower limbs but it was not long before my feet found their way into a slow rhythm, the one Thorir had beat out onboard the dragonship. I moved in time to it, faster, then faster again. It was very cold. The howl of the wind took on the plaintive cry of the reed pipes. A melody arose in my mind. It was a reel I knew, one I had heard a hundred times at home. *How odd that Thorir's drumbeat should underlie my old Scots tune,* I thought. I began to weave and step and kick to the melody I heard in my head and on the wind.

My toes tingled painfully but I kept on. Keeping warm was vital. The tempo increased. I closed my eyes against the stinging snow and imagined figures dancing with me, keeping me company, weaving and blending and exchanging places, arriving home again, only to begin anew.

The snow disappeared, and the cold and the howling wind. Pipes sang and a goatskin drum vibrated in my ears. A fire crackled and the voices of singers roared along, high and low, boisterous, joyful. Arms swung me about, warm hands took mine and laughing faces twirled by in the dance. I spun in the figure the frenzied dancers created. I was flushed and sweating, dancing for my life.

A dancer swung me around. I swayed past her to catch the hand of my next partner and as I twirled her she laughed. I moved on to catch the next one and watched as her skirts flared when she twisted away with a coy smile, barely touching my fingers. A hand grasped my arm. I turned to receive my next partner, but as my body moved in the flow of the dance, I was jerked to a stop. I opened my eyes and saw, staring at me with a mixture of fury and disgust, Thorbjorn Klerk.

I was saved.

The dancers and the music, all were gone.

Of course they were. They were in my head. Yet I had felt them too, as surely as I felt Thorbjorn gripping my arm, too hard.

"What are you at, you idiot?" he demanded. "We have been searching for you and here you are *dancing.*" He shook his head incredulously. Other faces bore looks ranging from impatience to indignation and not a few said, *there is something wrong with this one.* I realized then how it had looked to them. The Scots boy dancing, alone, in the middle of a blinding blizzard. My cheeks flamed.

I wanted to explain what had happened but the earl was already issuing orders. "Everyone hold on to the man before him. We will not lose anyone else today."

No one spoke to me. I took hold of Thorir's cloak and felt the tug as someone took the end of mine. We waited for the procession to begin again.

Thorir spoke into my ear. "Malcolm, tell me one thing." I strained to hear him. "Was there music?"

I thought he was ridiculing me at first, but his face was all seriousness. I slowly nodded.

He squinted at me. "And did you see anyone?"

"Yes!" I gasped with relief that quickly turned to confusion. "Why do you ask that?" Surely I had only imagined myself some company in my fear and loneliness. Had I not?

He regarded me gravely. "Malcolm, you must not go off alone again."

I began to protest that I had never intended such a thing

in the first place but he had already turned away. We moved again into the stream of the wind, but this time we were joined to one another, our cloaks a cord that would keep us safe, God willing.

• • •

When the wind shifted something inside me shrieked in horror. It had pushed at my back for what had come to feel like forever, and suddenly, without warning, it wheeled around and struck me full in the face, pouring down such a blast of frigid air that I sprawled in the snow again.

I got to my feet. Thorir's cloak had been wrenched from my hands. After a moment's panic I realized that everyone had stopped. Dark shapes collected around me. Arms gestured and pointed and argued. Heads shook. Haermund pushed in closer.

"Now we're done for!" he bellowed into the side of my head. "No going forward, no going back!"

"Why?" I shouted back.

He raised his arm to the sky. "We're lost. The weather will only worsen now, coming from the north as it is. We must stop."

It was less than ten miles from Hamna Voe to Firth, a few hours march at the most for fit men, yet it seemed to me that we had been dragging our feet through snow for much longer. There was no telling the hour, for the sun had been banished from the world, but as a gloom fell over us and snow continued to drop from the dull heavens it was clear that night was upon us.

"It can't be much farther," I cried.

"Who can tell?"

I looked around me. He was right. Even a man who had spent every day of his life on Orkney would not know if he were about to step into a farmer's yard or into the sea. We were like kittens, blind and helpless.

And then I saw it. A blue light, faint and flickering and then gone. It flashed again, dancing like the northern lights on a clear night, and disappeared.

I was not the only one to see it. Word spread quickly, from one huddled group to the next, as men peered into the wind and pointed. Others crossed themselves. I did too, for good measure.

Angus came to relay the earl's orders. We would seek the light and hope it meant shelter. I thought it was good news. Thorir did not. He stared a moment at Angus and, exchanging a meaning-laden look with Haermund, he broke away from us, bending into the wind as he made for the earl. I followed.

The look on his face had frightened me, and what I saw when I reached his side was no comfort either. In a manner entirely foreign to him, Thorir Honey-Tongue was vehemently protesting the earl's orders.

"We must not go there, my lord!" he said boldly, and when Thorbjorn tried to interject Thorir put his hand on the older man's arm and said, "No." It was a mark of Thorir's passion that Thorbjorn did not argue further.

The earl studied the face of his poet. "Then where?"

"There," said Thorir, pointing to the right of the blue light. At first I saw nothing. Then a soft amber glow grew more pronounced and I could almost feel the warmth of it stealing out into the white world, drawing me in. ☙

17

mighty is the bar to be moved away
for the entering in of all.
shower thy wealth, or men shall wish thee
ill in every limb.

~WISDOM OF ODIN~

The dread on the farmer's face when he slowly drew open the door only softened to dismay when he saw that it was men and not spirits who demanded entrance. The stack of shields that grew by the door as his house was filled with strange men did not bring him relief.

I could almost read his thoughts and those of his wife as they spoke with their eyes across the room. *Who ventures out on a night such as this? And what do they want with us?*

All I could feel was the sweet relief at having found shelter. For one terrified moment as we'd drawn near I had thought the light an illusion, for the farmhouse was completely covered in snow so that even the door and single window didn't show, except for the faint glow of the light. But inside it was definitely a house and it was wonderfully warm. My skin prickled with the sudden change and my limbs throbbed as they thawed. Smoke from the fire stung my eyes so that I could not see clearly at first. We pressed our way in like a school of fish swimming into a net. Piling all our weapons at the door was not done for any honour to our host; sixty is a large number of men to fit into a modest Orkney farmhouse and there was no room for men and armor both. As it was, some were forced to shelter in the byre with the beasts at the far end of the house and all had to stand, including the family who got up from their benches to make room for us.

The two smallest edged into a corner at a word from their mother, whose eyes were white and round as eggs with alarm. Thorir had said it was the custom to keep doors shut against spirits after dark—though unlocked, for spirits do not like the inhospitable house—but I could see that it was not the spirits the woman was fearing.

The earl was not blind either. "Mistress, I beg your pardon for the intrusion on your family. We are in need of shelter, but we will not put you out. I give you my word."

"Well then, your word. And what might your word be worth?" she demanded, her chin tilted in challenge. Her hair, where it poked out in wisps from her head scarf was fair. The thick knot of it bobbed on her neck as she turned on the earl. Fear had given way to defiance.

"Is the word of the Earl Harald Maddadson good enough for you, woman?" growled Thorbjorn.

Her face dropped. "The earl … oh, my lord, I did not know. How could I know?" The woman's voice rose in distress as she looked from the earl to her husband but she was recovering quickly. As her eyes roved around the room I was quite sure she was counting how many of us there were.

"Earl Harald? Of course! Now that I see you better. What an honour, sire!" blustered the farmer. "You are welcome here. We are your supporters, m'lord. I gave you my vote, for what it was worth, and I've been ill-pleased with your cousin's rule …"

"You honour me," said Harald, stopping the man, whose name was Olaf. "It is good to know I have the luck to find shelter with loyal folk, for we are in need of support this night."

"Aye, m'lord. It was a shock to see you at my door in the dark of a Yule night. And the more so because you aren't the first to appear there! Indeed, there was a man here shortly before you came, and one last night as well, only he was looking for Earl Erlend, he was."

"What did you say?" demanded Thorbjorn. "You housed a supporter of Erlend?"

The wife answered before her husband could. "Did you think we should demand to know who he liked best of the earls before we let him in? The laws of hospitality have not changed so much, have they?"

As she spoke a girl rose to slip an arm through hers. She looked to be about my age, and she was certainly the woman's daughter, with the same white-gold hair and sky blue eyes, though the colour in her cheeks was not yet faded by age and care. The woman patted her hand, but kept her defiant look.

"They have not," answered Thorbjorn. "How long did you shelter him?"

"Long enough for him to share a meal and to ask us the whereabouts of Earl Erlend," said Olaf.

Earl Harald's eyes glinted with excitement. "You know where Erlend is?"

"That I do not," sighed the man, "though I have heard he's in Firth. The other man agreed on that."

"Another man, you say?"

Olaf laughed. "Yes. He was here only a few hours ago and he was looking for you!"

There was silence. Harald's face had gone dark. "For me?"

"I tell you, when you arrived at the door I half thought you were coming to ask where Earl Rognvald was!" He grinned at his joke.

No one laughed.

"What did you tell him?" Harald asked quietly.

"Tell him? What I knew, which is little enough, clearly. I said you were in Caithness as you had been since ..." He cleared his throat in embarrassment for drawing attention to Harald's recent banishment from Orkney. "But as I say, I clearly know little, for here you are."

"Where did the man go?" Thorbjorn asked. He looked even more grim than Harald did.

"Off into this weather, and alone," answered the wife. "We tried to persuade him to stay but he would have none of it."

"Would not be surprised to hear he'd perished this night," said Olaf. "An old thing he was. Not frail, you know, but doddering." He waved a finger at his temple. "Went on about how he had business with you and how important it was and all of that. And then he was gone, up and out the door and gone. The storm just swallowed him up."

Thorbjorn was scowling. "We should find that man."

I noticed Thorir was following the exchange with interest. "For what? Because he said he had business with Earl Harald?"

"I'd like to know just what business," said Thorbjorn. "But you're right. He's probably dead in a snowdrift already."

"I hope not," said the girl, who looked to be about my age. Her voice was soft and low-toned. "I thought he was for you, my lord. And he was terribly wise. It strikes me that we need all the wise men about us that we can get."

"Agreed!" said Thorir. He toyed with the braid on the end of his beard, thoughtful.

Earl Harald bowed his head to her. "Well, you thought him wise and your father thought him mad, but either way I hope he lives, too. Now," he said turning back to Olaf, "if we could but use your roof to shelter us for a short time, we can make our plans and leave you to your peace."

The wife did not try to hide her relief. According to the laws of hospitality she was required to feed whoever came to her door. Her distress was understandable.

The two young ones had overcome their shyness and were playing a game of chase through the forest of legs that had sprung up in their house. They pursued each other, squealing with excitement whenever they brushed up against one of the men. Their mother scolded them, but the older girl murmured comfortingly, "Let them be. They are doing no harm."

The mother relented. After the two had run their erratic circuit through the maze again, the older girl caught the boy by the hand as he darted by and whispered a word in his ear. He thought for a moment, kissed her cheek, wove through a few more legs for good measure and then dragged his little sister to a bench where the two could stand high enough to oversee all that happened. Four brilliant blue eyes topped with hair like the down on a chick drank in the room, concocting, I was sure, great tales to share with the neighbour children another day.

The farmer's son had joined his father and the earl. He was a few years younger than I. However, I could see by the light in his eyes that he meant to make a man's contribution to the day.

It was decided that Olaf would host a third of us—though he insisted to his wife's annoyance that he could do more—and the rest would be billeted at nearby farms.

"I'll take 'em, Da," the boy said eagerly. "To uncle's? I can do it. I know the way like I know the yard."

Olaf bit the inside of his cheek, uncertain.

"It would be a great help if he could lead us," said Harald.

"Of course, my lord. It's just that he's a bit of a wanderer, this one. Knows the yard, he says, but he loses his way quick enough when there's work to be done."

"Da! I know the way!" The boy's ears were crimson. I felt a pang for him.

"Well, we can't very well stand here all night," said Thorbjorn. "Get us some ropes and the boy will tie on. If he gets lost he won't be lost alone. It's not so far from one farm to the next. They'll find a place to shelter before the night is out and no one will be the worse for it."

"It's not the snow his father is worrying about, sir," snapped the woman. "Seems it's only the ones who live off the land remember the land," she muttered. "There's other things happening in the world tonight than snow falling and you'd all do well to remember it. But we'll send Arni with you, for there's nothing else to be done about it." She had thrust herself through the crowded room to reach the boy. "As long as he does not get caught up in whatever business you're on. He'll have no part of that, you'll promise me!"

"But Mother, if I can help the earl—"

She stopped his words by taking his face in her hands. "You'll not get involved with whatever these men are about, son. Don't you stray off. Get there the quick way, you mind."

The boy let his mother wrap a wool blanket around him. He readjusted it as soon as she turned away.

"Olaf, how many can your brother take?" asked Thorbjorn. "A third of us, perhaps?"

"Oh, he can take twenty in Sudbister and not grumble about it. Just tell him I've got a score of men here and he'll want more."

Twenty men were led back out into the storm to follow their young guide to his uncle's farm to the south. They would return to Olaf's farm at dawn to reunite with the rest of us and together we would make for Firth. The door shut with a bang and all stretched reflexively in the space that had opened up. Thorir had naturally found his way to the children and was reciting rhymes for them that had the boy ringing out in gales of laughter. His younger sister watched Thorir with entranced eyes, her rosebud lips parted as she hung on every word.

The older girl laid some peat on the fire, smiling at Thorir's words and at her siblings' delight. I slowly edged towards her side of the fire.

To my surprise she spoke to me. "You're no Orkney-man."

"No. No, I'm not." I searched my mind for something more to say.

"Well, then, where are you from?" She flashed a smile at me that was meant to be friendly but made me more nervous. She was very pretty. Her hair was carefully bound in long shining braids and firelight danced red on the simple, but well-wrought brooches that pinned her blue dress at the shoulders.

"I'm from Moray," I said.

"Moray. Well, that's in the land of the Scots, no? I hear tell your land is covered in trees. Mountains covered in trees. Is it so?"

"Yes."

"What a wonder. I'd like to see that one day," she said with a sigh. "We only have weak, spindly things to call trees, shrunk by the salt air and the wind. The only real trees we see here are already cut from the ground. The sea washes them up on the shore," she said, patting the bench where she had sat down. Similar stone benches topped with wood planks protruded from all the walls. She patted it again. I sat next to her. Thorir raised a brow at me as he entranced the children with a tale of water beasts in the dark lochs of the south. I ignored him.

"Tell me what Moray is like," the girl said.

I hardly knew where to begin. I looked around me. The farmhouse was a long rectangle divided by a number of partial walls. Over each door, the one we'd entered and the one straight across from it, hung a heavy tapestry, for keeping out the cold. One was in bright threads of red, green and deep yellow, a complicated scene of beasts and men, all intertwined. The other was older and faded. I could not tell what the design had once been, though it looked to be an emblem of some sort. Whatever it had been it served no purpose now but to keep out the draft. The crosses of twisted straw that adorned every wall said that the house was Christian enough.

I told her of Dunailech, perched on its hill in a haphazard jumble of buildings, of our small family chapel and the kitchens where I often went to keep warm and steal a bite.

When I told her of my sleeping chamber she stopped me. "You have a chamber all to yourself? Go on. How big is it?"

I told her. I was about to ask her where her chamber was, when the memory came to me of how we'd slept at Dingwall, on stone benches that lined the walls of our small chamber. I was in her chamber and quite likely sitting on her bed.

She did not notice my discomfort. She was busy marveling that my chamber was so high above the ground, that I had a window of my own with a view of the valley. She'd seen stairs, she said, at the cathedral they were building in Kirkwall, and even coloured glass, but in a *house*?

I was enjoying seeing my home through her eyes. I did not tell her that my room was cold as the icehouse in winter, nor that the window was only a slit in the rock, more for spotting enemies at a distance than for enjoying the landscape. I did not want to disappoint her.

She demanded to know more. I told her of my family.

"I knew when I looked at you that you grew up with women around you."

I thought silence the best response to that.

"Only men who have a good mother and a sister or two know how to be proper men."

"Sigrith," hissed her mother. "Don't vex the lad with your opinions."

"No, that's all right," I said. "I imagine my sisters would agree with ... Sigrith, completely."

"I would like to meet your sisters one day," Sigrith whispered. "I think I might like them."

I had been thinking the very same thing.

• • •

I was just feeling warmed all the way through when Harald beckoned to Thorir, who signaled for me to follow. A score of men would stay with Olaf for the night. The last two dozen or so would tramp through the snow to yet another farmhouse. I stole a look at Sigrith and hoped I'd be ordered to stay. I was not eager to go out into the night again.

"I'll take your men to my cousin's house now, m'lord. And you rest yourself here. My wife'll take good care of you."

"I thank you, Olaf," said the earl, "but it's only fitting that I go. I'll rest better knowing all my men are well cared for."

Olaf was flustered. Clearly he had been counting on hosting the earl. There was much to be gained from hosting the man who might well, if God were willing, be ruler of Orkney again in the near future. "M'lord," he said, "it would be my great honour ..."

"It will be his honour," interrupted Thorbjorn. "What is this, Harald? You'd have us out there again? Let these others go. You are too generous."

"Thorbjorn, you may stay, but I will go."

Thorbjorn snorted with disgust, but Harald only smiled and turned back to Olaf.

"You have already honoured me amply tonight," he said in a friendly tone. "Do not think that I cannot smell your wife's good broth there on the fire. My stomach has been rumbling at the temptation of it, but I'll not eat a bite of anything till my men are all safely housed. Better for the score who remain here that I go to your neighbour's house. But I promise you, friend, that when I next pass by this place, I expect to be feasted heartily and well, and I will do the same for you when I am lodged again at Orphir."

"Well, then, m'lord. If there's no way I can change your mind, let us be on our way," Olaf shrugged, his disappointment somewhat assuaged.

"Olaf!" said his wife. "I would speak to you."

"Not now, Gudda." He avoided the glare she had set on him.

"Husband," she said firmly. "I would have a word."

They had their word close enough for me to hear it.

"You'll not leave me alone here, without even my boy to be man of the house," Gudda said between her teeth.

"You'll have a houseful of men here, woman," protested Olaf.

"And all of them strangers. You cannot expect me to host them all, and alone."

"Sigrith is a good help."

"Sigrith is a girl. She is a good help, aye, but she is a *girl*. What sort of man leaves his womenfolk untended, I ask you?"

"Someone must lead them," said Olaf. His eyes darted to where the earl stood, pretending not to hear them.

"I'll go."

Sigrith had risen beside me. Her parents broke off their talk.

"You'll not go," said her father.

But Gudda was weighing out the matter. "Either way we're depending on the honour of these men for her good keeping. Why not send her? She can sleep with Frida and Eydis at Brekkasetter. They'll be glad to have her company."

"Wife, you'd rather send your girl out in the snow than your man?"

"We need you. If I lose Sigrith, God forbid and forgive me, child, but I would only die of grief, not hunger. And there's the other three to think of."

"You'll die of neither, Mother. I can easily find my way to Brekkasetter and these men will treat me well, will they not, Malcolm?"

"Well, yes, certainly," I said, startled. "You have my word."

"See, Mother? Malcolm will be my protector."

"Girl," said Thorbjorn, with a scornful laugh, "you could not have chosen more poorly."

Sigrith smiled mildly at Thorbjorn, holding his eyes until he turned away.

• • •

The first blast of wind struck my face like a slap and I almost lost my footing before managing to brace myself. We all huddled along the front of the house, which provided some protection.

If Sigrith was in jest about my being a worthy protector, it did not matter. The moment she offered to go I knew I would too, even if I had to fight to be allowed. Which had almost been the case; when the earl called for volunteers almost all had wanted to go, for these men were always competing to show their strength and courage, but in the end I managed to be included among those who were venturing out again.

Olaf shouted directions at Sigrith and stressed, repeatedly, that she must be sure to keep to the east. If we reached lochside, we must turn due south, and quickly, and if we walked for more than a half hour, we were lost for certain and should return or find the nearest shelter. I could see that it vexed Olaf to send his eldest child out on this errand. Sigrith assured him with a few words and a kiss.

Gudda had shown her concern too, tying up her girl's thick braids into a knot similar to her own and binding her head with a thick scarf. She insisted Sigrith attach a few of the chains hung with household tools I'd seen the women in Dingwall and Wick wearing between their paired brooches. She kissed her daughter briefly on the cheek and turned to the business of feeding her uninvited guests with the grace of proper hospitality.

If Olaf had to lose the Earl Harald as his guest he would only do so halfway. He had given us enough food and fuel that we would not need to eat anything his neighbour might provide, to Gudda's undisguised dismay. I could not understand what this was all about, for we only needed enough for one night, but it seemed it was a serious matter, this hosting of men in Orkney. I carried some boar-shaped oatcakes—a Yule tradition, apparently—a parcel of dried fish and a flask of ale. Thorir carried a ham, more ale and bricks of peat. I was not sure why we would need extra peat. Twenty bodies would add enough heat to a farmhouse that already had a hearth fire, but it pleased Olaf, and no one argued.

Olaf gave his daughter the end of a long coil of rope and put two spare coils into waiting hands. "Now, you're sure?" he asked, again.

"Sure enough as any can be on a night such as this. I've only been there a few hundred times, Father. Haki's daughters are my closest friends," she said to Harald. "My feet know the way, even if my eyes cannot see it."

"Still," said Thorbjorn, "I think that it would be well to have a strong arm at the head of this column. You lead, girl, and I'll be directly behind you." He took the rope from her and made to tie it around her waist. I wanted to strike the leer off his face just then, but Sigrith stopped him with a raised palm and a smile that was polite, but firm. She took the rope back and tied it around her waist with a sturdy knot. Then she handed me the end that trailed from her middle. Thorbjorn snorted with derision. I took the rope, stifling a groan as Thorbjorn grabbed on behind me.

Sigrith led us, keeping a good pace, even with the wind blowing so hard against her passage. The land was now utterly dark. The only light came from Sigrith's torch, which she held out to her side, at arm's length, to keep the wind from whipping the hungry flames at her. Others, behind me, had torches too, but they might as well have not existed for all the light they shed on my field of vision.

The world became the storm again. I was glad of the rope, for I had frequently to close my eyes, so hard did the wind drive the snow into them. Sometimes it buffeted me so that I stumbled. At other times the rope went slack behind me and I wondered if the men there had all suddenly let go. Sigrith moved steadily along.

A tug from behind, then another, harder, was the signal to stop. I held the rope taut and Sigrith came to stand by me. Soon we were all together in a cluster and I saw what the matter was. A tall stone loomed above us, twice as tall as a man. Torchlight flickered to reveal a large hole low in one side. Ofram had walked straight into it and was crossing himself furiously.

"We have gone too far north," shouted Thorir. "We must leave here. Now!"

"We will go due south. We might have wandered into the loch," said Sigrith with a shiver. I had to watch her lips to follow her words for the wind greedily stole them away. "This was unwise, setting out here at night."

"You said you knew the way," yelled Thorbjorn. "You were meant to take us east. How did we get here?"

Sigrith looked at him. "You are not a believer, sir, so you will not understand when I tell you that the land is not the same place tonight as it is on other nights. We should go south, get away from the loch and away from these stones. Especially this one!"

"I agree," said Thorir. His face was pale. His eyes lingered on the stone.

"I will lead this time," said Thorbjorn as he snatched the torch from Sigrith. She untied the rope and handed it to him calmly, as if to say *it matters little who leads.*

We turned our backs on the stone and set off again, Thorbjorn leading.

We walked for what seemed an eternity. I thought the night must have passed already, but it went on. The wind kept up its howling and there were times when I thought it dove at me, searching for a way inside my head. I pushed that thought away. *All will be well,* I told myself. I had felt it, on the ship, the sensation of being drawn to a place, a certainty, a *rightness.*

I heard a cry as the rope was jerked violently from my grip.

I could just make out a cluster of men. They shouted, waving their hands about in agitation. It was a moment before I realized what had upset them so. There was the tall stone with the hole in its side. We had found it again. *Or it has found us,* I thought. All that long time we had been marching about in a great circle, drawn back to the place we had so pointedly left.

Thorir knelt before the stone, his satchel and the food and peat he had carried scattered in the snow around him. He did not hurry to rise. He seemed oblivious to every-thing but that stone.

A furious argument erupted behind me. The earl thrust himself between the men and they stopped, but it was clear that fear had wormed its way into our midst. He would have to do something. I could see that register on his face, yet he stood, unmoving.

We must not stay here, I thought.

And then I saw it. A blue light, flickering, the only living thing on the invisible horizon.

"There!" I cried. No one heard me. With a new certainty I pushed through to the earl's side and tugged on his arm. He looked at me with surprise. "We go there!" I shouted, and pointed towards the light.

Now everyone was squinting to see where I pointed but it was soon apparent to me that no one could see the blue light. They had seen it before, so why not now? I had no time to think of the implications of that. My companions might be formidable warriors, eager to defy danger, but I knew we would not survive a night in that blizzard. I knew what I needed to do. "My lord," I shouted. "I see a light. I swear it by the life of my family."

"There is nothing there!" cried Thorbjorn. "The boy is mad." He was pulling me away forcefully when Thorir stopped him.

"No," said Thorir, looking intently in the direction I'd pointed. "I see it now. I see where he is taking us. We must have shelter. Let us follow Malcolm."

I stared at Thorir. Earlier he had been adamant about avoiding the blue light. Now he wanted to go to it? Harald and Thorbjorn exchanged looks and scanned the blank landscape. Finally the earl shrugged and nodded. There was no other choice.

It was only afterwards that I realized what Thorir had done. As Thorbjorn handed me his torch and I turned to lead our party towards the unearthly light in the distance, Thorir walked at my side, but he did not follow the light. He followed me. He had seen nothing. Alone, I led the earl's men towards the blue spark dancing in the winter night. ⊕

18

I told no one when the light vanished completely. All I could do was follow my instinct and pray that I led my companions to a safe haven. They followed me, unaware that I was as blind as they were.

When the mound rose up before us, blocking our way, there was a great consternation among the men. Many crossed themselves and some of the Orkneymen made a sign like a hammer being raised. A few did both.

But I had little thought for anything but my own reaction to our arrival, for that is what it was. An arrival.

I stood before the mound and time stopped. I heard nothing except my heart thudding in my chest. My mind grew perfectly clear and I felt a recognition as powerful as homecoming. I had been drawn across the waters of the Pentland Firth to this place. I was meant to arrive at this strange hill in the haunted heart of Orkney.

The hill—or howe, as it is properly called—was not like the fairy mounds at home. Those could be mistaken for any other hill, at least until one stumbled across the dark, secret gash in the earth where a man who is brave, or does not know better, can peer in. This howe had steep, rounded sides and I knew at once it was not naturally occurring; I did not imagine, there in the blizzard, in the dark of a midwinter night, what, in fact, it was.

A shout rang out from the top of the mound and a torch flamed. We scrambled up the steep sides to find Fergus cursing loudly and testing the ground before him with his sword. He had stumbled over a hole and almost fallen in. Thorbjorn knelt over the opening, illuminating its ragged edges with the torch, kicking free loose rocks and turf. Emptiness gaped below. He signaled to Angus to give him rope and in no time he had cast the torch into the pit and was sliding down the rope to follow it. Sigrith knelt next to me. She shook her head as she watched him go.

The wind flailed at us but we remained like a circle of stones around the hole, watching the light below flicker and dim, then brighten again as Thorbjorn came back into view and looked up at our expectant faces. He raised his torch in triumph and shouted something that was torn away by the wind. No matter. His message was clear.

No one questioned the wisdom of it, at least not aloud. We were that desperate for shelter. I watched as men lowered themselves under the mound, climbing down the rope efficiently and without hesitation. My thoughts swirled like the snow. I knew I was meant to be there, so why did I suddenly have the urge to slide down the white slope and run, fast and far.

My turn came. I sat on the edge of the hole, slippery with snow, grasped the rope in both my chilled hands and squirmed awkwardly forward. The wet cold seeped into my clothes but still I sat. I did not want to enter the mound.

The strange confidence I'd felt on the passage from Wick was utterly gone. Thorbjorn's face grinning up at me did not help matters. I wished I could leap in bravely like all the others. Warriors did not inch carefully into a pit, even a pit of hell; they leapt in eagerly. But I lingered and cursed myself for it, and still I lingered.

A foot in my back sent me swinging wildly. Laughter chased me into the emptiness below as I clung desperately to the rope.

I hung on tightly as I swung in circles and the arching stone ceiling whirled around me. More laughter erupted from below. I had a night of ribbing to look forward to, I was sure.

"What are you waiting for?" called Vermund, who was peering over the hole.

I didn't answer. I lowered myself down the rope accompanied by voices that called out in teasing and encouragement, those from below echoing around me, the ones from outside only ghostly snatches of sound.

"The puppy can fly!" hooted Thorbjorn.

"You're almost there," someone else said from below.

"Almost?" said another. "He's almost to the top as well!"

Laughter carried on the wind and sounded off the walls. I set my jaw as I proceeded carefully down the rope.

"Take your time."

"Get another rope or we'll all freeze!"

"Intruders!"

I stopped dead. Terror burrowed at the base of my spine and scurried up into my neck. The voices of the men faded in my ears, and though their mouths kept working, I heard nothing of what they said.

"Damn them. Damn them all. I will not have it, not again!"

I searched desperately for the source of the voice that resounded in my head. The men below joked amongst themselves, ignoring me for the moment. Shadows from the torches flickered on the stone walls of the chamber but all I could see was the men who had entered the mound before me.

It's the wind, I thought. I took a breath and began to descend again.

"I will not have it!" the voice boomed.

My limbs went slack and I had to will myself to hold on to the rope. The low voice, like a rumble in the earth, had not come from the mouth of a man, at least no man I knew the like of. As I slipped to the end of the rope I stared about me at familiar faces, praying I was wrong, knowing with a sick feeling that I was not. The voice had not come from any of the men.

It had not been heard by any of them either.

In a daze, I tried to disguise the fact that my knees did not want to support my weight. The men jostled me good-naturedly, and someone gripped my arm for a moment while I regained my balance.

As I stumbled past Thorbjorn he held up his torch to illuminate my face. "Afraid of ghosties?" he whispered, his features ghoulish in the torchlight.

"No, are you?" I hissed back.

"Ha!" Thorbjorn bellowed. "The puppy has teeth! Milk teeth!" A few others joined in on the joke as Angus came sliding gracefully down the rope.

"Are you afraid of ghosts too, Scot?" asked Thorbjorn as he slapped Angus on the back.

"Aye, I am," said Angus, "until I know if they be friend-ly."

"Well said," laughed Thorbjorn.

I stumbled to a wall and slid down to sit hunched against it. The others dropped, one after the other, to the floor of Orkahaugr—for that is what the place was, and is, called. Orkahaugr, built by the people who have no name.

While men hung from ropes, fighting to secure a large tunic over the opening to keep out the elements, others got to work making our shelter fit for the night.

And I sat against the cold wall, searching the shadows. Once I thought I glimpsed a shape hovering low in the corner, but it disappeared when I looked at it straight on. *It's a trick of the light,* I hoped. After the day's events and Thorir's stories over the past week it was not surprising that my imagination might run amuck in the dim light of such a mysterious place. I was just being foolish, allowing child-hood fears to overcome me. The mound was simply that, a mound. The only things living in it were of flesh and blood, like me. All was well as I had known it would be on the firth.

"Friendly indeed," rumbled the voice in the shadows as the tunic was secured and the last of the men dropped to the ground.

• • •

Our rough meal was done and a skin of ale and another of mead were passed from hand to hand. The peat fire in the centre of the chamber cast a red glow over the faces crowded around it. Earl Harald and his lieutenants made up the inner circle with Sigrith among them. From the shadows I watched as Thorbjorn leaned against her arm to whisper something that made her shift away. He laughed but I saw the scowl that flashed across his face a moment later.

Getting out of the storm had been all that mattered when we first entered the howe, but now that we were sheltered and fed and with nothing to do but wait out the night, some cast wary eyes around them and up to where the wind tugged furiously at the tunic covering the hole. Muttering and an air of disturbance moved through the group. I was not the only one ill at ease.

With the torches doused to save them for a more needful circumstance, the only light came from the peat smoldering on the stone floor. It cast our shadows high up into the ceiling of layered stones, the height of three men, at least. Rivulets of melted snow wound their way across the floor, steaming as they went.

The main chamber of Orkahaugr had great, solid buttresses that occupied the four corners like paired standing stones. At hip height in three of the walls was a dark, square hole, large enough for a man to crawl through. These tunnels in the thick wall led to three small chambers. This we knew because Simon had immediately searched out each one.

Our quarters were tight. Two men could stretch out, head to toe, either way across the chamber, but for the twenty of us, and with all the rubble on the ground from the broken roof, no one could recline without sprawling over the next man. All the space was above us and it was an awesome space, hollow and echoing. Whoever had built Orkahaugr had meant it for some special purpose. The place might be no larger than the hall of Wick, but it was more impressive than any castle I ever heard tell of.

As the muttering wore on, I wondered that Thorir did not break in with a tale to fend off the dark thoughts, but he seemed to be preoccupied. He gazed into the fire as if seeking something in its orange glow.

Finally Ofram coughed. "My lord," he said abruptly. "I feel I must speak." Harald had been talking quietly with Thorbjorn. He raised a brow, but nodded for Ofram to proceed.

"My lord," said the burly warrior, with a shake of his head that sent his long, silver whiskers swaying, "I cannot say I am pleased with the abode you have chosen."

Nods of agreement punctuated his words.

Sigrith was kneeling by the fire. She caught the earl's eye. "I must agree with Ofram," she said. "This is not a place to be, tonight, or any night, but tonight …" she said, her voice drifting into the silence that had fallen over the others.

"I know it is not the best of lodgings," shrugged the earl, "but what choice did we have?"

"We can still leave," Sigrith suggested. "If we set out directly south from here we can return to my home."

"We tried that. The storm confused us."

"Or it turned us," said Thorir.

"We have a fire here, and food. It will only be a few hours

till light," said Thorbjorn. "You have nothing to fear," he added in a tone one might use with a child.

"On the contrary, you do not know this place, nor its power," said Sigrith tightly. "This place belongs to another, and he will not be pleased that we have come."

The voice I had heard echoed in my head.

"Another?" asked Angus, with interest.

"My ancestor. The founder of our farm, who was buried here more than three hundred years ago. He protects us, brings us prosperity while we please him. But our being here will not please him. I know. We have not fared well since the mound was broken."

Thorir's head snapped up at her words and he regarded Sigrith with interest. "You say the mound dweller is your ancestor?"

"Yes," she answered.

"I would hear more of him," said Thorir, smiling for the first time since we'd arrived. "And about the visitors to your house, especially the old man you mentioned."

My own interest was piqued. It was odd indeed, the story of those men at Olaf's door.

"Who broke the mound?" asked the earl.

Sigrith answered unhappily. "Your cousin, Earl Rognvald. He and his men broke in when they passed on their way to the Holy Land. They angered the spirit greatly with that dishonour and we have had hard times since. Our crops have been poor, our animals have gone lame and barren and the milk of the cows has dried up. If my mother seemed inhospitable to you, my lord, it was not that she is ungenerous. It is that we have just enough to see us through winter, and even then we will be thinner come spring than we have been other years."

"And you blame this on Rognvald breaking open this mound?" Thorbjorn scoffed.

"I do," she asserted. "All was well with us until Earl Rognvald's ... visit. Since that night the weather and the land have turned against us."

"Girl, you've heard too many tales by the fire," said Thorbjorn. "There are always bad growing seasons. Such is farming. Ours are the only spirits in this place."

"You cannot see everything that is, sir."

"Where are the grave goods for Valhalla, then? Three hundred years ago he lived? Was he a warrior or a thrall, because I see no battle gear. Nor a body."

Eirik spoke. "It seems to me that whoever made that hole in the roof would have already taken her ancestor's treasure."

"Perhaps," said Sigrith. "And perhaps not."

I wondered what she meant.

"We should search," said Vermund. "What a boon that would be, to find treasure here!"

"You intend to rob the spirit even while we invade his home?" asked Thorir.

"Do you actually believe in this superstition?" said Thorbjorn, incredulous.

"I believe that a spirit dwells here and that we should not. Would you like for men to break through your roof on a winter's night and take up residence?"

"Sometimes I think you are half mad or else a fool," Thorbjorn snorted irritably.

Thorir's answer was calm. "Sometimes there is little difference between the two, and both look much like the wise."

But Thorbjorn was unmoved. "I realize it is your duty to entertain the men with your fanciful tales, and you do it well, but it is a fact, Thorir, that when men die, they move on, whether that be into the earth to rot, or into the bellies of the ravens and the wolves. There's plenty of proof for that and none for your spirit worlds."

"You speak of the things of the spirit, of the Otherworld, as if you had earned the right to judge." Thorir's eyes glittered. I had not seen him thus before. "Are you an expert?"

"No," said Thorbjorn, "I am just an expert in sending men there!"

That provoked a few laughs. Thorir smiled.

"Oh yes," Thorbjorn continued, his voice flooded with mockery. "I am a great raven feeder myself. I have supplied your beloved Odin with many warriors for Valhalla." He drank from the skin of ale Simon passed him.

"I'm sure he is indebted to you," said Thorir quietly. "But he is the god of wisdom and poetry as well as of war."

"You send him words, I send him men. What I do is real. You, you act like your stories have substance, like flesh and bone, as if you believe them yourself."

"I truly do."

"And that Odin protects you."

"He does as he wishes. If he calls me I will go. If he says my life is to end, I will die."

That was too much for Thorbjorn. "If he calls you? Will

you hear him? Will he thunder from the heavens? I think you love to hear your own voice, but you are afraid, like a child is of a thunderstorm."

"I am afraid, but not the way you tell it and not in a way that can keep me from my duty."

"Good then," said Thorbjorn with a gleam in his eye that told me Thorir had given him some advantage. Thorbjorn waved his hand at the fire. "I don't think I should have to spend a cold night here because you left our fuel out in the snow. I intend to be as warm tonight as if I had a plump woman in my bed." He winked at Sigrith, who pretended not to notice. He turned back to Thorir. "Go get the peat you dropped."

"There is peat enough for tonight," answered Thorir.

"Not enough for my liking. I want a roaring blaze to keep the ghosties at bay."

All eyes took in the exchange, faces saying little.

"We do not need more peat for this short night." Thorir's voice was soft.

"I do," insisted Thorbjorn, "but if you are a coward, stay."

No one spoke. I writhed in my place by the wall, wishing Thorbjorn would go out into the storm himself and never return. He watched Thorir, expectantly.

Slowly Thorir inclined his head. "Thorbjorn, I am no coward, but no man walks alone in Stenness at Yule."

"Well, a few men do, but no superstitious child, fearing the ghosties and goblins."

Why was Thorbjorn doing this?

"Sir, Thorir is right," Sigrith cut in. "None should walk

alone until the power of the spirits is diminished."

Thorbjorn shook his handsome head with disdain. "Your people are simple farmers, girl. It is understandable that you accept such foolery, but this man, he is educated, an earl's skald. He cannot possibly believe in such things. No, I call him a coward. Let him prove otherwise."

Thorir sighed. "You do not believe in the spirits or the gods, do you, Thorbjorn? Nor in their power, for good or ill. No, you believe in yourself, and that is not such a bad thing. But there *are* other powers. The spirits walk, and the god will fly tonight, and denial will not protect you when the truth is revealed. It is easy to claim bravery when you fear nothing. Some day you will see that." With that he stood up and pulled his cloak around him.

Sigrith stood too. "I will guide you."

Thorir bestowed his warmest smile on her. "No, dear girl. It is not far. You are brave, though. You fear and yet you would venture out. That gives me more than your presence could."

"Then I will go," I said, too late.

Thorir shook his head. "Not you either, friend. Stay where it is warm."

"Why not take him?" said Thorbjorn. "You can appease your spirits with an offering and save your own skin."

No one laughed this time. Thorir made his way to where the ropes dangled from the hole.

"Wait, Thorir," said Harald. "Wait." He turned to his foster-father. "Thorbjorn, surely this is unnecessary? My skald is valuable to me. I cannot have him being carried off by the Hunt!" He attempted to make light of what had passed, to allow both men a way out. It might have worked, had they been other men.

"As you wish," said Thorbjorn. "Sit, coward. Your lord has saved you."

"Earl Harald," said Thorir. "I promised you a poem to honour your deeds on this venture and you shall have it, but your foster-father has maligned my name. My honour suffers at his hands. I have no choice but to go."

"Thorir, he is teasing. Sit yourself down and in the morning we will leave this place, together and in full daylight."

But Thorbjorn was not teasing and all knew it. Thorir shook his head. "My lord, do not order me to stay. You order me to dishonour myself. Let me go."

Earl Harald looked unhappy, but after studying Thorir's face he relented. Thorir lit a torch and held it in his teeth. Everyone watched as he climbed the rope, hand over hand, to the top. He struggled to move the tunic aside and almost fell in the process. Angus leapt up from his place by the wall and caught the end of the rope, pulling down on it to help Thorir steady himself. Thorir laid the torch down on the snow and hauled himself up to his waist and then heaved once again so his legs cleared the hole. The cloak was replaced and only the faint glow of his torch quivered behind the woollen weave to show where he was. Then it, too, disappeared.

All under the mound were silent. Above us, the wind howled relentlessly. Angus stood looking at his hand on the rope, his look reflecting my own thoughts. *I should have gone. Why did I hesitate? He would not have.* I was getting to my feet when Angus spoke.

"My lord, Earl Harald, I cannot bide here while that man is sent like a common servant into a night like this one. I must, on my *own* honour, aid him. Spirits and gods aside, it is a blizzard out there. He should not be alone."

The earl regarded Angus. He had made a mistake and knew it. But I felt no sympathy for him just then. He was the leader or he was not. He should have done better.

He decided. "Go if you will, Angus. You are right. No man should be out tonight."

"Now *you* talk of spirits?" scoffed Thorbjorn.

Angus turned on him coldly, cutting off the earl's response. "Thorbjorn Klerk, I am not as good a man as Thorir Honey-Tongue," he said, "nor as wise a man, but I know this. There are things I do not understand in this world. I have felt them pass me in the dark of night in the glens and mountains of my own land and I feel them here. You may ridicule those who acknowledge their existence but I will show them the respect they are due and hope they see fit to leave me be! Now, someone hold the rope for me. I have a poet to catch!"

Several men hurried to aid Angus, and when he was up the rope Ofram crossed himself three times and followed Angus into the night. ☙

19

let the wary stranger who seeks relief,
keep silent and hearing sharp:
with his ears let him listen, and look with his eyes,
only thus will he spy out the way.

~WISDOM OF ODIN~

mead and ale passed from hand to hand. No one spoke. For some time the only sound was the wind crying a long ululation of furious lament, impossibly loud. It groaned and howled in torment until it seemed to fill the space around us.

"What was that?" Vermund whispered.

"The wind," answered Thorbjorn drily.

"No, it sounded like someone calling," said Vermund, unhappily.

"Maybe it's the mound dweller inviting you to a game of knucklebones," snorted Arnfith, who had had more than his share of drink already. "I need to piss," he said, getting awkwardly to his feet. He looked up at the hole in the roof, but dismissed that idea. He looked around him at the crowded space and finally headed for one of the large square holes in the wall. He climbed in on hands and knees and disappeared from sight.

Sigrith chewed her lip as she watched him go.

Haermund saw it too. "Well, unless we intend to hold vigil for Arnfith until he returns I say we have a tale. Sigrith, tell us more of this mound, if you will. My farm is on Westray. I have passed by this place many times but know little of it."

Sigrith saw his intent and smiled gratefully. "I will tell you what I can." She drew herself up, pursing her lips as she sought a starting place and then began. "The mound was here when my ancestor came to Orkney," she said. "It only became fully his after death. I suppose it housed the guardian of the dark people before ours came. I don't know."

It was common knowledge that the mounds preceded the memory of the people, as did their original purpose.

"My ancestor was a great warrior. He fed many men to the ravens and the wolves," she said with a nod to Thorbjorn. "He was a giant of a man, in body and in character."

"What was his name?" Fergus interrupted. "Perhaps we have heard of him."

Sigrith shook her head. "Oh, we do not speak his name. That would bind him."

"Bind him?" asked one of the other Scots.

"To knowingly speak the name of one who has passed out of this life but not fully into the next is to tie him to a place, to hold him back. His name has not been spoken since he died."

"But you do speak of others who have passed."

"Yes, but as the founder of this farm it was his duty to remain here after death to guard and protect his children."

"What of Valhalla? Is that not your warriors' paradise?" That was Fergus.

This was all sounding familiar to me. Thorir had spoken of a man who guarded his kin, though he was long dead. *Thorir should be here now,* I thought. I looked up at the tunic undulating high above.

"He died in his bed, an old man, but marked with the

sword, so Odin would know he was for Valhalla. He will leave us in time. Some say the others have all left, you know, that they have been called and the other mounds are empty. They say the voice of the land is changing. Yet he remains." She shrugged again to say she was not privy to the reasons for her forefather's situation. "This mound is a portal between the realms so perhaps he can move between them. I cannot say. All I do know is that as long as he is here we honour him, and he rewards us with abundance. And at times he shows his displeasure." A shadow passed over her face.

I came from a people who could recite the names of their forefathers into the dark recesses of ancient times. A man hoped for eternal life in heaven, but he expected to live on in more earthly ways too, through his children, but also through his name, and hopefully the inclusion of that name in a tale told by the fire on winter nights for many years after his breath had left him. The ways Sigrith described were very strange to me.

"You don't speak his name, but do you know it?" I asked, overcome by curiosity.

Sigrith searched for me in the shadows and smiled when she found me. "His name has been secretly recorded in runes to be read with the eyes, but not with the mouth. My father could tell you more. One day he will pass to the next world for good. Then we will speak his name aloud and recite his great deeds. Until then we honour him well, for his power is great."

And what power is that? I wondered.

She answered my unspoken question. "I said our crops

were poor the past few seasons. That is not his only power." She waved a hand in the air. "He can call up the winds and deaden their power. He can do the same with men. He can cause them to fear, to grow angry, to go mad. And other things." A particularly loud shriek of wind punctuated her last sentence, causing many of us to jump. There was nervous laughter.

Thorbjorn was unaffected. He had begun rolling his eyes as soon as Sigrith spoke of the powers of the mound dweller. "We all know about the mound dwellers."

"No, we don't," Fergus said. "We have our own mounds and stories about them, but I'd like to hear the lass speak if you don't mind."

Thorbjorn shrugged.

Sigrith gave Fergus a charming look. "He came with the first Northmen who ventured to these isles, when they denied Harald Fairhair dominion over them, wishing to live free of his restraints. My forefather killed many of the dark people of Orkney and sent many others fleeing." Her voice took on a sing-song quality, much like Thorir's when he relaxed into a story. "Some say they still live in the hills or in among the standing stones. My mother says they became seals, and their sad eyes watch us living where they once did. All I do know for certain is that my ancestor took the land for himself."

"Your dark people. They were the Picts. Cousins to *our* forefathers. The story is an old one," Fergus grunted. "What else have the Northmen done but steal the lands of others, not to mention their lives?"

"It may well be as you say, Fergus, but I stole nothing. I

only tell the story as it was told to me. I was born and bred here and no living member of my family has ever been to Norway, nor have they ever gone viking. I am a woman of Orkney, as surely as those dark people once were. They were too weak to hold it. It is the strong who survive here."

"I only state the facts," said Fergus.

"You Scots have not always been so saintly in your doings," said Thorbjorn.

"No, but we did not make it a custom of ours to steal from others for our daily bread."

"You steal cattle from each other as if it were a sport!"

"And avoid bloodshed, not seek it!"

"Gentlemen!" cried the earl with a laugh. "You interrupt the lady!"

Fergus and Thorbjorn exchanged dark looks and then withdrew.

Sigrith mused for a moment. "You may think it childish, but in my imaginings I feel that the dark people are still much a part of Orkney and always will be. After all, their spirits remain and mingle with those of our ancestors," she said with a gesture to the vaulted space above. "In that way, our peoples have become one."

Fergus relented.

"You lose track of your story, girl," Thorbjorn said impatiently. "I would hear of men tonight, not ghosts."

I shivered at the flashing image of swirling dancers in the snow. Thorir and the others were taking a long time.

"Good enough," Sigrith responded. "I will begin *again*." That elicited smiles. The interruptions were not evidence of good manners in her audience. "He who lives under the mound built our farm and he put the land to work to feed his family, which grew large and spread upon the land. He wintered here and in summer he went viking across the seas.

"They say he travelled to many lands. He took his drag-onships down the rivers of Rus and encountered strange peoples and brought back much treasure. His family be-came wealthy. Every year he wintered here at his farm and burnt the log and drank Yule with his family and his men, honouring the ancient customs. He was lord of Stenness and obeyed by those who lived here. He was even loved, something most leaders cannot, I think, claim."

"What of his adventures?" someone asked.

"There are many, but I will tell you one of Orkney." Her eyes were on me again, as if she were telling the story for my benefit. "One summer he went viking. He took his many sons with him on his travels, each one captain of his own ship. He was away when the great worm came."

Thorbjorn snorted.

Sigrith did not seem to notice. "It breathed fire over all the fields of Orkney and the lands were scorched so that the people would have no bread to eat from it. They prayed it would leave soon so they might plant another crop to see them through the coming winter.

"But the creature did not leave. Instead it lay in the fields, in the ash and soot of the crops it had stolen from the people, and it tormented them mercilessly.

"Finally some men escaped and crossed the sea to take word of the dragon to my forefather. Weeks passed. It was feared the sea had taken them. The people became desperate as autumn drew near. Then one day, as the nights were growing longer, word came that many ships were mustering in Caithness. The women and children should flee to the refuge of the Giants' Dance, and the warriors would do battle with the dragon.

"The Dance is the stone circle that lies between the two lochs, but in those days there were no lochs there. My people feared the stones, knowing that the ancient spirits of the dark ones dwelt in and among them, but they feared the dragon more, so they went.

"My forefather brought men who gloried in battle, who always ran eagerly towards danger. To defeat a dragon a man must have a dragon-like spirit. To battle a dragon is the perfect path to Valhalla." Again, I imagined she spoke to me, for her eyes sought me out in the shadows.

"He led his men in a dragonship of seventy oars and with him came his good friend, the greatest warrior of those days, Ragnar Lothbrocks."

There was an outburst of laughter and exclamations. Obviously it was a name familiar to everyone. Everyone but me. I would have to ask Thorir about it later.

"Was he dressed for the occasion?" grinned Haermund.

"I did not hear," Sigrith said with a laugh. "Let us say he was, shall we?"

I was the only one not laughing.

"They met the dragon very near to where we are now, and they did him battle. Many men were killed, but finally the worm was destroyed and a great wind from the south came and lifted its carcass up, scattering it across the seas to the north. Some say the smaller isles of Orkney and Shetland arose from its teeth. They also say the two lochs that lie on either side of the Dance are from the depressions his body made when he lay resting from his ravaging of the land."

"So with the dragon gone, what happened next?" asked Ogmund, who was enjoying himself.

"They went raiding for provisions so the people could survive the winter."

"In Scotland, I suppose." Fergus looked rueful.

"It is the nearest place," said Sigrith, with a shrug that said she could not change it. "He went raiding every summer, as my people did then. It was the way."

"It still is for some," grunted Thorbjorn. "Svein Asleifarson still raids twice a year, and has the gall to attack his own lord …"

Harald laid a hand on his foster-father's arm. "We will deal with Svein soon enough."

"Not soon enough, but not tonight, I know." Thorbjorn turned to Sigrith. "If your ancestor lies in the mound, why do we not find him here? Why are there no bones? No treasure?"

Sigrith took it in stride. "I am but a farmer's daughter. I do not claim to understand the ways of the gods, of the dead, at least not any more than I need to. One day Odin will claim him, for Odin takes the best, always. He is not a wasteful god. Then we will name him, aloud, and his deeds will be recited at the feasts."

Sigrith talked about this Odin much as Thorir did. And yet her home had been decorated by an abundance of straw crosses.

"So, when he is gone, who will protect you?" asked Earl

Harald.

"Perhaps you will," she said softly.

He gave a short laugh. "Not if I have to be buried here."

"Ha!" she laughed. "Well, my lord, that was the old way, but I think that way is passing. People do not hear as they once did. When the wind blows for so many weeks and days, we stop hearing the roaring of it. No, however the land chooses to speak next, it will be different."

"Not everyone is deaf," said Ogmund.

"No, but too many are. When even Earl Rognvald is willing to break this mound to give his men a place to swill their drink I cannot say I have much faith in the state of things. Are we not headed for war even now?" she asked Harald, anxiety present in her voice.

"War?" he replied. "Why do you think it?"

"Why would I not? You have come to Orkney with many men in the dead of winter. One day we have three earls, the next we have two, then one, then two again? Do you imagine that it does not touch our common lives? It does! Certainly my forefather voices his discontent over the breaking of his mound, but do not think he is silent on the matter of all this strife. You cannot know, because you have not been here, but things are awry. This cannot last. I hope that peace is coming, because if it is not, war is."

I could almost see Marjory nodding vehemently in agreement. Sigrith was right. The two would like each other. I only understood part of what Sigrith spoke of, and it was too pagan for my liking, but I admired her spirit.

No one else seemed to know how to respond to her speech.

Harald said, "I can only apologize for what my cousin and his men have done and promise that we will do better. Men will be men, you know. I am sure the drink made them foolish."

She nodded, but did not look satisfied.

Vermund cleared his throat. "Speaking of drunks, where has Arnfith gotten to?"

"No doubt he's fallen asleep in his little hole," said Ogmund. "Leave him."

Harald was looking intently at Sigrith. "One thing you must keep in mind though. Earl Rognvald is earl here."

Sigrith paused to compose her thoughts. "My lord, I mean no disrespect, and surely whoever rules here has rights, but the man who rules the land must in turn be ruled by the land. And the people are of the land. One way or another they will have their say. Give the people what they need and they will support you. If they, we, are disappointed, so will you be."

"I'll get you!" a voice echoed loudly, cutting off Harald's reply. Then there was a scrambling and muffled curses and Arnfith came spilling out of the hole he'd entered some time ago. "You think you're so funny," he growled, face livid with fury. "Whose idea was it?" He glowered around the circle of us, all gape-mouthed with surprise.

"Was what?" Haermund asked, puzzled.

"Don't toy with me!" Arnfith bellowed. "You!" he shouted, taking a step towards Thorbjorn. "It was you! 'Leave this place … leave this place,'" he said, in a mimicking way. "I know it was you. Don't deny it."

Thorbjorn put up his hands in mock surrender. "Witnesses to my innocence?" he said, gesturing at us. Shrugs and nods supported his claim.

"You liar," spat Arnfith, stumbling towards Thorbjorn. "You block me in there, trap me in the dark and then make those sounds … you bastard—"

"What are you babbling about?" cried Thorbjorn.

"Leave this place! Leave this place! Over and over and over. Your *game* is over, now admit it!" Arnfith roared.

"Drink some more," scoffed Thorbjorn, holding up the skin of ale.

Arnfith flew at him, faster than I would have thought possible. Everyone else leapt up, to join in or to separate them, I could not tell, for I could see nothing with so many men blocking my view. I heard a blade scrape out of its sheath. I pushed my way to where I could see the earl in the thick of it, gripping Arnfith by the shoulders, pulling him back. Thorbjorn was just raising his fist to smash it into the man's face when there was a cry from above, an eruption of shouting and then a rebirth of the wind as the covering was torn free of the hole. The fighting stopped abruptly.

Harald leapt up and thrust a torch above his head. Something caught the light, flashing red. Angus' hair. He lay on his belly, looking down through the hole.

"Help us!" he shouted. "He will not come willingly." He disappeared from view.

Vermund scrambled up the rope. Thorbjorn followed. We waited but heard nothing except the ever-present wind. Where was Thorir and what was taking so long? And who was *he*? Eirik stood under the rope, looking up into the darkness. Finally he could wait no longer. He went up and out, and then his brother followed. The rest of us waited.

Something large tumbled down from the hole onto the pile of rubble beneath it. Smaller objects followed. Vermund dug two bricks of peat out from between some rocks and Haermund picked up the sword that had fallen, still housed in its sheath. It was Thorir's.

Benedikt shouted for a rope. He caught it and disappeared again. None of us could take our eyes off the hole.

What I saw next caused my heart to leap into my mouth. I could not move as I stared at the cloak-shrouded bundle that was lowered slowly down from the vaulted ceiling. Thorir's tousled head protruded from one end of the bundle. Eirik slid down another rope and stood where Thorir's motionless body would come to rest. Benedikt followed, but he dropped at the rate of the bundled man, guiding his descent.

Every eye in the mound was wide with shock. *It is a nightmare,* I told myself desperately, but I knew it was not.

I saw his eyes flutter before he began to flail. Thorir jerked his whole body in a violent spasm, knocking against Benedikt so hard that he swung one way on his rope while Thorir went the other. His contortions caused the ropes to slip. He was dangling from the waist, head down and howling a stream of meaningless words. He thrashed madly, trying to get free.

Benedikt swung back and grabbed him, but Thorir was slippery as an eel, and he wrestled out of Benedikt's grip, pushing him away. It was as if he *wanted* to fall and dash his brains on the ground. We all watched in horror as he writhed free of the rope that bound his legs. Benedikt had him again, but just then Thorir got loose. Benedikt lost his own grip and the two dropped from a height above our heads to the jumble of stones below, knocking Eirik to the ground beneath them.

I ran to them. Eirik groaned and extricated himself from the pile of limbs. Benedikt sat up and ran one hand over his head, feeling for damage. Thorir lay where he had fallen. When I reached his side he was staring blankly up at the night sky. Snow fell in his hair and on his face and in his eyes. When he suddenly blinked relief washed through me. *He will get up in a moment and tease me for being a worrying hen,* I thought.

I caught the end of his beard in my hand and began to berate him. "What were you thinking?" I cried. "You could have killed yourself!"

He did not even look at me.

I was in no mood for games. "Enough, Thorir. Get up and come to the fire. Get warm," I said, and reached around his shoulders to haul him to his feet.

As I pulled him into the crook of my arm he gazed up at me with a look of naked joy. "I must hang on the tree of life to hear the true words of the god. He has touched me with his hand. I will be reborn!"

I stared at him. "Thorir, you are not amusing. Stop it. Now."

He regarded me with that same odd smile.

My anger was quickly replaced by bewilderment. The man before me was clearly Thorir, but when I looked into his eyes, a stranger looked back at me. I had walked alone in the storm and been found. He, it seemed, had not. ♦

20

a guest must depart again on his way,
not stay in the same place ever;
if he bide too long on another's bench
the loved one soon becomes the loathed.

~WISDOM OF ODIN~

eirik had a bloody nose and one of Benedikt's eyes was swelling into a purple bruise. Thorir's calm had not lasted long. While Angus and Ofram attempted to describe what had happened out in the storm, Thorir had tried, more than once, to climb back out of the howe. He had needed subduing each time. He was wild and vicious in his fighting, not like Thorir at all.

The ropes were now arranged so that they dangled far out of his reach; he was bound for good measure. He would need help to escape Orkahaugr.

When they sat him near the fire with his arms tied to his sides and his legs bound together his frenzy diminished abruptly, the way a sail droops when the wind falls, but he did not return to us. He sat staring up at where the wind whistled through the gaps between the rock and the tunic, cocking his head as if he were listening, and murmuring what he'd cried over and over throughout his delirious battling: "He commanded me to stay. He will return. I will obey. Let me obey." Those last words were almost plaintive.

When Sigrith knelt by him, everyone tensed and I held my breath, afraid he might lash out again and harm her but he did not, nor did he pull away when she took his hand. He did not respond in any way. His eyes seemed to look beyond Sigrith, beyond us and the mound. He had left us.

"What happened?" demanded the earl.

"When we got to the top of the rope he was gone already," explained Angus. "We headed for that stone where he dropped the peat, hoping we would find him along the way."

"Odin's Stone," whispered Sigrith.

I stared at her. Odin's Stone? No wonder Thorir had been so shaken.

"But he was already there," said Ofram. "And he was … well … he was strange." Ofram's brows knotted at the memory.

"Strange, indeed," said Angus. "Reciting poetry, his back to the stone, his arms in the air, calling out. I thought he was …" He gave a rueful chuckle. "To be true, I thought he saw us coming and was toying with us, but when we came near he began to rant and would not let us closer and it was clear that … well, that something else was happening. He shouted many things. Most of them we could not hear over the din of the storm."

"What *did* you hear?" Harald asked.

Angus hesitated before clearing his throat to recite: "'He has brushed me with his fingers, he has marked me as his man, he is coming to take me to the tree.'"

Thorir straightened at Angus' words. He turned to the red-haired man and whispered, "He rode upon the belt of stars, thund'ring hooves, all eight, and his fingers passed over my eyes and shook the blindness off them."

Angus sighed. "He has said that a few times as well."

"He's clearly gone mad," said Thorbjorn. "He always was fanciful."

The earl scrutinized Thorir. "Perhaps it is shock. Storms can play tricks on a man."

"He's mad," said Thorbjorn.

"You should not have sent him out," Harald said, shaking his head. He watched as Sigrith and I wrapped Thorir up in his cloak. I made a pillow for him with his satchel and he laid his head down on it without a struggle.

"It was his choice to go," Thorbjorn retorted looking at Thorir with distaste, as if he had committed some sin for which Thorbjorn could not forgive him. "His superstitions have caught him up. He has chosen to believe in the stories he tells. Nothing out there did this. He made it come to pass. You cannot blame me."

Harald did not reply.

"Whatever the cause, the man is mad and we have to decide what to do with him."

"Do with him?" I asked. I had my hand on Thorir's arm. I pressed it, hard. There was no reaction. It was as if his body were an empty shell.

"If he's like this tomorrow we can't take him with us," said Thorbjorn, matter-of-factly.

"He won't be," I said angrily. "He just needs sleep and he'll be himself again."

"And if he's not?" Thorbjorn demanded.

"We'll wait for morning," said Harald.

Sigrith was smooring the fire so that only red seams of coal glowed between the black bricks. Thorir had gone to sleep. I sat beside him, with my hand on his arm. I had said he would be well in the morning because I needed to believe he would be. The thought of Thorir mad terrified me. If he could break so easily, then what of me?

Shame stung me. Here Thorir was, his brilliant mind torn in shreds, and all I could think of was myself. *No,* I decided, *he will be well. He is too strong, too good, not to be.* In the morning Thorir would be returned to himself and we would leave Orkahaugr. We would go to Firth and find Erlend and ...

With everything that had happened I had all but forgotten about my original dilemma. Paul had been right. Harald had said himself that he was willing to kill Erlend. Yule would not be over for another two days. If Paul was also right about Svein and about the people and their feelings about kinslaying, Harald would doom himself when he killed his cousin.

And me. If I am supposed to save my family by attaching myself to this man, then his downfall is mine as well.

I knew I should tell Harald everything. And then Margaret's man would know and he would kill me and send word to destroy my family.

But what if I could be certain who Margaret's spy was? Ah, there was a chance! If I could find a way to speak to Harald alone, without the spy knowing, I might be safe.

But who was the spy? I looked around at my companions to discover that they had all fallen asleep. Every last one of them. *How odd,* I thought. *They were all awake a minute ago.* Or had it been a minute? Time was strange in that place where night and day blended together, and it had been a very long day. I turned my thoughts to recalling whom I had seen Margaret with.

Angus. I dismissed that idea quickly. He had served Margaret and Maddad but he couldn't be the one. I knew it instinctively. But I had seen Vermund and Arnfith speak with her. How did they know her? Had they been at Atholl or did they know her solely from Wick? Was there another connection? Neither of them were very much to my liking. Nor was Simon, and he had appeared to be quite close to his dangerous grandmother as well. It could be him. Friendly as he was to me, I did not take to him either.

And Thorbjorn, of course. He would silence me without a qualm. But would he work against Harald? I thought not.

I sighed. It was no use. Her spy might very well be someone who had met with her in secret, very much as she'd met her lover on the moor.

I suddenly wished Marjory to be there. She was always the one who could get me out of my mental circling and set me straight. I touched her hair on the amulet and for a moment I felt she was not so far away. What would she tell me to do now? To have faith, likely. But faith in whom? I had no one to help me. The only person I really trusted who was near at hand was lying beside me muttering mad verse in his sleep.

But he will be well in the morning and I will tell him all of it. Ah, that was the answer! Thorir would know what to do. He would listen to the whole story and help me to decide what was right.

I laid my cloak over him. "Sleep, my friend," I whispered. *And awaken restored.*

I put my chin on my knees and settled my eyes on the low-burning fire. Now and then a gust of wind breathed on it and a pale flame threw a shadow up on the wall.

I could see Sigrith on the other side of Thorir, the pale skin of her cheek like a cloud-covered moon. Again it struck me as odd that all, seemingly of one accord, should drop into sleep without me noticing, especially since sleep evaded me so completely. *And what if they don't wake?* came a thought. I recoiled in disgust. Where had that come from? It was a frightening thought, an ugly one. I shook it off.

The wind tugged rhythmically on the tunic that covered the hole. The fire glowed more yellow and shadows danced lightly on the great stone blocks of the walls. Suddenly the air felt hot. Hot and close, the smell of smoke heavy around me. The fire sparked and flared, the shadows rose and began to run, beating hard against the ground. I felt panic in the air as a stampede stormed all around me, desperate to escape. Escape what? The fire! I choked on the smoke of it and on the terror I smelled on the air.

And then they were past me and in an instant the air was appallingly cold.

"Leave me be!" came a great cry. "I will not be demeaned! Torment me no longer!"

The sky came crashing down.

I fell to the ground and wrapped my arms around my head. A horrible cry rose up and became a great roaring in my ears that only intensified when I covered them. It went on and on. Then, amid the din, I heard the baying and barking of dogs and the scream of a horse and men's voices calling out names, a multitude of names in such an uproar of mad howling and wailing that they fell apart and ran together again, rising and falling into one great, unholy keening.

For what seemed an eternity, that torrent of names sailed on the wind that encircles the seas, voices raised in summoning, crying out the names of men and women, a multitude of names. There was no escaping the tumult, nor the great anguish of those who cried. They were lost, lost in the storm with no place to alight, no place to rest.

They crashed through the turf and stone of the mound as if it were made of water, swirling around and past me in such an ecstasy, such a complete abandon that I ached to let go and join in the flow and crush of the storm, the great journey of the wind.

I felt a touch like birds' wings brush across the back of my head and I shuddered as if struck by lightning. I felt death in that touch.

Death to set me free! screamed the thought. *Free!* I had only to let go and I would be free of all of it. I drowned in a terrible joy.

I listened with all my heart, all my strength, but did not hear the name I sought.

A lamentation rang out. It came from within me. *I do not want to be lost!* I cried. *I do not want to be left behind!*

I did not understand any part of the happenings at that time, so I did not know why the omission of my name from that eerie roll caused me such a great despair. And such terror. It was like standing on the edge of a cliff in the wind and wanting to sail off it to join the birds that flew there. That I could not fly did not matter. All I knew was that I was left behind and it grieved me, I who did not even know where I wanted to go.

Then, as suddenly as the din had erupted, it was gone.

"Torment me no longer," I whispered.

"It is true then!" the voice bellowed. "You intrude twice over. Into my hall and into my thoughts."

My pulse beat like war drums in my head.

"And you fear. That is good. You should fear."

Someone is playing a trick on me! But even as I clutched at the hope it slipped away. All my companions lay in silence on the floor, hearing and saying nothing. *Either I am mad or they are dead,* I thought in terror.

"You are not mad, and they are not dead. Yet." The laughter that resounded at the end of those words was thunderous. I could not see what produced it. The only movement was of shadow upon shadow. I shuddered, my hands clamped over my ears.

"You cannot shut me out that way," said the voice.

What is this thing? I could feel my mind falling apart at the implications of what I sensed to be true. Whatever spoke to me did so *inside of me*, was hearing my thoughts as if I spoke them aloud, as if it thought them with me! It *would* drive me mad if I did not shut it out of my head.

In desperation I conjured up the image of a door, a heavy oak door with strong hinges and I pushed it closed, feeling how futile it was even as I did it.

"A good effort!" said the voice, this time through my ears. I relaxed my hold on the door and the next words echoed inside me again. "But a wasted one. You are too weak. Listen now. Tell them to leave this place."

"We want nothing more!" I cried. "Please, let us leave!"

"I do not hold you here."

"But the storm."

"Is not mine."

"But you brought us here," I said. "The blue light …"

"WAS NOT MINE!"

The shadows rose up to tower above me and took on the form of an enormous man whose beard and hair were long and silver, his brows heavy, hiding his eyes. He wore great arm rings of gold and a long, weighty sword. His cloak billowed and whipped in a wind that did not touch my face and all around him glowed a soft blue light, except on his breast, where a disc of gold spun. From the centre of that disc a form was born and revolved and leapt with spread wings to alight into the sky. It was a lion, a dragon, both, a beast of great beauty and greater danger.

"He sent you to try me, but I will not weaken. Dishonour me and feel my wrath! Murderous hearts! Kin-slayers! Hunters of the leader of the land! Yes, I hear *all* your thoughts. I read your hearts. I see what you have done, what you will do! I should devour you all in the flames, make this your funeral pyre!"

"Why don't you?"

"I cannot harm the pure heart. And he touched you before I could. But I will find another way. He will not defeat me."

My mind reeled with all of it, but one thought stood out. If he saw all our thoughts he could tell me who the spy was. How I thought of such a thing at that moment, I do not know, but mad occurrences breed mad thoughts.

He proved he could hear me. "I will tell you nothing but this," he growled. "I will do my duty. I will nurture my honour. You will not banish me, not now or ever. If you do not heed me I will speak all the louder. I will instruct you more carefully."

"I do not know what you are saying," I cried.

"Then you will be punished with them."

I persisted. "You know all our thoughts. Tell me who would kill me and I will wake them all now and we will leave!"

Silence. Then, "You promise a thing you cannot give and you ask a thing you could do for yourself. You deserve nothing from me but torment." Suddenly his head snapped up and he gave an enormous cry of fury. "I will not go," he exclaimed, as the howling rose and hooves began to beat on the edges of my mind again.

I heard another voice whisper *then I will* before I fell to the ground, curling into a ball as the cacophony struck again. The same ululation of names—and, now I heard it, the call, the beckoning I had not comprehended before.

"Ride with us!" cried the storm. "Ride tonight! Ride the storm!"

"Where do you go?" demanded the shadow defiantly and I knew he had said those words many times before.

"Ride with us!" came the answer. "Ride tonight and see! It is over! Be free!"

"I will *not*! Do not come again!" the voice howled in great despair as he tore apart his armour and I saw the mark of the sword etched in his breast glimmering blue. "I will feast in the hall of the god, or in my own! I will not join your honourless rabble!"

"Ride! Ride! Ride!" was the only reply.

From the corner of my eye I saw them for one flashing instant: wild horses and rampant hounds and men not living flowing past me, all silver, blue, grey with one flash of pale gold, not bright like the gold that comes out of the earth or from the sun, but dun, the colour of straw and of hair. And then they were gone, like fog whisked away.

All around me my companions slept miraculously on.

The shadow spoke to the sky, his voice barely a whisper. "I will not give up my place. I will not stoop, nor fall. I will not lose what is mine."

What is yours? I asked, amid all the other questions that roiled in my mind.

He answered my silent question, his voice soft as a breeze, ominous as the stink of death. "I have what few men own, though it lies outside the reach of none. I have the only thing a man takes to his grave, the only thing none can steal, but a man from himself."

He spoke in riddles, as Marjory did and Thorir and my father. It was beyond bearing.

"Leave me be!" I screamed. "You drive me mad! Leave me be! Leave my mind!"

I stood railing at my nightmare vision, the man clothed in blue light, whose head soared up to the vaulted ceiling again and then he was gone.

But I was not alone. All around everyone had sat up and were looking at me. Someone quickly stirred the embers and the light grew brighter. *They have seen!*

"You are not mad," whispered the voice of the shadow along the edges of my mind like a stray thought, mocking me.

"I am not!" I shouted. "I am not mad!" I looked to my witnesses, for confirmation.

All were staring at me, to a man, and there were many things written in their eyes in the faint light. Concern, alarm, pity, even fear. But all spoke one thing.

The boy is mad.

I had met the one who had gone under the mound, so many, many years ago. But in that I was alone, for I knew then that no one else had seen anything but me, shouting at the night like a madman. ❦

21

hidden runes shalt thou seek and interpreted signs,
many symbols of might and power,
by the great singer painted, by the high powers fashioned,
graved by the utterer of gods.

~WISDOM OF ODIN~

Vermund grunted, "He's a funny boy."

"Not so funny," Arnfith muttered as he rolled over and began immediately to snore.

"Go to sleep," Haermund said to me, not unkindly.

I stared at them all, trying to understand how it was that they had seen nothing! "But …" I stammered, "but I saw …"

"What did you see?" the earl asked.

"I saw …" I began, but could not finish the thought. What had I seen? "Nothing," I finally said. "It was a dream."

"Well, dream more quietly next time," muttered Haermund, trying to make light.

Sigrith was propped up on her elbow and I could not see her face. She lay down again giving no hint of what she thought.

I did not wonder long. Sleep caught me up quickly this time, bringing a very different sort of dream.

A red fox sat on a little hillock, looking at me. That was all it did. It sat and looked and I looked back.

We were far apart, the fox and I, yet I had the strongest sensation that the fox was *with* me. Yet the more I felt the fox was with me, the more I felt that I was alone. It is the sort of thing that must be felt to be understood. But I was not afraid. I realized that was what the fox was telling me. That I was alone, but that I should not be afraid. I should have faith. All would be well. How I thought all this from a fox simply sitting upon a hillock, I do not know.

Nor do I know why the whole time I looked at the fox, all I could think of was Marjory.

• • •

A sharp blow to the leg wrenched me from my sleep. Someone tripped over me, cursing. All I could see was men leaping up and stumbling in one direction. Were we under attack? Something cool brushed my face. I swiped at it with alarm. A torch thrust into the embers of the fire flared, illuminating large clumps of snow falling down around us. I looked up. The tunic that had covered the hole was gone. The wind shrieked furiously, gusting down at us.

The commotion fizzled into a collection of men standing under the hole, staring up at it, unmoving. *What are they waiting for?* I wondered with annoyance as a blast of icy wind gusted a new smattering of wet snow in my face. I shivered. My clothes were still not dry. Wool is warm enough when wet, but the damp linen beneath my tunic clung to my skin unpleasantly. Worse, my head pounded so loudly I thought the others must be able to hear it.

"I don't understand how it can have happened," Eirik was saying. "They're heavy. Can it really have whipped them up and out?"

"What else could it be?" asked Harald.

"Who came down last?" demanded Thorbjorn.

"I did," said Vermund. "And left them hanging where they were."

"So where are they then?" Thorbjorn was furious. "Who had the watch? Did I not set a specific watch on the ropes?"

The ropes. The ropes that had hung down from the roof of the howe had vanished.

Tempers flared as men disagreed over who had been set to watch and who had slept and who had not. I alone knew that none had kept awake. None but I, and I slept some of the time or I would have seen what had happened to the ropes, wouldn't I have?

I joined the others in peering between rocks and lifting shields in search of the ropes, for they were more likely to have fallen than have flown, but though we searched the rubble well we found no sign of them.

That was discussed loudly as well.

"It makes no sense, I say," said Benedikt. "I can see how the wind might take the tunic, but the ropes? No, there is something more to it than that."

"I think you look for sense in the wrong place," muttered Ofram. He sat on a rock, scowling accusingly up at the hole. "There's something more to it, sure, but what? And do we really want to know?"

"Oh, stop that," Thorbjorn snapped. "It's simple enough if you don't get caught up in some superstitious explanation before you find your way to the plain one."

Sigrith gave Thorbjorn a look and then returned her attention to stirring the fire. While the men argued she coaxed the half-dead embers into flame with a practiced skill that somehow reassured me. It was so normal, what she did. She was like the eye of the storm, calm and cool while all whirled on around her.

As I watched her it suddenly occurred to me that the delay might be fortuitous. Paul had said to keep Harald from killing his cousin. As long as the two were kept apart Erlend would be safe and so would Harald.

Even as I thought it panic gripped me. Fragmented images showered my mind, feelings of terror and fury, of a voice demanding ... something. The urge to flee was violent in its intensity. It was imperative that we escape. How could I have thought otherwise?

It was as if my mind did not belong to me. It ran in nightmare circles.

I sucked in a deep breath, willing my heart to slow its furious beating. I breathed, slowly, in and out. *It was a dream. A terrible dream, but only that.* For once I had to agree with Thorbjorn—tales by the fire had sown a seed in my mind that had blossomed in the night. I was giving my dreams too much power in the light of day. I must not let them overrun me or I would indeed go mad!

Whatever my thoughts, it was a fact that no one was going anywhere. Our only way out was through the hole in the howe's roof, and our only way to the hole was with the ropes.

Sigrith laid another brick of peat on the fire. She looked subdued. I could not blame her. She would be wanting to get home to her family.

Thorir. I had forgotten about him. I needed to speak with

him, now more than ever. I would even welcome whatever he had to say about my bizarre dreams.

I scanned the chamber. He was not beside Sigrith where I expected to find him. Sigrith, when our eyes met, offered me an oatcake but after she handed it to me she turned away, unsmiling, before I could ask her where Thorir was. A strangeness hovered about her and I suddenly wondered if she were afraid of me. Was it my outburst? I did not relish the others thinking I was mad or a fool, but it bothered me even more to think Sigrith might. I would speak to her as soon as I found Thorir.

I searched the cluster of men, hoping he might have risen from his strange trance, healthy and whole again, and be adding his own wise counsel to the agitated discussion. He was not. Suddenly I looked up at the hole in the ceiling and then at Sigrith in horror. I saw from her look that she already knew what it had taken me so long to realize.

Thorir was gone.

The side chambers! I got up eagerly, gesturing to Sigrith, but her expression stopped me.

The bickering of the others seemed suddenly so petty. I wanted to shout at them to stop, but all my energy had left me. My voice was flat when I spoke. "Thorir is gone," I said. No one heard me. I moved closer, standing just behind Haermund. "Thorir is gone."

Haermund turned to look at me curiously. "What?" he asked, but he had heard and his eyes were already searching the interior of the mound. He, too, nodded towards a side chamber and when I shook my head he pursed his thick lips a moment and puffed out a heavy breath. He pushed his way to the earl where he stood looking up at the hole, chewing his lip in thought.

When Haermund spoke the earl's face seemed to fall for a moment before growing puzzled. "But why?" he said, shaking his head.

"Why?" I cried. "What does it matter why? We must go after him. He will die out there!"

"And shall we fly out?" barked Thorbjorn. "Did I not say he was mad, your poet? Or maybe he was playing. Maybe he's a spy for Erlend and he's trapped us here." He was working himself into a lather now. "That would suit your cousin well, would it not? Like fish in a barrel? Oh, yes, your poet is no fool," he raged. "He's quite brilliant. It's we who are the fools!"

"Thorir is no traitor!" I shouted, furious. "Do not say it again!"

Everyone stared at me in surprise.

"Malcolm is right," said Harald. "Thorir is no traitor. We will learn what transpired when we see him. Until then we have other matters to discuss, like finding a way out of here."

If we see him. That's what he should have said, I thought with despair. *Who knows what has happened to him.*

Maybe, with God's help, he had found his way to some shelter.

I sank down beside Sigrith, clutching that prayer, feeling even as I prayed it that it was hollow. That's when I saw what lay neatly piled beside her: Thorir's shield and his sword and, worst of all, his cloak. When I looked up there were tears in my eyes and Sigrith's sad smile did not comfort me.

275

●●●

When one of the men commented that it was a wind born of Niflheim itself—Niflheim being the Norse hell, which is as icy as the Christian hell is hot—I found myself agreeing as I shivered under my short cloak from the wind that blew in from the hole. I immediately asked for forgiveness for my blasphemy, but every blast of wind after that put me in mind of it.

Nothing felt right or normal, not the place, not the dark turmoil of the dream that still laid its impression on my mind, nor Thorir's absence. It is true that I had only known him for a very short time, but I *knew* him. He would not just leave us there, trapped and exposed to the storm. He was not that sort of man. *But if he was mad ...* I could not believe that either.

Whatever had happened to him, finding a way out of the mound was the business at hand. It was not proving a simple one. Even when the earl, the tallest of the men, stood on Benedikt's shoulders, he could not reach the hole. There were enough rocks to build a heap on which one man might boost another up to the high ceiling, but they were small and did not pile up well. It would take time to build anything steady enough to climb out on. That all twenty-odd men wanted to build it their own way did not help. I helped by keeping out of the way.

The wind played havoc with the fire, now causing it to flare so that it burned the fuel too quickly, then almost snuffing it out. Sigrith watched with concern. She would not like resorting to her flint. The custom of her people was to keep the fire burning through Yule; having to do the work of starting it again was not proper.

When someone trampled over Thorir's and my things, I hurried to move them. I rummaged through my satchel checking for damage and found the axe handle, the work I had not laid a finger on since the day I had made my bargain with the earl's mother. *Only two days ago,* I realized with a jolt. It seemed like two weeks.

Sigrith watched me as I drew out my knife, balancing it in one hand, the handle in the other. Softly she reminded me it was not proper to work during Yule, but I told her it was not work for me. She raised a brow at me. I did not know how to explain to her that carving was more play than work.

I ran my finger along the wood. The pattern of knotwork was very rough, but I had managed to sketch it out in its entirety at Wick. Only that one space still lay bare and my imagination offered nothing to fill it. I decided to stay away from that part for now, to see what would come to me later, when my mind was less troubled. I had more than enough to do refining the knotwork.

I felt the muscles in my shoulders ease, and I forgot myself for a time.

The morning wore on as the men built their tottering tower of stone that kept falling apart as soon as anyone tried to climb it. At least I assumed it was the morning. There was no way to know.

Angus was resting when he made a discovery that was to change the events of that day, if not all the ones to come. He had leaned against the wall nearest the growing pile of snow when I saw him turn with a curious look on his face.

He began to run his fingers over the stone, squinting as he examined one block.

Finally he caught Ofram's eye and asked, "What are these odd scratches here?"

Ofram pushed between the wall and two men who were hoisting up a large rock and stooped to look where Angus pointed. "Let me see," he said, moving his body to the side so the firelight could fall on the stone.

"Runes!" he cried. "Would you look at that! These are runes carved here, my friends." He traced the spidery lines with a finger. "Treasure!" he cried excitedly. "Treasure, hidden here!"

The men crowded around for a closer look.

"'It is told to me that treasure is hidden here,'" read Eirik.

"It is told to you?" asked Fergus.

"No, that's what it says, on the stone," replied Eirik.

"But who wrote it, and who did the telling?" asked Vermund.

"That I cannot say. Only that there is treasure. Or was."

"Is, I'll wager. We're fools not to look, wouldn't you say?" That was Vermund.

"And if there's a hoard, what good will it do you in here?" demanded Thorbjorn. "Find a way out and come back to search all you like when your duty is done."

"You make it sound like we'll die here," scoffed Ogmund. "At the worst we'll wait a day or two till the others come looking for us—"

"They'll look for us in here, will they?" Thorbjorn asked mockingly.

He was right. Who would think to look for us inside Orkahaugr? But his observation only stopped Ogmund momentarily. "So we'll find our own way out, but we're not going anywhere right now, Thorbjorn, and you know it. Even if we could get out, the weather would not allow. We're as likely to find our way into a loch or the sea as find the right farm in Firth. No, this place is small enough to warrant a quick search," he insisted, daring Thorbjorn to disagree.

The glare he got did not deter him. "Look," he said, pointing to the dark opening in the wall. "I'll bet it's in there, in that little room. That's what it means by 'here,' don't you think? Can it hurt to look?"

Simon protested that he'd already explored the side chamber but no one listened. The hunt was on.

It was rather a shameful affair. While I had only known these men for a few short days, I had learned in that time to feel some respect and liking for them, but now, before my eyes, they became like large, rough children, all clambering about in their eagerness for gold. Their behavior seemed very out of character, especially for those who had been worried about offending the supposed inhabitant of the mound.

Men squirmed through each of the three openings and there was the sound of a sword being drawn from its sheath and of metal hitting stone, but no cries of discovery. Soon all the explorers had made their way back into the main chamber.

"Nothing," said Arnfith. "Not even a bone. Not a coin. Just stone and more stone."

"I told you," said Simon, from where he leaned against the fourth wall, examining it. "Next time listen to me and you won't waste your time—"

"Watch your mouth, you cocky—"

"Because I have something here!" Simon cut Arnfith off, and I saw the tips of his fingers suddenly disappear from view. "This stone, it's not part of the wall."

Thorbjorn pushed Simon out of the way and knelt to examine the gap around the stone. "It's a separate block, and it's enormous," he said, "but we'll move it."

"A way out," said Earl Harald. Thorbjorn nodded.

"All right then," said the earl. "Two jobs in one, men. Move the stone, and if there's treasure found on the way then we are all richer for it."

There was no way of gripping the edges of the block to pull it inside the mound so they began to push, in turns. Bit by grunting bit it moved to reveal a lengthening tunnel. They had a great competition, all vying to be in the dark hole the longest, none willing to admit when he might need to rest. When I tried to take my turn Eyolf pinched my arm and declared it unfit for pushing boulders and the others laughed in agreement. The strength I had to offer was not worth the space I would take up and so I kept to my own task.

Vermund found the next runic message. Men flocked to him.

"It says … it is unclear. Yes, it says … treasure was carried away!" Vermund said angrily.

"Wait," said Benedikt. "Read it properly." He crouched to scrutinize the scratches that began at hip height and travelled up the narrow edge of a tall cornerstone, almost to its peak, and then trickled over onto one of the large, horizontal blocks. "Here it is. It says, 'That will be true which I say, that treasure was carried away. Treasure was carried away three nights before they broke this mound.'"

"Three nights before *who* broke it? And who took it away? And to where?" The men were indignant, as if they had been robbed of some fortune they'd already counted as their own.

"It is very odd," said Angus. He turned to Sigrith. "Who could have written this? You said Rognvald was the first to enter here. Who else has come?"

"None that I know of. We've stayed away, other than to make our offerings. In the summer my father tried to mend the hole, but more rocks broke off and fell in, so he gave up, fearing to make matters worse."

"We don't care about that now," said Vermund rudely. "We want to know where the treasure is!"

"That I cannot say," said Sigrith.

Vermund was suspicious. "Cannot? What does that mean? Do you *know*?"

"I do not know," said Sigrith, but her eyes were wary.

"It is a trick," said Thorbjorn. "Someone, one of Rognvald's men, has played a trick."

"Perhaps," said Arnfith. "And if it's not? What if there is treasure here, or nearby, for the taking. Do you want to pass it by? Let someone else have it?"

"We are not here to find treasure. We are here to regain Harald's lands," stressed Eirik.

"Would it hurt him if his men became rich in the process?" asked Vermund.

"You are here to serve the earl in this mission, not the other way around. Remember it."

"There is no treasure," said Harald, firmly, "but even if there were, we must be able to leave here for it to be of any use. Only know that when we can leave, it will be for Firth. And if it is too late to go today, we will go tomorrow, but not because you decide it."

"And if we go tomorrow," pressed Vermund, relentlessly, "is our time today our own?"

The earl shook his head in frustration. Whatever he meant, the men took the gesture as a leave to proceed. While one squad of a half dozen men worked on the stone, those with more knowledge of the runes searched for inscriptions, no doubt hoping to find more clues as to where the treasure might lie.

Sigrith looked on with a frown. She had not said a word to me for some time.

"Does it bother you so much?" I asked, indicating my carving.

"No," she said, shaking her head. "That's not it. He will not like it, this search. He will not like their trying to take what is his."

Her use of the word *he* stirred up a flurry of panic that I ruthlessly quashed. "You mean the treasure?" I asked with false calm. "There is none here. You saw for yourself."

"But there is," she whispered. "If not under the mound itself, then nearby. The stories are true, whatever mockery some make of them. This is not good, Malcolm. He is not kind when he is angered. We must leave this place. When we can we must leave. Tell them."

I stared at her. "I think they know it." I hesitated, my frustration tinged with fear. "They will not listen to me." But it was coming back now. *He* had demanded we leave and he had threatened if we did not. All the terror of my dream was returning to me now.

"They know it," said Sigrith. "But I am not sure they know why. What is it? What's wrong?" She grabbed hold of my arm, her eyes troubled.

"Nothing," I mumbled. "I don't like this place. It makes me ... strange."

"Yes, well, it makes us all strange," she answered, her remark taking in all the men in the mound. She patted my arm consolingly. "But you will do what you are meant to do and all will be well," she said. I waited for more but she just leaned to prod a brick of peat, her enigmatic statement dangling between us. ❧

22

I was methodically flicking out bits of wood to clarify the first row of knotwork when Haermund roared so loudly I almost took off the tip of my finger.

"My eyes are as sharp as my axe!" the squat warrior cried. "Sigrith, look at this. It seems your tale of last night is more than just a tale, my good girl!"

Sigrith gathered her skirts and wove her way through the men to the wall where Haermund peered excitedly. "I do not have much learning of this magic yet, Haermund. Please," she said as she ran her fingertips along the strange markings etched in the block of stone.

This magic? I stared at her straight back, her hair still modestly knotted on her neck in its multiple braids.

"Well then, just you wait till you hear this. You oafs, shut your mouths a minute and hear. It says that the mound here is very old, that it was here before Ragnar came. Lothbrocks! And," he began to chuckle, "it says that *her* sons were bold and smooth-cheeked men!"

Gales of laughter echoed through the chamber. Even Angus and Fergus and the other Scots had wry smiles on their faces. I was the only one who did not appreciate the joke.

Ofram noticed my confusion. "Lothbrocks means 'hairy

breeches.' There's a tale told of Ragnar that he boiled his trousers in tar and covered them in goat hair, and that's what he wore to fight his first dragon. Got his first wife that way."

I shrugged. I still didn't understand all the mirth.

"Well, that was in his youth, but he received his nickname from the event. He never could rid himself of it, no matter how wild his feats. I am surprised you don't know of him. He was famous across the world for his exploits. Ragnar thought himself very ingenious to protect himself thus, but perhaps he might have liked to be called another way."

"When he was an old man he became obsessed with outdoing his sons," said Harald, "who were considered even greater than he, and they managed their feats in their own skins. His pride was ... overly strong."

"He died trying to outdo them," Sigrith explained as she returned to the fire. "Sometimes old men grow foolish as their strength wanes. But he was a great man, Ragnar was, hairy breeches or no."

"Great, perhaps, but in the end the English king killed him," said Thorbjorn.

"Yes, but all must die," said Sigrith. "And his sons did avenge him and took England in the process."

"And outshone him in the doing," added Simon, who lounged with one leg crossed over the other.

"He fought to the end. He was brave and died defiantly," said Thorbjorn.

Ofram crooked a brow. "He had a nasty habit of attacking Christian cities on holy days."

"So? He was not a Christian. The days were not holy to him." Thorbjorn rolled his eyes.

"He took unfair advantage." Ofram was a Christian, I knew, if only from the heavy cross he wore about his neck.

"That is how men win. They scan the field and then find the surest path to victory," scoffed Thorbjorn.

"No matter what they trample to take it?" Ofram's face had gone red. "I still say nothing was holy to him but his own name."

"There are worse things," said Thorbjorn.

"Like what?" said Ofram.

"To be thought a coward."

Ofram stood so that he looked down on the younger man. "Do you call me a coward, Thorbjorn Klerk?"

"I do not," Thorbjorn growled as he got up to glare eye to eye with Ofram. It was true. I was surprised that Ofram, who was usually an even-tempered sort, would take offense so easily, though I confess I was not unhappy to see someone challenge Thorbjorn.

"Didn't you?" taunted Ofram. "You've said it before, of others here, and it was unearned then."

Thorbjorn's eyes narrowed as he assessed Ofram, who was a very large and able man. Then he said, "You slept on a particularly hard rock, Ofram, and it has fouled your mood. I've never called you a coward. Other things, perhaps." He squinted at the older man and then stepped towards him. "An ass, for one, but never a coward."

Ofram did not break off his stare. Everyone waited. Thorbjorn's hand hung loose at his side hovering just over his knife. Ofram didn't need to look down to know that.

"An ass, you say? Well," said Ofram, shifting slightly so that his stance was broadened, "better an ass than a coward."

Now it was Thorbjorn's turn. I held my breath with the others. The wind whistled through the hole above our heads. It had become so much a part of that little island under the earth that, though it never actually diminished, at times I forgot to hear it. At others I thought I heard laughter in it and shouting. Now it sounded taunting.

The tension in the room was as brittle as the icicles that had formed on the ceiling. The men who crawled out of the tunnel just then must have felt it too, for they kept silent. All were intent on Thorbjorn and Ofram.

Neither of the tall warriors moved for a long moment. Each weighed the other with his eyes. I felt the urge to thrust them together, to see what came of it. I wanted to see them fight. I held my breath, eager for the first blow to land.

When, after a long spell, Thorbjorn finally stepped forward to clap a hand hard on Ofram's arm I jumped. But there were no blows. "You are neither, Ofram, though I'm obliged to tell you, as a friend, that your breath is truly as foul as your mood."

Ofram did not blink. Then, still scowling, he slowly raised a hand to grip Thorbjorn's arm with his own massive hand. Hesitant smiles broke out around the chamber and the tension dissolved like salt in water. A new shift of men crawled into the tunnel and others settled in by the fire to while away some time. It was as if nothing had happened. And yet I felt a queer sort of disappointment. I had wanted to see what would happen, like everyone else, but the truth was that a part of me had wanted to see harm come to one or both of them. That was no surprise as far as Thorbjorn went, but Ofram? It was not like me. Nor had Ofram been his usual self. I wondered again at his odd behaviour. The man might be a warrior but he was not hot-headed. And Thorbjorn had made peace. Perhaps he was just a coward, more than willing to torment someone like me but not so eager with Ofram, who was likely his match.

Or he was simply practical? I hated to admit that he could choose not to fight because it did not serve him, but it was possible. Brutal violence was not his flaw.

And yet I had wanted violence while Thorbjorn had made peace—that gave me a bitter taste in my mouth. I was confused. I wished, not for the first time, that Thorir were there. He would have shed some light on the matter, among other things.

And when we find him I will tell him everything, I swore.

"Have we done now with quarrelling or shall we all cut each other's throats and finish the subject of who gets the treasure?" Vermund stood with his fists on his hips, his brows raised so that he looked like a mother scolding her ill-mannered young.

"I say we just cut a few throats," said Ofram.

"I agree," said Thorbjorn.

"You are both asses," said Vermund. "All of you are. While you've been squabbling like children I've been doing something useful. I think I deserve the lion's share for this find, for surely, this is the key to all our fortunes."

"You'll deserve a knock on the head if you don't get on

with it," said Arnfith.

"Listen then," said Vermund. "It says, 'In the northwest great treasure is hidden.'"

"In the northwest? The northwest of what?" said Fergus. "And which way is northwest!? You sounded like you had gold trickling from your fingers already."

"Listen, Scot, you've not been to Orkney before, but I grew up here and I'll tell you that to the northwest of here there isn't much. There are the lochs, like two lungs in a man's chest, and in between them a little sliver of land that is the heart of Orkney. That's where it is, I'm sure of it."

"Where?" demanded Fergus.

Vermund laughed. "In the only place it could be. In the centre of the stone circle. The Giant's Dance."

"Why do you think so?" asked Sigrith.

"It's the only place that makes sense," said Vermund.

"I'd say very little here makes sense," said Angus.

"Why could it not be *in* one of the lochs?" asked Sigrith. There was something odd about her tone, but her face hinted nothing.

"Ah ha! The girl is bright." Angus' eyes danced with merriment. "If I were trying to hide my hoard from grave-diggers like yourselves, I'd toss it in the loch so you'd drown seeking it! Excellent, girl. I'll not be going out in this blizzard on a death-hunt."

"Why would any man throw his goods in the loch?" demanded Vermund.

"Any man?" scoffed Haermund. "You rump on a donkey. This is no *man's* treasure we hunt. We seek to steal from the dead!"

His words were like the crack of a whip on flesh. If any had managed to forget they had slept a night in a tomb, those words brought him back to reality. For a moment the only sound was the wind howling up the tunnel.

"Aye, he's dead," said Angus. "All the more reason not to rob him."

"Maybe you're the coward," said Vermund. "Or maybe just a womanly sort."

Angus leveled a look at him. "It seems to me that women are more often than not the only ones with any common sense about them," he said, nodding towards Sigrith, "but I'm no woman and only a blind man or a brash one would suggest it."

"You'll keep the hearth-fire warm for my return, darling?" asked Vermund, with a wink.

"Aye," said Angus, shaking his head wryly, "though I must be the ass to keep watch for one such as you."

Thorbjorn interrupted the laughter that ensued. "I think your brains have all gone to seed. Has someone found a way out of here and not informed me?"

Amid groans, the work began again. The tunnel was now angling ever so slowly upwards. After endless hours—for we had lost all track of time—it had grown longer than the chamber itself, yet it still did not open out to the air. I left my carving once to peer into the darkness that was lit at intervals with knobs of glowing peat, and I wondered just how deeply we were sunk in the earth. How long before we could get out and find Thorir?

There were times that day when I told myself he was sitting by some farmer's fire, charming all the women of the

house, making firm friends of the men, all in the telling of a
single tale. And there were others, horrible moments, when
I imagined him lying half-buried in snow, his lips blue, his
eyes vacant. But I could not entertain those thoughts for
long, even the happier ones, for there was the smell of a lie
about them that I could not explain.

I would find him, I swore, even if it were only to give
him a proper burial. I wondered how a worshipper of Odin
was buried and if I would have to sin to bury him thus. I
shook myself. It was wrong to think of Thorir as dead. That
in itself was a betrayal.

Haermund gave another cry. His excitement was as in-
fectious as a child's. I went to look.

The runes were cut into two blocks of stone to the right
of one of the openings. They were tall, spindly markings
that danced along the surface of the wall. They held no
more meaning for me than the veins of colour in a stone
might, but to my companions they were another sort of
mystery. Even dour Benedikt, with his monk-like calm,
looked like an eager boy when he came to look.

"It says something about Jerusalem-farers. Could be
Rognvald and his men on their way to the Holy Land, as
Sigrith said," said Haermund.

"Unless they were coming back and laden with trin-
kets and barbarians' gold, I care not," said Vermund. "I
see something far more interesting just below it. Benedikt,
make way."

Benedikt moved aside so that Vermund could sink down
on one knee with a torch in his hand to read what was
scored into the lower half of the stone block.

"Here is real treasure, my friend. Oh, yes!" he cried ex-
ultantly. "If there was any doubt, here is something to as-
suage it. It says, 'It was long ago that great treasure was
hidden here,' and then, 'Happy is he who can find the great
wealth.' Now, does it not sound like we shall find mountains of gold here? You doubters, you stay here by the fire
and keep warm. We adventurers will feast you with our
spoils when we return, rich as kings."

"Does it tell you which stone to look under? How deeply
to dig?" Benedikt shook his head. "Or perhaps which loch
you should dive into to find your mountain of treasure?
And you have neglected to read the last line. Shall I?"

"No. I can, though it's faint." Vermund got right down
to look along the lower lip of the stone where it curled
slightly under. "It says ... it says ... Hakon alone carried
treasure from this mound."

There are words that enter the ears like any other words—
an announcement of death, a declaration of love—yet they
resound in the mind as if they were made of a different
stuff. For my companions, those words sparked off a new
debate about whether this Hakon had taken the treasure
away and used it up or buried it, somewhere near, somewhere far. Some even thought Rognvald might have found
it and was spending it in the Holy Land.

For me, they created a space, a distance between my
companions and me, in which one word rang, as if it were
the only sound in the world.

I was not the only one struck strangely by those words.
As Vermund spoke them, Sigrith's bowed head suddenly
lifted. She looked at the men crowded by the wall. When

she turned back to the fire she caught my eye for an instant.

We do not speak his name. It is not for me to bind him here. That was what she had said.

There was no binding then, though I only learned that later. But there was a response which, though it came from outside of me, trembled in the core of my own being as surely as if it had been born there.

• • •

When the next shout came it was one of both alarm and victory. I scrambled with the others into the long, low hole that stretched away, angling gradually upward. There was a light! Faint, hardly discernible, but a light that stood out against the blackness of the tunnel. At Harald's command I hurried back to the fire to bring him a torch.

The gigantic stone—a door, so it seemed—was hidden away now. After its tedious progress down the passage it had abruptly slipped to the side into what must have been its intended home, a niche in the wall cut to just its dimensions. Once the men discovered it and redirected their efforts, the stone took up its place in the row of other stones that lined the walls of the tunnel.

Standing stones. That is what they appeared to be in the flickering torchlight. Two long rows of standing stones, a processional leading down into the earth, into the land of the dead.

And also out of it, I thought. There were some harrowing moments breaking through the far end, which was overgrown with sturdy Orkney grasses. There must have been damage to the outer end of the entrance, for as the men worked to widen it so we could pass there, it collapsed, showering the men with rocks and dirt. Fergus was struck unconscious and had to be dragged back into the chamber to be tended by Sigrith.

If anything, the minor collapse invigorated the others and in no time they had pushed through and all of us crawled out of the mound. We had found a way back out into the world of the living. ⊕

23

the herd knows the hour of its going home
and turns from the grass to the stall;
but the unwise man is slow to learn
how much his maw will hold.

~WISDOM OF ODIN~

he weather had not improved. The wind blew with the same ferocity and the snow fell so heavily it hung like a dense curtain between us and the world beyond. We might be free of Orkahaugr, but leaving it would not be easy. After everyone had gone outside, more to prove to themselves that they could than anything, they all hurried back in again.

"Get your gear on, boys," Vermund crowed, as cheerfully as if he'd just stood under a perfect summer sky and was off to pluck some sweet maiden from her fields. "We're going hunting!"

I thought it was an odd way to describe searching for Thorir, but I went to where I had lain his things and put his cloak on over mine. He would need it when we found him. Until then it could keep me warm.

When Arnfith saw me, he asked, half way between scoffing and surprise, "Coming with?"

"Of course," I replied impatiently.

"Thought you preferred wood to gold. A little unnatural, that," grunted Vermund as he fastened on his sword.

They had forgotten him.

"Thorir is out there," I said, keeping my voice low because I was afraid of how it would come out if I did not restrain it. "He's out there."

Some of them had the decency to look uncomfortable.

Angus looked at me sympathetically. "Aye, he's out there, Malcolm, but I doubt he's out there alive."

I stared at him. "But what if he is? We have to try!"

"We don't," said Thorbjorn. "We can quite safely assume Thorir will reappear when the snow melts, but not before. What we need to do is get on our way to Firth."

"We're not going to Firth in this!" exclaimed Vermund with disgust.

"Then where do you think you're going?" growled Thorbjorn.

"You know very well," Vermund retorted.

The argument was boiling over as I slipped through the tunnel and out of the howe.

I must have been mad to think I would be able to find anything in that storm. I suppose it was a matter of wanting to believe combined with being quite ignorant. As soon as I had taken two steps away from the mound I was swallowed up. Only snow and wind existed. And me.

I aimed myself in the direction I thought was north; I had no idea where Thorir would be, but after the way he had reacted before the Odin Stone, it seemed the best place to look. It quickly became apparent that the wind was intent on choosing my path—the wind that was coming from the north. I fought it, to no avail. I was realizing the folly of my actions and thinking how likely it was that when the storm passed there would be two bodies found in melting drifts of snow when something touched me. I shouted in terror.

Hands held my shoulders as a face pressed up close to mine. Sigrith grinned as she saw me recognize her. She enjoyed my panic, but I did not care. I had never been so pleased to see anyone in my life.

We linked arms and plunged together into the swirling snow.

We wandered for a few minutes or it might have been hours. There was no way of knowing. The world was nothingness. Time vanished. We thrust ourselves forward into the featureless landscape, never knowing if we had moved forward except that now and then we stumbled over rocks that had not been under our feet before.

The great stone appeared as it had the day before, as if it had risen out of the earth at our approach, as if it had found us.

Thorir was nowhere to be seen.

We searched the area all around the stone, in case he had lain down on the snow—the thought made my heart sink painfully—but he was not there. All I found was a brick of peat, which I put down my tunic. We huddled together for warmth while we decided what to do next.

"There is a farm a little to the east of us. He might have gone that way."

"How can you tell which way is east?" I cried, a little desperately.

She gave a great cry of amusement. "From the way the stone stands. Trust me."

How could I not? I took her arm and we set off purposefully. This time I counted steps. We had gone at least a hundred when Sigrith stopped suddenly. She had hit her shoulder against something and was rubbing it.

The Odin Stone.

I looked at her in puzzlement. She did not say a word. She set her jaw as she took my arm and set off resolutely to the east again.

The third time we found the stone neither of us said a word. I read in her eyes what I was thinking: our destination was not up to us. Not that night. We turned our backs on the stone and allowed the wind to propel us.

Snow muffles sounds, wind carries them. The click of metal on metal rang like a dented bell. There was a shout of anger and a great guffaw, and then they were almost running us down.

"There you are!" shouted Arnfith merrily.

"Hurry up!" Ogmund boomed, giving my arm a slap as he careened past me. "We're bringing back the gold!"

I could not tell how many there were, but it looked to be most of them. They galloped by like ungainly sheep on the run from some temperamental shepherd, swirling around us where we stood, unmoving, until they passed. They were giddy, wild, out of control. Whatever had infected them, it was not what touched us.

As the last of them disappeared from sight, I thought: *They are out. They were supposed to get out.* My skin crept. I half-saw a towering shadow in my mind. Yes, they were supposed to go and, as the fear of my dream washed over me again, I was glad for them. Upset as I had been by their forgetting Thorir, and for their lust for whatever gold might lie nearby, I now felt relief. Relief mixed with fear. What if I was wrong and they were all lost, if all of us were lost?

We found the mound a moment later, as we'd expected to. They'd covered the entrance with someone's garment. We ducked under it and were trudging down the tunnel when we heard voices.

"We should all have gone," grumbled Simon. I was surprised he had not.

"No one should have gone," Angus replied.

"They were too long cooped up in here like hens. Better for everyone that they get out for a bit. They'll be back," said Benedikt.

"And we have a little peace," said Eirik.

Everyone turned to look at us as we entered the main chamber.

Benedikt gave us a nod and continued. "Talking will change nothing but busy hands are a cure for any ill, so I will leave you to it." Putting a torch to the fire to light it, he took his knife off his belt and crawled into one of the holes in the wall. A scratching sound a moment later told us what he did.

I dropped the brick of peat on the stone floor.

Thorbjorn looked from it to me. "What are you doing back here?" he asked as he took a sip from his horn. "I thought you'd be off with that pack of animals. Or were you off on your own treasure hunt?" he said with a broad wink at me and a look at Sigrith that made me want to shove the brick of peat down his throat. "The boy has finally started to act like a man," he was saying when we were all abruptly engulfed in a terrifying blackness as both the fire and Benedikt's torch were snuffed out like candles.

Someone shouted. I was crushed beneath the full weight

of a heavy body and my face was ground against the stone-strewn floor. A hand pressed hard into my back as the man on top of me pushed himself up again.

I staggered to my feet, breathing hard. Shouts echoed off the walls of the howe, but I could not tell what was happening. *Sigrith! Where was Sigrith?* She had been right beside me. I groped about in the dark where she should have been but she was gone. I shouted her name into the commotion.

"I am here," she said.

"Get out your flint, Sigrith," Thorbjorn commanded.

Silence.

"Don't give me any nonsense about the holy rules! Light the fire. Now."

"Yes, of course," she murmured, but I could hear fear in her voice.

A spark winked like a shooting star and was gone. Then another. Darkness. It went on, that casting of sparks that died the instant they were born. Once, twice, I thought she had it, but the darkness was not relieved and the sparks began again. The sound of striking flint became a reassuring pulse to counter the fear that hung like a cloud in the darkness.

"Give me that," said Thorbjorn impatiently. I heard the flint strike once, twice, and then there was a burst of flame. "Touchwood," he explained, as his face sprang out of the darkness. "I always have some with me. A man never knows when he will need to make a fire. You should be better at that, girl. A woman needs to know how to keep her hearth fire going."

In the growing light Sigrith's mouth curved minutely. "It is good you had this touchwood along," said Sigrith. "I seldom have a problem lighting a fire. Perhaps my hand remembers that it is forbidden even when it is necessary."

"Well, good thing I'm here then. If it were left to you we'd freeze in the dark."

My hands shook as I watched her blow on the fire until it was light enough to see that all were accounted for. Unnerved, but present.

"I said we should have gone," muttered Simon.

No one answered him. I knew we were all thinking the same thing. Just as fire may start in an instant, set by the hand of man or God, so is it killed, by water or wind or smothering earth. But it does not die without help. And yet it was the opposite possibility that plagued me as I watched Sigrith nurse the fire like a newborn until it had grown bright enough to cast our shadows onto the walls again. Whatever hand had doused our fire with such ease might just as easily send it the other way.

"I am beginning to think we should not be here," said Harald, after a long silence.

"No, we should be in Firth and gone already," said Thorbjorn.

"That is not what I mean," said Harald, tersely. "This," he said, waving his hand at the fire, "and the storm and Thorir disappearing and all of it, they begin to strike me as omens."

I cocked my ear at that.

"Omens? Son, don't start talking nonsense. This has not gone right, obviously, but we can't let the ghosties into our heads. Keep your head straight."

"My head is straight," snapped Harald. "But I am feeling, more and more, that this is all folly." He poked at the glowing turf with his short knife, causing sparks to rise up from it. "When nothing goes your way it may be that you are going against God's will, don't you think?"

Simon came to sit beside me. He pretended to watch what I was doing, for I had taken up the axe handle again, but really he was listening to Harald and Thorbjorn.

"Ah, so you expect God to make things easy, and that is how you know his will?"

"No," said Harald. His heavy look dissolved into a wry grin. They shared a look that told me they'd had similar discussions in the past. Harald shook his head with frustration. "I hear what you are saying, but can you see my point? With so much resistance …"

"Resistance means you give way? Come, Harald, I know it does not look good, but we will get out of this place soon enough and take care of our business in Firth."

But Harald did not look so certain. "I need to think."

With all that had gone on I had almost forgotten about the whole business of Erlend, in particular the part that concerned what I alone knew.

"You have already thought on it. What exactly are you thinking of doing differently?"

"All of it."

I bowed my head to hide my excitement.

Thorbjorn had to work hard to put down his fury. "Harald! What is there to think about? Erlend is a flea that has taken up residence where he does not belong. Only putting the fire to him and all that he infests will put you out of your misery."

Harald sighed. "Thorbjorn, I hear you. But he is my kin. What would I do then? Pay the weregild for his life, or claim it?"

"Who will pursue the matter?"

"Rognvald, for one."

"Rognvald," Thorbjorn snorted. "We don't even know if he'll come back. We'll deal with him when he does. Deal with Erlend first."

But Harald was looking at him strangely. I realized I had missed something. In the lengthening silence I knew that the others were all listening as hard as I was to hear what would come next.

"Deal with him? You mean in the same way?" And when Thorbjorn simply shrugged, Harald continued, softly, "You would have me kill Rognvald as well as Erlend ..." Then he exclaimed, loudly, "My God, Thorbjorn, will I bathe all of my lands in the blood of my kin to make them mine? What has come over you? I fear I do not know you at all!"

I was swimming in relief. Harald was finally seeing Thorbjorn clearly.

But Thorbjorn knew his business well. He raised his hand to stop Harald. "Harald! Your imagination runs wild, son. I said no such thing. I want us to be rid of Erlend, yes. I have never felt, or spoken, otherwise in that matter. He is a treacherous one, with no honour to speak of, and he shamed you. Do you know how that pains me? I cannot help but despise the man. But Rognvald, he is reasonable, intelligent, a good enough leader. My only hope is that he will be a fair partner."

"I expect he will," said Harald, his voice flat.

"And you are probably right to expect it, though you should be prepared for the worst. You do not know him as well as you think."

"What does that mean?"

"Only that he is not the saint the people think he is. Never forget that while your mother was the one who took from her brother to give to you, Rognvald was in total agreement. He enjoys his position. He could even better it and decide to rule alone, not to share with either of you, if it suits him."

"You come back to that same thread." Harald sounded weary.

"And you prefer to avoid it. Erlend is our immediate problem. Only realize that even if all goes well here your troubles may not be over. That is all. But I am not suggesting going against Rognvald and none can say I have."

Harald looked thoughtful. "You are knowledgeable and experienced, and I know you are thinking of my best interests, but this thing you propose ..."

"I know you are having trouble with Margaret, but she was right about this—"

Harald's face turned to stone. "You discussed this with her?" he demanded.

"Margaret and I are old friends as well as kin. And she is your mother!"

"That does not make her my ally."

"Harald," said Thorbjorn, "you are better off with her as your ally and you know it. She has always worked for your good. She would not turn against you."

I looked up then to see if there was any hint of a lie in Thorbjorn, for I knew that what he said was not the truth, whether he did or not. *What if he really is the spy?* I wondered suddenly.

The earl's brow shadowed his eyes and his thoughts. Thorbjorn regarded him a moment and then said, "And son, even if she would turn against you, you know I would not. No matter if all your men desert you and you lose all your lands, I will always be here. Know it."

"I know it," said the earl. "I do know it."

And I, looking at Thorbjorn, heard the truth in his words then. I might hate the man—hate him enough even to *want* him to be the spy—but I could not deny that he loved his foster-son. He truly was in the younger man's service.

"And Harald," Thorbjorn said, as he leaned forward across the fire to look into the younger man's eyes, "I spoke of omens. It may seem that the storm keeps us here, but if I read the message in this fire correctly, we were being told to leave. So whom will you heed? Wind or fire? You must choose and then you must act."

For once I agreed with Thorbjorn, though I was quite sure I would not agree with him on what was a wise course. But, looking at Harald then, I saw what Thorbjorn saw. Earl Harald was confused and he was lost. That was perhaps more frightening to me than anything, for if he did not choose the right course for us, we would all suffer the cost.

Sigrith laid another brick on the fire and I continued with my carving, my head full of thoughts.

The only part of the handle that was still naked was the place I'd left open for the beast. It was as if a hand was held before my eyes to block the sight of that one small part. It annoyed me greatly, but I knew from experience that I could do nothing but wait until I knew what belonged there.

I began rubbing the wood with the pumice I'd been given at Wick. I was well pleased with the way the lines of my design ran, weaving in and out of each other, complicated and yet well balanced. I was rightfully proud of my work. The only part of the handle that was still naked was the place I'd left open for the beast. I had entertained the possibility that it was a dog, and I liked the idea. Dogs signified loyalty and Thorir had hinted that my varden might be that of a dog. But every time I brought my knife to it I stopped. It was as if a hand was held before my eyes to block the sight of that one small part. It annoyed me greatly, but I knew from experience that I could do nothing but wait until I knew what belonged there.

Vardens. Thorir was gone and I thought of vardens.

Thorir was gone.

And I was not so loyal as he'd thought. I wondered what the earl would think if he knew what I kept from him. I watched him as he pushed the tip of his knife into the red coal of the fire, studying the double-glow reflected in the metal surface and said a little prayer that he would prove out his bloodline after all. If he, with the blood that was in him, could not sort out such complicated plotting, how could I hope to?

Simon had been watching as I worked, which I did not

much like but it was close quarters in the howe and I could hardly send him away.

"So, there was no sign of Thorir," he said.

I had not expected that. I shook my head.

He shook his too. Then he leaned nearer to murmur, "What do you think of all this?"

I was as surprised at the question as I was that he asked it of me. "I think killing is wrong. But what does it matter?"

"That killing is wrong or that you think it?" Simon asked, winking. "Of course, you are right," he went on before I could answer.

I decided to take it as an insult. "Your grandfather did not seem to think my father too low to ask him his opinion."

Simon smiled at me with genuine delight. "Ah, so there may be a bit of your father in you then. A bit, I say, because so far you have kept your thoughts to yourself and he always has a ready opinion. Probably wise," he said.

I wished he would go away. A moment later he did. Thorbjorn got up and went down the tunnel, presumably to relieve himself. As soon as he was out of sight Simon stood and nodded to me. I felt a creeping sensation up my spine as I watched him sit by Harald.

"Uncle," said Simon. "In light of what I have just heard you say, I feel I must tell you what I know, for it may have some bearing on your plans."

Harald, who had been deep in thought, looked at Simon with mild annoyance.

Simon did not seem to notice. "You should know that Svein Asleifarson visited us in Atholl last year. He was there when Grandfather died."

That caught Harald's attention as well as mine. What did Simon know?

"I heard Svein speak more than once on the necessity of having only one earl in Orkney. But he said, and I agree with him, that whoever rules Orkney must be strong enough to withstand rivals sent both from the Scots and Norse thrones, and send rivals they will, for they never like a strong Orkney.

"My father made a comment after Svein was gone that might interest you. He said at times it sounded, when Svein spoke of the need for a strong leader, like he might be speaking of himself. Of course, he could never rule as earl," he said, waving a hand dismissively, "but as his counsellor …"

"More likely his master," growled Thorbjorn, from the entrance. "And he's already doing that," he said.

Harald's nodded in agreement and his look of interest faded.

I, on the other hand, had suddenly become very interested. I did not know what Simon was trying to do, but I had just realized that if Harald followed this line of thought long enough he might uncover, simply through his own musings, the truth. It would not be a simple unravelling, but with a few clues laid out for him …

"It seems to me that if Svein is really so powerful you should make him your friend again," continued Simon, with the tone of an old advisor.

"It might be wise, but there is too much bad blood," said Harald looking at Thorbjorn. *If Simon is wise he will*

leave off suggesting Harald embrace Thorbjorn's greatest enemy,
I thought, but I did not really think he was unaware of it.
Something else was afoot.

Thorbjorn was still studying Simon, as if he were decid-
ing what to do with him.

"There is honour involved," was all he said.

"On both sides," said Harald with a nod.

"Honour?" Simon huffed. "Honour or pride? It seems to
me that this honour you speak of stands as an obstacle to
the proper enhancing of *your* honour, uncle."

"Keep your opinion to yourself. You know nothing about
this." Now Thorbjorn's anger showed, but Simon kept on.

"Fine," he said. "I only think that you should not ex-
clude such an excellent option."

"He would not leave Erlend without cause," said Harald.

"And what if Erlend was no more?" said Simon.

"That might change many things," said Thorbjorn in a
new tone as he eyed Simon thoughtfully.

The firelight glinted in Harald's eyes as he chewed on
what had been said. I had a sudden memory of Margaret
sitting beside me on the bench in her chamber, of her hand
on my arm, holding me gently in place while she spun her
web.

"It would," he said, almost to himself. "It would."

Simon nodded with satisfaction. *Why was he pressing
Harald in this direction,* I wondered. What did he know?
Was he Margaret's spy? I stifled a shudder. Is that why he'd
asked me those questions? Was it a warning?

But if he were in cahoots with Margaret, why would he

bring up Svein? Would Margaret not want that kept secret? I was dizzy with the implications. Unless he was *against* Margaret … but that made no sense either. None of it did. Simon was heir to Atholl. He would serve at the right hand of the king one day. No, the most likely answer was that he was serving his pleasure, indulging in a game of plotting and manipulating, as those born to power are wont to do.

I was thinking this when a gust of wind announced that someone had entered the howe.

A light formed at the far entrance of the tunnel and then a shadow grew in front of it and lurched in a grotesque gait towards us. Light and shadow quivered over the rock as the form neared. I remembered the blue light that had enticed us in the darkness and Olaf's face when we'd appeared at his door.

As the strange apparition reached the threshold of the chamber we stared, mesmerized, caught up in a spell that was only half broken when Ofram's face was revealed. He stumbled towards the fire, beard and hair frosted white, like an old man's.

Behind him came the others, all rimed and aged by snow and bitter cold. While those of us who still bore colour and life moved back for them, they clustered silently around the fire. ✥

24

wise in measure should each man be;
but let him not wax too wise;
for never the happiest of men is he
who learns too much of too many things.

~WISDOM OF ODIN~

*I*t was like sunshine turned to rain, the change in their demeanor from departing to returning. Unease hovered about them like the tang of cold air and snow, stealing our questions from our tongues. They held reddened hands to the fire, but none looked up or spoke, as though they all were still far away from us.

Even Thorbjorn did not demand a report.

I saw Harald count heads more than once and assumed from his silence that all were present. No one had been lost in frozen lakes or to spirits dancing in the blowing snow.

No one except Thorir.

It was not long before the colour returned to the cheeks of the treasure-seekers and to their hair and clothing. Beads of water sizzled in the fire when they stood to shake it off their clothing.

When the story was finally begun, it came in fits and starts, mumbled descriptions of snow and wind and getting confused about which direction to take; I could hardly hide my impatience. Something more had happened. I could smell it. We all could.

"I don't know what to tell you," said Vermund, scowling as he pushed his finger through a tear in the knee of his trews. "We got lost, just like when we came here." He darted a glance at Ofram, who looked away.

"So, no treasure then?" said Thorbjorn sardonically.

Vermund threw a scrap of torn wool into the fire where it flamed and then sank into the coals. "Wherever that treasure-hoard lies, it will lie there a good while longer." He sounded uncharacteristically subdued.

"This is quite a turnabout!" said Thorbjorn, scanning the faces. "What happened to change you all from brave Vikings to shy girls, running from ghosties and fearing the dark?"

"The dark?" Ofram barked a humourless laugh. "If I tell you what happened you will scoff and I won't even be able to blame you. If these others hadn't been witnesses to it, I would think myself mad."

"Oh, so something did happen," said Thorbjorn. "Well, tell us, please. We lack a trained skald, but I'm sure with all this drama you've created you will be able to entertain us."

"Good enough," said Ofram, rising from his place by the fire. "One of you entertain him. I've got something that needs doing." He stepped over men and gear to reach the place where he'd slept the previous night. He got out his knife and began to etch something into the wall.

"Well?" said Thorbjorn.

"Patience, man," growled Vermund. "Ask for a tale, but don't dictate the telling of it!" He looked about him as if seeking guidance, but when none came and Thorbjorn had cleared his throat twice, he pulled his knees up and, gripping them, began. "It's like this, then. We headed north towards the lochs but we got all turned around and ..."

"Aye, we got turned around," Fergus laughed, slapping

Vermund on the back to cut him off. He took up the tale in his own style. "So much so that all we could seem to find was that stone with the hole in it. We just kept running into that damned stone. It was like a bitch in heat, drawing all of us to it, no matter what we did." He spoke as if he were in jest.

Sigrith caught my eye and held it a moment.

"Well, I can tell you that none of us wanted to see that thing again. We kept trying to get away from it, but it was as if this whole bloody island could swing around on its axis, like we were floating, a bubble over the earth, and setting down wherever the wind blew us. One minute we were beside that stone and then we were up to our knees in water and not sure if it was salt or sweet. I swear, the way we moved from one place to another, not of our own volition, it was not possible. And yet, there we were, one minute in the water and the next, in the middle of that ring."

"The Dance," Sigrith whispered. Her eyes glowed in the firelight as she watched Fergus.

"Aye, the Dance," said Fergus darkly.

"What happened then?" asked Eirik.

Fergus hesitated, then threw up his hands and exclaimed, "They *danced*, of course! What did you think?"

Everyone burst into relieved laughter. Fergus beamed. He had broken the spell that had fallen upon all of us.

"Yes, you should have seen it," drawled Arnfith, who had found the ale and was already in his cups. He waved his hands around dramatically. "They all lit up with a blue light and then danced around us. Slow as the stars, it was, but dance they did. And we became the stones. While they, the *stones*, moved around us, and we could not move—"

"Such an adventure," Thorbjorn interrupted dryly.

"Aye, it was," said Eyolf, humourlessly. "You should have come."

"And the treasure?" Eirik asked.

"Is for someone else," growled Ofram from his place by the wall.

"How did you find your way back?" asked Sigrith. I alone knew why she asked.

"By some miracle, to be sure," snapped Ofram. His words were punctuated by the scratching sounds his knife made. "We could not break free of the ring. We were … trapped. And then there was this horrible sound, a keening howl like death riding over the world and I swear, it thundered like an army in the distance, but I didn't see a thing. The sky was black. Even the stones were black. The snow. Everything."

"You closed your eyes?" offered Benedikt lightly.

Ofram grunted. "I may have, and I may have pissed myself too for all I can tell. I'm soaked to the bone."

"So, death rode over the world?" prompted Sigrith.

He answered with another grunt.

"Ach, he's just sinking back into his pagan roots," said Fergus, waving away Ofram's version of events. "From there we gathered our wits and turned tail and made our way here, as fast as we could."

"You were gone for hours," said Harald.

"We were gone for years," Ofram muttered.

There was a long, uncomfortable silence and then Thorbjorn began to clap his hands together. "I want to thank you for your tale, gentlemen. You have entertained us well. I'm sure a proper skald could not have done better. I'll tell you what I think. You hiked down to Olaf's house, had yourself some ale and a meal and concocted the whole thing," said Thorbjorn.

"And then we soaked ourselves so we could happily freeze the way back," spat Vermund. "Think what you like."

"I think you should have brought us some of that ale," said Thorbjorn.

"That I'll agree to," said Ofram from where he worked. "I hope you didn't drink it all while we were gone."

And that was the end of it. The ale went around and, as if by silent agreement, those who had gone and those who had stayed left the subject of what had happened out in the storm.

But I was not fooled, nor do I think Sigrith was. Something had drawn us to the Odin Stone and back to the mound again and it had worked on the others as well. But what had sent them out into the storm, only to draw them back?

Soon the evening meal was underway, with just enough food reserved for the morning. For, as the earl joked, Erlend would have drained both the food and the drink from whomever had been unfortunate enough to play host to him and we would likely have to get our own.

Whatever tension was left over from our adventurers' strange tale, everyone did well at ignoring it, busying themselves with talk of mundane things and preparations for the coming day. But Ofram, for one, had not even paused to eat and was still carefully chipping at the wall with his knife. I got up to bring him some salted fish and a skin of ale.

"You'll need to sharpen your blade before morning," I said and was immediately sorry for I had startled the big man. His knife skittered across the stone. When he regained it he looked at his bleeding palm, then put it to his mouth. He waved off my apologies, taking the ale from me.

"What are you carving there?" I asked as he drank.

I could not read the runes, but I recognized the crosses that encircled the pagan symbols. Six of them and perhaps one in the centre, though it was hard to tell in the dim light; the strange stick-like markings resembled poorly formed crosses themselves.

"My name is there," he said, indicating the runes. "The crosses are a protection, a barrier between me and—"

He didn't finish, but I knew what he meant.

"Did you hear voices?" I suddenly whispered. "Names …"

Ofram looked into my eyes, as if trying to read the heart of my question there. "No," he said, turning back at his work. "Why do you ask?"

"I don't know," I answered.

He shrugged. I did not press him. We had traded lie for lie. I returned to the fire.

"Why did you ask him that?" asked Sigrith.

I shrugged. I had hoped no one had heard me, but no one could really speak in that place without being heard.

"He hears voices all the time, this one does," said Thorbjorn.

"It's better than being deaf," I said. I meant to sound defiant but it came out peevish.

"Surely it is," he said and looked very serious. "Tell me what you hear."

"Nothing," I said.

"Let us hope you have not gone deaf!" said Thorbjorn with mock concern. "A man can only lose so many of his faculties before we must find another name for him."

I gritted my teeth but managed to hold my tongue. My eyes returned to Ofram's strange inscription, a mixture of pagan and Christian. How did he reconcile the two?

"The runes are holy," said Sigrith over my shoulder. "All things die, you know, even the ancient gods, but the runes, they live on as long as the stone or wood or cloth or bone they are marked on remain. It is a binding of sorts. The name of a man can be breathed back to life long after all who knew him are gone. His spirit, though it lives in the next world, can still be blessed in this one by the uttering aloud of his old name."

"And if he is not gone?" I asked quietly.

"Then we must be careful," she answered, her eyes saying what her words did not.

"You should bless yourself, Malcolm. You seem a little touched by this place," said Vermund, quite sincerely.

"I think I'll just leave my mark here," I said, holding up the axe handle.

"A blessing would not hurt," said Ofram. "I can do it for you, if you like."

"Thank you, no," I said. How was it all these Christian men, not to mention Sigrith, spoke so easily of such things? I added, "I have some Latin. I can write my name in that way."

"I do not think it is the same," said Benedikt. The cross around his neck gleamed. "I do not think God will be upset if you write in the letters of the North or the ones of

Rome. He will do His own will either way."

That, at least, I knew was true. But I did not join the others as they bound themselves to the stone in that place. I worked on the handle, satisfied that my silent prayers would protect me as they always had.

It was not long before they gave up with their carving and began to draw nearer the fire. I suspected this was as much for the warming of the spirit as of the body. The night was cold, even more so than the first one had been. How Sigrith managed to keep the fire so well on so little fuel, I do not know, but she certainly put Thorbjorn's slander to the lie.

It had been quiet for a few minutes and the mood was feeling more subdued than was usual when Ogmund spoke. "I have a tale fit for this night."

"Not one of dancing stones if you don't mind," said Thorbjorn.

Ogmund nodded his head in mock servility. "There may be a few stones in it, but I'll do my best, my lord," he said.

The rest of us were eager to be distracted and quickly settled ourselves so he could begin.

"One night, many years ago, when my grandfather was a young man, he was coming home from my grandmother's house—for they were children then, but already in love—when he was caught out alone with the Hunt bearing down on him. It was a night like this one," he said with an upward tilt of his chin, "with a great wind howling and tearing about, though with little snow. Whenever he told the tale, he always agreed he was a fool to have gone, what with it being Yule and all. And then he would laugh and say that being a fool is part of being a youth, and it is not always ill-fated.

"He may have been a fool, but he was not stupid, so he took shelter where he could, ducking behind some large rocks. But there was no hiding from those riders.

"The hounds were baying and the horses screaming. The thundering of hooves took much of his hearing that night, or so he liked to say when we were little and had to shout for him to hear us. His fear was upon him, he said, but he knew what he had to do if he wished to survive and with all his parts intact."

The hair was standing up on my neck. I put down my work to give him all my attention.

"The Leader swept to the ground on his fierce mount, and all eight of that great steed's golden hooves flashed in the night sky. The Leader, he threw back his head, and just as he began to call my grandfather's name, just as it was issuing forth from those magical lips, my grandfather stood tall, in the face of that grave danger, and interrupted him. Aye," he said, grinning round at us, "he was a cocky one."

"'Oh Great One,' he said. 'One-Eyed Allfather, Giver of Life and of Death, I most humbly ask a boon of thee.'

"Sleipnir and his rider froze there for an instant. It seemed the god would decline and trample my grandfather to his death or take him into his army right then, for even in his youth he was a fine figure, tall and strong and of a proud bearing. A warrior to tempt the god.

"But the rules of the worlds are not only for men. The gods must abide by them, too. My grandfather had begged his blessing in good form and so must the god reply.

"'What would you have of me?' demanded Odin.

"'A mere sprig of parsley, as a man has a right to ask,' my grandfather answered humbly.

"The god regarded him with his one piercing eye and then he spoke. 'Your words are humble enough, and you do not lack intelligence, but you have much to learn. Still, I grant your boon.' A sprig of parsley appeared in his enormous fist. He let it drop and it was carried by the wind to my grandfather's own hand. It was as long as his forearm and solid gold.

"He held it, knowing what it meant, knowing that his future was made, and as he gazed upon it he dreamt a glorious life to come. In that instant he forgot the god. Odin drew his reins and Sleipnir reared up again, so that his golden hooves struck my grandfather in the head."

"But he lived," Vermund interrupted with a shout. "Unless he got your grandmother with child that night!"

"He lived," answered Ogmund, with a grin. "And my father was not among his bastards, though perhaps yours was. Cousin?"

Vermund laughed loudly. "Carry on, storyteller. Tell us what happened next."

"He got up from the ground in the morning and thought he'd had a dream, but then he saw the proof in his hand. The sprig of parsley shone as bright as the morning sun."

There were sighs of pleasure at that. I grinned to myself. The gold lust was not going to leave them quite that easily.

"But something had changed. He found that when Sleipnir had kicked him, he'd landed such a blow to the left side of his face, that all of his teeth had been knocked out there. They called him Havard the Lop-sided from that day onwards."

"And your grandmother still took him."

"She did. She said when she saw that he had half the teeth of a man, she hoped he'd have half the appetite as well."

More laughter.

"It was a good tale, Ogmund," said Harald as he passed Ogmund a skin of ale.

"But it is not done," Ogmund pouted. Harald raised his palms in apology and Ogmund resumed his tale. "He went home that day and all the neighbours came to see his golden sprig and his injury and he told the tale to all of them. One of those who came was his cousin, a right half-wit according to my grandfather. That one decided that he, too, wanted a sprig of gold for himself, so the next night he went out into the dark, alone.

"But he got himself quite drunk first, for he was a coward at heart and not prepared to face the Hunt or the god or much of anything without an aid to his courage. Others tried to stop him, but he would have none of it. Off he went, bragging that he'd ask for an oak bough!"

"Did he meet the god on the road?" asked Eyolf.

"I think he did, though none ever knew for sure. They found him, curled up in the very spot where my grandfather had hidden the night before. His hands were empty and he was dead.

Heads nodded with satisfaction around the fire, but I did not understand and I very much needed to.

"Why did he die?" I asked.

Harald explained. "Either he answered the god wrongly or he was asleep when the Hunt came. The people believe that a man who would sleep under the stars on a Yule night does not show proper regard to the spirits or the gods."

"He could have died from any number of other things," said Thorbjorn, "from a fall to an unfortunate meeting with an ill-tempered man. But I'm curious, Ogmund. What made you tell that story on a night like this."

"I couldn't say," Ogmund answered. "Thorir used to claim that the god decided what stories he would tell on a night. This one seemed fitting."

There was silence at the mention of Thorir's name.

Thorbjorn grunted. The howe grew quiet again as each man sank into his own thoughts.

I, for one, was thinking that I might have solved the mystery of who had brought us all back to the mound. I felt the truth of it sitting in me, sure as the stone under me. And yet I fought it too, for what did it mean, if Thorir's world and mine were both true?

• • •

Not long afterwards, when all had been quiet and still for a while, there was a movement, a shadow that wove its way among the sleeping men. I was about to leap to my feet with a shout of warning when something in the shape of it spoke to me. It was Sigrith. *Making sure of the fire,* I realized as I watched her bow her head, busying her hands with some invisible task.

But she did not touch the fire. She only hovered near it a moment and then she moved away again and lay down so that I could not see her among all the rocks and bodies that lay strewn about the floor. ◈

25

*more blest are the living than the lifeless.
'tis the living who come by the cow;
i saw the hearth-fire burn in the rich man's hall
and himself lying dead by the door.*

~WISDOM OF ODIN~

One moment I was leaning up against the wall in the darkness listening to the lullaby of snoring, the next I was staring up at the towering shadow of he who lived under the mound.

He was so still that in the first instant I thought my eyes played tricks, that he was simply that, a shadow. But what my eyes could not discern my heart did, for he emanated a fury as violent as the storm that raged outside. It rolled off him like heat from a great fire, but at the same time it seemed to come from within me, a flaring coal in my breast, leaving no room inside me for calm or reason. That was his power.

"You did not heed my warning!" His voice struck like a blow.

"I thought it was all a dream," I gasped. Was that true? Now, standing before him, I wondered how I could ever have thought it.

The disc of gold on his breast radiated light like a small sun, the figure upon it flaring with life. The glare from it was so blinding I averted my eyes.

"They did go!" I cried, desperately.

"Because I sent them." He was pronouncing his judgement on me.

"Not all of them," I murmured.

"Not all men are tempted by the same thing. They will leave too, in their turn."

He wanted me to cower. I summoned my courage. "But the ones you sent, they came back! Why did you bring them back?"

His silence and the rage that boiled beneath it told me I was near to a truth. A truth he did not want me to touch upon. He could feel me treading near it, as surely as I could feel him willing me away from it.

"Why didn't you destroy us all? You said you could burn us up. Why haven't you?"

"The pure protect the impure."

"It was a test," I said.

"You owe your lives this night to her." Approval, pride, even a distant sort of love washed over me, though they were not for me. That I had not expected.

But now I knew we had some sort of protection, so I asked the real question.

"Why are we here? Who keeps us in this place? If it is not you—"

His only answer was another volley of rage cascading over me. "You hide beneath his cloak and think to taunt me?" He raised a fist and I felt the breath sucked out of my lungs.

Who keeps us here when you want us gone? I cried with my mind. My body screamed with need, for air, for release, for any change to occur that would end that hanging moment.

That is when I saw my body lying on the floor and knew that I was not that body any longer. Or rather, I was not that body *alone*. The form of myself the dweller of the mound gripped by the throat was another part of me.

Suddenly I had the greatest need to see the part of me that was being held, suspended, breathless. I stuck my hands out before me, but saw nothing. Was I dead? What was this body of mine that the shadow was throttling?

With a wretched gasp I was breathing again. *This body breathed?*

"You do not want to see the form of your spirit," the shadow whispered. "You are an ignorant wretch, but I will tell you that much. See it and you will die."

You cannot see your own varden, of course, not unless you are dying. Thorir's words.

"I can see you," I panted.

"I am already dead."

Without warning, the sky came crashing down upon my skull. I dropped to the hard stone floor and curled up like a hedgepig, sheltering my head with my arms, and I prayed, to whom I can not honestly say. Horses stampeded, dogs bayed, close on the scent of the spirits they hunted. The hallooing of the huntsmen and their Leader cried out in a deafening cacophony for the dead to rise and join them.

They called his name. Over and over they called it and I knew they would never stop.

I realized then what a feat Ogmund's grandfather had performed on the night when he had kept his wits and made a demand of the god. I was all but swept away by the force that tore through the mound and through my mind.

It was worse than the first time. Like an enormous wave, it caught up all in its path and rendered it no more than flotsam on the flood.

How did *he* withstand it?

An eternity passed while the Hunt hurtled through the mound. An eternity, an instant, and all the while they called his name. And all the while he defied them, with no fear and no doubt. I knew, for nothing he felt escaped me.

That was part of my gift.

When I finally looked up again, dazed, an agonizing pain thudding in my temples, I saw him where he sat on the pile of rubble with his great hands pressed over his ears, like a child who has been told no when he wanted to hear yes. No light glowed about him now. Even the shining brooch on his breast was dulled.

"How can I leave? Who will speak for the land?" He spoke in a whisper to himself, the whisper of a man who has lived alone beneath the earth for hundreds of years. But I heard him.

"What is happening here?" I asked in a new voice, one hushed by awe.

"You cannot understand. You are not a warrior, nor a poet."

Waves of despair washed over me. I felt the stirrings of a curious pity for my tormentor. He was trapped. He was left behind. Sigrith had said the others were all gone. And yet I could feel his great defiance, his utter refusal to leave. I could even admire it.

"Keep your pity for yourself," he growled, his anger rising again. "I know what you fret about, what you whine and wish over. I have your thoughts, your heart, before my mind's eye. I *see*. You could too, but you close your eyes. You dream the truth, but you sleep and do not see."

I saw the fisherman, one eye milky and blind, the other seeing everything.

"You know him," he grunted with bitter humour.

I knew who kept us in the mound.

"But he is not the only one with power!" he bellowed and I felt myself drowning under the waves of his rage.

In my mind I closed the oak door I'd conjured up the night before. I had a moment's reprieve before he blasted through it.

I was sitting in Margaret's chamber, her hand on my arm as we made our bargain. The memory was as real and clear as it had been the day it was made, only this time I could see the glint in her eye that I had not seen then. *He* showed it to me now. *He* reached into my mind and presented my own past to me. He knew it all. Shame blossomed, then anger. How dare he see the truth! How dare he thrust it in my face! He did not know what had truly happened. His judgement hung from my neck like a weight.

"I am doing my best," I said, and was assaulted with an image of my father, looking strained. *He will be obedient and will do his best.* That was what he had said. Why had I been so displeased? How had I not seen the strain on him then, the worry in his eyes?

"I see all of you. I see who is traitor, who is kin-slayer."

I stared up at him. He could read all our thoughts, not just mine.

"You know who would betray Harald?"

"Besides you?" he laughed mockingly. "I know. When the leader of the land is adrift, all become wreckage on the shore."

"Tell me. I will do anything you ask!"

"You cannot give me what I desire."

"You want us to go. We will. I promise."

"You promise a thing beyond your power. Your word means nothing. They will go, driven like beasts by the darkness of their hearts. And they will fail."

I knew that he meant I would not go and that it was not permission, but prophecy. And that he did not like it. He wanted me gone as much—more even?—than the others.

But what did he mean about them failing? Would they fail at finding Erlend or at killing him?

"Can you see nothing? Weak and foolish wretch! If he kills you, you will not be welcome in this place."

"Kills me?" I cried, bewildered.

"Your enemy. I cannot touch you, but he can."

"And why can you not touch me?"

Damn him! It was a howl of fury, so deafening that in the silence that followed I thought I had lost my hearing, like Ogmund's grandfather.

And then: "Who are you talking to?"

The question shuddered through me. The shadow was gone but Thorbjorn crouched so low over me I could smell his breath.

"I was dreaming …"

"Who were you talking to? What are you up to?" He leaned over me menacingly.

He is the spy! He will kill me now!

I fumbled for my dirk but it was not in its sheath. I had left it lying on my satchel.

Was this why the shadow had said the others would go, but not I? Had he seen my death?

Thorbjorn was not moving. He had me at his mercy, with no witnesses to stop him. What was he waiting for? Cruel, cruel, to draw it out so torturously!

And then he was turning away. "What a waste of meat you are," he mumbled before stumbling back to his place by the fire.

I watched him stretch out by the makeshift hearth without another look my way. He could have killed me and the only witness would have said nothing.

• • •

An eagle circled high above the land of gently rolling hills. He was hunting. I could feel it.

A cloud blotted out the sun. The eagle disappeared. It was dark all around me. I shivered with cold.

There he was again, circling so high above I could barely make him out.

And yet I could sense the keenness of his seeking, his pursuit, as if it were my own. The sun gleamed on his wings as he tilted, drifting lower, sweeping upwards again.

But the eagle was not the only hunter. I *felt* that other presence lurking so near me, and yet all I saw was shadow upon shadow.

That was his gift! To hide himself, to hide his true nature! Whoever he was, this one who lay in the shadows against the earth, he stalked the eagle. And yet the eagle flew with the clouds, while this one—I was certain of it—was earth-bound.

There was a flicker of movement in the shadows. The eagle tensed.

Again, movement. The eagle dropped from the sky like a stone.

The hunter waited beside me, perfectly concealed, patient and sure.

I tried to call out a warning but my voice had no power. In the instant that the eagle swept the earth with his wing, a great shape hurtled out of the shadows.

It was a boar, silent as death, and it was flying straight for the eagle.

All vanished. The sun, the eagle, the boar. Only the sky remained, stretching bloody red banners from horizon to horizon.

Black came the wings against the red sky. Hope surged in me. Was it the eagle? No, there were two of them. Odin's ravens, the harbingers of death? *Please, no!* I cried wordlessly.

Fire burned in my heart like a knife wound. It was happening too fast. I could not stop it!

Then I saw that the creatures were not ravens at all. Two great dragons circled each other in that endless red sky.

I say there were two, but the truth is that I only saw the one that soared on black wings, a dark, familiar reflection of the other. The other—the instant my eyes lighted on it a pain cut into the core of me that seared like a blade entering my soul. Tears streamed from my eyes and inside me there was an ache that made me wonder if I'd looked too long.

But my breathing continued. I was alive. Slowly I opened my eyes, keeping my gaze low. Nothing moved. The world of rolling hills was blackened, burned to ash, dead. It was still as a grave. It was a grave.

A dark head rose up from the water. Enormous eyes found me. The seal. It looked at me, long, calm, then vanished under the water again.

I lay there, dazed. I lifted a hand. It was my own.

The seal, the fox. I knew what they were. *Who* they were.

I reached a trembling hand for Marjory's amulet and the fox appeared before me. Fox, I say, but more accurately, she was a vixen.

"Tell me what to do," I said to her.

I felt her presence as if she stood before me, but she offered no answer to my request.

"Tell me!" I begged.

The fox became Marjory standing in my chamber with my green tunic over her arm. I knew she was telling me something. What had she said to me that day in my chamber?

So many things, but she had only ever told me one thing, advised me one time.

She, knowing me so well, had told me to listen to our father.

And of all the things he had told me, one stood out now as brightly as that form that had so dazzled my eyes. All his warnings, his lectures, they had meant nothing compared to this. One thing he had told me, the shadow had told me. The one thing I feared the most. ❧

26

little the sand if little the seas,
little are the minds of men,
for ne'er in the world were all equally wise,
'tis shared by the fools and the sage.

~WISDOM OF ODIN~

here is a particular quality to the sounds men make when they are preparing for an important day. The most mundane act echoes with a fresh urgency that gives each old sound a new tone, as on a holy day when every event is coloured by the bells ringing at their determined intervals.

That is what had woken me, that feeling. From the sound of it, the storm had not let up one bit, but that was not stopping my companions who ate while they checked their weapons and gear. Their eagerness to leave was contagious. I began gathering my things together.

Sigrith nudged me and dropped a handful of dried fruit into my palm. Only then did I realize that she, alone, was not preparing to leave.

The earl seemed to have realized it at the same time. He crouched beside her. "Sigrith, I had hoped the storm would have broken by now—"

"I will stay here," she answered, as if she were speaking of something as commonplace as lingering a little longer in her friend's kitchen garden and not a burial mound in the midst of a fierce storm. "I will be safe."

"Safe? I'm not so sure about that."

"I assure you, my lord, I am in no danger, but if you want someone to stay with me, I would not mind the company."

"You are a brave young woman," said Ofram. "I wouldn't be staying here alone if I had another choice."

"But I am not you," said Sigrith with a smile. I knew what she meant, if Ofram did not. She did not need a man's strength to protect her in that place.

Then Thorbjorn said, "Let the boy stay," as I'd known he would. Had there ever been another possibility?

"Malcolm?" asked Harald, looking to me.

"He can get lost in the storm again for all I care, but he'll be little use when we find Erlend. And I'm sure these two will be quite happy to have the place all to themselves."

I had no time for his insinuations. It was still Yule and Harald was setting out now to kill his cousin. Could I let him go like this, without telling him what his actions would mean? How had I left it so long? So the mound dweller had said they'd fail. I still didn't know what that meant. I still didn't know what to do.

I looked around at the earl's men, my companions of the past few days. One of them was the man sent to kill me if I spoke out. The mound dweller had not told me I was to die this day. Did that mean I would not? Did that mean I could speak and I would not be killed? He had not said I would *not* die.

It was enough to drive me mad, but it was no longer so easy to be a coward. I took a deep breath. "My lord, I have something I need to say to you."

"Say it," he said, as he adjusted his sword.

Everyone was watching me. One of them watched as Margaret's eyes.

"May I speak with you alone?"

"And where would you like to go to do that?" he snapped. He was agitated, distracted. And why not? He was about to take back his earldom. *Or attempt to,* I amended. *Do I hope the mound dweller's prophecy is correct?*

"My lord," I said, "I am glad to stay with Sigrith. I wish I could be a greater service to you today, but I wish you Godspeed and," I fumbled around for the words. With all those eyes on me my burst of courage had faded. "And I hope that … I will set eyes on this cousin of yours, this Erlend, that I may see him cast out, and you raised up again to your proper place and …"

Harald's eyebrows had arched as soon as I'd said Erlend's name and by the time I'd finished he was giving me such a look of annoyance and disbelief that I was wishing I could disappear.

"This is what you needed privacy for? My God, Malcolm, are you trying to say something, or are you not?"

There were looks of amusement all round.

"Only that I hope this can be resolved peacefully. So did your uncle." It was the first time anyone had mentioned Paul since leaving Wick. Harald gave me a dark scowl. I persisted. "He talked about how bloodshed had been the bane of Orkney for so many years, among your ancestors, the earls—"

Thorbjorn cut me off. "Harald, can we go now?"

"Yes, let us go. Malcolm, your well wishes are kind." Harald shook his head in bewilderment and turned away.

I felt like an idiot.

The howe was slowly emptying. Men traipsed out through the humbling tunnel, a few calling out farewells to us as they went. I sank down beside the fire as I watched them go. I thought I felt at least one man's eyes on me in a way that did not feel comfortable at all.

Then they were gone and I was left to wonder if what I'd said constituted a confession that might cost me, cost my family, everything.

But what could I have said, I thought in my own defense. It was not as if Harald would believe me if I told him that Svein and his mother had connived together, that if he killed his cousin he would kill his own future. Thorbjorn would knock such words away like a pestering fly. And yet it was the truth. I knew it in my bones. So should I have said it? If I was going to risk my life, should I not risk it for something more grand than a roundabout warning so cryptic only someone who already knew it to be true would recognize it as such?

In the silence that grew after their departure the only sound was the faint popping of the fire. I looked up at the vaulted ceiling, saw the pagan scratchings in the walls, and I felt that other presence watching us. Watching me.

"The quiet is peculiar, isn't it?" said Sigrith. "The silence opens up worlds. But there is nothing here now that was not here before."

"How can you be so calm?" I asked.

"I know what to fear," she answered. "You just need to find your bearings. A stranger must follow the ways of the land he is in to avoid getting lost. I will show you how to find your way in Orkney," she said.

"You really weren't afraid to stay here, even if I went?"

"He won't hurt me." She handed me one of the boar-shaped cakes. "No," she said, lightly touching my wrist to bring my hand away from my mouth, which I had been about to fill with the cake. "Like this." She took one for herself and broke it in two, laying it on a flat stone by the fire.

This was what she had been doing in the darkness each night. Making an offering. Again I had the disconcerting feeling that I did not understand her at all.

But she already understood me well enough. "It is a pagan thing, I know, but it is what we do here. This is *his* place." She gave a slight laugh. "I never thought to be doing it under the mound. We always leave it on the table for him during Yule or on the top of the mound. But the purpose is the same. We give respect where it is due. It cannot hurt."

I was about to tell her that it might well hurt, that such an act might well mean eternal damnation, but life was not so simple as I had thought it, and Sigrith was right. I was not in my own land anymore.

I broke the cake and laid it on the stone beside hers.

I do not know if it was the gesture itself or my show of faith in Sigrith or if I actually appeased the spirit of the mound, but in the instant that my fingers left the cake, I felt my spirit lift with them, as if the mound dweller had taken his hand off my heart.

Sigrith nodded approvingly.

"Now, let me show you what I found. It may help."

She made her way towards the corner to the right of the entrance.

At first I did not see what she pointed at. I had to stand on my toes, and when I realized it was a series of scratch marks in the face of the corner stone I was all the more puzzled.

"I don't read runes, Sigrith," I said.

"No, but I do. Enough."

"I thought ..."

"It was more enjoyable for them to read the runes. And I have not had much practice. But this is only two words."

I laughed at that. She had fooled all of us. More than once, I suspected.

"It says—" she paused and I realized that she was in fact nervous, or excited, or both. "It says *Thorir*, Malcolm. *Thorir* and the word *fomir*. Fomir means ... it means to be mad." My heart dropped. "Mad in the face of the god," she whispered.

Mad in the face of the god.

He has touched me with his hand.

But where had Thorir gone?

"There is something more. This figure," she said, reaching up to run her finger along a curving line. It was as long as my hand with short lines branched out from the bottom of it. "It is the mount of the god. It is Sleipnir, who carries the god in the Hunt, Malcolm! Thorir marked this stone. He had the wherewithal to mark this stone. It is good news!"

• • •

Some time later we were sitting quietly, each with our own thoughts, when Sigrith said, "You were trying to tell Earl Harald something earlier."

I did not know where to begin. For a brief moment I thought I might confess the whole thing to her but something stopped me. She liked me. I did not want to see that change when she heard the truth.

"He could not hear you, you know. Not now. He had to go."

"Well," I said ruefully, "I didn't exactly say it very well."

"Perhaps not, but I don't think it was the time. You must have some faith, Malcolm. Fate is in your favour or it is not."

"How can you have faith in it, then?"

She laughed. "It will happen as it happens. I will do my part. The rest is beyond my control, so why worry?"

I scrutinized her. Was her ancestor's ability to read my thoughts something Sigrith could do as well? I hoped not.

"But things happen. There are clues, you know. Clues to what is coming and if you pay attention you will hear the whispered hints, see the signs."

Just then a thought flashed through my mind. "Sigrith, you said a man came to your house before we did."

"Which one? The young or the old."

"Both," I whispered. When I'd asked the question I had a sensation that the *other* one, the one who listened from the shadows, had leaned forward to listen more closely.

"The old man was very mysterious. He had this odd way of smiling when he spoke, as if we were missing his point and he thought it quite humourous that we did not understand him. My father assumed he was mad."

"And you?"

"I thought he was odd. If he was mad, he was harmlessly so. There was no dark intent in him." She stopped. "No dark intent. I said he was mysterious. There is always something dark in that. What I mean is that I did not sense he meant anyone harm. He was just going about his business."

"What did he look like?" I asked, knowing what she would say.

"The old man was ... old. I don't know. I think he must have been very tall once, but he was quite stooped over now. Old and thin. And he was blind in one eye."

"And the young one?"

"He was quite handsome," she answered. "He was young, with very fine features and his hair was quite unusual, I suppose. It was blue-black and terribly shiny. It looked very much like a raven's wing—"

It was her turn to stare. "Are you all right, Malcolm?"

"Fine," I said. "Fine." But I was thinking very hard then about fate and faith and what on earth my best might entail.

• • •

For a time Sigrith let me be. She could see that I was preoccupied. But the longer I sat trying to sort out all that I had just learned, the less I was able to understand. I was certain that the young man was Margaret's lover, but why was he in Orkney? I had a hundred theories, none of which I could prove. And then the old man. I had no theories to explain him at all. How did anyone ever find the right way through such a quagmire?

When Sigrith began to talk I was grateful to be rescued from my useless musings. She told me the stories of her ancestor. I knew he listened. I wondered if he heard the pride in her voice, her pleasure in the telling of his deeds, this girl who was the child of his children.

There were more tales than could be told in a day, she asserted, but she would tell me the best ones, her favourites.

More than once I thought how Thorir would have enjoyed the day.

While she talked she undid her long, pale braids and picked out the tiny knots the wind had tied in her hair. I stopped carving to watch her. When her hair was all shining and smooth again she ran her fingers through it and came up with three strands, which she rapidly whipped into a long, neat braid.

"Your ancestor was friends with this Ragnar," I said. "It seems I am the only one who does not know about him." *Thorir would have already told me the whole tale in all its varying forms, I thought. And he would have found a way to irk me and make me laugh with every turning of his story.*

But Sigrith was no mean storyteller either. She talked and I carved, my hands doing their work to the pleasant sound of her voice. She did not comment about my working that day, for I think she understood by then that it was medicine, for my spirit and for my mind. Both were greatly restored in the hours we passed thus.

The handle was almost complete and it looked very good indeed. Once begun it had almost carved itself, except, of course, for that one small part.

While I smoothed away the rough spots Sigrith told me how Ragnar had been a man with the wanderlust, and how he had raided in faraway places. He had been the king in

Rus and made a hundred men's fortunes from ransoming Paris. His first wife, Thora, he rescued from the snake that her father had given her, which grew so large it encircled the tower where she slept, biting its tail and letting no one near her. His second wife, Aslaug, was the daughter of Sigurd, the dragon-slayer. She gave Ragnar four sons who avenged him when he died in England, bitten to death in the snake-pit of King Ella. As he was dying, he cried out, 'How the little pigs would grunt if they knew what had happened to the old boar!' And they did. They killed King Ella in a horrible manner and took his kingdom for themselves. They were known everywhere for this triumph.

"It sounds like he would have hated that," I said when the series of tales was done.

"And yet that was his failing, don't you think? A man should wish his sons to achieve the highest glory they can. No good father holds his son back, for any cause."

I thought of my own father and then of Ragnar's sons, for I had been looking at the one bare spot on the earl's handle while Sigrith told her story and I suddenly knew what belonged there. I knew what beast resided in the wood. As I cut the first tusk I thought of my father. He had held me back many times, but always and only to keep me safe, to keep me from wandering out alone before I was ready.

Which meant that when he sent me out into the world he knew I was ready.

• • •

Hours later I was stretched out beside the fire, having decided that Sigrith's way of celebrating Yule, with idle hands, was a good one. I was feeling more at ease than I had since leaving home. My head was cushioned by my cloak on one rock and my feet were propped on another one and I gazed lazily up at the ceiling, trying to figure out how exactly it had been constructed. The stones layered inwards from the wall, narrowing until they reached the domed top. Except for the ugly gash Earl Rognvald's men had made in it, which we had expanded, it was a perfectly balanced structure, simple seeming, but beautifully engineered. I wondered who had made it, why, when. I would never know, but I enjoyed wondering nonetheless.

I was violently jolted from my musings. The tunic was torn away from the hole. The end of a rope dropped into our midst, to be followed by a pair of legs and then the rest of the man. Clumps of snow fell in with him. A grim-looking Haermund dropped to the ground before us. ⏃

27

the ill-minded man who meanly thinks,
of all things a mockery makes:
he does not know, as know he ought,
that he is not free from faults.

~wisdom of odin~

horbjorn came in long after the others were already warming themselves by the fire. He dropped his sword and shield noisily against the nearest wall and sat down by the fire where he let off waves of his own simmering heat. The rest of us gave him as wide a berth as we could.

The earl's eyes flickered in Thorbjorn's direction more than once, but he said nothing. He nodded distantly as he accepted the drink Sigrith offered him, but his look was ponderous.

And why should it not be? They had failed. And Harald was saved. And I might be condemned, but I could not worry about that. I had decided to trust in fate.

But a small war was waging, with Harald ignoring Thorbjorn and Thorbjorn growing ever more furious, glaring openly across the fire at the younger man. For a few minutes Harald ate and drank, not saying a word, while Thorbjorn fired angry looks his way.

They finally found their mark. "Are you going to say it or are you just going to burn holes in me with your eyes?" Harald said in a voice that was surprisingly loud after a long silence.

"Doesn't seem I need to say it, but I'll tell you, *my lord*," said Thorbjorn. "We should have kept going. I've said it. Does it please you?"

"Oh, it pleases me greatly. Do you have any more helpful advice?" Harald's face twisted with a bitterness that turned it ugly.

Had they chosen to turn back? I imagined Thorbjorn would see it that way.

"If you think sitting here does us any good ..." Thorbjorn began.

"Being out there didn't get us anywhere," interrupted Haermund. Others nodded in agreement but neither Thorbjorn nor Harald paid any heed.

"You want my counsel, but you don't—"

"Enough!" growled the earl.

Thorbjorn shrugged. "As you wish, but you know that we'll have to go searching for him now. He won't be where our spies said, not anymore, so we really should be making yet another plan and taking all of this into ..."

"Enough, I said! We were out in that blizzard for hours. We're all wet through and night is falling. Tomorrow we leave here, no matter what the weather, and we find Erlend. Tomorrow! Now have done with it!" The veins in his temples bulged. I could see him swallowing the words that wanted to come. He had looked just this way at Wick, with his mother.

There was much similarity between the two of them, between all three, really. Harald, Margaret and Thorbjorn were family. Perhaps anger came to them in their blood, alongside lust for power and God knew what other dark things.

Harald was glaring into the fire, clearly seeking to compose himself while Thorbjorn scrutinized him with his own heavy-browed intensity. I had seen that look before. He was seeking a foothold. *Now,* I thought, *Thorbjorn will touch another nerve.*

I was wrong. When Thorbjorn spoke it was in a voice altogether too composed to be true. "As you wish," he said and began rifling through his satchel as though nothing had happened, leaving Harald looking like he'd swallowed a hot rock.

But the argument seemed to be over, at least for the time being. Everyone else was busy dividing up the last of the food. It was not much, just a few biscuits, some dried fruit and bits of dried meat tossed away as scraps earlier. Snow was melted for water—the lack of other drink was the only real cause for complaint. I felt mildly guilty for having eaten so much during the day so I didn't take much for myself.

No matter. It would only be one more night. It could not be more.

It was Arnfith who started it up again. "Thorbjorn is right, you know," he said with a look of disgust on his face after taking a large gulp of warm water.

"No one asked you," said Haermund, without looking up from the knife he was sharpening on a strip of leather.

"I'm just saying," Arnfith muttered.

"Don't."

Arnfith shot Haermund a dirty look and proceeded. "We should never have stopped here at all. We should have gone round to Firth straight off and wet our swords with Erlend's blood that first night! Over and done with. This," he said with a wave at his hand to the men scattered around him, "makes me feel like an old woman."

"Aye, well, you smell like an old woman," Haermund growled, glaring at Arnfith in warning, "and you think like one. That's why you are a hired sword and not an earl. No one was getting to Firth, that night or this one."

Arnfith belched. "I'm not an earl because *my* mother was a fisherman's daughter."

Haermund was up quick as a snake, his knife buried in the thick bush of Arnfith's beard. Arnfith's eyes bulged with alarm.

"You will shut that mouth of yours," Haermund hissed into Arnfith's face, "or I will." It was hard to tell just where the tip of his blade was positioned, but the way Arnfith kept pressing his head back at an increasingly awkward angle suggested it was pricking flesh.

"Leave him be, Haermund," said Harald.

"Not till he begs your pardon."

"Leave him be, Haermund," warned Vermund.

"Leave *me* be," growled Haermund as he leaned harder into Arnfith, producing a high-pitched yelp in the younger man.

"I won't," said Vermund. He shoved me roughly out of the way, his own knife high in the air. I was just righting myself again when I saw that another figure had added itself to the fray, and another, and then it was impossible to tell who was who anymore.

Thorbjorn was shouting. The earl looked on, his expression grave. Some of the men seemed to be trying to end the fight while others appeared to be joining it. Arnfith and Haermund were hidden from view but when they did reappear, the latter had an angry Vermund attached firmly to his back and Angus was standing beside him, one hand gripping his tangled locks and the other holding the point of his dirk neatly to the base of his skull.

"Get off me, you stinking Scot," growled Vermund.

"I will," said Angus. "Just as soon as your blade finds its way back into your sheath."

Vermund made a move that was not in keeping with Angus' request but Angus did not move and a slow trickle of blood trailed down the back of Vermund's neck.

First blood. I held my breath, waiting for Harald to say something. He didn't. He appeared to be waiting.

Thorbjorn did not hesitate. "Enough," he said, in a tone that left no room for disagreement. "Enough. And Arnfith, the next time you insult your lord, I'll cut your throat myself."

The violent tableau dissolved, though not without a few shoves and unpleasantries.

"And that," he said, with a look to Harald, "is how you lead men."

Whatever I thought of Thorbjorn, he had that much right. The men listened to Harald but Thorbjorn willed them to heed him. I wondered that Thorbjorn had not taught his foster-son that.

• • •

When Sigrith reminded us that it was the last night of Yule it struck me how far removed from the world we had become. At Dunailech my family would be preparing to celebrate the Feast of the Epiphany. If we'd been anywhere else, it would have been a night of great celebration, of the best food and drink and entertainment, the last and the best day of the Christmas season. As it was, we drank melted snow and licked at crumbs.

But feast or no, the men were determined to spend it well. The air felt like it does just before a lightning storm. If some of them suspected what was at the root of the flares of temper in some and fits of gloom in others, none admitted it. They were intent on escaping in the only way they could that night.

Ogmund, with his voice as deep as a pit, sang a song that made me blush, but which, to my surprise, caused Sigrith to clap her hands with a glee that encouraged more songs of the same sort. Apparently, I was something of a prude.

Competitions in poetry gave way to contests of insults called flyting, which were brilliant to hear. My people can be fined for insulting a man's or a woman's honour, but my companions delighted in it. The game was to receive an insult and deliver a greater one, and to never show anything but grace and good humour, whether giving or receiving. No man could lose his temper at any point in the match. It may not have been the best game to play in our circumstances—at times moods seemed precariously perched on a blade's edge, in danger of falling into either mirth or murder—but there was no real trouble. The men kept themselves occupied and the night wore on.

I spent my time carefully picking away at the last fine details of the earl's axe handle. I would have liked to oil the wood properly, and I did not know if it could be fitted together well enough for him to carry the next day, but it was complete, and I was very pleased with it. The weave of the knotwork was beautifully balanced and fitted the shape of the wood perfectly.

Even the beast at the heart of it belonged there within the weave of those intertwined lines. He stood, legs splayed, ready to dart off the handle. The boar of my dream, of the amulet that hid under my tunic. Was it a protection or a warning? I did not know. All I knew was that it was meant to be there. The work was done. All that was left was to present it to Harald. The only problem was when.

For, while moods seemed to have improved in general, the earl's had not, and neither had Thorbjorn's. The two sat, islands of glowering, brewing anger, in the midst of all that forced merriment. I waited for a break in the weather.

Vermund had perched himself on top of a rock and was holding a torch over his head, illuminating the wall high above the tunnel. The last of the peat had been added to the fire and the howe was the brightest it had ever been, so that his shadow danced darkly across the walls. "I've found another one," he said. "This one tells of a Viking come under the mound."

"That's me," said Eyolf.

"What would you know of Vikings? You on your Shetland farm with only your sheep for neighbours," Vermund laughed, making the sound of a decidedly drunken sheep.

"I've been farther than you'll ever go," said Eyolf haughtily. "I went over to the Hebrides and Ireland a few years back and we did well."

"Yet you ended up herding sheep on your rock again!"

belched Arnfith. "You're a shepherd, not a Viking!"

"None of you are Vikings, nor do you have the makings in you. That breed has died out, more's the pity." Everybody stopped to look at Thorbjorn; it was the first time he'd spoken in hours.

"What do you mean by that?" asked Ogmund.

"Take whatever meaning you will," said Thorbjorn.

The earl shook his head with irritation.

Thorbjorn caught me watching him and gave me a withering look.

"How did this Viking get up there?" someone asked.

"Easily," said Eyolf and he grabbed Angus' arm and pulled him to a place near one wall. Vermund saw the plan and cupped his hands for Eyolf's foot, boosting him up and towards Angus, who cursed as Eyolf clambered roughly up him to set one foot on each of his shoulders. The two swayed dangerously. Angus tripped over the rocks at his feet tipping Eyolf forward against the wall where he tried to hold himself up, leaning so far forward I thought he would surely fall as Angus struggled to straighten. They received applause and advice and a few jeers for their performance.

"You've proven your point!" said Angus. "Now get off!"

"Not yet," said Eyolf. "Move to the left there a little and when I'm done I'll teach you how to bless yourself properly. Hold steady."

"I'll thank you not to speak to me as you would your horse!" said Angus.

"My horse has better balance than you do," laughed Eyolf as he pulled out his knife.

Angus responded by moving so far back from the wall

that Eyolf spluttered that he was surely as strong as his horse; the red-haired man obliged by moving back to the wall.

Now others had their knives out, and Haermund his axe, and were carving their legacy in the walls of the howe. Angus was writing his name under Eyolf's tutelage. Even Harald was watching with some amusement. Thorbjorn was another matter. The lighter the mood got, the darker his became.

Simon dropped down beside me. He examined the finished handle approvingly. "It's all done, is it?"

I nodded.

"Well, aren't you going to give it to him?"

"I will, just not—"

"You have to stop hanging back!" he cried as he tore it from my hand. "Harald, have a look at this. Malcolm finished it. Maybe that's what we've been waiting for," he added with a laugh.

But Harald never got to see the handle because just then Thorbjorn leapt up and snatched it out of Simon's hand and whirled to wave it in my face.

"You finally finished, did you?" he sneered. "Well, something good has come of this misadventure then, hasn't it? This is what you have to show for yourself, for all your expense, your effort?" He was no longer speaking to me. The handle was in Harald's face. In a flash it sailed from Thorbjorn's hand and into the fire.

Sigrith leapt after it, God bless her, but Thorbjorn shoved her aside with his leg as he plunged his foot down to press the piece of carved oak into the coals. Sigrith tried again to grab for it, but it was no use. She pulled back, rubbing her arm where he had hit her. For the first time, I saw real anger in her face.

Thorbjorn stayed there, one foot in the fire, oblivious to the heat, glaring at Harald as if he had committed some unforgivable offense. When he finally lifted his foot out again it was because the handle was beyond saving. Flames were already hungrily licking at the fresh fuel.

I was so angry I was robbed of my words. I stood gaping up at Thorbjorn like an idiot, red-faced and mute.

"Look at him, cheeks flaming," he said with contempt. "He's more girlish than the girl."

"That was ill-done," said Harald softly.

"It was a trinket!" Thorbjorn said, shaking his head in disbelief. "You wonder why we fail? You bring children on the most important venture of your life and encourage the childish antics of the ones who *are* men!"

"We are *here*. What should they be doing?"

"You encourage their tomfoolery and lack of discipline. You foster weakness. We should be eating Erlend's food tonight, but we let the weather keep us indoors, like women."

Eirik stood, frowning. "Thorbjorn, the weather is beyond any man's power …"

"To control! But it can be braved, whatever the cost! That is how warriors go. Against the grain, into the fray." He turned on the earl, accusingly. "You have stopped short of confronting your cousin. You cannot deny it."

"I cannot." Harald was exasperated. "I did not force my men to continue on to their sure deaths. I did not choose to sacrifice them to my ends. To futile ends! There is fate wrapped up in this weather. We have tried to leave! None of us is stronger than the wind or the snow."

"Fate!" Thorbjorn spat out the word. He spun on his heel with his arm raised to take in all who sat, staring, in the howe. "He speaks of fate. He says he held back to protect you lot. What do you think of that? Do you love him for his gentle kindness? Maddad wouldn't have stopped, given up. Think on it, son. Your father would have been in Firth by now, and Erlend would be on his way to hell."

Harald took a moment to collect his words before he spoke. His eyes were on the handle that was slowly being eaten by flames. "Evidently I am not my father, but I do not believe he would have sacrificed himself or any of his men on a fool's errand. Nor do I believe he would have killed his own kin." He ignored Thorbjorn's snort of derision—all knew Maddad had been party to the abduction of the Earl Paul. He pressed on firmly. "He would have read the signs, I think, and seen that the time was not right. This whole expedition was a mistake. We should have waited, been more patient."

"You mean timid! And *signs*? We're not going back to that!"

"He's right, you know," a voice interrupted Harald's response.

"Arnfith," warned Haermund.

"Well," said Vermund, with a glint in his eye, "if I'm being asked, I have to say that spending yet another night in this place is not to my liking."

"It is easy to criticize when you are not expected to offer

better avenues," said Benedikt.

"Well, we're trapped, aren't we?" retorted Vermund. "I see it. But we were out and if he'd said we keep going, I'd have gone. I know my place. And as for what to do about Erlend," he went on, obviously enjoying the attention, "well, it seems obvious to me."

Heads were nodding at that. I watched, dismayed, as Harald saw it, as uncertainty took hold and, for a moment, he looked like a boy, young and lost. He recovered quickly enough but the frown of responsibility and doubt darkened his face.

How I hated Thorbjorn then. He had won and he knew it. He held his face carefully composed but I read victory glittering there like the flashing of silver fish in dark water. He had used the others to find the earl's weak places and thrust there with hidden daggers. Now he stepped forward to grip Harald's arms, but I knew he was using the time to choose his words. He was going to get his way. Yule might be ending and Margaret's plot be undone, but the danger had not passed. How could I only have seen it now?

It did not matter *when* Harald killed Erlend. It only mattered if he did.

My father had said Harald had the makings of a good leader, but what if those around him stopped him from becoming such a leader? What if they undermined him, took away his strength? What if his followers doubted him? Harald was a decent man, but he was young and he was worn. And now, alone, he seemed about to bend under the pressure of it all.

It was time for me to serve my lord and to do it well.

That was what my father had told me to do. It was every man's duty. I must find a way to show the others that they had turned to serving Thorbjorn and whoever was working against Harald. And I must do it in a way that did not destroy my family.

I was no better than my companions. I had pledged to convince Harald to kill his cousin, never intending to do it, but neither had I supported him. Thorir would have done better. He would have found a way to protect those he loved and support his rightful lord. For all his strange ideas, he seemed to always do what needed doing.

What had Thorir said at Dingwall? Something about his people choosing their leader and influencing his choices? A Thing. That's what he called it. *Where all men gather and are heard. Where men may even decide the fate of their lord.* Was this not the way of the people of Orkney? Harald had lost Orkney due to the decisions made by the people. Why not win it back the same way? Some of the men would be ripe for bloodshed, but not all. If they all had to speak their minds Thorbjorn's damage might be undone.

"My lord," I said. The words came too fast, but I knew that if I slowed I would stop. "Thorir told me about a custom of yours, one that I found strange, but very … interesting. He said the men of a community meet and they all give voice to their thoughts on matters and the lord hears them and then makes his choice with all the wisdom of the people at his disposal."

Everyone was looking at me. I kept my eyes on Harald who was studying me with the strangest of looks. His hooded eyes were shadowed but I saw the glimmer there. Very slowly a smile kindled at the corners of his wide mouth and he reached out a large hand to rest on my shoulder.

"Well then, we've talked enough of fate the past few days," said the earl, "but we do not really trust it, do we? We think we can make it serve us, but its workings are truly unfathomable. I have been looking in the wrong places for what I need, it seems. They say wisdom comes from the most unlikely sources, from children and madmen, do they not?"

He continued to regard me a moment longer. He squeezed my shoulder and turned to the room of now silent men. I could not even feel unhappy about how he had described me. I was holding my breath as I waited to hear what would come next.

"Gentlemen," he said. "Gather yourselves around the fire. I have need of your wisdom. I will hear from all of you and together we will decide what is best. Prepare to convene a Thing." ⚛

28

well-groomed and washed, wend to the thing,
though in garments none too new;
of thy shoes and breeches, be not ashamed,
nor for the quality of thy steed.

~WISDOM OF ODIN~

Sigrith rose to move away, for the Thing was a gathering of men, but Harald waved for her to sit back down. "Where will you go, Sigrith? You can speak for your father."

"Why not let her speak for herself?" said Thorbjorn. "And then we can ask everyone we meet along the way from here to Firth and perhaps a few of the sheep as well."

"Sheep have more respect than you," growled Haermund.

"What harm can she do?" asked Angus. "She has a level enough head. Give her a say."

Sigrith was crouched half way between going and staying.

"Don't listen to him, Sigrith," said Harald. "He is uncouth when he does not get his way. Please, sit. If you have anything to say, we're glad to hear it."

"And you wonder why your plans fall awry," said Thorbjorn with an ugly grin, but he said no more. Sigrith sat back down, her face a careful mask.

The earl stood. "I will begin. We have only one order of business today. We have come to reclaim Orkney and yet we have had nothing but ill luck. It may be that we have not chosen the right path to our goal and that is why God does not smile on us. The question we must answer here, that you must help me answer, is what course we take on the morrow."

"We can't go back!" interrupted Eyolf.

"The earl is speaking," said Eirik.

"No, he's right," said Harald. "If I retreat now I fear I am done for." The look on his face said he was already tasting that failure. "So, the issue at hand: Thorbjorn believes that Erlend will be a danger to my claim in Orkney as long as he breathes and that he should be killed. And I am less certain."

"Seems to me there's no need for further discussion," said Simon. "Kill him and have done with it."

"We have all night," said Fergus to Simon, "and I'd like to clarify a few things for myself before you decide my opinion for me." He addressed himself to Harald. "My lord, the people of Orkney chose Erlend over you, did they not? And you vowed not to contest the decision. And, he had a legal claim, as the son of an earl?"

"Why are you asking me this now?" asked Harald with displeasure.

"I just want the facts. I don't know much about this Thing business, but I do know a man needs all the facts for his opinion to be worth hearing."

"Fine. Erlend's claim is legal insofar as his father was an earl. And yes, the people chose him and I agreed to their decision, but I was not free to make an honest decision. There was, shall we say, a knife to my throat," said Harald grimly, for he had been held captive by Erlend and Svein and had only given up his rights in order to obtain his freedom. "But Fergus, they did not have all the facts either. They bought the horse before they'd checked his teeth. Now they see that his teeth are all rotted and his insides, too. I think, given another choice, they will buy a different horse this time."

Fergus grinned to show his teeth and Harald's face brightened.

"There is little doubt that the people will choose you over him now. The issue is how long will it be before he comes back to stir up trouble," said Thorbjorn. He gestured impatiently at the circle of faces. "And this is unnecessary. You have advisors to direct you."

"To direct me?" asked Harald with a wry laugh. "Is that what you do?" He seemed to be recovering himself.

Thorbjorn thought a moment, then shrugged. "Perhaps it is time then for me to step down. If you have outgrown me you need only say it and I will keep my thoughts to myself."

His words were a bluff and all knew it.

Harald sighed wearily. "Thorbjorn, I tell you, I hate my cousin with a fire like a knife in the belly, but my spirit is chilled each time I think of how this will all fall out in the end. And you are right when you tell me uncertainty is dangerous," he said, talking over Thorbjorn's attempt to interrupt him, "but that is why I am doing this. I am uncertain of my course. I hope that when I have heard what other men think I will be less so."

"You want *them* to decide for you!"

"I will hear them!" Harald snapped.

Thorbjorn put up his hands in a gesture of surrender, but

I did not miss the glare he sent my way as Harald began again. He would not soon forgive me for suggesting the Thing. I did not care. It was underway. He would soon feel his power wane. Or so I hoped.

"So," said Harald, "two paths are laid out. One is to meet with Erlend and seek a new arrangement. The other is … well, more final."

Haermund cleared his throat. "My lord, as I recall it, you had talks with the man before. "What makes you think you will fare better this time?"

"I only know that the field has changed and that the minds of some men have changed too. And I am no captive this time. My position is stronger."

Haermund nodded as he arranged his thoughts. "I agree. The field has become overgrown with neglect. The farmers will welcome a new master, but only one who does not set those fields on fire. Erlend did not shed your blood to wrest Orkney from you. I do not think you should stoop below his level."

I suppressed a grin of satisfaction. I should have known I could rely on Haermund.

Thorbjorn leaned forward to answer him. "Erlend dealt with Harald as he did because he knew Harald would be honourable in his dealings. That was Svein's doing, his plotting." He waved a hand at Harald. "But it seems even Svein can be wrong sometimes, for here you are, breaking your oath just by being in Orkney! So, how likely do you think it is that Erlend won't come back if you let him go?"

Haermund was nodding thoughtfully as Thorbjorn leaned back.

"You're right," said Eirik. "He'll do everything he can to turn the tide in his favour again. All know it. But killing him undoes all that we gain, angering kings and other lords and giving Harald a bad name. Otherwise I'd be all for it. Erlend has cost us much. If God sees fit to strike him his final blow tomorrow I'll not grieve, though he's kin to me as well. But it must not be seen to come from Harald's hand. The people will not stand for it."

"Nor will God," said Benedikt.

"Are we discussing religion now?" asked Thorbjorn.

"Should God's will not always be a factor in such weighty decisions?"

"God's will is not knowable until it is done, so I don't trouble myself with it," said Thorbjorn. "What we should spend our time on are the other words your brother spoke. He admits he would be glad if Erlend died, as long as it was *not seen to come from Harald's hand.*"

Eirik interrupted. "That is not what I said."

"It is exactly what you said," Thorbjorn said coolly. "And you were right. And as for angering the kings, do not grieve yourself on that front. The kings will plague us only as long as we appear to be weak. Once they learn to fear Harald properly they will leave Orkney alone. If they do not, it is war we'll see."

My father had spoken of war too, but he'd said it would come about if Harald failed. Could he kill Erlend and succeed? I was sure he could not. Not if what Paul had said was true, as somehow I knew it was. No, Thorbjorn was twisting Eirik's words and Eirik was not the sort of man to stand for it.

Eirik chewed on his lip, eyeing Thorbjorn a long moment. Then he gave a curt nod of his head. "Well," he said. "I suppose you're right at the end of it. A strong earldom will keep the wolves at bay." He got out his knife and began paring his nails.

I stared at him. The others looked puzzled as well.

If Thorbjorn thought it odd he gave no indication. He stretched his legs out towards the fire and crossed his arms over his broad chest.

"Why don't we take him as he took Harald," suggested Angus, "and call a Thing of the farmers of Orkney and—"

"The farmers of Orkney would rather hang out their wives washing," Thorbjorn said.

Angus regarded him carefully. I could see the words running a second time through his mind. Then he nodded in grave agreement, as if Thorbjorn had just made the most sage of statements. I could not believe it. They'd rather do their wives washing than attend upon their earl, than have a say in their own fates? And Angus, usually so quick and honour-bound, said nothing.

And so it went on. When any ventured an opinion that differed from his own, Thorbjorn batted it away as if it were a drunken fly, too bloated to dodge a swat, and it fell dead. At first even he seemed mildly surprised by the lack of effort required to defeat any arguments, but as it grew apparent to him that he could not lose the debate he began to counter every point made with one more ridiculous than the last. When Ofram said it might be better to wait until summer, he said flowers bloom happily in winter too. When Benedikt said they might pray on it, he replied that God had his ears stopped up with wax. The result was always the same. The argument stopped there. Thorbjorn's delight grew.

My heart had sunk down into my knees. What was happening? Had they all gone mad? Had their minds and spirits been drained from them? These were not the men I had come to know, the men who had turned out to be fine men, most of them, men of honour, men whose word meant all to them. And now, it seemed, it meant nothing.

Through it all Harald sat, motionless, silent. Panic rose in me.

Just then Sigrith caught my eye and my dismay plunged to the deepest of depths. Her face wore a small smile. She did not see it either! I was alone in this. I was alone in a world gone mad.

She shook her head. I gave her a quizzical look. She directed her glance downward to where her hand rested on one of the hearthstones and tapped the stone with her fingertips. The stone where we'd left the broken oatcakes.

I looked back to her face. Her eyes did a sweep of the ceiling.

She was not mad and neither was I. She had said the spirit of the mound could weaken a man, draw him down to his lowest level. The spirit was having his revenge on us after all.

And then I realized that, since I had first mentioned the Thing, something had been missing from me. I had been too preoccupied to notice it before. All I had been feeling had been my own. My own thoughts in my head, my own heart in my chest beating with my own anxiety. Not his.

The ancient warrior had shut himself off from me completely. For the first time since we'd entered the howe I was free of his presence.

But surely he was not gone. He could not be. He had only shut himself off from me. But why?

The debate—if it could be called that—went on, but it went nowhere.

Harald's face was unreadable. He did not even seem to be listening. He slouched in his place by the fire. I would not have known him for an earl just then.

So, whatever the spirit is up to, he's practicing it on Harald, too, I thought.

There was a lull, with low murmurings passing through the group. Sigrith's eyes locked on mine. No one stood against Thorbjorn. All were in agreement: we should find Erlend and kill him. All my hopes were fading like smoke against a cloudy sky.

If Thorbjorn wondered where his new-found power came from he gave no sign. He gloated, unrestrained in his arrogance. He winked at me as he began to address the men again.

"I think," he said, "we should teach the farmers a lesson here in Orkney. After all, they did turn against their rightful earl last year. They have suffered by their choice, to be sure, but should they not be punished beyond that, to discourage further such behaviour?"

Some of the men present were, of course, farmers of Orkney. Their looks were bland.

"So I say we burn every farm between here and Firth, and then we burn down the house that hosted Erlend this

Yule, burn it down around the ears of his treacherous hosts and all their guests, and when we are done there we tour a few of the other islands and dispense some more lessons in Earl Harald's mercy among the people. We will defeat Erlend and show our strength all at once. Scotland and Norway will think twice about flexing their muscles in our land again."

No one spoke against him. His grin, in the flickering firelight was ghastly, but the true horror of it was that not a single man brooked an argument. Harald had not even looked up.

My eyes swung to meet Sigrith's. She mouthed a word at me. The third time I read her lips aright. *Speak,* she said.

She was right. She and I were the only ones not under the sway of the spirit. All of them had been turned already to their darkest hearts. I must turn them back.

I opened my mouth to speak.

And nothing came out. As the first word formed on my tongue a storm hit me from *inside* and drove all the air from my lungs. Terror, all the fears I'd ever had, rushed over me at once, like riders of the Hunt, and screamed their horrors into my heart, mind-tearingly awful.

The spirit had kept his thoughts from me for this. He could touch me after all.

I could not breath. I could not move or even think. I would drown in the torrent. A scream came up my throat as the urge to go tearing out into the storm shot into my limbs and I felt myself scrambling up.

"May I speak?" I heard beyond the din in my head. Sigrith.

"You have something useful to say?" said Thorbjorn, his voice far off.

"I believe I do," said Sigrith. She looked at me, sat up straighter and drew a breath. "I believe that if my father were here, he would say that to kill is an evil thing. And to kill kin, more evil. Even with the holy time coming to an end, the sin of a kin-slaying is one many will consider unforgivable."

Even in my state I could see she was glorious. She opened her mouth to continue but Thorbjorn was prepared for her. "Unforgivable, you say? And if men—kin!—came to your house, drunk and with evil intent towards you, your mother, even your pretty little sister, what then? Would your father fight, even kill, to save you, or would he stand by and watch, or," his lip curled in contempt, "would he run away and hide?"

"He is no coward," answered Sigrith.

"So he would kill."

"Yes," she said, "to save us, of course he would, but he would not plan for it."

"A raid on your farm and a raid to regain an earldom cannot be compared."

"Then why did you compare them?" Sigrith asked.

She was holding her own. She did not bend as the others did. She would save us. I was still swarmed by the fear imposed on me but I felt the slightest degree of relief.

"To show that there are situations that require strong measures."

"Then we agree. The laws allow for killing in self-defense," she answered confidently.

"And in battle. And this is battle."

"It need not be," she said quietly. She would have him in a moment. The others would see she spoke the truth.

Haermund cleared his throat. "I have to agree."

Hope nudged at fear.

Everyone looked at him. "With whom?" growled Thorbjorn.

Haermund looked puzzled. He cocked his frog-head to the side. "Why, with you of course. Sigrith, you're a lovely girl, and you know I mean it, but you should keep to your place. There's a reason you wear skirts and not a sword. Come to Westray with me and be my wife and talk all you like, but leave men's work to the men."

Sigrith did not move.

"Aye, girl," said Angus, "you've a pretty enough face, but you should leave the thinking to the men."

"Shall we talk about her place, then?" Vermund leered.

Arnfith reached out a hand towards her. She flinched. I jerked up from my seat to push between them. She flew up as well, to stop me from going further but Arnfith snorted and withdrew. My heart thudded in my ears, this time with rage. Rage that had, at least momentarily, loosened the hold of the spirit on me.

"You see now how the land lies?" said Thorbjorn to Sigrith.

"I see that the wind is blowing, though you cannot see it, Thorbjorn Klerk, though it blows into your face, and brings death on its wings. You look with closed eyes. You close the eyes of other men when what they need is opening."

She spoke to Thorbjorn, but she looked at me. I must speak. I knew it, yet I could not. What could I say that they would hear? They had become strangers. My lord sat, dejected, drained of his purpose. Thorbjorn had succeeded. He had made Harald his puppet, just as the men had become his sheep. If I told them why Harald must not kill his cousin they would laugh. If I told them the rest of it, all of Margaret's hand in it, my family and I would die. And they would not heed me! I would speak and lose all, and for what?

I stood looking into Sigrith's sky-blue eyes and began to shake my head, to tell her that I could not risk it. Then I stopped. My own fear was reflected in her eyes. Her own fear, for her family, for her land. How had I not seen that before? That by saving my family I might condemn all of Orkney. I felt a flare of shame. I would speak.

A new and vibrant onslaught of terrors assailed me, such horrors done to my loved ones that I whimpered in agony.

The spirit put such poison in my mind. He might hide himself from me, but I was not hidden from him. He knew my thoughts. I fought to breath. I found Sigrith's eyes again and held them as if in a vise. We stood facing each other for an endless moment while she lent her will to me. The others were murmuring amongst themselves. I breathed in and out, each breath a chore, as I pushed back the fear with all the strength I had in me and said a silent prayer. That God's will and mine might be aligned. That my father's gift might prove true. And mine as well.

I opened my mouth, not knowing what I would say. I suddenly thought of Thorir, who had said his words were given to him and I knew what I must do. Another breath and I put my trust in fate and in powers greater than the one who lived under the mound. I trusted and these words came from mouth:

"There was once a young eagle," I said, my voice cracking, "who fell from his nest before he learned to fly. A woman came along and found him on the ground. 'How fine and strong he is,' she said. 'I will put him back in the nest until he is ready to fly.' The woman put the eagle back in the nest and tied a leash to one of his legs, strong enough to tether a bear, but fine as spider's silk, so that it was invisible to the eye. 'To repay me for my kindness he will hunt for me,' she said."

"It is not time for tales," Thorbjorn said.

I focused on Harald, in my mind and with my eyes, and continued. "In time the eagle learned to fly and he hunted for the woman. Only sometimes did he long to see what lay beyond the horizon, but every time he tried to fly beyond the woman's lands, he found he could not. Still, his life was good. He flew daily and hunted for her and killed all manner of creatures for her table and she ate well and was pleased with him.

"One day the woman said, 'My enemies have prepared an army against me. They come to kill me. Destroy them.'

"He flew to find the woman's enemies, but they were not marching on her castle. They were farming their fields. He went back to the woman.

"'Your enemies are not marching on you,' he said.

"'They will be soon enough,' she replied. 'Kill them.'

"And he saw the evil in her heart and he said that he was

tired of hunting for her.

"'You will not leave me,' she said, 'for we are bound to each other.'

"The eagle flew away, but he found she spoke the truth. Though he could not see it, he felt the leash pulling on his foot. No matter how hard he tried he could not cut himself free. 'I would rather die than be her slave,' he said, and he flew into the sun."

While I spoke Harald had slowly looked up and was now watching me from shadowed eyes. The others, too, were intent upon me, but they were not my concern. I spoke to Harald.

"The sun grew so hot the eagle's feathers began to burn. He flew on. Finally the tether burned through and the eagle was free. Down from the heavens he flew, only to find a vast ocean below and nowhere for him to land. A current of wind caught him up and he followed it. It was a long time and his strength was all but gone when he finally saw green fields in the vastness of the blue sea."

"When he finally reached the land he was so exhausted he fell from the sky.

"A man found him and lifted him up. The eagle was badly hurt. The man carried him home where he nursed the bird for a long time, so that by the time the bird was well again he had grown a deep love for the man."

Harald was sitting straighter now.

"On the day the eagle was ready to fly the man sent him out into the sky and said, 'Fly as high as you will and come back when you will.' And the eagle flew to where the air was thin and he saw the world spread out before him and was filled with joy, and then he returned home. He hunted for the man and they lived together and all was well.

"Then one day the man said he had an enemy to the east, one who would take his land from him if he was not stopped. The eagle was angry. 'Where is this enemy?' he demanded. 'I will kill him for you.' And he did. The eagle went out and killed the man's enemy and when he flew home to tell what he had done the man was well pleased.

"The next day the man said to the eagle, 'My neighbour to the south has taken over my fields that border his land.' The eagle found the neighbour and killed him.

"The next day it was the same. The man complained of his neighbour to the north and the eagle did away with him as well.

"On the fourth day the man said that he feared his neighbour to the west would harm him one day soon.

"'If I kill that neighbour there will be no one left,' said the eagle.

"'Then no one will be able to harm me,' said the man.

"'But who will you turn to in your need and in your loneliness?' asked the eagle.

"'I have you,' answered the man. 'Do you not love me?'

"The eagle said he did, and so he flew to the west looking for the man's neighbour. But all he saw was a child playing in the fields. The child was innocent, hurting no one.

"The eagle flew back to the man and told him of the child.

"'That child is the heir who will grow into a man to rob me one day. You must kill him.'

"The eagle refused. 'The man is just like the woman,' his

sorrowing heart said and he flew away. But when he came to the edge of the ocean he found he could not fly any further. Something held him there. There was no tether to his foot. This one was to his heart.

"He went back to find the man, to speak to him, to cool his hatred. But he could not find him in his lands. He went searching in lands nearby. His love for the man would turn his heart. He was sure of it.

"He flew to the north, the east, the south. Finally he sought the man in the west. He saw the child playing among the flowers. The man walked up behind him. The eagle hovered upon the currents of the wind. Then he saw the blade of the man's knife shining in the sunlight. The man raised his blade and the eagle he knew what he must do."

I stopped. Every eye was on me and I knew how Thorir felt when he stood in the hall.

"Well, what happened?" demanded Eyolf.

I shook my head.

"Did he kill the man?" asked Arnfith.

"No, he took up the child," said Haermund.

They thought I toyed with them, but the truth was that the words had dried up. Yet they had done their work. My companions bombarded me with questions. They had returned to themselves. Even Harald, who sat up and cut me with his scrutiny.

I shook my head. "I don't know," I said, looking back at Harald. "I don't know yet."

I could see Sigrith's excitement bubbling in her like a spring. Thorbjorn was perplexed, angry, but he made no protest. I could see he wanted to, but it would not come out. He had his ally and, it seemed, I had mine.

Ogmund tugged at my sleeve. "Why not a falcon in your tale, Malcolm? Is it not unusual for an eagle to be kept tame?"

"It is, indeed," I said, standing up straighter to meet Harald's penetrating stare.

Thorbjorn finally found his voice. "So he's become a skald now, has he? Do you think to advise with the moral of his tale?"

I could see him fighting to conjure up an argument, but what argument was there to make? I told a story, a fable. There was nothing to counter without giving more power to the truth.

Harald was still staring at me. Suddenly his gaze swung away, to look at the fire, then over the men sitting around it, then to Thorbjorn and back to the fire.

"He's as mad as the poet was," growled Thorbjorn.

Harald put up his hand to stop Thorbjorn. His eyes were on the fire. Everyone watched him. Had he fallen into his stupour again?

Firelight softens most faces. His was made more harsh. It looked like the very bones in his face had grown heavy.

"Why did you burn the handle Malcolm made for me?" he asked softly. I had not expected that. Even clever Thorbjorn was a moment digesting it. But only a moment. "It was a trinket. Unnecessary, and—"

"It was for me. It was made for me, to serve me, to wield the strength of my arm in defense of the land I was born to rule. And you destroyed it."

Thorbjorn seemed at a loss. He made an agitated motion with his head. He was about to speak when Harald put up a hand. "Such a headache I have. Be quiet so I may think."

"Harald—"

But Harald put up one hand while the other rubbed at his temple. He sat that way for a minute, then more. We all sat too, in silence. I stole a glance at Sigrith. She watched the earl.

Finally Harald looked up again. "I thank you all for what you have said here. I will weigh your words carefully." He looked at Thorbjorn, then at me. "Then I will decide what is to be done. Either way, tomorrow we leave this place." There was weariness in him, and, when he looked at Thorbjorn, I saw a flash of sorrow. Thorbjorn saw it too and, for the first time that night, doubt passed over his face.

I exhaled the breath I'd held too long.

I did not know what Harald would decide, though I strongly suspected—nay, my heart told me what his choice would be—but that was no longer in my hands. Harald must decide it and I must attend to my own purpose. In the dimly lit howe, with the wind screaming above and the firelight flickering, I felt a thing I'd not felt before.

I had encountered a new power: my own. And with it, a clarity I had not imagined before.

From deep inside of me a voice spoke, wordless, to tell me my work was not done. It was confirmed by other evidence, for, just as the spirit had shut himself off from me only to attack me so profoundly, now I felt him again, his thoughts pulsing just beyond my reach, his anger more immediate. One truth we both acknowledged: more was yet to come. There was still another night to pass under the mound. The last night of Yule, the holy season, the time of the spirits, of the Hunt riding the heavens. Tomorrow it would be done. By tomorrow it must be done or it might never be.

• • •

Much later, when all was quiet, Sigrith rose and I joined her. Wordlessly we broke the last of the oatcakes, one Sigrith had hidden away for just this purpose, and left it on the stone. Then she went to her dreams and I to mine. ❧

29

he must rise betimes who from another,
wealth or life would win;
scarce falls the prey to sleeping wolves,
or to slumberers victory in strife.

~WISDOM OF ODIN~

*I*t was as if some creature that had lain dormant in my breast from the very start, unbeknownst to me, had ignited my heart with a new fire. Not the hot-flaring fire of childish fits of temper, but slow-burning, enduring, true.

My companions were still stirring. The other nights they had all dropped off almost as one. I knew that he kept them awake. He would avoid me this night if he could. I smiled to myself in the darkness. It hardly mattered. This night was coming, no matter what either of us wanted. They would sleep, eventually. I was sure of it.

And there were things to sort out while I waited. I lay on my back looking up into the darkness of the high ceiling. An eagle had flown there, and a boar had lurked nearby, enshrouded in shadow. Marjory had given me a boar. One had appeared on the handle that had been turned to smoke and ash by Thorbjorn's temper. I knew who the eagle was, but who was the boar? And those other creatures … only another dream could answer my questions, and I did not know how to summon one of those.

Finally I sensed that I was the only one still awake. Still he remained hidden. I could feel him there, near but removed. It was as I had expected. He would not appear to me. He would delay until it was too late. I could not let him have his way.

And how did I know these things? The change that had taken place in me had done away with much of the clutter in my mind. Many had tried to guide me: my father and Thorir, Sigrith and the old man at Beauly. I was finally ready to hear them, to use their wisdom with my own.

I took out my knife and went to one of the tall standing stones that supported the roof of Orkahaugr. I said a small prayer and scratched my first line in the stone. The cut was hesitant. It was dark in the howe, so that I could hardly see anything. I closed my eyes until the image glimmered at the edge of my memory, refusing at first to reveal itself. It grew clearer and my hand blindly began to record it on the stone. Patiently I worked, feeling no need to hurry, feeling that all was as it should be.

I do not know how long I worked that way, recording on stone the image I held in my mind, but I knew when I had achieved a fair reckoning because the lines on the stone began to glow like coals, as if a fire burned beneath the surface of the stone, seeking escape. I worked faster and faster, joyfully carving what was now seared into my vision. The image in stone and the one in my mind were one. As the intensity of the light that shone from them grew, I prayed that what had once sent me careening back into the world of waking could take me where I needed to go.

I laid the knife down on my satchel and waited.

The strange beast that had emerged in lines of fire now heated the stone so that it glowed and, ever so slowly, it became, not stone, but a disc of gold. The light that shone forth from it was dazzling. I stepped back, not for the brightness, but to make room for the shadow that had grown behind the disc of gold, the brooch on the breast of the dweller of the mound.

Had my eyes not told me of my success the chilling cold that poured from him was proof.

"You are still here," he said.

I stood my ground. "I had little choice in the matter."

The low rumble of his laughter coming from within me no longer shocked me as it once had. That he laughed at all was something of a surprise.

"And you summon me. Is that foolishness or bravery?"

"Are they so different?" I replied with a momentary flutter in my heart. Or was it his? "It seemed better to choose than to wait."

Again he laughed, soft and dangerous. "You might have waited forever."

Fear rippled through me. I saw all my companions lying dead in the howe, sprawled in death as they had been in sleep, their bones stripped of flesh. He had said we would be punished! Sigrith lay among them. I felt a voice deep inside me begin to scream.

It is not real, I told myself. He was only showing me what he could do if he liked. The most dangerous beast is one that is cornered. *And why had he not done it?* I wondered. Was it true Sigrith was our shield? If so, would she still be if this night did not pass as I sensed it must? No, the spirit must leave or we would never leave. Sigrith had said it that first night: the other mounds were empty. This one should be too. He had been called. He knew this night ended Yule. But did he realize what I suspected, that after this night he would be free of the Hunt that relentlessly called him to join their ranks? Free forever.

The Hunt was leaving the world. That was what I had read from all that was happening. That was why they beckoned so fiercely. Thorir had told me that one world was ending and another beginning. Paul had, too. The old powers were waning, departing, but they were not yet gone, and if they left and he remained, only then realizing it was too late—

This was what I kept hidden from him behind the same door he'd blown through so easily twice before. I was not sure for a moment that I was strong enough to do it, but I had no choice.

"Why do you summon me?" he demanded.

I turned my attention to him again. "I wish to know if you can see what comes tomorrow."

He did not respond for such a long time that I thought I had fallen out of the strange place of waking and dreaming.

"You ask two questions."

I had not guarded my thoughts. He was right. There were two. Had he seen them both? I could only hope he had not, for if he had, all my instincts said we were lost.

"I only wish to know if my lord will fail tomorrow," I said, keeping my mind clear.

"It is not all you wish. Do not think to deceive me. You have power, but it is but a faint echo of mine."

"I know it," I said, as I held the door in my mind fast, praying it would prove a sufficient barrier. It was all fumbling in the dark for me that night, all instinct and faith and hope. "But can you see?" I asked, desperately afraid of the answer. I had to be sure!

"Speak your mind or leave me be."

I could feel him prying, unsuccessfully. His anger boiled in my chest, but he did not simply silence me. I was stronger now.

I plunged on. "It is your power to see, just as it is your power to change the winds and make it rain, to dry up a cow's milk and a man's courage, to kindle his heart in anger, to kill the crops before they bear fruit. But you are just, aren't you? You do not punish where you are honoured, where the balance is maintained. Sigrith says that you have given protection to the people who have honoured you for many generations. So you care for the people on the land. It seems to me that providing them a good leader, the best possible leader, would be part of that. I only ask to know, is tomorrow a day of good fortune for my lord?"

Is he a good leader? came the thought. His? Mine?

"My purpose here is not your concern. I have all the powers you speak of, and more. Remember it."

"I have honoured you even though it went against all I believed," I said, silently thanking God for Sigrith. "Now I think you were not worthy."

I braced myself against the outpouring of his anger.

"Where is Ragnar?" I asked and I knew that I had taken him by surprise. "Your friend, Ragnar Lothbrocks. That is who you are, isn't it? The one who slew the dragon with Ragnar. Where is he?"

"Ragnar? How would I know where he has gone? No

man does until he arrives there himself." Tension vibrated like drumbeats. I moved closer to my goal.

"Yes, you see little from here, don't you, buried under the earth as you are? Yet you remain." I knew that I should be wary but the business of that night must be done. "Where has Ragnar gone?" I demanded. "And Sigurd? Do they sit in darkness under the earth? I think not. Their names are spoken of around the fire. They are honoured as they should be. They are remembered. But not yours. Your name is unspoken. Unspoken, that you not be bound."

His anger was mounting again. It might be true that he could not kill me, but he could strike me down again and delay me long enough to keep me from fulfilling my task.

"And yet *you* are bound," I said softly. "Trapped, as we are."

The brooch pulsed on his breast, burning my eyes with its intensity.

"I have honoured you with my presence."

"Honoured me?" I cried. It was what I'd waited for. "You have tormented me! And do not say that you chose to speak with me, for we both know that we were thrust together here, and neither of our own volition."

"I do nothing against my will."

"You *choose* to speak to me, you say, but you know it is not wholly true. I can hear you as you hear me. You speak to me because you must, because someone *else* put me in this place *to hear you speak*. And we must speak because we are alike!"

"Never were two more different!"

"You cannot lie to me." The words flew from my mouth,

as they flew into me from some other source. "You were a dreamer when you lived, when your spirit was still wrapped in flesh. You saw what others did not. You tried with all that was in you to die in battle, for you saw your future! You dreamt it, didn't you?" I cried, my voice a shrill challenge. "You saw you would die in your bed, but nothing beyond that. And you feared that future, for you would have a warrior's death, and a warrior's life after it. Instead, for all your great deeds and your duty to your kin, you achieved this reward. A dark hole in the ground, and no one left to honour you."

"I am no tame Christian ghost! I have no need for gentleness!"

"I know it. You are as pagan as any man ever was, and you have lived here in the darkness, as pagan things do. But the others are gone. You, alone, do not heed the call."

I was sure now. I looked quickly to where my body lay. Yes, I was in that other form.

"What do you know of it?" he howled. I was very aware of all those sleeping around me and of their vulnerability, but if I did not press on now, they would not last the night.

"I know that I listened to names called on the wind," I said, "and did not hear my own, though there was a listener deep within me, in a dark, wild, frightened place I had not known existed, and he yearned to hear his name, my name. But that was not my path. I do not know how I would have resisted if it had been."

"I will remain here forever."

I had no choice.

"You cannot. Your honour here has dried up. You must find it elsewhere." I took a deep breath. "*Hakon of Orkney*, it is time to leave this place."

I waited for the great storm of fury to strike out at me, at my companions, but it did not come. All that happened was that the light that shone from him, the gold on his breast and the pale blue that shimmered like a cloud before the moon faded like a dying coal. For a moment I thought that I had fallen asleep—or awake—for in those days I was ignorant of such things, novice that I was.

But nothing happened. My eyes searched in the dim light and the shadows were indistinct. Had I done my work simply by naming him? It could not be. I reached out with my mind and I felt him there still.

Along with someone else.

Thorbjorn moved stealthily, stepping carefully around sleeping men. I saw him glance over at me, the sleeping me, lying at the foot of the buttress stone where I had carved the dragon. I thought I looked very young with my hair a tousled mess and my mouth hanging open.

Now Thorbjorn was stepping over someone's legs. He paused when he came to Sigrith, who lay curled on her side, and I felt a sudden thrill of fear. But Thorbjorn only looked at the sleeping girl before stepping over her. Then he was standing over me where I lay, defenseless.

I was awake and asleep. I had stumbled into the method of separating my two halves but I had no idea how to become whole again.

I could only watch while he knelt beside me and reached towards my face. Ah, what a fool I had been! Hakon could not touch me, but Thorbjorn could. Hakon could easily turn his hand to an act he already had a desire to take.

I could see how it would happen. Thorbjorn would cover my mouth and nose with his hand to smother any outcry, and then, if I did not die quickly and quietly enough, he would crush my throat with his experienced hand.

"They will know!" I cried aloud. But Thorbjorn could not hear that voice. And even as I said the words I knew what he would say in the morning. 'The boy died in his sleep. There are a dozen here, at least, who could have done it. Perhaps it was your nasty ghost, or perhaps the pup died of fear.' Knowing Thorbjorn he would even find a way to use it to his benefit. And I would be dead.

But if I died … I did not know if I had succeeded in my efforts with Hakon. I did not even know if my instincts had told me true! I could not die. Not yet.

But I could not move either. Not in either form, and so I watched as hands lowered down over my face. I could almost feel their warmth, almost smell him. I watched as he began to murder me and I wondered that I did not love life enough to spring back into my body, to leap up, to shout, to roll away, to somehow save myself!

Willing it was not enough. The spirit was right. I had overstepped. Now I would watch myself die.

The thundering struck like a summer squall, with no warning. It pounded in my heart and in my head, like a hammer on an anvil, like a thousand hammers beating out a thousand swords.

I cowered instinctively, but even as I was curling my spirit form into a ball to protect myself from the deluge,

I saw that Thorbjorn was unmoved. He still bent over me, his hand now on my mouth, his elbow pressed against my chest. He did not hear it! I marveled that he could be so oblivious to the storm that had descended upon us, for now the hounds were baying and horses shrieked and voices screamed, but Thorbjorn was like an old man whose ears no longer know the world. I waited there to learn what death was like, to see what would happen to me when my other self was no more.

And so it was that I saw the Hunt in all its terrible glory. Two nights it had passed with me lacking the courage to look fully upon it. Now my eyes lifted up from my killer's back and they were transfixed.

The walls of Orkahaugr had dissolved. I stood under a black sky strung with beads of white fire and the host that bore down on us, glowing a pale, unearthly blue, and all tearing madly towards the open space where the mound had been.

The dead rode with a senseless oblivion, intent only on their wild spinning across the sky. The stampede of horses and riders and hounds crashed all around me, hooves pounding, riders howling in their grief and their exultation, dogs baying in their rampant pursuit. They trampled the air around me and then wheeled sharply into the sky like a flock of silver birds.

My mind began to bend under the Hunt's appalling splendor.

And then it was gone, but for one form that dwarfed all others. The Leader rode a horse the colour of starlight, as beautiful as it was dreadful. It had eight legs instead of

four and each was taller than a man. It filled the space between the eight great standing stones of the mound. When
it reared up, its hooves sparkled like shooting stars as they
thrashed at the air. All I could see of its rider was his great
arm as he waved it across the sky, shouting a command.

With such grace that it seemed a caress, one shining hoof
hit Thorbjorn square in the head and he dropped like a
stone onto my inert form.

The voice that roared out from above made me whimper.
"You would let my servant be slaughtered by one such as
this?"

I remembered the feeling like wings brushing against the
back of my head the first night in the mound. I knew how
I had been protected.

"Your servant?" cried Hakon. His voice which had so
overwhelmed me before was a pale reflection of that other
voice. "He does not worship you. He does not even believe
in you!"

"I do," I whispered. "I wish I did not, but I do."

The Hunt swirled above like banners streaming in the
wind, like stars dancing.

The Leader turned his one fiery eye on me. I was forced
to look away.

"You have heard my whispered words in your heart," he
said in a voice not kind and yet not pitiless. "You have
served me well and received your reward," he said.

I did not know what he meant, not then. "I thank you,
my ..." I began.

The god Odin threw back his head, his beard shaking,
and laughed at me. He reminded me, fleetingly, of my fa-

ther. "You keep your old ways," he said. "It is well. You are doubly blessed, twice-gifted."

Then he turned to pin Hakon with his one-eyed gaze. "Now I will take what is mine."

"I am not yours."

"But you *are*!" cried Odin. "You do not choose me! I choose you!"

"You have said so these many years," cried Hakon, defiantly, "and yet here I remain! Do you come to offer me a place at your table? Am I to enter the Great Hall?"

"Your duty here is done. You spoke for the land in the days when men had ears to hear you. But no more. You know it! They turn from you, as they turn from me. The horizon beckons us both."

"I will remain here for all time and I will be honoured, if the land must bleed for it! You thought to take that from me, didn't you? You thought to strip me of even that honour, but you will not. Even your boy honours me! And these men who sleep here like animals in a byre, they fear me and that is near as good as honouring me." Hakon had risen to his full height as he spoke, certainty growing with every word to meet the gaze of Odin.

His voice rose, victoriously, "And your servant, he has not served you so well. He has bound me here, the little fool! Oh yes! He has called my name and bound me under the mound forever. Call me all you will. I am invulnerable."

Odin stared back with his one eye. I wondered then, for a flashing instant if I had done wrong. Hakon was all defiance and pride and he did not flinch.

Then Odin threw back his head and howled, and I thought that I would not hear another sound again in my life. That cry was greater even than the one my own spirit had sent up on the first night in the howe. But when I looked up at the god I saw that he did not cry out in anger or grief. No, the Allfather, Thorir's lord of poetry and of war, his savior, howled with pleasure.

"You were ever an arrogant one, Hakon, always above your place, always too proud, too certain that you knew all and others knew nothing, always doubting their good faith." I could feel, as if it were happening to me, Odin's eye boring into Hakon. "Do you imagine I do not know why you deny my call? Do you think I do not hear your thoughts, your heart? I have drunk from the well of Mimir. I gave an eye for wisdom yet I see further than any man, living or dead. You think Malcolm has bound you here?" Laughter battered me like blows.

"Look upon him. He is a *good* servant. He follows the path laid out for him, though it was not the one he desired. He bound you. He did. As he was meant to! For he bound you not to this place of stone and earth as you think! When Malcolm spoke your name it was not in the dust of his body, but clothed in his spirit. You are freed of the mound. Nay," he laughed joyously, "you are expelled from it! You have fought the power of the river long enough. It is time to be carried into the sea."

Odin glowed so fiercely I could see nothing else. I could not deny him. No one could have. Not even Hakon. I could not see Hakon. I wondered for a moment if he had vanished.

He had not, but he was changed, transformed, his defiance and rage shed like an old skin.

I strained to hear him, for the din of the Hunt had come closer again, trampling the air above my head so close that I crouched involuntarily.

"My lord," said Hakon, "all my days I served you and all for the honour of sitting in your Hall one day. But you did not take me. I awoke here and I was neither dead nor living. And here I stayed, and did my duty well. For all those many generations of my children I did my duty. And they honoured me, some more, some less. But all things end, do they not? So I waited for you. And then you came, with these," he said, waving at the heavens, "and offered me an eternity of riding the waves of the skies, a spirit torn from its reason, its honour. Some think it a glory but it is not what I deserve! I served you well, my lord. I long for the company of my equals, for the Battlefield and the Feasthall. I will not go elsewhere."

Odin's answer was a whisper. "You think this boy weak, but he took the path he feared and he has become a man."

"Will you promise me?" Hakon persisted, pleading. It was terrible to hear.

"I will not. You will know your fate when you heed my call." That was a father speaking to a son, brooking no argument.

"Who will take my place?"

"Your place will be filled."

There was a long space of silence, then, "I will obey."

"Bring a mount!" cried the god and a silver stallion with flashing eyes screamed as he dropped from the sky to hover just above the ground where Hakon stood, smaller now than he had been in his defiance, but taller than two men nonetheless. I was forgotten as the rallying cry for the Hunt was sounded and the din roiled up once more and dug like knives into my skull.

Hakon swung himself onto the broad back of the un-earthly horse and I saw sudden joy spark on his face. The uncanny beast pranced in place, all icy fire and turmoil, and Hakon laughed with an exultation that spilled into me as his rage once had. I longed to follow him, to know that joy forever. We were one in that moment. And in the next I could feel him drawing away.

"But I am not gone yet!" he cried to me.

Now he will punish me, came the fleeting thought.

But it was not that. He looked down upon me. "Only now do I see how you have served me." His form lost substance even as it grew brighter, glowing and wavering like moonlight. There was no threat in him now. He was like a warrior going to battle, already halfway there. "I see now what will come tomorrow. You will serve well here in my place."

In my place? He *was* going to punish me.

He gave a great shout of mirth. "Ah, this night is not only for *my* fate!"

I trembled. I had done my duty. They had both said so. Was this what I had earned? Was I to replace Hakon under the mound?

Odin spoke, amusement in his voice. "No, that is not your path. You will serve above the earth as Hakon did beneath it. The land requires a new voice, one the leader of the land will be able to hear. But Malcolm, before you can be that voice, your honour must be intact. You know of what I speak."

I did. I bowed to acknowledge the truth of it.

Then Hakon spoke to me, with something nearing benevolence. It was as overwhelming as his rage had been. "And so you came here to disturb me and leave as my heir. My treasure is yours. You will find it at the feet of the god," he said with a laugh. "For one who has seen so far you should understand."

Behind him Sleipnir reared up, four of his eight legs kicking out at the air, just above my head, and he let out a piercing scream that rang out from the mound to resound across the isles of Orkney, across the world.

"Hakon!" cried Odin, his voice ringing above the din, and Hakon's steed writhed with desire to be gone, tossing his mane and tail. Hakon's brooch flashed blindingly and I cried out.

And then they were gone. All the spirits of the Hunt and Hakon, too.

The night sky was alive with light and the land spread out beneath it, at peace, at rest. Snow glittered on the ground and water shimmered. The silence was complete.

I tested voice and ear with a whisper. "I do not know what my reward is." Then I knew that I was alone for there was no answering voice. It was done. My purpose there was fulfilled.

The walls of the howe encircled me again. How like a dream it was, to stand there alone in the mound of Hakon while my companions slept, oblivious to all that had transpired. How like a dream, already grown pale as dreams do when they are over, and yet it was more real than anything I had ever known.

I was suddenly incredibly weary and I found myself returned to my place by the wall with Thorbjorn lying across my legs. He had tried to kill me. The nape of his neck was exposed. If I wanted to I could take my knife, the one meant for carving wood, and I could cut into that flesh. Harald would be free of his poisonous influence, and so would I. Had he not tried to take my life? Would he not try again?

Hate flared in me then, and rage for all that he had done to me, for the way he pushed Harald to be more like Thorbjorn himself, more like Margaret and the Vikings who were his ancestors.

I felt around and found my knife. I stared at his neck, the bare skin so vulnerable. Then he moaned and moved, pulling himself off of me. His eyes were unfocused and he did not see me. I do not think he even knew where he was. He pulled his cloak around him and curled up like a child on the floor.

And I lay down my knife and my head and fell into sleep like a stone falling into the depths of the sea. ⊕

PART 3

30

"Malcolm."

A hand rested warm on my arm. I slowly opened my eyes and immediately shut them again against the dazzling light. My head thundered with the most enormous headache I'd ever had. I blinked a few times, then squinted up at Sigrith. Her hair was lit from behind like gossamer

Light streamed down from the roof of Orkahaugr in angled shafts filled with spinning dust motes. Weaker beams crept down the tunnel, casting the standing stones pale gold.

Harald stood in the middle of the chamber shaking his head in child-like wonderment.

I would tell him everything that day. Odin had been right. My honour was not intact. I knew that I might ruin all my prospects by confessing so late, but it didn't matter. Whatever Harald did with me, I could not let that day end without disclosing everything. For all I knew his whole future might hinge on it.

I would speak to him as we made our way to Firth. Already my heart felt lighter.

There was no food left, only melted snow to wet our

mouths. A runner had already been sent to Hamna Voe with orders for the ships to sail around to the bay at Firth. Two others were leaving to gather the rest of the men from their billets. Almost everyone else was already waiting outside, extremely happy, I was sure, to be out under the sky again.

Sigrith was busy at the fire. I started to tell her to come along, that this particular fire did not need to be kept alive any longer, but then I saw what she was doing. She had gathered up all the bits and scraps we'd discarded and was heaping them on our temporary hearth. Of course. She would purify Orkahaugr of our presence as best she could. But if Hakon was gone, did it matter? A quick inner check told me he was. I began to tell her, but realized we were not alone. Thorbjorn was still there, leaning up against the wall, watching her.

She took no notice of him and when she looked up at me I saw that there was only one thought in her mind. She knew. Somehow she knew.

So why did she take such care of the fire? Looking around at those ancient walls I had my answer. For whomever had built the place, long before Hakon had ever set foot on the shores of Orkney. She did the right thing. It was always good to honour a man. *Or a woman,* I thought, as I watched her.

Thorbjorn hadn't moved, nor had he spoken. He might have become one of the stones, but for the gleam in his eye. I got up with some difficulty—my bones and even my skin seemed to ache—and walked past him to the entrance of the tunnel. He did not look at me. Did he remember that he'd tried to kill me? Did he know how close I'd come to killing him?

Someone outside called my name. *I'll be there soon enough,* I thought.

Again they called and I answered, rather peevishly, that I was coming. The world seemed determined to keep me endlessly moving. Sigrith was done with the fire. She gathered up Thorir's and her things and took one last look around her before ducking into the tunnel. I turned for a final look as well.

It looked different with the light of day shining in it. Wrong, somehow. The hole would have to be mended. I knew I would never see the inside of Orkahaugr again, knew it with that sureness I was only beginning to understand. I would never enter the place again, but a part of me would never leave it.

But what was Thorbjorn doing? He had gone to kneel by the fire. All I could see was that he had his horn in his hand. Had he lost something? Was he paying some last respects in utter contradiction to his character? Perhaps the events of the night had actually affected him.

Whatever it was, I did not care. I would not fear him any longer. He must have felt me standing there but he never glanced my way, even when someone shouted my name again through the hole in the roof. Grumbling, I bent to shuffle my way out of the howe.

Immediately my arm went up to shield my eyes against the intense blue and searing white of the landscape. It was a moment before I could see anything more. Then, to the south, I saw men approaching. Sigrith ran towards them. I recognized Olaf as he warmly embraced his daughter.

They got here quickly, I thought. The runner had only just left. I watched as Olaf fussed over his child with a multitude of questions.

"Malcolm!" I heard again, from above.

"I'm coming!" I said, between a grumble and a shout, and then began a clumsy scramble up the steep slope of the mound, wishing that whoever demanded my presence didn't also insist on making me climb to find them.

I was irritated and wet when I reached the top, for I had fallen twice, but it seemed the urgent matter had grown less so because no one even looked at me when I reached them. They stood in a cluster, all talking at once. Then Angus saw me and, with a strange look on his face, beckoned me over.

At first I could not believe my eyes. I simply stood rooted to the ground, not sure if I was going to laugh or cry.

Sitting on one of the stones that had been pried loose from the mound was Thorir. He was just fastening his cloak about his shoulders and he looked as though he had just gotten up from his sleep like the rest of us.

But not like the rest of us. And not like himself either. He smiled at me and I knew that he was … returned, but in a way that none of the others would ever understand. Perhaps not in a way I could either. But he was not mad, if he ever had been, of that much I was certain.

But he is touched with a new colour, I thought, *one that few men have even seen.*

"We thought you were dead," Eyolf was saying. "Where the hell did you go?"

"Let us say I was well-hosted," answered Thorir with his familiar wink.

There was a barrage of questions, but his answers were elusive and it was not long before the questions dried up. *More quickly than they should have,* I thought. Everyone was clearly happy to have him back, and yet they soon began to drift away. Perhaps they thought he teased them, withholding the truth so that he might save it to make into a tale later on.

But that was not it and I knew it. They could sense the change in him too. *They do not want to know. They will happily forget what they can of what has happened here. They will accept his story full of gaps rather than hear it whole.*

And I could not blame them. The sun shone now. That other world was far off. I would have joined them in forgetting if I could.

Thorir and I were alone. He did not speak. There was such a stillness about him that the questions brimming in my mind stopped when they reached my tongue. A half-smile played on his face. I followed the direction of his gaze.

The land spread out in low swells, pearly white and dazzling where the sun shone, silver-blue where the gradual hills cast their shadows. Every shade of blue was displayed there, in the shimmering ripples of the lochs and in the sky, naked and pure with its heavy shroud gone. Even the standing stones in their circles wore purplish hues.

Three days I had been in Orkney, and this was the first time I had set eyes on the land itself. At least *these* eyes, for the land spread out before me was the land of my dream.

I glanced at Thorir. He was not taking in the view. He had been looking intently at one thing all along. The Odin Stone.

There was a mystery there still. But not one that would be solved that day.

A voice called. We were departing.

I stood to go. Thorir caught me by the sleeve. "You look a little the worse for wear, my friend." It was the first thing he'd said to me.

"I am well enough," I said, which was a lie because I had never felt more wretched, "though my hosting was not all that gentle."

He gave a short laugh. That was the most I ever told him about the events of that night—for some reason the words always failed to come when I tried to tell him more—but in that moment I sensed he knew more than I could have told. And I understood why he'd answered the others as he had. I understood that Thorir and I were different, and that we would both be set apart all our days for our difference.

We made our way down the steep slope of the mound.

"But how did you know we were here?" Harald was asking Olaf.

"Well, we were told, of course," answered Olaf, puzzled. "Last night. You sent him, did you not? I mean, I thought it was odd, him being there again, but also that you would send him, in particular, and in the storm again, and—"

"What are you babbling about?" demanded Thorbjorn, and received the coldest look I'd seen Sigrith deliver in the three days I'd known her. He was oblivious.

"The old man," answered Olaf, his enthusiasm undeterred. "He said we'd find you here at midday. Said not to go sooner, but midday. So here we are and here you are too and—"

Thorbjorn cut him off again. "We didn't send any old men. I want to know who he is. When we're done here I'm going to find him and teach him a lesson."

Thorir smiled placidly. "Thorbjorn, you'll find him one day, I'm sure, but I doubt you'll be the one doing the teaching."

I thought Thorbjorn turned a shade paler than usual. Was that a flicker of recognition of a memory returning? Most likely he thought it was all a dream. That was the pity of it. If he had been able to admit what had happened it might have made all the difference.

"Well, whoever he was, he had it right," said Harald. "We seem to have slept the morning away. I'm not sure how that happened, but we must make up the time as best we can. Ready yourselves."

He was right, I realized, gauging the sun, which was just nearing its zenith. I shivered. It was no accident that we had slept so long.

Was anything an accident? Or was it all bound, as the land and sky and sea were bound up in a constant dance, beyond sight, beyond comprehension, but there nonetheless? The strands of the web, Margaret had called it. *But she has only seen part of that web,* I thought. *Only a very small part.* Already I knew more than she, and there was much yet to learn.

Harald was invigorated and eager to be off. He took no time to dwell on why we had all slept so late. He was on to the remedy for it. I was certain this remedy was one I could live with, though he gave no sign.

Sigrith stood with her father, who was looking both relieved and excited. He was going with us. "Malcolm," she said, "may I have a word before you go?"

I felt my ears go red. I followed her a short distance from the others who were having a laugh at my expense.

"I will see you again," she said. It was not a question.

I nodded.

She hesitated. I had not seen her look uncertain before. It was rather charming. She leaned close. "Malcolm," she whispered. "Will you tell me his name?"

I shook my head in wonder and I told it to her.

"Yes," she said with a satisfied nod. "It is as I dreamed. You freed him. Thank you, Malcolm. Now we will care for ourselves and look to God for help."

As she smiled at me I could not help but notice that her eyes were the same colour as the winter sky. She grinned, then took my face in her hands. She kissed me and was gone.

I watched until she disappeared behind a low hill. I turned to find Thorir waiting with a broad smile on his face. I shrugged, feeling prouder and happier than I had ever thought to feel. The others were already off, Harald in the lead and setting an eager pace, by the looks of it. Thorir and I followed, falling into step with each other like an old habit.

The sun, weak as it was, felt good on my back, but exhaustion from the night's events was sinking into my bones. I would be glad when the day was done. When this day was done! The whole purpose of coming had yet to unfold! After all that had happened, we had still not done what we had come to do.

And I still had to speak to Harald. But what would I tell him? The entire story all at once or what I thought he needed to know this day? Could I tell him of my dreams and vardens? Hardly. I must sort that out myself first, for I no longer had any doubt that my dreams meant something. I glanced over at Thorir. He might be able to help. But Eyolf and Haermund and Simon were running nearby. I couldn't speak of such things in front of them.

And what should I ask him? Harald was the eagle but the boar still eluded me. He must be someone I didn't suspect, someone adept at keeping hidden. Was that not the essence of the boar, to be secretive, skulking, deadly dangerous? So I should suspect someone I was not inclined to suspect? Just once it would be very nice for something to come easily! I looked at the men trotting along before me and around me. Even if I knew which of them was the boar, did I know what he was going to do? Better, did I know what I was meant to do?

A wave of weariness passed over me, bringing doubts. It was hopeless. I sucked in a deep breath of fresh air. It was good to be outside again, above the earth rather than under it. I had survived unbelievable events. I must have faith. I would find out soon enough what I was meant to do. Of that I could be sure. I plunged on through the snow feeling moderately better.

Our shadows lengthened and faded as the sun dipped behind a hill. The day was hurrying to a close already. We'd slept the better part of it away. Only an hour or two of good light remained. Smoke rose in black smudges from the backs of hillsides where farmhouses hid. We avoided them. It was not easy to know who was a friend and who might send out a runner to reach Erlend before us and spoil our plans. *Harald's plans,* I thought with relief, *not Thorbjorn's.* My need to speak to Harald nagged at me but he was far ahead. *When we stop,* I promised myself.

From Stenness to Firth is not a long way but it seemed so to me that day. When we arrived at a farmhouse, which Olaf insisted belonged to a man loyal to the earl, I was so exhausted I could only drag myself, head pounding, chest wheezing, to a bench beside the door. Harald and his lieutenants had already gone inside. *When he comes out again,* I told myself, *I will speak to him.*

"Drink this," said Thorir, handing me buttermilk he had charmed from the farmer's wife. "You look like you need it."

I drank gratefully.

"The time for rest will come," he said, stretching his legs out before him. "Not yet, but it will come. Now is the time for living stories. Later will be the time for telling them." His smile was the one he reserved for the pleasure of annoying me.

We sat in silence.

Soon Harald and his lieutenants emerged from the farmhouse looking pleased.

"The farmer here drank Yule with Erlend two nights ago," he announced. "We are close," he said, his eyes glittering. He was off without delay. His exuberance and my exhaustion were conspiring to keep me from him.

I got up to follow. My heart beat high and fast in my chest. The reason I'd been sent north was coming to pass. The others were almost jubilant in their anticipation. Their high spirits fueled me in the last leg of our journey.

And yet something dragged at me as well. I thought it might be my physical weariness, but when I thought back later, I realized it was more than that. Harald was leading us and leading with a plan that I was quite sure would be both moral and wise and that was very good. Yet something was not right.

I was both surprised and relieved when we stopped only a few minutes later.

"My cousin is in the house on the other side of this rise," Harald said in a voice just loud enough to carry. "Listen well. We will surely outnumber him and I do not want him to think we are attacking, so half of you will remain here. I will enter the house as a guest. To talk."

There was some buzzing among the men. Those who had quartered with the farmers did not know of the Thing. I wondered what they had been expecting.

"My cousin and I will speak," he said, "man to man."

"And if he comes out with sword drawn?" asked Angus, with a quick look at Thorbjorn.

Harald shook his head. "We will not shed blood today. Do you all hear me? I will knock at this door in peace, and will do all I can to persuade Erlend to sit down and make a new arrangement. None of you must do anything to provoke violence. You will be ready to meet it, to defend yourselves, if Erlend chooses to fight, but only then.

"I will not bloody my hands to regain Orkney. Any who disobey me in this, except in defense of his life, will be stripped of all his wealth and banished from my lands. I will not bend on that point."

There was a new authority in Harald where there had been hesitation. I saw the others take note of it. There were some raised brows, for there are always men who prefer bloodshed to peace, but no protests. And I noted with satisfaction that men like Angus and Haermund and Eirik, who had been swayed away from their hearts in the mound were now in accord with him.

Thorbjorn had not moved throughout Harald's speech. This I knew, for I had watched him closely.

And so I saw what the others had not. He had stood immobile as a standing stone while Harald spoke, but his face had slowly, almost imperceptibly come to life as a certain string of words were pronounced. When the earl had said *I will not bloody my hands*, something shifted within Thorbjorn's whole body. The power of motion returned to the big blonde warrior as he turned to look at his foster-son with a new light in his face.

I knew then that my lord's fate was not yet certain. ❧

31

put not thy trust in the first sown fruit,
nor in the son unproven;
weather undoes one, unwisdom the other,
and both are subject to fate.

~WISDOM OF ODIN~

*I*n the days since I had betrayed Earl Harald by keeping secrets from him I had always managed to find myself a good reason not to confess what I knew. All such reasons evaporated now. I had left it too long. *Something was wrong.* I could feel it in my guts and in the part of me that had come alive in the mound. I was a fool in the ways of the world, the world of politics and war and power. Harald was not. I saw it now. What I had not been able to sort out he might have.

And now it was too late.

"Earl Harald," I said, forcing my way to his side.

"Yes? Oh, you'll stay here, Malcolm."

"I know. But I need to speak to you. Now."

"What is it? Quickly. The sun will set all too soon."

"Alone," I insisted.

Harald was not pleased. He was impatient to be off, but he assented. "What is so important?" he demanded when I had him far enough away from the others. "There is no room for delay now, Malcolm."

His impatience rushed me and as I tried to begin the long, twisted story the words jammed in my throat. My faith that it would come together when it needed to failed me. There was no time to explain it sufficiently and giving him half the picture would do more harm than good. I cursed my stupidity. But I had to say something. He had to know that I felt treachery afoot. He had to be on his guard.

"My lord, you will hear more about this later, but at the moment I will just ask that you trust me. I have withheld information from you, not with any intent to do harm, but now is not the time explain in detail. What you must know is that something is amiss here. Something is …"

I must have sounded ridiculous to him. And yet he waited.

"The man in your mother's chamber, the young man. I believe he has been here. I believe he was at Olaf's the day before we arrived. He was the one seeking Erlend."

Harald's eyes narrowed. "What exactly do you know of this?"

My face burned with frustration. "All I know is that he was here and that your mother has a hand in it and that she has aims that you do not know of."

He gave me a look of suppressed exasperation. "Malcolm, my mother always has aims I do not know of. You are exhausted and not making sense. But consider me forewarned. You can tell me the rest tomorrow." He took the sting from his words by patting me on the shoulder before turning away.

I had to say it. I knew what might happen if I did, but I had to tell him.

"Wait," I called.

He stopped and looked back at me, his brows raised with

barely suppressed exasperation.

"Don't kill Erlend," I said. "You must not kill him." Men were watching. I knew Margaret's ears might be listening, but I felt nothing but relief at finally having told him what I should have told him at the start.

He looked at me for a long moment. "Did I not just say there would be no bloodshed today?"

I nodded.

"Thank you, Malcolm," he said, and he strode back to the others.

"We go," he said to Thorbjorn.

"I will take up the rear," Thorbjorn answered.

Harald's chin jerked defensively. Thorbjorn had always insisted on being at his side. "Just in case Erlend is not as eager for peace as you are," he added mildly. To Haermund, who was in charge of those who stayed behind, he said, "Remain at the ready, and if you hear anything untoward, come quickly rather than quietly." He crooked a brow at Harald to ask if the order met his approval.

"You will come in with me to meet with Erlend." It sounded a little too near a question for my liking, but Thorbjorn simply agreed and Harald gave a curt nod to his foster-father and another to Haermund and then he was gone, flanked by Eirik and Benedikt.

The western sky was filled with red clouds like lines of breakers on an otherworldly sea. Any sailor will say a red night sky is a good omen, but that night I shivered at how it bathed the men in its light as, one by one, they disappeared behind the hill.

Thorir widened his eyes at me as he passed.

Thorbjorn was nearby, waiting for the last of the men to pass him. Simon stood beside him. That struck me as strange. I realized I'd never actually seen the two of them together, at least not alone. For some reason I'd always assumed they disliked each other.

Now Simon took a step away from Thorbjorn and I could no longer see him, for Thorbjorn stood between us. But Simon was speaking and I suddenly had the most intense desire to hear what he was saying. I went closer. Still I could not see or hear him. He stood in Thorbjorn's shadow.

There was a ringing in my ears. I saw the great shadow in my dream sweep across the sky, black wings concealing that other form, the threat I'd felt nearby. One darkness hiding another.

Simon was the boar. The rest of it did not matter. I stood, rooted, as the implications of my dream engulfed me.

The two were disappearing around the side of the hill as I recovered myself. I knew what I must do. The instant Haermund turned his back, I slipped away.

The hill was not high but it was broad, part of a series of hills that, in the falling light, cast dark shadows to blacken the path before me. A few times I feared I might have lost my way, but I kept the solid darkness of the hill to my right and hoped that the scent of smoke or a glimpse of a companion, even an unfriendly one, would guide me.

A shadow separated from the darkness. I saw Marjory in the blackberry patch, the boar skulking in wait, ready to sink his tusks into her young flesh. I saw them as I had in my dream all those years ago.

My dirk was already drawn and hidden behind my

thigh.

"What are you doing here?" Simon hissed.

Thorbjorn must have gone ahead. Whatever he was about, there might still be time if I could get past Simon. "I must speak to the earl," I answered.

"You have done quite enough of that," he said, moving closer.

Paul had told me his great mistake was to assume Margaret thought as he did. Simon would not believe me innocent. He was a plotter, a conniver, a sneaking, skulking boar. He would think all others were as tricky as he was. He was not stupid. And I was not capable of lying as he did.

I stepped back. There was still a chance. If he thought me innocent and ignorant as I'd surely appeared to be …

"What are you doing here, Simon?"

"If you have to ask me that you confirm my thoughts of you."

It hit me. He knew about my father and about me. Everything was cast in a new light. Simon was a spy.

I had no time to dwell on that. I had to get past him. I took a leap. "Whatever Thorbjorn is planning, it cannot be good. Don't you see that he is corrupt, that he will ruin everything if he has his way?"

It was a moment before he reacted. Then he snorted. "So the oak did not send forth an acorn, but an apple seed. A shame. Yes, Thorbjorn has his little plot which will fit in nicely with mine, but that is all it is, a little plot."

Suddenly he darted forward, quick as a snake, and gripped me by the throat. "You did not keep your bargain," he hissed.

I saw Margaret and Simon by the gate in Wick.

"What did she offer you?" I demanded.

"An earldom," he replied.

I gasped.

He gave a harsh laugh. "Not Orkney, Atholl. Killing Harald to take Orkney for myself is my idea. My cause is my own. At one time I thought you might help me in it, but I see now that I was mistaken—" and with no pause, no warning, light glinted off his blade as it flew at my chest and struck, hard.

But it did not sink into my heart as it was meant to. It struck the amulet dead on, severing it from its thong. I felt it slip down my chest inside my tunic and catch at my belt.

I slashed at him with my dirk. He cursed in surprise. Satisfaction flared in me, but then I was leaping back as his weapon whipped out at me again. Heat seared across my throat. I threw myself against him, and together we rolled to the ground. I landed hard on my side, the snow scraping my cheek where it had frozen to crystals.

The breath had been knocked out of me, but he was quickly on his feet. I tried to push myself up. A sharp kick to the ribs sent me sprawling again. I couldn't move. I lay on my back, gasping for air as he put his toe under my chin and turned my head with it. He grunted with satisfaction.

"Talk all you like," he said. He delivered another well-aimed kick and was gone.

I lay there for what seemed an eternity. Finally I was able to turn over and support myself on hands and knees and then, slowly, get to my feet. The pain in my side was excruciating and, as if in sympathy, the pounding in my head that had gradually subsided during the trek from Stenness had returned in full force. I put my hand to my throat. It came back wet with blood, though the wound did not hurt. It would later, I knew.

I stumbled after Simon, the scent of peat smoke guiding me to a farmhouse nestled in back of the hill. The house stretched to the east in a direct line with the angle of the sun, long and ambling, an old structure added to over generations. The waist-high stone fence that framed the yard did not nestle so closely at the southernmost end, leaving room for a kale yard, where there was the most sunlight. A door on the end of the house led out to it. There would be two more doors, at least, one on each of the long walls of the house.

Harald would be at one of those doors, or he might have already entered the house. I could not tell which. He was nowhere to be seen. Nor was Simon. In fact, there was no sign of anyone, no sound but the wind blowing. I might have gone rushing in, but for the air of secrecy, of waiting, that hovered about the place.

The only movement was of the wind teasing at the smoke as it twisted up from the turf roof. I thought I detected the low murmur of voices coming from inside, but surely not all the men would be in the house, even if Harald was. So where were they?

At the other door, I realized. *The front door.* The hills would let in more light on that side; it would be much less threatening to open the door on a face that could be seen than on shadowy men. For all I knew the murmur of voices might even be the earls talking together.

But where was Simon?

I nearly shouted in surprise as the door at the end of the house opened and a woman stepped out. The orange glow of the hearth-fire and the sound of men's voices carried out into the night for a moment before the door closed.

She moved into the yard. Her gait was slow, as if she were enjoying a moment's respite. She was of middle years, tall and full-figured, her hair neatly bound in a scarf the colour of her apron-like dress. Rust red, like dried blood, with white flowers embroidered down the front. They looked like snowdrops.

I did not move. Startling her would send her running into the house, raising the alarm.

I sensed a presence at the back door of the house. There was a slight movement and the black dragon cut across my vision. Flames belched from his mouth and lit the world on fire. I knew that presence. Thorbjorn. He had not forgotten something in the howe. He had been scooping a coal into his horn. Thorbjorn, with his foolproof touchwood. He was going to burn the house down around Erlend's ears.

The house would be smoky already, with the fire that burned on the hearth. It would take a few minutes before those inside knew what was happening. Did he mean to block the door that they might not escape? But the door to the yard was unguarded. Was the plan really to burn them all alive or just to start a melee? Surely someone would look up and they would see that the thatch above their heads was alight, and they would know they were under attack, and they would, naturally, run out the doors of the house.

Out the back door they would meet Thorbjorn, who would cut down the men who meant nothing to him in order to get to the one he wanted to kill. And if Erlend went out the other door? Swords are drawn in an instant. Peaceful intentions or no, the fight would be on.

Thorbjorn had accepted Harald's plan because it mattered not. He followed his own plan.

My eyes were on the woman as she knelt to knock snow off a head of kale. Thorbjorn still hovered low by the door. She was turning to go back into the house. She would be inside when the fire was lit. Would the men save her or would they trample her in their urgency to get out and engage the enemy?

A faint glow hinted from where Thorbjorn hid, then was gone. The coal. In a moment it would meet his touchwood and be bursting into flame. The need to find Harald screamed in me. Simon had said Thorbjorn's plan helped his.

What was that plan?

Thorbjorn was waiting for the woman to return inside. She would go in, he would light the fire and the battle would begin.

Where was Simon? What should I do? I could wait for Thorbjorn to act or—

"Fire!" I shouted, leaping up. "Run! Fire! Fire!"

The woman's hands flew to her mouth, her eyes went wide with terror. She screamed, piercingly, then caught up her skirts and fled into the house, slamming the door behind her.

The door where Thorbjorn had been hiding flew open,

spilling out men. I saw his face as they came for him. He was grim, ready, focused. His sword flashed and I heard him shout furiously and then I was running around the end of the kale yard towards the front of the house.

I rounded the end of the yard in time to see men swarm out the other door. Harald leaned against the house within feet of the door, his sword sheathed. Ofram, Angus and Eyolf were fending off any who came near. But Harald was not standing quietly by. He was shouting one word loudly over and over. "Erlend! Erlend! Erlend!" The only answer to his cries was the clash of swords and men grunting and cursing.

There was no sign of Simon.

The doorway was clear. Harald ducked his head in and back out again as a man charged out at him. He parried the man's blows easily, then stepped back to give his bodyguard room to manoeuver. Angus quickly dispatched the man.

It was almost completely dark. A dozen battling men blocked my view of the earl. I edged along the fence to keep him in sight.

The last rays from the dying sun ran flat along the ground and shone directly in my eyes so that as hard as I squinted to catch sight of Harald, all I saw were haloes dancing around the shadowy forms of the men who fought between us. The fighters no longer looked like men. They swung their arms and their weapons gleamed in the fading light but their bodies were distorted. It was not just that they blurred. They were changed, taking on new forms entirely. Familiar forms.

I rubbed my eyes and then jerked my hands away. They were sticky with blood. I looked down to see blood staining the length of my tunic. Even the ground was dark with it. *Simon has killed me,* I thought as my hand went instinctively to my throat, but I felt none of the fear I should have. It was what I saw before me that made my knees go weak. I clutched at the stone fence.

It has happened, I thought. *I have gone mad. I have died and found the gates of hell.*

For it was a hellish sight I beheld indeed. The men were gone and in their places bears and stags, bulls and foxes, wolves and hawks, and all manner of other beasts, cavorted in the failing light amid men's cries and the clash of weapons. It was a hideous dance, a nightmare. I covered my eyes with my bloody hands and felt my strength ebbing away.

I looked again and a shaft of light seared my eyes, momentarily blinding me. The beasts were still there, but now they were not alone. From the corner of my eye I saw the men too and how the ghostly beasts danced about them, like wisps of fog contorted on the wind, like clouds of breath on a winter day. I saw Ofram and a bear loomed at his side. By Angus a powerful stag kept watch, by Thorir, a dun horse.

The pale gold horse I had seen once before.

The last of my strength was leaving me. What was I meant to do? I saw their vardens, but *why*?

I must reach Harald. I moved further along the wall. It was all shadows. Where was he? Then I saw the ethereal form of an eagle soaring above the house and knew Harald had to be just below it.

But where was the boar? I shoved my hand down the front of my tunic and found the amulet. The prayer I sent heavenward was wordless. I squeezed the tiny boar, hoping desperately.

From the corner of my eye I saw a darkened dragon sweep around the end of the house as Thorbjorn came tearing across the foot-churned snow, his face flooded with rage as his eyes frantically searched the scene.

He saw Simon at the same time I did. He knew now, too. But then two men fell on Thorbjorn with their swords and he was fighting for his life, his dragon varden twisting black above him.

Few with a dragon spirit have the strength to overcome the darkness of it. I felt an inexplicable pang even as I swung back to see Harald step into the doorway. A man sat at a table inside. He gestured, an invitation. There was no threat in it. Harald took another step.

And so did Simon.

"Harald!" I screamed, but my voice came out a whisper. A fresh trickle of hot blood ran down my chest.

Harald moved further into the house and Simon went in behind him, reaching for the door with one hand. In the other he held his knife. The door closed. Then all I could see was their vardens.

I cried out then, as loudly as I could, but my voice was gone and my strength with it. Simon had done his work well. I clung to the wall like a burr, even as I felt myself slipping to the ground.

The flutter of wings stirred my hair. A dark form dropped to the wall beside me and a hideous cry rang out, raven's song, a death knell. I had failed to save the earl.

The raven cocked its head and peered into my eyes. Then

it opened its beak wide and let out another volley of strident cries. The defiance in that black eye screamed into my heart.

I clutched the amulet so tightly it bit into my fingers. I sent up a prayer into the night sky and then I followed it.

"Simon!" I screamed, but it was not the voice I'd always known to be mine that echoed resoundingly against the hillsides. This voice was as deep as thunder and as angry. It belonged to the part of me that woke in dreams and spoke with spirits and gods. It was incandescent, flowing and pure, golden. Voice and spirit rose up into the sky and I dropped down onto the murderous boar that was Simon of Atholl.

• • •

The next thing I remember is a green sky scattered with stars of blue and gold and brilliant white. The sky became a field of hardy grass, sprinkled with a multitude of flowers.

My shadow lay across a tall, broad stone. Through the hole in one side of it I could see low, gentle hills rolling away towards the sea.

Sigrith wore a blue gown over soft white and a blue scarf over her hair, so that only wisps of pale gold danced in the wind around her face. She smiled at me and I smiled back. Then I took a knife and I thrust it into the earth at the base of the stone.

The sun shone over my shoulder and into the rich earth I had exposed. When I moved and my shadow fell across the hole. The light hidden in the earth did not diminish. It burned, golden and glittering. I put my hands into the earth and drew out the sun. ⊕

32

not great things alone must one give to another,
thanks often comes for small gifts:
with half a loaf and a half-drained cup,
i have found me many a friend.

~WISDOM OF ODIN~

I awoke in a world of flickering firelight and warmth and far off voices. I did not know where I was, only that I was at peace.

A face bent over me. *Thorir*, I thought. In some wonderful dream Thorir had returned.

But it was not Thorir. It was Harald.

"We thought you were done for," he said.

I stared at him, trying to remember something, something important.

"Simon!" I gasped.

"I know," he said, with a hand on my chest. "Rest."

Was it all a dream? I wondered, looking around me at the unfamiliar room. *It must have been.* Then, as my eyes began to close again they fell on a woman's back and when she turned I saw the white flowers trailing down the front of her rust-red dress.

"Rest," said a voice and I obeyed.

• • •

From the light that spilled in through the door when it opened, I guessed it was morning. The door closed again and the room was illuminated more gently by the fire and a few oil lamps. From the bench near the fire where I lay I guessed there were a dozen men present.

"So, what do we do with him then?" someone asked.

"Harald said what would happen if any tried violence here." That was Angus.

"Give him to me," said a voice I had not heard before. "Once we had great sport together. What do you say, Thorbjorn?" It was a rich voice, deep and full of mischief. I strained to see who the speaker was, but as soon as I tried to sit up I was pushed back down.

"Banish him," the woman in the rust-red dress muttered softly as she opened the bandages that swathed my throat. She was none too gentle, though I sensed her anger was not with me. "Or drop him into the sea." Our eyes met. "Killed my man, he did, and tried to burn my house down around my ears. Banishing is too good for the likes of him."

"The likes of me doesn't have to hear from the likes of you," said Thorbjorn.

Harald spoke. "Thorbjorn, you might keep your peace for now. This is a serious matter."

"Serious indeed, if you let a farmwife and this one decide my fate."

"A farm *widow*," challenged the woman with ferocity, her chin trembling.

"True enough," said Harald. "We'll be paying you compensation for your loss."

The woman was silent.

"And I'll be paying you for Erlend's indulgences," said the stranger.

This time when I tried the woman let me sit up. From the

pleased looks on my companions' faces I judged that they had not expected me to be sitting up so soon, if at all.

Thorbjorn's face was the only one that didn't change at the sight of me. He was sullen, simmering. Something was happening here indeed.

Harald looked distinctly unhappy. "The trouble is, this isn't only about defying my orders, is it?" He glanced over at me. "I have reason to believe that there was quite a plot brewing here, that treachery was even closer to home than I'd imagined."

I scanned the room. Where was Simon?

"You really think I would take part in trying to assassinate you?" exclaimed Thorbjorn. He sounded shocked and hurt.

"How am I to know what you're taking part in anymore?" Harald cried.

Thorbjorn shook his head. "If you can believe that—"

"It seems I can," Harald answered softly.

I cleared my throat then. "He's telling the truth. He wasn't part of it."

"I don't need you to speak for me," Thorbjorn barked.

"Be quiet," said Harald. "Go on, Malcolm."

"I can only guess about most of it, but from what I can tell Simon either acted alone or with your mother, though I cannot say for sure if killing you was part of Margaret's plan. It may have been," I said, apologetically. When Harald shrugged, as if to say it didn't matter, which of course it did, I went on. "But whatever Thorbjorn was doing, and even if he agreed with Margaret regarding killing Erlend, he wasn't part of anything larger than that. She used him, and so did Simon. But he didn't mean to harm you. I'm sure of it."

My rather lengthy statement was met with silence. How they all must have wondered how I had come to be in possession of all this knowledge! Thorbjorn just glowered on. It must have disturbed him greatly to have me, of all people, rise to his defense. He was not alone in that. It rankled not a little with me.

"You should have killed Simon for what he tried," Thorbjorn muttered.

"You are in no position to talk," said Harald, curtly.

So, they did know about Simon. But where was he?

"What I would like to know," said the stranger, "is who is this young man with all the answers?" A lazy smile spread across his face as he spoke, but there was nothing lazy about him. I could feel his mind, sharp behind the facade, and the rock of his will beneath that. A dawning suspicion as to his identity was growing in me.

"Svein," said Harald, "this is Malcolm, Alasdair Roy's son."

I met his shrewd, amused eyes. I did not look away. I knew who he was. What he was.

"I should have known it," said Svein Asleifarson. "Welcome to Orkney, Malcolm. I am sure we shall know each other very well in the future that is to come."

I knew his words for what they were. Not a pleasantry, but a prediction. He had recognized me too.

The story came out then, or at least most of it. I'd been right. The young man who had come to Olaf's door had indeed been Margaret's lover. He had been sent to warn

Erlend of Harald's approach, but that was not all. He had
been sent to offer Erlend a bargain. Margaret and her bar-
gains. That woman alone might undermine all that was
stable in the North if she were given free rein.

But even I was shocked when I heard the plot spoken of
aloud. Margaret had sent word to Erlend that if he managed to kill Harald she would side with him against Rognvald. She and her infant son, alongside Erlend, with Svein
as uncle and foster-father to the infant, to advise them all.

Erlend, of course, had not trusted Margaret—he was
not a complete fool—but he had felt himself warned and
wasn't about to leave the comforts of stout walls, food and
fire in the midst of a blizzard, and he had remained until
the weather broke. When we still hadn't arrived by noon he
had gotten skittish and left on one of his ships.

He had been gone only a few hours when we arrived.

"And where were you in all this?" demanded Thorbjorn.

Svein gave Thorbjorn a wolfish grin. "I was about. I am
always about, my old friend. We were all caught in that
storm, were we not?" He crooked a brow at me and I suppressed a shiver. I would have liked very much to know
what he knew.

"Well, it was all very flattering, as you can imagine,"
Svein was saying, "that she should want me there with her
in her newly made kingdom, but I must be growing old,
for Margaret's plots have become rather wearying to me."

I noticed he said nothing of Paul and just enough about
Margaret to make the story ring true. I could feel that keen
mind spring like a deer from thought to thought, always an
instant ahead of the rest of us, I suspected.

Formidable, indeed. If he'd been of noble blood ... but no, this man was exactly where he should be. He might be brilliant and even honourable in his own way, but he was not a leader. Power was a game to him. He played solely for the sake of exercising his superior skill. He loved the game too much to be trusted.

"You should know that Erlend had the wherewithal to say he'd be happy to join in with Margaret and bade Erlend the Younger to take that word to Margaret."

I noted that he made no mention of Paul or their bargain or how he intended to let fate play out as it would.

Then I heard him clearly and everything fell into place. I turned to Svein. "That name you just said. What was it?"

"Erlend the Younger? Margaret's pretty lover who she sent on this not-so-pretty errand."

Now I understood it all. When I had asked Margaret to tell me the whereabouts of Erlend she had thought I meant her lover who was off laying the groundwork for her attempt to take over Orkney. And when Paul had stepped in to stop her from tearing me to shreds, he had known that I meant that other Erlend, Harald's cousin, the usurper earl.

But he did not tell me! Ah, how he must have savoured that small morsel. Me, utterly bewildered as I stepped into Margaret's web, and Margaret frothing at the mouth, thinking I had *seen* into her plans and might undo them at any moment. But of course I had not seen her plans at all, and yet they had come undone just the same.

• • •

We left not long after that. Svein had taken his leave

and was off to meet Erlend. He had a duty to fulfill, he explained, but he was well-pleased with how things had gone and was sure he'd be in our company again some day. I was quite sure it would never be safe to trust him wholly, but I trusted his words.

That Svein was well-pleased did little for Thorbjorn's mood. Thorbjorn had been released and there were mixed feelings about that, but no one spoke them aloud. Thorbjorn was only one small part of the venture that had gone bad.

Svein left us, stalking across the hills to the north, turning to wave just before he disappeared from sight. He was hiding his destination, of course. I had to smile at that.

Others were heading for the ships in the harbour. Eirik and Benedikt had left at first light with a prisoner who was likely to bring a good ransom. Three more prisoners were already onboard another of the birlinns. They would be freed for a moderate sum or to earn some goodwill, depending on who they were. Harald would return to Caithness to bide his time until he could make another attempt. Some would join him there, others were to disperse to their homes, and all should keep their ears keen for any intelligence they could glean over the coming months, especially those in Orkney.

I sat down in a spot where the sun would shine full on my back to chew on a hunk of stale bread bought from the newly made widow. She had tended my wound well, but it had begun to burn nonetheless and swallowing was painful. Though my strength had rallied somewhat I did not relish travelling just yet.

Beyond the bay, rising up like the backs of whales, lay the islands of Orkney. The teeth of Sigrith's dragon. Sunlight sparkled on the water, like a thousand silver coins floating there.

The earl sat down beside me, stretching his long legs out before him. He accepted the bread I offered, and we sat there, chewing, looking out at the water.

"I will go with you to Caithness then?" I asked. It would not be easy now with Thorbjorn. It might well be worse, but I had survived him in Orkney. I could survive him in Caithness.

"I think not."

My heart dropped. "Then I will return to Moray?" The intensity of my disappointment surprised me.

"Not yet," he replied. "Remain in Orkney until spring and learn what you can for me. The men from Atholl will ride home then and you can go with them."

"The land route suits me well," I assured him, relieved at not being wholly dismissed.

He grinned, then grew more serious. "You understand that it is only because I think it best that you not accompany me now."

I nodded, not really understanding.

He gave a dry laugh. "I thought Thorbjorn despised Svein but the way he looks at you, well, I would not wish any man to hate me thus. It is my fault, in part. You will join me again, in the future, but for now …"

I did not think Thorbjorn would hate me less in the future but I did not say it.

"He is the closest I have ever known to a father."

"Yes."

"I know what he tried to do," he said, more to himself than to me. He gazed out at the bay where three of his ships lay waiting, where Erlend's ships had been so recently.

For a moment I thought he was referring to Thorbjorn's attempt to murder me, but then I saw that he was not. I wondered if it would make a difference if he knew.

"And I know what others would do with him," Harald was saying, "but I cannot bring myself to it. Not yet. I will lean on him less and perhaps we will find a new balance. He might become more temperate." Even as he spoke, I knew he did not believe his own words. He spoke of hopes, not of likelihoods.

"I do not think I will make much of a spy," I said wryly, changing the subject.

He chuckled. "I'm not so sure of that. You might make the best sort of spy. Who would suspect you of subtlety? What I mean is that you are not the sort of person who skulks in the shadows plotting against others. You are honest, and that can be a very useful thing."

He called me honest. He'd forgiven me too easily. That can be more uncomfortable than having forgiveness denied.

"Haermund wants you with him on Westray. Stay a few weeks, then go to Olaf." He handed me a small pouch that contained, from the weight of it, no small amount of coin. "Give Olaf enough for your bed and board and keep the rest for your journey home. Explore Hrossey. Get to know the people. People will talk in front of you. Listen to them and tell me what they say. I'm sure Sigrith will take you to meet her neighbours." He smiled. "She's an excellent young woman."

My face turned a deep shade of red and Harald grinned. "It seems my orders are in keeping with your wishes," he said. "Good then." He rose to leave. "When you arrive home," he said, extending his hand, "give my thanks to your father for the gift of service he provided in you. Tell him that I will not forget it and will do what I can in return. And when my situation improves I will try to remedy it entirely."

Then he pulled up his sleeve. "For your service, Malcolm mac Alasdair, I give you this in payment." He removed from his right wrist one of his finely wrought armrings. Gold. A fortune in gold in that one ring.

"I do not deserve this," I gasped.

"You deny me the pleasure of gifting my retainer as I see fit?" he said with mock anger.

"No, but—I betrayed you!"

He frowned. "You behaved wrongly, yes, but out of ignorance, not malice, and you remedied it."

"But you did not receive anything," I protested.

"I received this," he said, pulling the eagle I'd carved at Dingwall out of his scrip. "And your words, your story, helped me more than you can know. And now Thorir tells me you saved my life, though he will not tell me how. But Honey-Tongue does not tell lies. Perhaps he will tell me one day, or you will, when we meet again. But until then you will do whatever you can here in Orkney and when you return home cut the strongest, finest piece of Moray oak you can find and carve for me a handle fit for a king's hand. Do you hear me?" he said, his face hard, his eyes twinkling. "And do not worry about this business with my mother. Simon will reach her before I do, but Eirik will get there before him. She will send no messages, south or anywhere. Your family is safe."

"How did you know—"

"Simon." His face went dark. "I let him go. Had I known about that," he said, pointing to my throat, "I might not have let him off so easily. He tried to kill me. It was my choice what to do about that, but—well, it is done. He is kin, more close even than Erlend. If I could spare my cousin for what he's done, I had to spare Simon, didn't I? He's young, and my mother had her hooks in him."

He shook his head. "Simon will be dealt with by his father, as is right. You see, it appears that you and I were not the only ones he intended to kill. Whatever came over him last night, I do not know, but I do believe he confessed to every crime he ever committed, as well as the ones he dreamt he might! Simon had some grand dreams, to be sure. After he was rid of me he was to go home and hasten his inheritance."

"With Margaret's help," I said.

He was surprised. "You knew?" He would be wondering how much he could trust me if I was not careful. Svein might be good at telling half-truths, but I was not.

"Only just before the end," I said, and felt him sigh. He trusted me. I must make sure he always could. I really would tell him all of it. All that I was able to.

"So he said. Mind you, he was babbling like an idiot at the time. You might have thought he'd gone mad. I even hoped it was not true, but of course it was. He was in no state of mind to be lying. It was only my promise to keep the golden dragon from devouring him—Malcolm? Are you all right?" He crouched to take me by the shoulder.

I could feel the blood drain from my face. "Yes," I said. "I am fine. Fine."

He didn't look as if he believed me, but he went on. "So the short of it is that Simon will return to Atholl where he will satisfy himself with an inferior position at his father's court. He smiled wryly. "I told him that if his father did not live to a ripe old age Simon would not outlive him by much. My brother will know all of this soon enough. Simon will never be Earl of Atholl."

Harald gazed thoughtfully out at the bay again. His pleasure had disappeared as quickly as it had arisen. "And me? I will try again." He nodded, as if the matter were settled. "There is nothing for it but to try again."

His kin had tried to kill him and the father of his heart had betrayed him. That Thorbjorn had meant to serve did not matter. Harald was surrounded by men who loved and supported him and yet he was alone. The ground upon which he stood had shifted and it would take time for him to find his footing again. But he would. The seed was planted. The harvest would come.

"My lord," I began, and then I almost changed my mind. I remembered my father hesitating in that same way. When Harald turned his sharp gaze on me I drew a deep breath. "My lord, I must tell you a thing. You may do with it as you will."

"Another secret? You are a mysterious one, Malcolm."

"Well, mysterious it is," I answered. And so I told him of a dream of an old man dying in his bed in Orkney, a powerful leader surrounded by loyal men who grieved his passing and I told him that I believed in my deepest heart that, mad as it sounded, the dream was a mystery, but not a lie. I had no proof to offer. Proof would come in its own good time.

That I lied, in part, must be forgiven, for I did not tell whose dream it was. I let him believe it was mine. It was the dream, not the dreamer, that mattered just then.

He did not answer me at first. His eyes searched me as they had the day we'd met.

"Malcolm, return to Orkney when I call. You will serve me as craftsman but also as … well, I will have to think about what we will call you in the hearing of others." He laughed. "Yes, my father's description of his friendship with your father makes much sense now. So, you will carve for me, and we will wait together to see if your dream proves out."

I could not answer. My eyes had filled with tears. I dropped to one knee. I had thought he was sending me away, but he was honouring me.

He gave a short laugh and hauled me to my feet. "I told you that you never needed to do that, Malcolm, for the sake of our fathers, but for your own sake as well." He shook his head. "They didn't make it easy for us, did they? I don't know about Alasdair, but I see now that my father dropped just enough hints, said just enough, that I would see the truth of it on my own, if the truth was before me."

A chill had crept over me. Was he saying what I thought

he was?

"Alasdair was my father's friend, to be sure, but more, he was his guide. He was—though I do not believe my father ever let the word pass his lips, not regarding your father or any other person, for he was a completely rational man— his seer."

"We are not the same, my father and I," I said, quietly.

"Are you saying you do not have second sight?" he asked, in as low a tone.

I was a moment getting over the shock of hearing him say those words aloud. I took a deep breath. "No, that's not what I'm saying. Only that I see differently."

"Well, however you see, see for me. See for Orkney. That is all I ask. And now," he said, brushing crumbs from the front of his tunic as he stood. "You know what you are to do. I thank you, my friend, for telling me of this peace. For that is what it means, does it not? A man who dies in his bed must have known some peace." He looked hopeful.

It was not what I had said but I nodded.

"They are welcome words," he said. "We leave soon," he called to Thorir, who had been waiting nearby. "I will give you a few minutes to say goodbyes."

He gripped my shoulder, squeezed it and then left me.

"My lord!" I called, running after him. He stopped, a curious look on his face. "I have one more secret to reveal." When I near enough that I could be sure no others heard I told him where he might find his infant brother.

He shook his head in amazement. "You truly have earned your keep, Malcolm." Then, "I will not harm him."

"I know," I replied and watched as he strode away.

"There *will* be peace, won't there?" I asked softly as Thorir came to stand beside me.

"In time. And then there will be war again. And then peace."

"All that was done before?" I said.

"You listened to me!" he exclaimed.

"What did you tell Harald about me?" I asked. Harald might know of my second-sight, but could he know what had actually happened?

"That you saved his life."

"You didn't tell him ..."

He shook his head. "No, but I'll tell you."

He pulled himself up as he always did when he told a story. "The sun had almost dropped away and a bleak darkness was falling. I tell you there was an evil in it. The fighting was heated and I was kept busy with my sword and then, in the midst of that chaos and the creeping darkness there was such a burst of light that I thought for certain that ..." he stopped, his eyes wide, "that *someone* had appeared!"

I knew who he meant.

"But it was not him," he said softly. "No, *this* light—it was a creature *made* of light—it soared skyward, like lightning born of the earth! The next instant it plummeted back down and disappeared into the house.

"The door flew open and Simon came charging out, howling like a madman."

"Say it," I demanded. "Say what it was." There could be no doubt, but I needed to hear him say it aloud. I needed for the words to be spoken, for the truth to be made real.

"It was a dragon."

I drew a deep breath. It was the truth. My varden was that of a dragon, the greatest of all beasts and the most foul, depending on how a man chose to make it. I would have to trust Thorir on that. He had said what he saw was beauty, a glory. I knew I would have to work to keep it that way. For I had seen what would happen if I did not.

"Thorir," I began, but the words disappeared from my tongue. "You have done so much for me. You saved me, you know."

He shrugged. "I only did my part."

"All your stories, all that you taught me, and you saw where I was going wrong—"

He stopped me. "Do not credit me too much. I tell the stories I am compelled to tell. I do not always know why at the time. As I said, I did my part." He grinned his customary grin. "I told you, I belong to him."

"It seems I do, too." I was still not comfortable with the idea.

"You do, and you do not. Something has changed. He still exists, to be sure, but I believe he has done his final work here. I could be wrong. Perhaps I will hear him thundering by next Yule. I would like to. But either way I think that you may feel right in holding to your own god."

We grinned at each other, savouring our shared knowledge. No one else would have understood. We did not need them to.

"And now, my friend, I'm afraid it is time for our ways to part. But we will meet again, I know, and when we do, I will have a great poem ready for you, about a young dragon who gained his treasure and was not enslaved by it. I will tell it by the fire in front of everyone and only you will rec-ognize the truth of it."

"I look forward to that day," I said. "And perhaps I will hear of your adventure one day?" But even as I said it I saw the look that crossed his face.

"If I could …"

"A poor shadow of the god's thoughts?" I asked, softly.

He smiled. "You hear me well."

The others were making for the beach where the ships had come to shore. I began to walk towards them. "Well, I do hope you can find the words for another composition. I have a story for you that may be the beginning of your great saga." And so I gave him, as we walked together down to the sea, the name of Hakon of Orkney.

I watched him climb aboard the Sea Eagle and lose him-self among the other men. Another figure caught my eye. Thorbjorn, standing on the foredeck of the great longship.

I never saw him again. ⚘

33

young was i once, i walked alone,
and bewildered seemed in the way;
then i found me another and rich i thought me,
for man is the joy of man.

~WISDOM OF ODIN~

The snow had melted from all but the highest peaks and April was already drawing out pale buds from the trees when I rode down the familiar trail. Flocks of tiny birds feasted on bright berries and fluttered up in agitated, twittering clouds at my approach.

I had missed the snowdrops, but I was home.

I was alone for the first time in months, the men from Atholl having parted from me that morning. I did not mind so much, but it did feel strange. We had grown close on the long journey south.

The sun poked in shafts through the trees that lined the trail and fell on the ears of my horse, a lanky grey I had purchased in Thurso with some of the coin from Harald. We had stopped there on our way south to pass on what little news we'd gathered from Orkney.

I had met many people, both on Westray and Hrossey, but had gleaned little that did not have the saltiness of rumour to spoil any bland truth that might have resided in it. Men talked much of what had befallen Harald and the rest of us—few of these imaginative stories were recognizable to me—and of where Svein and Erlend were, putting them throughout the scattered isles, along the Scottish coast and in Norway, often on the same day.

The earl, who was too busy to meet us in Thurso himself, sent Thorir and he had much to tell. It was a happy reunion, if brief, though the news Thorir brought was not good.

Harald's troubles had been unceasing since the debacle at Firth. Thorbjorn had been stirring up trouble with his temper, and Svein had begun his raiding early that year, attacking all up and down the coast and among the islands as well. He had said he was not Harald's enemy and I believed him; that did not mean he would not have his sport.

Most importantly, Margaret had disappeared from Wick before Harald had been able to reach her. She was in Shetland with Erlend the Younger, who was offering Harald his support in exchange for being allowed to marry Margaret. Harald was more inclined to kill the man.

Another flock of birds sent up a chorus of protestations at my interruption of their midday meal. They flitted around me, scolding raucously, and then, as an entity, swooped up and over a clump of bushes to drop down among safer branches.

I was almost home. A tingling grew in my feet, an eagerness to leap off my horse and run the rest of the way. I restrained that childish impulse. No one was watching, yet I did not want to appear a boy. I was not a boy. Not anymore.

Haermund had done his part to ensure that. He had decided that I should become an adept of the battleaxe and had proven himself a fiendish taskmaster. Every day I spent with him I trained and every night I dropped into my bed, a mass of bruises and throbbing muscles. But by the time I left, I think even Thorbjorn might have credited me with some skill in my weapon of choice.

When I parted from Haermund he honoured me by giving me one of his best axes, a lovely old thing that a great-grandfather of his had carried into battle many years before. That he had died with it in his hand seemed to enhance its worth to Haermund. And thus to me.

At a bend in the trail stood a massive, gnarled oak. Behind it hid Marjory. Or so she thought. I had known she was there since the tree had come into sight. Her varden did not appear to me as clearly as it had in my dream—in the light of day it was more something I saw from the corner of my eye—but it was there. As was my father's. He would be sitting somewhere just around the bend in the trail. I smiled to myself. I should have known what form his spirit would take. We truly were alike.

The fox was positively twitching with excitement. I held my face steady.

Marjory leapt out onto the trail. "I told you it was today!" she crowed triumphantly.

"How did you know?" I demanded, pretending astonishment.

My father limped onto the path. "Actually, we argued. She said it was today, but I waited here yesterday for a time as well. It seems I do not see as clearly as I would like to think," he said with a smile, but his eyes were searching mine, much as they had the day I'd left home.

I saw him truly for the first time. He did not search me to find fault. He sought the boy he had sent away, the angry, proud, foolish boy I had been.

I slipped down from my horse and went to him. I gripped his arm, to help him to balance aright.

"I do believe, Father, that you have the clearest eyes I have ever known. You were right. About everything." And then, as if that hadn't surprised him enough, I threw my arms around him and held him tight.

• • •

I told them everything I possibly could in what had remained of the day, entertaining my family and the servants until I was dozing in my place, lulled by the warm comfort of home.

My sisters questioned me ruthlessly, wanting to hear it all, reliving my adventure with me. What I kept to myself was little enough with such interrogators.

My mother was her usual calm self that night, listening attentively, smiling proudly now and then. The thought came to me that she, who had no gift of sight, seemed to have been the least concerned for me, as if she had access to some other assurance.

As I talked, my father's eyes drifted repeatedly to my throat and the scar that was etched there, ugly and permanent. I thought I saw pride in his face and perhaps a little regret.

I must have drifted off for a time, because one moment I was telling them all about crossing the Pentland Firth for the second time and the next the women were all gone and my father was sitting on his stool, sipping his drink, watching me.

"Why didn't you tell me about you and Maddad?" I asked.

He nodded. He'd been expecting the question. "I suppose I didn't want to colour your view of things."

I crooked a brow at him, inviting him to clarify.

He smiled. "Well, it's like this. I didn't know how your gift would show, just as I didn't know how mine would before it did. I could feel a certain power in you, but I couldn't be sure, and so I didn't want you to have expectations. I wanted you to find your own path. And you did."

"But you did not see my path? You said that you saw Harald an old man—"

He gave an ironic snort. "Ah, I thought you would come to that. Yes, I saw him. It took me some time to know it was Harald Maddadson, I'll have you know! The dreams may come easy, but they don't mean anything easily, as I'm sure you already know."

I nodded emphatically.

"But I never actually saw you there. I thought I sensed you, but did not know if it was just hope stirring my imagination."

I waved a hand to say there was no need to explain.

"What else do you wish to know that cannot wait until tomorrow?" he asked.

"Only one thing," I answered. I thought a moment how best to put it. I took a breath. "Father, why did you spare Earl Maddad's life on the battlefield all those years ago? Why didn't you kill him? He was your enemy."

He grinned broadly at me. "Ah, you come to the start of it now, if it can be called the start. If anything can." He put down his cup with a far off look.

He leaned closer to the fire. "I might have killed him, you know. He led the attack that ruined us. I did not know who he was, all caked in mud and blood and looking as much a wreck of battle as the rest of us, but I knew he was someone. Someone important. My father had just been cut down in front of me and I was half mad with grief and terror, and then this man appeared before me and I wanted nothing more than to rip the life from him, to see him drown in the muck. I wanted to kill everyone in that moment. Brother, enemy, friend. All were the same."

He was seeing that long ago day. Now he looked me in the eye. "The bloodlust was screaming in me. I raised my sword to strike. And then I saw his face." He stopped. "You have to understand, I really did not know who he was. I grew up here, as you did, away from the world he lived in."

"So why didn't you do it?"

He smiled. "Because when I looked into his face, I knew I had seen him before. In a dream. And I knew then, knew it more surely than I had ever known a thing before, that if I killed him there, I would be ending my own life. For I had also dreamed you, Malcolm, and Harald, and I had seen the two of you together, him leading and you guiding, supporting. I knew if I killed Maddad, I would be killing my future. I would be killing you.

"I dreamed what would come if I killed Maddad, and I chose."

We sat for a time in silence. Then he got up and limped over to me. He leaned down to kiss my hair and he went to his bed.

•••

When I got to my room Marjory was waiting.

"It's late," I said.

She was sitting on my bed with her shawl wrapped around her knees. "It is, but I have grown used to surviving on only a few hours of sleep a night with all the dreaming I've been doing. All about you!" she cried, as if I were to blame. "With you back, maybe I will get some good sleep. Now that I've got a decent dowry it wouldn't do for me to lose my looks!"

So, she'd dreamt too.

She winked mischievously and I laughed. Harald might have been busy in the weeks after our Yule venture, but he had taken the time to send money to Dunailech, along with a letter describing his plans to intercede with the king, his cousin, on our behalf. My sisters had their dowries. My father had his land.

"I must confess something to you, Malcolm." She bit her lip, narrowing her eyes at me. "I was jealous of you. Jealous that you were going on such a grand adventure and that I had to stay here, and all because I am a female. It's not fair, you'll warrant," she sniffed. "Give me a sword and I can handle myself at least as well as you!"

I laughed. "True enough. But you *were* there, you know. In a way. I dreamed about you."

"Bah," she retorted. "So you dreamed about me. How does that make me there?"

I didn't know how to answer her. Tell her that her spirit had flown across land and sea to find me, in the guise of a fox? I might, one day, but not just then.

"Well, it was my duty to get you a dowry, not to provide you with adventure. What, am I to do everything?"

She flashed me a broad grin. "You are not. And I will have my own adventures, I assure you. Until then, I must say that dreams are quite a good second to real adventure. I was not in jest! Such happenings! There was a beautiful woman with sharp teeth and then you were caught in a web for a long time and trampled by horses and sometimes I thought we spoke, but I could never sort it all out. Enormous warriors and an eight-legged horse and a dragon! My goodness, my nights were very strange! It is good you finally saw fit to come home."

She *had* been there. Why was I surprised? I reached under my tunic and took out the boar amulet, on its new thong. I pulled it over my head. "This is yours," I said, giving it to her.

She did not argue. She held it in her palm, looking at it long.

"Why did you give it to me?" I asked.

She looked up at me and her smile was strange. "Because I dreamed that I had given it. The night before Father told you that you would go north."

"So you don't know why."

"About the boar, no, though I did dream of a boar. But the hair, I think that was to keep me near you. All I know for certain is that I was meant to."

I looked into my sister's blue eyes. "That I understand very well."

• • •

It was almost six years before I returned to Orkney to

take up my role as Earl Harald's craftsman and his friend, for those are the titles he finally chose for me, not finding more accurate ones that he could speak aloud.

Much had changed. My father had received a full pardon and even some favour with King Malcolm. My sisters had all married men I was happy to call brothers. And I was as tall now as my father and as skilled with the battle axe as he was with the sword. And those other skills of mine, those had been honed too, with much effort and the guidance of my father.

Harald was now the indisputable and sole Earl of Orkney. Earl Erlend was dead, at the hands of Margaret's husband, that other Erlend, or so he had bragged the day it happened. Unfortunately for him, he did so in the hearing of Svein Asleifarson, who paid him in kind and left Margaret a widow once again.

Margaret disappeared after that, not from the world, perhaps, but from the world of power. I do not know how he did it, but somehow Harald finally succeeded in tying her hands. Her infant son was raised by a good family who never knew how close their adopted son had come to being an earl.

Earl Rognvald was dead too. For a time he and Harald ruled together, peaceably, but Thorbjorn could not forget his old dreams. He ambushed Rognvald one day while he was hunting and killed him.

Harald had called Thorbjorn father, had loved him, but Thorbjorn had gone too far. Harald's men insisted he must die for his crime, and though it pained him greatly, Harald saw the truth: if he spared Thorbjorn again, he would lose all the others. His people would turn against him.

And so Thorbjorn's victory was brief. He made Harald sole Earl of Orkney and passed from out this world.

Thus my own life in Orkney began.

On the day that Sigrith took me to the heart of Stenness, the sun was shining and the ever-present wind was gently scudding wisps of cloud across the sky.

My first sight of Orkahaugr, after all that time, stirred something in me, but it was not fear.

Though I didn't go to see, I knew the hole in the top had been mended. A few days after we'd left it, Sigrith had gone with her family to cover it over with sticks of driftwood and then rock and soil. Grass would take hold there and, with time, the place of the ancients would be returned to those who made it.

We walked past the mound and through a small ring of stones that jutted up like broad, flat blades into the sky. This small ring was but a child to the larger one that lay between the lochs, where my companions had briefly touched the next world.

Our destination was the giant holed stone of Odin, Thorir's god, who had become mine even while I kept my old faith. How this could be, that two faiths, two worlds, should coexist, I have never understood, but I know the truth when it touches me.

The Odin Stone looked very different in the light of day, but no less magical for all that the sun shone on it. Some things no amount of light can turn commonplace. Shadows in the corners of a dark room are revealed to be empty of monsters in the light of day, but not in Stenness. Its mysteries do not evaporate in sunlight, for they are seen by the other eye.

Sigrith and I stood before the stone. It had not felt right to go there sooner. I had waited, secure in the knowledge that what lay hidden in the earth waited only for me. Now I knelt, drew my knife, a gift from the earl, and plunged it into the thick grass at the base of the stone. The turf peeled away easily and I began to dig with my fingers. Smells rose up, of damp, cool earth, the sweetness that transforms decay. I sank my hands deep into it.

They struck a surface that was not earth or stone. I was careful now, gently stroking the dirt from each object as I drew it out and laid it on the linen cloth Sigrith had brought. When I was sure I had them all, I pushed the earth back into the hole and carefully covered it over. I bundled up the cloth and we walked to the shore of the loch where I laid the whole thing into the water. I pulled back the corners of the linen.

The gold sparkled in the water, catching the rays of the sun and throwing them back in brilliant defiance. Seven gold arm-rings, the ring-money of a great lord and hero. Seven spiraling twists of gold, meant to bind a leader to his men.

And one other piece. On a disc of gold flashed a beast, a proud dragon, pierced by a sword but living on.

It was just as I'd seen it flashing on Hakon's breast, just as I'd carved it into the stone of Orkahaugr, only now it shone in sunlight.

I had a sudden urge to hurl the thing up and into the loch that had been a dragon's bed, to send it after Hakon, wherever he was and I was about to do that when I caught Sigrith's eye. She was smiling, with all her usual patience and understanding. She took the brooch from me.

"You know," she said, as she stood on her toes to unpin my old brooch. "This was made for the one who lives with one foot in this world and the other … elsewhere." She smiled as she pinned my cloak with the gift that was my inheritance. ⚛

MORE THAN FIFTY YEARS HAVE PASSED *since those nights spent under the mound. My hands are not so clever now as they once were, nor is my other gift so keen. Both talents served my lord and me well.*

Neither can serve him any longer. In recent days my lord, my friend, Earl Harald Maddadson, lord of Orkney and Shetland, Caithness and Sutherland, passed from this world to the next.

He ruled for nearly seventy years. I will not lie and say he was a gentle ruler. The times would not allow that. But he was a strong one, and just, and he brought more peace than strife. In this world where war is still cherished so dearly in the hearts of men, he did better than most. And I did my best to help him to the path of peace, the path that would best honour the people and the land they live upon. The void he leaves will call men to fill it, with war or with peace, as fate should decree.

Fate. I once thought it so cruel, but I see now that mine was kind. Still, there were losses. There are always losses.

Svein, who had long been a thorn in Harald's side, became his friend again and would remain thus for the rest of his days. He became mine as well.

One day at a meal my lord asked Svein to give up his raiding. "The old ways are passing," Harald said to Svein. "You should avoid war, rather than seek it."

Svein answered him with a roguish grin, "This comes from a man who has less peace in him than many, but I will agree, if you will grant me one last venture."

Svein Asleifarson died somewhere in Ireland with a sword in his hand. And with him, Harald's son, who was Svein's foster-son. And Thorir. Thorir Honey-Tongue, who had gone to make a great poem of the last exploits of a legendary man.

I like to think Thorir fell composing that poem, that his face spoke of joy, not agony. I hope I imagine true. There was no dream to tell me.

But he did make that other poem. The sound of it still rings in my ears, the shape of those words in their intricate metre, breathing the name of Hakon of Orkney into the world again. I remember Sigrith's face glowing in the firelight the first time she heard that name spoken aloud in the earl's hall, her fore-father's honour reborn in the world of men. And the hint of a smile on Thorir's face when he came to the end and told of the golden dragon that had lit the dark Orkney sky like a comet, bringing light to a dark time.

That poem was Thorir's greatest. I pray it lives as long as men tell stories by the fire.

Thorir never told me what happened to him those three nights he was lost to us. And I never told him what had befallen me under the mound, though I yearned to. I assume the words always stopped in his mouth as they did in mine.

But fate provides.

There is a young man here in Orphir who sits in a candle-lit room scratching down the words that flow from his mind—the words I have given him—as if he will lose them if he tarries. He is a skald from Iceland, trained in the same school where Thorir once learned his craft.

He has found his great tale, he tells me eagerly, the making of his name. He sets it down for the sake of future generations, a record of the earls of Orkney, a history of those men, great and not so great, as the case may be. In his jagged scrawl of letters lies their immortality. Once they would have been embalmed in the roundness of the spoken word, passed from lip to ear, down through the generations. Perhaps this is better. I cannot say. Whatever the case, the earls of Orkney will live on and I am glad of it. It does them honour and it is always well to do a man honour.

I have done my best to recount for him the tales of Harald Maddadson, for there are few left now who can do so. In the beginning I felt awkward. I talked out of a sense of duty, but as the days wore on, with that eager young face drinking in my words, my tongue grew loose and I told him more than I expected to. More than I had ever told anyone.

And so, he heard of my dreams, of the voice in the howe on that stormy night, of vardens and the god on the horse with eight legs. The more I told, the faster the words came, as if I were running down a steep hill. What did I care? I was an old man with nothing to fear. A great burden was lifted from my spirit. Only then did I realize that I had been afraid to tell the truth, even to Thorir. Fifty years had passed and I was still hiding my true self!

I came to the end of my tale, saying a small prayer of thanks for the gift of this young fellow who had released me. And then I looked at his face.

Why did God give men tongues, when it is the eyes that tell all a man's thoughts? Those bright eyes looked back at me and said, a mad old one, this one. Poor thing.

I'd been given a confessor whose ears were deaf to the one true story I had to tell.

That night I lay down upon my bed and laughed, hard and loud, for a very long time. God, whatever name we give Him, whatever form He takes, has His own plan, whatever plan we hope to make.

I sat down the next day and began the work that you hold now in your hands. The lad had not heard me because it was not his tale to tell. My story is my own, the telling of it was a gift. If you are reading these words now, I thank you, for you have breathed new life into my name. I live on.

It will not be long now. My children are grown, and my grandchildren are scattered from Moray to Orkney, thriving like snowdrops in spring. I have lived without my Sigrith for a few long years now. Only Marjory is left to me. She lives yet in Dunailech with her large brood, all red-haired and warm-hearted, clucking about her.

I have not laid eyes on my sister for many years now, but soon spring will come and I will set out on my last adventure in this fleshly form. I will leave the brooch for the one who comes to take my place, whoever he—or she—may be. I have done my part. Now, if fate allows, these old bones will rest in the soil of my forefathers. But not before I sit by the fire with my sister and we tell the tale, together, of that time under the mound. ◬

afterword

Both Orkahaugr, known today as Maeshowe, and The Ring of Brodgar (The Giant's Dance) still stand in the heart of Orkney, much as they did in 1153. The Odin Stone was destroyed in 1814 by a farmer fed up with people traipsing over his land to visit it. The section of the stone with the hole in it is believed to have survived as the anchor to a mill-shaft until the 1950s when it was finally smashed to pieces by a young man unaware of its history.

The ruins of Harald's stronghold at Wick can still be seen today. Of Dingwall castle little remains and what has been described here is wholly fictional. Dunailech never existed outside the pages of this book.

Under the Mound is ultimately a work of fiction, but its setting is historical, as are many of the characters. With the exception of Malcolm's family and a few of the Atholl men all the characters in the book received their names from historical record or from the walls of Maeshowe where they can still be read today. Aside from Harald, Thorbjorn and Margaret none of the characters depicted hear bear any resemblance that I know of to their namesakes.

All the runes described in the book can also be found on the walls of Maeshowe. Translations were borrowed from Michael P. Barnes meticulous work *The Runic Inscriptions of Maeshowe, Orkney* published by Uppsala University in Sweden in 1994. The chapter epigraphs are from the Norse poem Hávamál and are amalgamations of my own words, Olive Bray's translation of the poem, and Lee M. Hollander's translation of *The Poetic Edda*, published by the University of Texas Press, 2nd edition revised, copyright in 1962 and renewed in 1990. *The Orkneyinga Saga, The History of the Earls of Orkney*, translated by Hermann Pálsson and Paul Edwards, published by Hogarth Press in 1978 and by Penguin Books in London in 1981, was a major source of both information and inspiration.

Many wonderful people gave of their time and energy to support me in writing this book. I truly could not have done it without them. Special thanks to Jennifer Burkholder, Ben Bedford, Angela Lavery, Farah Nazarali, Kristine Webber, Justine Blicq and Danielle Dove who read drafts at various stages and provided feedback and encouragement. Also to Christianne Hayward and her Ravenous Readers at Christianne's Lyceum in Vancouver for reading the manuscript as a work-in-progress and for voicing such honest and helpful opinions. A special thanks to Stanley Hayward for his rave review, which encouraged me immensely.

I am eternally grateful to my dear friend and editor Melanie Wilkins-Ho, for the many, many hours she spent hashing out scenes, arguing plot points and putting me back on my feet when I was sure I had bitten off too much to ever chew. Thanks also to John Kieran Kealy who stepped in to help the manuscript find its final form and to Dean Curtis and Chris Canewell who taught me about dreaming big and then making it happen.

I have only been to Orkney once (and not during the 12th century) so when I needed to get in the spirit of the place Sigurd Towrie's excellent website Orkneyjar.com was the next best thing. I often found the inspiration I needed by wandering through those well-crafted pages. Thanks also to Freda Rapson of Jacobite Cruises in Scotland who kindly answered what must have seemed a silly question at the time. Without her input I might have tried to sail my boys directly from Loch Ness into the Moray Firth, which would have been quite a feat considering the rather lengthy drop from the one body of water to the other. Thank you for saving us all much discomfort.

Finally, most loving gratitude to my family for your faith in me, and especially to my parents who have never doubted I could do anything I set my mind to.